Spoofed and Spiked

John Alexander

Bright Pen

Visit us online at <u>www.authorsonline.co.uk</u>

A Bright Pen Book

Text Copyright © John Alexander 2010

Cover design by Millicent Alexander ©

British Library Cataloguing Publication Data.
A catalogue record for this book is available from the British Library

This is a work of fiction. Names, characters,organisations, places and events are either the product of the author's imagination or are used fictitiously.

Accounts of the sinking of the Titanic are drawn from 'Titanic Survivor--Memoirs of Violet Jessop' published by Sheridan House Inc. Scripture quotations are taken from the New International Version of the Holy Bible.

ISBN 978-07552-1221-7

Authors OnLine Ltd
19 The Cinques
Gamlingay, Sandy
Bedfordshire SG19 3NU
England

This book is also available in e-book format, details of which are available at www.authorsonline.co.uk

About the Author

John Alexander worked for regional newspapers in the south of England for more than 30 years and in 1978 received a National Press Award commendation for investigative reporting. He later became a tutor in a new training centre for would-be journalists, before taking up an editorship in Bedfordshire. When he became a Christian later in life, he joined a Christian research organisation and for several years managed the Keep Sunday Special Campaign.

Dear Nick,
    To be read with
  a smile on your face.
  Best wishes,

      John

Acknowledgements

A golden rule of writing a novel, I was told before a sentence of this book had been written, was not to drift from one genre into another. Two or three of my close friends, who volunteered to read the original script, told me that was just what I had done and it didn't work! Their comments sent me back to the drawing board. I closely examined the change of gear they said had taken place in part two and agreed that a little more subtlety was definitely required. What I didn't agree with was the contention that two of the main characters of the book could not possibly have undergone such drastic changes to their philosophies, beliefs and attitudes in the manner and time-scale I had described. All I can say to that is I have the strongest possible evidence that this can happen and leave it to you, the reader, to make up your own mind.

Thanks to all those who gave precious time to reading an author's first novel, something most publishers have ceased to do because of financial restraints and a mistaken idea that only people with celebrity status can attract public attention.

My unpaid editors were a combination of journalists and non-journalists, Christians and non-Christians. All contributed something and I would like to thank Pauline Goss, Eddie Duller, Sue Anderson, George Elsbury, Jack Taylor, Aileen James and Ian Stone for the conscientious way they approached their task.

I am indebted to my granddaughter Millie, showing great early promise as an artist, for her front cover illustration and her father Nick, for digging me out of one or two theological holes I was in danger of falling into. My daughter-in-law, Sara, gave sound advice after making *Spoofed and Spiked* her holiday reading and my wife, Susan, kept her calm under extreme circumstances and always had a useful piece of advice ready at hand. Without her support this painstaking, but I hope thought-provoking first offering, would never have taken shape.

To Adrian and Nick

CONTENTS

(Part One)

(Part Two)

Part One

1

(1970)

Monday Morning Enlivened

The yellowing, crumpled newspaper clipping, which fell from one of my coffee-stained notebooks, was just about readable. Its continued survival amid other less distinguished material served to demonstrate how reporters love to gloat over their little triumphs. I was no exception. To me this particular piece of newsprint was very special, a front-page banner headline, sweetened by an acknowledgement that the words were created by Damon Jenkins. It had led to my first and only award for diligent investigative journalism so always brought a glow of satisfaction no matter how many times it reappeared from a grubby corner of my office desk.

The story recorded the day when Stephen Spicer, at the tender age of 19, decided to throw in the towel and admit to the world that he was not, after all, the Western world's most gifted psychic. From that time on, he wanted to be known as a 'mentalist', an announcement few people understood but one that, I felt, fully justified the months I had spent trying to convince people this mendacious young man was taking them for a ride.

Others with more vivid imaginations and different agendas would have me think otherwise, but it was pure coincidence that the cutting resurrected itself at the moment a commotion broke out in the newspaper's reception area. It was not unusual for the girls manning the front office to be entertained from time to time by the bizarre behaviour of one of the town's eccentrics but in the hubbub, two names had penetrated far enough to reach the ears of one very short-tempered news editor.

Eric Driver didn't like Monday mornings at the best of times, certainly not after a weekend marred by the arrival of uninvited and unloved guests. He had already spent the first moments of a new week moaning to everyone in earshot about the constant jabbering of the female members of his unwanted house party.

To the relief of those who were being forced to listen to the Monday morning rant, Eric switched his attention to the unseemly din threatening to test his health and temper even further. 'Damon, was that your name I heard above the babble?' he shouted across a room vibrating with a cacophony of typical newsroom noises, most dominant being jangling telephone bells which might have created the impression to a stranger that something important was happening. Usually it meant no such thing.

'If you're to blame, you'd better go and sort it, pretty sharp,' snapped Eric who always felt he must act the hard man with me despite our long relationship. It was rumoured he had a warm heart but few ever felt the glow. I was probably alone in being able to strike his sensitive spots, when the occasion demanded.

'I didn't hear the name Stephen Spicer as well, did I?' queried Eric, stubbing out what was already his fifth cigarette of the morning, 'I'm putting that down to impaired hearing. Most things I can cope with but not the re-birth of that slippery charlatan, Lord forbid!' he said swivelling wildly in the news desk chair that had been management's special gift. It was the directors' acknowledgement, grandly made on his 40th birthday, that Eric spent long periods at an uncomfortable desk, sifting and redrafting copy, much of which would shame a primary school pupil. He liked to use his chair as a front line assault vehicle, sometime hurtling towards unfortunate juniors who watched in dismay as their precious stories were turned into confetti before their eyes.

I, too, thought I had heard Stephen Spicer's name, ruling out the possibility that both of us were mistaken. But would this discredited man, who exploited any gifts he may have had for financial gain, return to the stage he left in disgrace? When the Stephen I remembered decided to make himself scarce and disappear into a world of phoney healers and health diviners, there seemed little chance he would reappear to face the wrath of his many accusers, especially his irate publisher. This gullible woman, who had put so much faith in Stephen, lost a fortune when his second book was denounced as perfidious and committed to the shredder.

I stayed glued to my desk for a few more minutes, hoping our burly security man, Wilf, would quickly return the front office troublemaker to the street from whence he came. But what, I wondered, had happened to that curiosity and boyish enthusiasm which had so enlivened me in days gone by when a good story started to take shape? I certainly wouldn't have stayed glued to my seat, wishing a potential informant would go away.

Sadly, three years of banality, more often than not locked to a desk where a voice on the other end of a telephone provided the only contact with the outside world, had eroded those essential senses of excitement and anticipation so important to the effective journalist. Worried about the decline of their industry, overwhelmed by the advent of new technology and accompanying union pressures, managements had long since decided it was far too expensive to let reporters off the leash.

How different it all was when the local newspaper stood tall in the community. Back in the fifties and sixties there was a real buzz in the newsroom and at the smell of a good story reporters competed for the privilege of getting out on the trail. Many of them may have been raw but they were keen. It was no boast to say I was one of the erstwhile enthusiasts and had moved to Trentbridge to help Eric galvanise his newsroom, a combination of old stagers and new recruits.

Being a chief reporter, as I had then become, still meant something but I knew I would have my work cut out enthusing a predominantly, inexperienced staff at the same time as helping my own young family settle down in a new house and new schools. It would have been nice to ease into the new job gently but Stephen Spicer and a disruptive poltergeist weren't going to allow that. Initially, it seemed to be such a stupid and predictable story, the sort conjured up in many towns and villages when the population disperses at holiday time, leaving local newspapers scratching around for something to write about.

But I could hardly blame Stephen Spicer for not taking my personal circumstances into account. He was already on his way to becoming a celebrity of sorts when I moved my tribe several hundred miles across country to take up residence in Trentbridge. Within a few weeks of our arrival, he had become a household name but not at this stage a threat to the harmony of my family. When his activities did become a matter of discussion it was usually because my two young sons, Marcus and Ian, had become fascinated by repeated references to poltergeists.

Such questions as, 'do we have one?' and 'can they be dangerous?'

5

were understandable in the circumstances but not welcome at a time when mounting tension in the Jenkins household threatened domestic harmony. I also had to take into account that my wife, Penny, was still smarting from the shock of being uprooted from her home town.

I soon discovered that despite intense national interest in poltergeists, confined mainly to the tabloids, the Trentbridge News' policy was to stay aloof. The hierarchy seemed to have an aversion to the sensational so in the early days cuttings about Spicer's activities were abandoned to a pending tray where more often than not they stayed. Many months were to pass before Stephen and I actually came face to face. What were considered more serious local issues received priority and non-proven spooky yarns, although supposedly happening on our doorstep, were generally ignored.

If the reports of Stephen's alleged contact with gremlins from another world had been brief and occasional, his rise to near celebrity fame would almost certainly have stalled. But once started, there seemed no stopping the columns of newsprint rolled out to describe the 'remarkable powers' of a boy not yet out of his teens.

'Who'd scoff at the supernatural after this' trumpeted one large circulation publication as it proceeded to treat every statement by Stephen as something approaching gospel truth. After one experience, while home from his boarding school, he was given the freedom of the press, the freedom that is to say almost anything in the knowledge that his words would be lapped up and splashed liberally over as many pages as were low on advertising content. Quotes often sounded as if they had been taken from a boys' adventure magazine. A typical example was:-

'One night while lying on my bed, I was startled by odd noises coming from an old cabinet in which I kept books and a few souvenirs. When I switched on my light, I could hardly believe my eyes. The cabinet was violently rocking as though someone or something was trying to get out. I wanted to shout for help but my lips froze. Suddenly the cabinet lurched one more time, then crashed onto its side. The noises stopped.'

Almost on a daily basis cuttings appeared on Eric's desk recounting ever more preposterous accounts of what was happening in the cottage home of Trentbridge's psychic wonder. Most of them were accompanied by a photograph of Stephen looking every bit the hippy freak---scruffy jeans, a patterned shirt buttoned at the wrists, shoulder-length locks and what looked like feeble attempts to grow facial hair into a moustache and goatee beard.

Passing the news desk it was not unusual to see Eric, in his bored moments, redesigning the face to resemble a teenage Hitler. The time would come when he would feel compelled to acknowledge we had a young notoriety in our midst, but during those early days, the gathering pile of clippings were given contemptuous treatment. Some of the more outrageous claims found their way into my brief case, put there to enliven chit-chat among friends in the pub that evening. Inevitably, carelessness on my part meant some of this material seeped into the Jenkins living room and was pounced upon by curious members of the family. Producing it in the school playground and associating it with the activities of their father probably gave ten-year-old Marcus, and Ian, his younger brother by three years, feelings of importance.

Long-suffering Penny recoiled at the mere mention of anything to do with the spiritual world and was not pleased when my editorial bosses decided they could ignore the story no longer. She was even less pleased when the assignment came my way. Domestic harmony was to take a jolt when calls late at night became the norm rather than the occasional.

Being disturbed by the harsh jangling of a telephone bell in the early hours was a frequent occurrence in my previous job but those calls were usually from an over enthusiastic fire brigade switchboard operator alerting me to a conflagration, not from callers convinced of strange goings-on in their spare bedroom.

There was plenty for me to do in my new job and disturbed nights did not sit well with a brief to re-energise a complacent group of would-be young journalists. Or to resettle a family still unhappy about the move away from friends and relations.

But there was no escape. Stephen Spicer had moved into our lives and wasn't going away in a hurry. I still wonder how he managed to get under my skin so quickly but evidence of his duplicity was mounting fast and soon had my sensitive journalistic antennae twitching. Stephen was, I thought, an unscrupulous young man, who was making a living by exploiting people's weaknesses. Some were gullible and deserved it, but not all of them.

His tour de force was 'automatic' drawings, which appeared on his bedroom wall at frequent intervals and were so well crafted even the experts had to agree they were passable copies of work by well-known artists. Good enough, they thought, to attract the attention of those who could see prospects of turning his skill into profitable, but most probably, unlawful activity.

My reminiscing was brought to a halt by Eric who, noticing that I had not moved a muscle, shouted: 'Get off your ass, Damon, and deal with that maniac outside.' All the troops, especially the younger ones, were now looking at us, anticipating another of our frequent verbal punch-ups. It would brighten an otherwise routine Monday morning, they were thinking.

This time I would disappoint them. In a bid to counter creeping lethargy, I headed in determined fashion towards the swing doors separating the newsroom from the outside world. The scene greeting me on the other side was comical, something akin to a sequence in a Whitehall farce with the characters frozen, as though caught by the flash of a publicity man's camera.

Computer screens abandoned, pens and paper scattered, the front office girls were leaning across the counter, staring down at a flustered, insignificant little guy half-lying, half-kneeing on the floor, trying to recover vast amounts of paperwork. Hovering over him was Wilf, who in trying to do his job protecting the paper's sensitive reporters from real-life members of the public, had landed himself in a situation he had no idea how to cope with.

The relief on Wilf's face was palpable when I appeared. 'It was you he wanted to see, Damon. I told him he would have to wait 'til I tracked you down. Kept on saying he had important information on a chap called Spicer, a friend of yours, he claimed. When he started to head for the newsroom I stuck out an arm and all this stuff he was carrying went everywhere.'

'So we'd better help him pick it all up,' I suggested, 'then perhaps this gentleman will explain his problem and why my name and that of someone long since dismissed as a calculating cheat, penetrated the hallowed sanctum of the reporters' room. It disturbed the slumbers of at least three overhung scribes!'

The two front office employees, who had been part of this strange tableau, obviously considered it not their job to take part in a paper chase, so it was left to Wilf and me, with some help from our as yet unidentified visitor, to grovel and collect.

By now I had half made up my mind I was dealing with a screwball

8

but nothing could have prepared me for his next statement which came in a half whisper, just loud enough to be heard above the noise of rustling paper: 'I know who killed John F Kennedy,' he announced, his face remaining deadpan.

'You know what?' I queried, dropping the few papers I had managed to gather. 'What the hell are you talking about?'

Monday mornings are usually painful but this one now promised to descend into total farce and probably would have done so if I hadn't made a connection between the article recently rediscovered at the back of my desk and what this visitor was trying to tell me. It was not the first time in my journalistic career that the two names Spicer and Kennedy had been talked about in the same breath. No stretch of the imagination would normally have conjured up a connection between a murdered American president and a nineteen-year-old English boy with grand claims to extraordinary psychic gifts. Nevertheless, I had the feeling that imaginations, and probably my patience, were about to be stretched to the limit.

It seemed unwise to start an interview with the participants still on hands and knees so I encouraged an organised completion of the salvage operation, giving me time to rake the memory for information that might intelligently feed and sustain the conversation certain to take place as soon as we returned to an upright position.

How long was it since I left the safety of the newsroom? Was it really only a few minutes ago that I came across a Jenkins keepsake recording a moment of glory when Stephen Spicer was exposed with the largest possible front-page headline. Now, here I was on hands and knees with someone who seemed to want to bring Stephen back into my life with a story bordering on lunacy.

The priority was to recall what had happened shortly before Stephen decided to disappear over the horizon and seek a degree of anonymity. Perhaps I had been so keen to wallow in his downfall, I failed to look carefully into the reason for his sudden trip to the United States and, more important, what had scared him so much that within the week he had headed back to Britain. Shortly before his departure, he had been making a name for himself, regularly appearing on television chat shows. He rarely got a tough interview because producers, wanting to excite viewers with as much of the spooky stuff as was available, rarely sought to challenge seriously the claims he was making. For a while, everything was going for him.

One man who didn't appreciate his rise to fame was Yasha Rashnin, a crafty manipulator who had made an international name for himself as a psychic metal-bender (cutlery was his speciality), a mind reader and a predictor of future events. Rashnin had led the field in this department for many years and Stephen was beginning to tread on his toes. Rashnin considered his worldwide reputation was being threatened when Stephen started to get the prime time shows and the celebrity interviewers.

The rancour between them intensified after the cancellation of a show in which Rashnin was going to demonstrate to the world how the out-pouring of his mind could bounce into homes all over the country and cause controlled chaos. Advance press releases promised cracked windows, clocks going backwards and invalids saying they felt better having met Yasha's gaze through a television screen. Rashnin put the blame for the programme's cancellation squarely on Stephen's shoulders, claiming his rival had influenced producers with a string of lies.

From my hands and knees position, I was about to recover the last few pieces of paper when I noticed eye-catching words printed in red at the top of two documents--- **TOP SECRET** on one **SECRET AND CONFIDENTIAL** on the other. For a moment, I couldn't make up my mind whether to retreat to the safety of the newsroom or stay and risk plunging myself again into the unpredictable but exhilarating world of investigative reporting. It was not the sort of decision one usually makes from such an undignified position.

'What are you doing with this?' I said, pointing to the words I had last seen while doing national service in the registry office of a secretive NATO department. The two of us were now almost eyeball-to-eyeball, the front office girls were trying not to giggle and even Wilf was starting to see the comical side of the situation.

'On second thoughts, don't answer, let's go and find a quiet office. Bring all this paper with you and we'll start again,' I said realising that this was probably a mistake and would lead me into dangerous territory. Dangerous? There was a time when my adrenalin would have started racing at the first sniff of a story with the potential this one appeared to have.

As we moved towards a small corner of the building that served as an interview room, I was able to get a better look at my visitor. Impressive he was not, with straggly, shoulder length hair and a physique as puny and unhealthy as I remembered Stephen's had been. No doubt after a few years hawking his wares around the world's cruise liners his body weight would have soared. It was all coming back to me now--Stephen had adapted his skills to healing, a more lucrative activity, he discovered, than 'communicating' with the dead, particularly in the world of the elderly blue-rinse brigade. The guy walking ahead of me must be about the same age as Stephen but obviously his way of life had been more frugal and spare flesh was not his problem.

Passing through the door of the interview room and before we could settle at a table, I was treated to a repeat of the most extraordinary statement any small-town journalist could expect to hear on an ordinary, dreary Monday morning. Throwing himself into a chair and dramatically throwing out his arms like a minister in a pulpit he declared: '**I mean it, I do know who killed the American president.**'

With hindsight perhaps, that was the moment when the interview should have ended. Mildly disturbed people frequently walk into newspaper offices with information they describe as 'exclusive' to give it more weight and a better chance of being taken seriously This was the moment I should have prised the lowliest reporter from his pile of wedding reports and delegated to him the task of listening, very carefully, of course, to the ramblings of the latest local crank. There were going to be several times in the future when I would regret not having done that.

I shuffled a few of the documents now lying on the table and turned up the papers with official warnings clearly displayed. 'It's not very wise to mess around with papers bearing hands-off warnings like this, you know. What are you doing with them? Why have you brought them to me?'

Getting no immediate reply to these questions, I tried a different tack. 'You tell me you know who killed the President of the United States. That suggests to me you have material denied to the top brass of the FBI, the CIA and the Warren Commission. They got it wrong, you have the answers. Is that the nub of it?'

Realising the Monday morning feeling was doing nothing for my manners or the professional approach I prided myself in, I decided that if I wasn't going to walk away at this point then at least I should probe the identity and motivation of the rather bewildered, sad looking person sitting in front of me. What was wrong with me? I hadn't even bothered to ask him his name.

11

'OK, let's start again. Tell me who you are and why you have come to see me. I'm sorry if we didn't get off to a good start. Your entrance was a touch chaotic, I think you'd agree?'

He didn't agree. 'It was your chap who scattered my files but don't let's worry about that now. I'm Christopher Howell, one of Stephen's old school friends, friend of the family for many years. If you've read his book, you will know Stephen's psychic adventures were not confined to his parents' home. They went with him back to the boarding school dormitory we shared. Looking back, I don't know how any of us managed to get any work done at all. Many nights were disturbed by bunks being moved around the dorm; articles, some of them quite heavy, were thrown in a dangerous manner and bottles were smashed with careless abandoned. I remember several nights when we had to switch on the lights and clear up the mess. The headmaster was not amused and threatened to send Stephen home. But he relented and set out to get help from people he felt would have a better understanding of matters ethereal than he had.'

'Hang on a minute, if you were as close to Stephen as you now say you were, you will remember that a lot of those claims were proved to be false and although I can't remember you being around at the time, you must remember this newspaper campaigned vigorously and revealed all sorts of trickery and under-hand practices. You must also know I was the leading antagonist so why have you come to see me today, three years after all this happened.'

'Because I fear that Stephen has got himself into really serious trouble, and no one will take his plight seriously. I'm just hoping your knowledge of what happened in the early days will help sort things out.'

'What sort of trouble are you talking about?' I wanted to know, 'It seems odd to seek help from the person who scuttled his career and deprived him of a tidy fortune.'

As we talked, Stephen's old school pal was searching feverishly through his paper mountain on the interview room table, presumably looking for something to galvanise me into action. It seemed right to give him a chance to gather whatever evidence he felt he had to throw new light on the situation.

A mere 45 minutes had passed since a cutting had fallen out of an old notebook and simultaneously Eric had prodded me into front office territory to sort out a disturbance. During that time, all sorts of memories had been flooding back, most of them relating to the manipulation, the lies, the tantrums, even the tears of a family totally in the thrall of their teenage son.

The number of people he managed to carry along with him was quite phenomenal. Tabloid newspaper reporters were easy meat as they sought ways and means of filling pages at all times of the year but particularly during summer silly seasons. Fringe investigators, who called themselves scientists, were sucked in, magazine editors with claims to paranormal knowledge and more amazingly, publishers with serious money at stake joined the Spicer bandwagon.

I rated myself one of the few who didn't toe the line and received letters, some quite abusive, from light entertainment television producers and others who wanted to preserve the image and titillate the viewing public.

Stephen eventually met his Waterloo, I received an award, courtesy of an august panel of national editors and the last I heard of Stephen's exploits was a report that he had joined a cruise ship and was soothing the brows of elderly widows, relieving them of substantial amounts of cash in return for promises of miraculous healings.

My thoughts were disturbed by Christopher Howell's shout of triumph as he unearthed a piece of A4, very faded but still containing words so preposterous one didn't know whether to laugh or cry. I seem to remember that in my case it was the former. *The Gemstone File* as it came to be known contained a whole string of outrageous accusations under the tabloid-style headline '**Who shot President John Kennedy? Was it really Lee Harvey Oswald?**'

Despite the fact that several years had passed since I last saw this document, I remembered every detail, not because of all the extraordinary allegations within it but because it led to a string of events causing the collapse of Stephen's planned career.

Things had been going well for him until he made a fated trip to America. He thought he had stumbled across something that if served up in a paranormal sort of way from afar would feed the interest of his growing band of followers back in the UK. Instead, he had to beat a hasty retreat when he realised that, possibly for the first time in his life, someone was taking him for a ride and an uncomfortable one at that,

'Why are you so pleased to find this long discredited document?' I asked Christopher, 'there was a time when every journalist in the Western World had a copy of the *Gemstone File* in their locker but no one chose to print it because of its unproven claims inevitably leading, many felt, to a sackful of expensive libel actions. Possibly a few death threats, as well.'

For the first time in this strange encounter, Christopher allowed some of the tension he had obviously been feeling to ease. Until now, his face had given no indication of any emotion lying beneath the surface. The mention of the notorious file changed his demeanour completely. 'That's why I'm here; it seems the *Gemstone File* was not as harmless as all you journalists decided it was.'

'How come? Every agency in the US raked it over word by word and eventually the Commission itself came to the conclusion that the content was make believe, an attempt to stir up trouble.'

'But they would say that wouldn't they, politically the desire was to close the investigations down,' suggested Christopher, 'despite all your diligent inquiries there was one question you never answered satisfactorily. Why did Stephen come back from the States in a such a hurry and why did he go straight to his publisher and say he no longer wanted to be described as a psychic, he wanted to be known as a mentalist?'

'Well, I thought my investigations had something to do with that surprise development,' I said trying not to sound too boastful. 'So what is your take on his rapid departure from the States, it must have been something he thought serious enough to abandon a lucrative lecture tour.'

'Stephen did tell me what happened and I have mentioned it to no one until now,' said Christopher, conspiratorially.

'Why now, then,' I asked, 'why come to the one person in the media Stephen would probably not want to have anything to do with?'

'Perhaps I am beginning to think some of the things you said at the time were not so far from the truth. But Stephen remains a friend and I am desperate to try to help him. What he didn't know when he went to the States the first time was that he was being targeted. I think someone, or an organisation, who wanted to promote a conspiracy theory about the death of Kennedy, decided to use Stephen as a kind of spiritually empowered go-between. They planted a document on him containing all sorts of dangerous allegations knowing that when in America Stephen would be tempted to claim he had received the facts on the death of Kennedy through paranormal channels.

'Of course, that is just what he did and much to Stephen's surprise he received a visit from a couple of characters who pretended to be top security officials. They wanted him to go with them then and there but Stephen managed to persuade them he had to fulfil a promise to give a lecture the next day. Frightened by their aggressive approach, he decided discretion was the better part of valour and headed for home. On his return to England he discovered he had been rumbled and renounced his psychic abilities.'

'But since then he's been making a small fortune on the cruise circuit. Whatever persuaded him to go running off to America for a second time?' I asked.

'Stephen eventually got bored with trips around the Mediterranean, persuading elderly women he could cure their headaches and sooth their arthritis. Despite his past bad experiences, he decided to cross the pond and try his luck again. He was always convinced there was far more interest in the paranormal on the other side of the Atlantic and the guys who had threatened him previously would probably no longer be around.'

I ventured the thought that having forsaken his psychic pretensions once, achieving credibility again would not be easy. There would be some who would remember the confession he made after scurrying home and they would not be slow in confronting him with that fact.

'That wasn't the way he was thinking,' replied Christopher, 'he thought he might be able to fix up a programme of lectures in the States, this time concentrating on what he considered to be some of the more serious aspects of paranormal research. But before he could make any headway something happened which indicated *The Gemstone File* might still contain sensitive material capable of muddying the waters again.'

'In what way,' I inquired, 'and how did you come to know about it?'

'He phoned me to say he had received a threatening note four or five days after his arrival. He had no proof but he thought it had come from the same source as previously. The next day he was due to deliver his first lecture in Chicago and apparently that went ahead. But when I contacted his hotel one of the organisers of the lecture tour said he had left the lecture theatre on his own the previous night and had vanished. The police had been told but no one had seen him since. I really fear something dreadful has happened,' added Christopher, with genuine concern in his voice.

I suppose this was the moment the adrenalin started to activate again; negative vibes I might have had previously began to dispel and

I had the feeling that before the end of the day, I would be knocking on the editor's door suggesting that the Stephen Spicer case was worth revisiting. It was one way of stemming the fall in circulation figures, I would tell him. It was worth a try. As I reached my desk I realised I had made one bad mistake, I hadn't asked Christopher Howell to explain the two top security documents which had slipped out of his file. Perhaps, at this stage it was better that I didn't probe too deeply. There would be, I was sure, an early opportunity to discover their origins and the reason why they had landed up in the hands of Stephen's best friend.

****

The strange drama which had taken place in the front office played on my mind as I drove home that night, home being a modest semi-detached five miles from the centre of Trentbridge. Its attractions, despite its size and situation, were an open vista across fields, a fertile vegetable garden and, inside, an open fire, a great comfort when the cold winds swept in from the North Sea.

Little time was going to be spent on the vegetable patch that evening; another more pressing operation was looming---a thorough search of the attic above my bedroom-cum-office for the many thousands of words devoted to Stephen Spicer's escapades three years previously.

As a matter of habit or misplaced pride, I had kept my clippings, ranging from a couple of paragraphs to two-page spreads, from the day I enrolled as a 16-year-old cub reporter. The early crop---reports of dog shows, funerals and golden weddings---were the efforts of the most reticent of young scribes, so timid in fact, that his daily practice was to seek the farthermost corner of the newsroom in the hope no one in authority would notice him. How he managed to earn a living acting in this way neither he, nor anyone else, will ever know.

Those acquainted with his more recent journalistic exploits, would hardly recognise this picture of little Damon struggling to prove he had a modicum of journalistic talent. The quality of the writing may have improved only marginally during the intervening years but the manner in which the material was gathered had certainly moved up a gear, demonstrating more determination, even aggressiveness. Penny wasn't around during the formative years and recalled that the man she married certainly wasn't shy, just pig-headed and in need of being weaned off a tendency to become a chronic workaholic.

Her husband's other addiction was nicotine but she had decided on the day they became engaged that newspapers would have died a death years ago if reporters had been told to extinguish their cigs, or fags as they were more commonly called in those days. The other necessity for the average hack was to drink above average volumes of beer but this was regarded as necessary fuel, just as vital to the smooth running of a typewriter as petrol was to a car!

Tolerating for the most part the long hours I chose to work, Penny did successfully convey with some force that there was more to life than work. Once the poltergeist saga had been wrapped up and Stephen had abdicated, life became less frenetic and for many months we were able to return to a more normal style of family life. Now I could see that this period of calm was about to be put in jeopardy as the content of a packing case, out of sight and out of mind for so long, came fluttering down from the attic, dust and all.

The worst arguments Penny and I had while Spicer was being pursued were invariably over the way I allowed potential informants to ring me at any time of the day or night. To my dismay, she admitted she was quite spooked by my constant references to poltergeists and alleged contact with spirits from another world. I tried to convince her it was all an elaborate game and she shouldn't take any of it seriously. Then, I realised her concerns must be listened to when in a nightmare she thought she saw distorted faces sneering through the glass of her dressing table mirror. Disturbed nights had become the norm.

These memories were vivid enough for me to decide to leave the packing case and its contents where it was until Penny had gone out to tea with friends. This I did but could not resist a preliminary skirmish into the vast quantity of printed matter, much of it so trivial I wondered what had possessed me to retain it for so long. Raking over the past can become absorbing and very time consuming and before I could safely store away the last remnants of my archive, Penny was backing her car down the drive. 'What are you doing up there?' she asked, as she came through the front door, 'Oh, nothing of consequence, darling,' I said, repeating the little white lie that must have been told by husbands from time immemorial.

As soon as another opportunity arose, I again buried my head into the

17

contents of the packing case knowing I needed to check out details of an earlier encounter with Stephen prior to his aborted visit to the States. In this pile of grubby, mouldy remnants of my life's work, I would find details of a brief meeting with the self-proclaimed psychic wonder man, some time before the poltergeist and other alleged phenomena became the centre of attention.

There would be occasions when I would wish that brief encounter had never taken place. But I would also have reason to thank Stephen for being an unwilling participant on a journey which started crazily enough but eventually threw up an episode in my life and his which would have a series of life-changing after-shocks.

2

(1967)

The Year of Invincibility

Nigel Ferguson was not the sort of editor to inspire confidence in his staff. The adjustments he needed to make to put the rumbustious capers of a Scottish national behind him and adopt the more down-to-earth practices of a subdued English regional were beyond him. It didn't take us long to discover why hard-nosed north of the border journalists had decided to dispense with his services.

His news sense was highly suspect and many of his decisions were based on personal prejudices rather than on the hard facts placed before him. This fault was so pronounced, he was known to compose a headline long before the unfortunate reporter had returned from his designated assignment and produced his copy. Ferguson also had a vicious streak that demonstrated itself in the way he toyed with his editorial staff, sometimes giving them convoluted briefs that were virtually impossible to fulfil.

I shouldn't have been surprised when one of these came my way. Called into his office during a particularly dull week he commanded outrageously: 'Damon, go and find out why everyone is meditating.'

Transcendental meditation, marketed as a technique for seeking peace and tranquillity, had been made trendy by the participation of the Beatles and other pop groups seeking eye-catching publicity in the permissive society. The sit-on-your-bottom and contemplate routine had become all the rage in university towns and Trentbridge was no exception.

'Did you say everyone?' I asked, trying to get off the hook. 'It's a fad, indulged in by immature academics and students with too much time on their hands. It'll die quickly enough when another cranky technique comes into fashion.'

My protest fell on deaf ears. 'Go, try it, Damon, the administrations of the Maharishi Mahesh Yogi with his emphasis on peace and tranquillity may make you less brittle. Find out, while you're about it, why he thinks his mind-cleansing technique will contribute to world peace within 20 years. The United Nations could do with someone like him.'

I realised Ferguson, who we knew had been bruised many times as a junior by the rough treatment of more than one battle-hardened news editor, was trying to wind me up but he was probably right in suggesting that in this case the kid gloves should come off. The Maharishi was raking in mega-bucks and had recently had the cheek to announce the year ahead would be *The Year of Invincibility*. If nothing else, I should try to make him explain what the hell that meant.

As a preliminary to his intended crusade of Britain, the placid, expressionless Yogi had sent a couple of disciples ahead of him. Their job was to launch 60 training centres in Britain and it was at one of these centres where I first met Stephen Spicer, then only 16 years old. He didn't know I was there as an inquisitive journalist; I didn't know at that stage he had an ambition to follow in the footsteps of Yasha Rashnin, the Eygptian conjuror-cum-magician who for a while had managed to secure the blessing of the pseudo-scientific priesthood by claiming to have psychic abilities. Rashnin was a well-known performer by this time and met claims he was a sham with lots of disdain but very little in the way of proof to the contrary. Spicer was still to launch his colourful career, cutting into Rashnin's territory, so it was not entirely surprising I regarded Stephen, at that first meeting, as just another sucker looking for the end of the rainbow.

The bizarre ceremony we experienced together in an atmosphere of reverence, designed to underline its importance, is not something you forget easily. We were each handed a small bunch of flowers, some fruit and a white handkerchief but assured that this was not a 'religious' occasion. However, our teacher added, the ceremony had a profound relevance to religion, for all religions were in essence concerned with leading people to inner awareness.

I recall trying desperately hard, but not very successfully, to disguise my amusement and scepticism to others around me but I do remember Stephen took it all very seriously indeed and was quite upset when I made a joke about the mantra, a personal password constantly repeated in the head to bolster the two periods of meditation a day I was now committing myself to.

'You mustn't make fun of it,' he implored, 'used in the proper way it will help us reduce stress, anxiety and nervousness. It could lead to a blissful state of relaxed creativity if we take our training seriously.'

Stephen had obviously swallowed the entire publicity blurb and sat there with a fixed look of contentment on his face. But how could I take it seriously when burning a hole in my pocket was the staggeringly naïve newsletter of our first local transcendental centre? No modest claims here, rather an announcement that the centre's activities along with others would eventually 'produce a coherence and harmony in the world so profound that countries would stop arguing with each other and live in peace.' As the state of invincibility took hold, we were informed, there would be no more wars and even natural disasters would be eliminated.

It struck me on the first occasion I read this piece of gobbledygook that even if some wars could be tackled by soothing the minds of world leaders, a religious element of some kind might be needed to deal with natural disasters. The statement continued: 'In every way there will be harmony, happiness and progress; but for that situation to come about it is obligatory for every sensible individual to spend 20 minutes morning and evening in meditation.'

I remember how difficult it was not to draw that statement from my pocket and subject the Maharishi's disciples to some tough questioning but my brief was to take a serious look at the meditation technique and it wasn't the moment to blow my cover. Apart from that, the newspaper's financial director had handed me a cheque for £300, which was to be used solely to further the cause of investigative journalism. I did risk one question about the technique required to eliminate natural disasters but this produced a 'better talk to me afterwards' type of answer.

Stephen and I didn't really come to know each other during that first meeting and I didn't give him another thought until months later when his name started to appear in various publications. I wrote my piece on meditation, concluding that it was a useful means of relaxing but there was nothing in the course, which couldn't be taught at a run-of-the-mill evening class.

To her credit, Penny managed to maintain a sense of humour during the three-month period I spent retreating to our holiday caravan in the drive for twice-daily meditation experiences. 'Haven't noticed any difference yet,' she said after the second month, 'except that I see even less of you now than I did before.' There was a slightly more worrying response back at the office where colleagues were saying I was losing my sharpness and a desire to go for the jugular when it was required. What they really meant was that instead of tearing around like a headless chicken, I was more composed, maybe they meant lazy and less focused. Of course, if that was the case then meditation could be said to be working—for me anyway. What it would do for the world if vast sections of the population just switched off, was another matter.

Sidney, cynical friend and next-door neighbour, was highly amused when I refused to divulge the secret, personal mantra I was using (strangely, to this very day I have never forgotten it). 'Please yourself,' he said after I had denied him the privilege of sharing my buzzword for the third time, 'the music of Mozart works just as well for me and it doesn't cost the exorbitant fee you hand over to the Maharishi.'

I should have been aware by this stage in my career that putting oneself on public display for the sake of a zany feature can have its setbacks. It was not the first time I had fallen into this trap. Trying to kick the nicotine habit and reporting on progress three times a week didn't do my reputation much good especially when I had to swallow hard and report shameful failure. Telling the world, well my little world, about meditation and its mollifying effects fuelled even more ridicule. When a vicious forehand or overhead smash passed my racket without any sort of retaliation, my tennis club chums suggested a replay so that I could meditate further on the shot I might have played in less competitive circumstances.

Meditation was soon to take a back seat when more universally popular feature material presented itself. The reappearance of Stephen as the supposed victim of a poltergeist activity didn't surprise me greatly. He had talked about the spiritual world at one of the Maharishi's debriefings, showing a lot more curiosity than anyone else on the course.

Poltergeist activity had reached almost epidemic proportions across the country, judging from daily reports of ever more extraordinary happenings. At a moment's notice tabloid newspaper editors were despatching staff to various parts of the United Kingdom with a mission to unravel the flimsiest of domestic mysteries, often precipitated it was frequently maintained by psychologists, by young girls struggling to cope with their early puberty years.

There seemed no reasonable explanation for the sudden explosion of cases in Trentbridgeshire. Suddenly the county had bobbed to the top of the list of places known for intriguing poltergeist activity.

'Perhaps they're planning a spooks' convention,' suggested Bob Harding, the most cynical of our photographers when given the task of providing some sort of pictorial evidence. 'How do you photograph a bloody ghost anyway?' he wanted to know.

The first story about the Spicer family, reported in sensational fashion by many popular journals, might have been the last if it had not triggered a wave of other reports often manufactured by failed scientists looking for a role in life. At the time, the meagre editorial resources of the Trentbridge News were being mopped up in pursuit of a noisy parrot accidentally let out of its cage by a local pub landlord. For a week or so, its recapture had been of vital importance to various sections of the population. Under a dozen trees, bird lovers sat, proffering cages laden with seed and other tantalising tit-bits which parrots were said to like.

So with a cross-section of our readers having sleepless nights waiting for news that Polly was back in the smoky warmth of the Queen's Head lounge bar, the arrival of a lively spook did not initially grab the attention. It didn't take long, however, for interest to be awakened once Stephen's parents declared it was their belief that Stephen was the catalyst. His mother, Maureen, a respected member of a branch of the Women's Institute, lit the fuse by deciding to tell the world how she was coming to terms with her son's supernatural powers. His father, Patrick, a local government employee and member of the Pentagon Club, a coterie for professional men, also surprised everyone when he described in detail how he had tried to trick the poltergeist into revealing itself.

One of my well-preserved cuttings contained an interview with Spicer senior, who recalled the morning when Stephen and his 13-year-old twin sisters, Caroline and Veronica, came under suspicion. Precious family heirlooms had been found lying on the floor of rooms some distance from their normal resting places, heavy furniture was moved and carpets lifted. Initially, the twin girls were accused of playing pranks but this theory was ruled out because of their physical limitations. A break-in was considered but nothing had been taken and no burglar, it was decided, would have left precious objects lying around when their acquisition would have paid for a night's work.

The Spicer family were well known and respected in the sleepy, picturesque village of Deepcote where the locals had certainly not prepared themselves for a riotous introduction to 'the pack'--- a popular description for a group of journalists who prefer safety in numbers when planning an invasion out of London and into the English countryside.

Being the local man at large I wasn't bound by the rules of the pack, and one of the clippings which had surfaced reminded me of the day I descended on the Spicer home hoping to put this burgeoning story into perspective. The cottage, with rambling roses over the front door and bushes of sweet smelling honeysuckle straddling a rustic fence, looked peaceful enough, not the sort of place to run into disturbed souls from another world.

Mrs Spicer came to the door, flinched when I revealed my identity, seemed about to shut the door in my face but then changed her mind and said: 'I suppose you'd better come in.'

'I'm not from one of the nationals,' I said, hoping this would underline my more responsible credentials.

'Well then, perhaps you'll start telling the story as it happened, not making it up as you go along,' she said witheringly.

'Is that what you think has happened so far?' I asked, and at that moment noticed a publication on a coffee table, which had the word 'paranormal' in its title. The front cover design indicated that it was probably a more academic offering than much of the material so far produced to back up claims of the extraordinary.

Mrs Spicer noticed my attention had been drawn to the magazine and spent, I suspect, a minute or two weighing up the chances of getting a more sympathetic hearing from someone with a local reputation to preserve than she had had so far from unscrupulous news-hounds from London. Threatening to sue me if I strayed from her version of the truth, she agreed to go over the details so long as I promised to report her words faithfully.

She took the publication from the coffee table, tossed it in my direction and invited me to sit down. She then explained that after a strange sequence of events in the cottage, initially frightening most members of the family (apart from Stephen himself) she and her husband decided to quell their fears and try to examine the happenings in an adult and logical manner. If necessary, they would seek outside help.

'Disturbed about loss of sleep as much as anything, we hunted in the town library for anything which might put our minds at rest and came across this publication which talked about mischievous spirits but admitted there was very little serious research into causes or outcome of such manifestations.' Distracted for a moment or two, she walked towards the lounge window and gazed into the distance as though searching for inspiration.

Then, with a suddenness that startled me she asked: 'Do you believe in an after-life Mr Jenkins? If you don't you might have considerable difficulty in coming to terms with what has been going on here.'

'I don't think I'm really sure,' I mumbled, 'In moments of quiet contemplation, we all like to believe in another place, I know, but most of us postpone consideration of such weighty matters until another time…a time when we're less busy,' I added feebly.

'Isn't that rather stupid?' queried Maureen Spicer, 'If God is left on our back burners we're going to be caught on the wrong foot at some time in the future.'

This was a disconcerting reversal of roles. Now I was the one being interrogated, and was by no means certain how to bring the conversation back under my control.

'Well, where do you think this troublesome little poltergeist of yours fits into the scene?' I asked rather hopefully, 'many people will write him off as a piece of nonsense created by the media; others faced with something similar might well be frightened out of their wits. My wife would be that's for sure.'

Struggling to pull an argument together I added: 'At the end of the day it probably depends on our view of the physical world, whether we feel every activity can be explained or believe there is something "out there" like God, angels, the devil or even spirits of some sort. I would hate to think all we have done down here, all the relationships we have formed, the daily struggles, the few things we have achieved, amounted to nothing.'

Maureen Spicer didn't respond to my pathetic little sermon despite the fact that it had been inspired by her own question. Instead, she returned to her account of what had been happening in the cottage over a period of time.

'Without saying anything to the children, Patrick and I decided to set a trap for our elusive night raider. Doors were sealed with sticky tape and we stretched strands of cotton across the stairs from wall to banisters. Next day the tape and the cotton strands were still in place but the same objects had been moved or thrown around again. How do you explain that?'

'At the moment, I can't, but I would very much like to talk to Stephen. Is he at home?'

'No,' she replied, a little too quickly as noises upstairs indicated someone was around and it was unlikely to be the twin sisters, still at school, or her husband who was presumably at his office. I decided not to push the issue as my conversation with her was proving to be quite useful in its own right.

Maureen Spicer then explained that after more disturbances in the cottage, they went further afield for answers and eventually Stephen and his sisters did come under scrutiny when one 'expert' after another confirmed poltergeist activity was usually connected with the presence of a child or adolescent.

'Have you thought of getting help from our local university?' I suggested, trying to maintain a helpful approach, 'They do research into this sort of stuff because they frequently send me handouts hoping to whip up the newspaper's interest.'

What I didn't mention at this stage were the problems many researchers had experienced when trying to track down competent and honest observers. Even boffins can be tempted to cut corners when funding pressures threaten the future of their research programme. Their colleagues at home and abroad usually uncover their deceptions eventually but a lot of damage can be done in the interim.

I was in the process of explaining this to Mrs Spicer when a door opened noisily upstairs and a voice called out, 'Is that another sodding reporter down there with you, Mum, tell him to go away. I'm sick to death of the whole crowd of them.' The door slammed. Stephen's mother, obviously embarrassed that she had denied he was in the house, tried to explain that he 'came and went' as he pleased. 'It was all a novelty to begin with,' explained Mrs Spicer, 'but he's beginning to get irritated by all the attention, much of it pumped up and malicious.'

'Tell your son I would have liked to talk to him,' I said as I left the cottage, 'and please tell him he might get better treatment from his local rag if he decided co-operation rather than conflict was the best policy. Ask him to get in touch if he changes his mind.'

After my first visit to the Spicer homestead, we decided to leave Polly the parrot to her own devices and deploy the entire investigative team of the Trentbridge Evening News (all two of us) on a quest to expose the mischievous poltergeist. It was no surprise that this decision and the arrival of yet more seekers after the sensational coincided with further outbreaks of even more dramatic happenings at Deepcote. All sorts of domestic and personal items ceased to be inanimate and found their way to every corner of the cottage, we were told in one publication.

So much furniture had re-located itself a posse of strong local neighbours had to be recruited to put it all back into position. They obviously felt they had strength and safety in numbers but that didn't stop one timid, potential helper turning on his heel and walking away from the cottage because he decided it was probably cursed.

Meanwhile, Stephen, according to one talkative friend, had to deal with a succession of weird requests. A record company tried to persuade him to make a pop record. 'There's a vast teenage market out there just waiting for you,' he was told. Stephen tried to tell them he couldn't sing but this didn't seem to be a matter of concern to those who wanted to exploit his notoriety.

With the less scrupulous press going into overdrive, I was coming under pressure from both editor and news editor to put our publication into the front line. 'I didn't like the story much in the first place,' said Eric, 'but we're saddled with it now so let's show them our local knowledge counts for something.'

Nigel Ferguson was even more scathing. 'Get ahead of the game Damon or we'll put someone else on the trail,' he warned. These comments did not go down well with me. Neither of them had shown any interest when the story first broke.

At home, our telephone started to get red hot and Penny's nerves started to jangle. She knew enough about the demands on a journalist's time not to reprimand me with the time-honoured words 'can't you leave your business at the office' but she was hoping this was a story that could soon be to put to bed and forgotten.

I felt the time had come for me to talk to the Deepcote residents, who had regular contact with the Spicer family. There was no shortage of people who liked to see their name in print. One close neighbour reported seeing a young girl, who she thought was Caroline Spicer, 'floating around her bedroom without any visible means of support.'

'It was really weird, the girl smiled at me several times as she drifted by in a horizontal position' was this eyewitness's impression of what had happened one quiet afternoon. It topped the list of absurd and unlikely sightings now growing in number with every passing week.

No photographs were produced, of course, but psychic 'experts', skilled at covering their tracks, usually claimed it was impossible to pick up camera images from the spiritual world. The media corps was also in a state of excitement about a new development---the appearance on Stephen's bedroom wall of 'automatic' messages written in fluent, distinct handwriting by who-knows-who. Even more intriguing were paintings and drawings 'signed' by famous artists. Of course, they're fakes we told ourselves but that left us trying to answer the question: 'If they are fakes, how did he do it?' The original artists must have taken their time but this phantom sketcher-cum-painter obviously thought in terms of completing a piece of work in a few hours, not days or weeks.

It was agreed in the newsroom that there were so many more questions to be asked and answered, so much nonsense to be stripped away to see if any hard facts lay beneath the surface that another visit to the Spicer home had to be next on the agenda. To our surprise, on this occasion the welcome mat was laid out for us.

3

Chicanery Denied

Despite his scepticism, Bob the photographer liked to accompany me on what he good-humouredly described as my 'crazy little missions.' Usually a quiet figure in the background with his camera at the ready, he couldn't control his mirth when told in all seriousness about domestic objects and furniture moving around the cottage. 'Easiest thing in the world to do a bit of rearranging while everyone is asleep or watching television,' he said with crushing logic. This injudicious comment nearly ruined our second visit but Mrs Spicer smiled weakly and ignored Bob's diagnosis.

I, too, was becoming irritated by the naivety of the parents, who appeared to be allowing their offspring a platform from which to launch a series of unsubstantiated claims, seemingly embellished by fertile imaginations. Unprofessionally, I allowed this irritation to surface and it led to the first skirmish in my rocky relationship with the Spicer family.

If the story had stayed centred on poltergeists, it would eventually have run out of steam. Poltergeists can be quite easily 'invented' and just as easily disposed of when more important worldwide topics come to the fore. But the automatic drawings, which plastered the Spicer's interior walls, were another matter because no one could fathom how they could be produced so adeptly, in great quantity and with such a high degree of accuracy. If Stephen was bringing them to life with his own artistic skills and ingenuity, there was still the puzzle of how he maintained this astonishing production line over a considerable period of time, without detection.

Stephen's mother was his greatest defender. Fixing me with an accusing glare in the early stage of our acquaintanceship, she said icily: 'One thing that saddens me is when ignorant people (she didn't need to add 'like you') write off this family as charlatans and cheats.'

If any reporter, pseudo scientist or curious villager suggested chicanery, she would march them around the family's 16th century cottage pointing out various drawings and writings, describing the many disturbed nights the family had suffered and then regularly pose the same question: 'Would any mature person with a busy life to lead be party to some sort of spiritual scam, just to keep the media amused?'

She spoke of Stephen as being a gentle, kindly young man who had an uneventful teenage until recent developments. But she did believe he might be burdened, or should she say gifted, with a brain that performed to a different and unconventional pattern. She didn't believe her daughters were involved in any way whatsoever but had no proof of that fact.

One man who offered his services to the family was, Nick Bertram, the new curate at Deepcote's village church. I had interviewed Nick when he moved into the area because he came with some innovative ideas on how to reinvigorate parishioners and recapture the interest of young people. Not long out of theological college, he was given a baptism of fire when he found himself tackling the vagaries of a local poltergeist. Nick thought an article in the parish magazine might help to stem the flow of misguided comments and sought me out to give a little journalistic guidance.

'The article was a great help,' he told me later, 'I didn't think Mrs Spicer would respond but I gather she's been telling members of the congregation that as a result of what has been happening around her, she's more certain about the possibility of an afterlife. So far it is the one good thing to come out of this whole affair.'

He was also pleased when Mrs Spicer decided to pay more regular visits to his church and became eager to spend time with him discussing spiritual matters. On one occasion, waiting in the church porch for a particularly fierce storm to blow over, she dramatically pointed in the direction of a streak of lightning and speculated: 'If there is a place up there, heaven I mean, then surely we can't rule out the possibility that spirits, good as well as evil ones, are bobbing around somewhere.'

All this was related to me when Nick decided to address a larger audience, using the News' letters page. 'Someone has to counter all the ballyhoo you newspaper chaps are creating,' he said with a hint of a smile. He saw opportunities as well. Activities in the Spicer cottage imagined or not, had encouraged some of his flock to think about matters outside their own little worlds. 'That's good so long as there is someone around to point them in the right direction,' he added.

'You'll take that on with gusto, I imagine?'

'Of course I will, but my first concern is for the Spicer family. They're playing with fire and Stephen, in particular, is in danger of getting his fingers burned. He needs help if his life is not to be plagued by more and more disquieting happenings, real or imagined.'

'But will he accept any help?' I queried, 'do you really think he's playing it straight?'

Nick's attitude worried me because I felt he was taking the Deepcote incidents far too seriously. As much as I liked him, his readiness to embrace the possibilities of paranormal phenomena before applying a measure of rational thinking, disturbed me somewhat. So far, no recognised mediator, religious or scientific, had set foot in the cottage to verify or challenge the family's story.

Inevitably, a rash of letters to the News accused Stephen of either fabricating or grossly exaggerating the incidents taking place in his home. Mrs Spicer hit back saying her son could not be blamed for something over which he had no control. 'I know my son rather better than the readers of your newspaper do,' she wrote, 'and I know he would not deliberately cause chaos in my home or anywhere else.'

One member of Nick's congregation, who I found waiting outside my office on another of those bad Monday mornings, thought I should know about an incident that shocked the Deepcote faithful. Mrs Spicer uncharacteristically put Nick Bertram on the spot by interrupting him in the middle of the previous day's morning service. His mention of spirits provoked her to ask him, in what most people thought was an unwarranted outburst, to explain how he thought evil spirits could interfere with people's lives. 'But you're not the person to answer that one, are you?' she shouted provocatively, 'you only deal with the good ones, or should I call them, the holy ones.'

Young ordinands are probably not trained to deal with this sort of interruption but my informant said he stayed calm and acknowledged her family was trying to cope with a set of unusual but very disturbing circumstances. 'It would certainly make life comfortable for me if I had only to encourage people already filled with the Holy Spirit,' replied Nick, 'but there are other aspects to my job, like trying to help those who are miserable, desperate and, yes, worried that they themselves or their loved ones might be under the control of evil influences.'

Maybe Maureen Spencer felt she had overstepped the mark because at this point she turned on her heel and walked out of the church without attempting to extend the debate. It kept the villagers talking well into the following week and letters to the News became so prolific correspondence on this subject had to be closed for a while.

****

What was not anticipated initially when we branded the Spicer case a space-filling, 'silly season' story was that we would still be trying to tie up the loose ends a couple of silly seasons later. It was the introduction of automatic writing and painting into Stephen's repertoire, which had moved the whole crazy adventure up a notch or two.

Cynics, myself among them, recoiled in disbelief when characters long since dead, allegedly started to make their presence felt in the Deepcote drama. Perhaps editorial planners across the country came to the conclusion that poltergeists were losing their appeal as out of the blue another ghost of more ancient origins made an entrance. My suspicion was that Stephen, upset by a drop in the number of column inches he was managing to mark up, decided a change of emphasis was required.

Charles Chatsworth, named in village records as a man who had resided in the Spicer cottage towards the end of the 17th century, decided he now had an opportunity to re-visit the world he had left behind. Or perhaps it should be said this was the popular version of the story grabbing the headlines almost everywhere.

To all who would listen, Stephen described a confrontation with Charles Chatsworth on the stairway of the family home. The couple, one earthly the other ethereal, had a heart-to-heart chat and the 'ghost' stayed long enough for his picture to be drawn on a door in Stephen's bedroom, resplendent in a frock coat, wig and wide-top boots. Villagers plunged into local records and found Charles' life and domestic arrangements quite vividly described. The possibility that perhaps Stephen, too, had been able to examine these records before the meeting on the stairs took place, inexplicably was never explored

One well-known journalist, sadly with little respect for his own credibility, went along with a decidedly dubious account of Stephen's experiences.

'*Hundreds of names accompanied by dates appeared over a three-day period. No one in the Spicer family smoked but the smell of tobacco was frequently noticed. On one occasion, Stephen followed the smell into his parent's bedroom and there came face to face with Charles Chatsworth again. This time he attempted to shake hands but there was nothing solid to grab hold of. Stephen did succeed in giving the ghost a present, a small silver ashtray. Chatsworth made a grab for it and dropped it into the pocket of his frock coat. Then, he faded away as a television picture fades away. The ashtray also disappeared. There was corroboration from Stephen's father, whose unmade bed was frequently made by unseen hands. Pyjamas left in an untidy heap were often found neatly folded. Strangest of all, Stephen's father felt pain in his right hip and lower right leg. Charles Chatsworth, it was revealed in village records, constantly complained to the locals about his sufferings and he was known to walk around the village with the help of a stick.*'

The headline writers had a rip-roaring time as the stories accumulated:-

From beyond the grave—an intriguing question.

The ghosts who write and run.

When chaos comes in the night.

Could my psychic powers be a secret weapon?

The headline speculating about using his powers as a secret weapon seemed destined to turn him into a laughingstock but Stephen smiled charmingly at doubters and said it was not up to him to prove or disprove such claims. Few cared if people, often sensation-seeking minor celebrities, were taken for a ride by Stephen's manipulations and predictions. It was all part of the psychic circus. But the seriously distressed who started to believe Stephen could reach out to the recently departed were usually left poorer and with their promises unfulfilled.

One story Stephen was ever ready to tell if it guaranteed more publicity, centred on an incident, which allegedly occurred when he was alone in the family cottage. While reading a book, he sensed someone was tampering with his precious motorbike. What started as a vague feeling developed into a strong vision that someone was meddling with the braking mechanism. He rushed to the garage and switched on a light. No one was there. He checked the machine and all seemed perfectly in order. But instead of feeling relieved, his anxiety increased. Was he being given a warning of danger? Was an alarm signal being triggered in his brain? This may have been the first time Stephen experienced a real sense of fear as a result of what he felt was going on around him. Perhaps reality was going out of the window and fantasy taking over.

A person beginning to play an important role in his life was his publisher and business manager, Melanie Cooper, an attractive but decidedly gullible woman in her early thirties. It was suspected that she had ghost written Stephen's early publications because the female touch was only too obvious in books bearing his name. Melanie's tendency to believe almost anything Stephen told her didn't discourage him from turning to her when any sort of crisis in his life was looming. He decided to contact her for a second opinion on his disturbing vision.

'That's really strange,' said Melanie, hearing but not immediately responding to Stephen's worried account. 'I had an unusual visitor this evening and I'm still trying to fathom what triggered his decision to call on me.'

'What do you mean an unusual visitor? Presumably he said who he was.'

'He said he worked in one of the country's intelligence departments. Attached to the Ministry of something or other.'

'Try to remember... the Ministry of Defence maybe?'

'Could have been,' said Melanie, who was more at home dealing with would-be authors and bookshop owners. Top-level civil servants were not the type she regularly encountered.

Melanie was something of an enigma; her friends and acquaintances could never make up their minds whether she really was so unworldly or pretended to be if it served her purpose. She was certainly bright enough or maybe attractive enough to twist Stephen around her little finger. She was said to have been looking for a toy boy when Stephen obligingly turned up on the scene

'It was no social call,' she ventured, 'He was trying to reach you because he had read about your powers of telepathy and how this enabled you to tune into some far away event or conversation, an ability he thought might be put to good use in the intelligence world. He was obviously weighing up the possibilities of you taking part in a series of experiments but had another reason for wanting to see you. He wouldn't go into detail but information had come his way which was quite disturbing and he wanted to warn you...'

'To warn me...about what?' Whether Stephen thought there was a link between his unsettling vision and the visit of an intelligence agent to the office of his publisher was not immediately clear but when he came to recount the story to the next hungry journalist, its importance had grown out of all proportion. Stephen was his worst enemy when he allowed his imagination to run riot. Now, he said, he was hot property and possibly in danger of being whisked off to the Soviet Union. His colourful stories even included a suggestion that some foreign country might be thinking of him as a long distance super spy. His fear, he told one inquirer, was that an attempt might be made to eliminate him to stop him being used as 'a secret weapon.'

Stephen claimed the intelligence officer had been so serious about his mission, he had laid down ground rules to ensure his future safety:-

He was given a list of countries he should avoid visiting

He must avoid becoming an instantly recognisable figure (rather too late in the day some might have thought)

He must refrain from publishing the results of any experiment.

He mustn't talk to the press without prior permission (not an instruction Stephen was likely to adhere to if previous behaviour was anything to go by).

It was probably significant that the Official Secrets Act was not mentioned, a strange omission if intelligence work was involved.

For the benefit of his growing band of followers, Stephen wrote in one of his own press releases: 'It's clear that in some government departments I am being regarded as a sort of espionage time-bomb. But I am adamant that I will not use my psychic powers for anything even remotely connected with military or intelligence interests.'

Despite the fact that Stephen was later to deny he had fed journalists with this sort of material, I felt I had to dig deeper into the piles of information colleagues and friends were sending me in every post. I wanted to fathom the mind of a man, who at one moment would boast about his powers and set out to illustrate them, and then complain about the treatment he was getting from the world around him, resulting in a period of sulk. Also accumulating were all manner of research documents some from recognised organisations dealing with paranormal investigations, others from…well, anyone's guess was as good as mine. The latest claim that he was able to use powers of telepathy to gatecrash the conversations and debates of people in far off countries was as far-fetched as any to date but Stephen made no attempt to dampen speculation.

Sometimes in his naivety, Stephen would walk straight into the arms of those who wanted to prove him a cheat---and I have to admit I was often first in the queue. My modus operandi, apart from challenging chunks of his book, was to discover flaws in every new episode of Stephen's spooky existence. I saw a real chance of putting one of his claims to the test when I read he had been invited to meet Lord Mayfield, head of a Whitehall Think Tank—a powerful group which advised the Government on a wide range of subjects.

A letter from Lady Mayfield had paved the way. In an attempt to disguise her own fascination with the occult, she told Stephen that her husband had always wanted an opportunity to study the kind of phenomena Stephen was experiencing. True or not, Lord Mayfield is said to have given Stephen 45 minutes of his time and had asked specific questions, such as where he had worked, which countries he had visited and what experiments he planned in the future.

There was no holding Stephen now. He started to throw caution to the wind and reveal details of conversations which if they were true should never have reached the public ear. 'Lord Mayfield wanted to know if I could physically affect things from afar. Could I make objects move? Did my power diminish with increasing distance? Did I think I could interfere with radar or wireless waves?' When asked about the answers he had given Stephen clammed up and said his replies were 'secret'. It was certainly the right sort of response to keep interest alive.

Although there had been several reports of this alleged conversation, what had never been firmly established was whether Stephen had actually had a meeting with a well-known defence chief or whether his vivid accounts sprang from a desire to be considered important, even powerful.

My initial reaction to reports of this unlikely collaboration was to leave it well alone. Then I started to wonder whether it could lead to a major breakthrough if I wanted to expose the Spicer dynasty for what I thought it was---a group of people working through a calculated agenda to exploit each and every aspect of Stephen's alleged paranormal powers.

Just a mile or two from my office was the Mayfield residence, a large refurbished Victorian house within substantial grounds. An impromptu visit seemed to be a good idea but it was with some trepidation that I set out on this mission.

What I wanted to know then, and would still like to know today, was whether there was ever serious consideration at top level of using ESP and psychokinetic phenomena as an intelligence tool. If there was how did one explain Stephen's indiscretion in revealing details of a top-secret conversation with someone in the upper echelons of the Government machine? A man of Lord Mayfield's status would certainly have insisted on an official declaration from Stephen that their deliberations should remain under wraps.

Predictably, the Mayfield mansion was at the end of a long drive and I shouldn't have been surprised to find that getting within a few hundred yards of the occupants would be no easy task. But I hadn't calculated that this Peer of the realm would have the sort of security system usually afforded to a vulnerable Northern Ireland Minister.

An attempt to introduce myself through the speaker system attached to the front gate brought an icy retort. My question about a reported meeting between Lord Mayfield and a local psychic was met with the time-honoured response 'No comment.' The interview ended with an ominous barking of guard dogs and the gates staying firmly shut. A letter to the Mayfield residence did illicit a reply of sorts, this time a denial that the Peer had ever had anything to do with Stephen Spicer and if he had, he wouldn't be talking to the press about it.

There were moments when I was tempted to drop the whole silly business, to relegate the little evidence I did have to the non-proven file, especially as my colleagues were telling me my time could be spent more usefully on local problems that really mattered. And if Stephen had decided to duck out of the limelight at this stage, I might well have wrapped up my inquiries with little remorse. However, I was not allowed to abandon my quest for the truth so easily. With impeccable timing, a psychical research team, based at the university, decided to set up a funded study into some of the uncharted functions of the human brain. Telepathy and parapsychology were to be re-examined under conditions which would rule out the sort of cheating which, in the view of many, had become commonplace.

The leader of the research team, Bryan Pettifer, a bright and cheery but very ambitious young man, asked me whether I would like to be a layman observer in a series of experiments. It was an invitation I found hard to resist but again I might have said no if I'd known it would involve entanglement with Stephen Spicer. And not only with Stephen but also with the international figure, Yasha Rashnin, who I had clashed with when seeking his opinion on another well-reported poltergeist case.

Many tried over the years to bring the Rashnin empire crashing down. But it was still as strong as ever. Programme after programme featured Yasha's spoon-bending marvels, clever use of mind games and sleight of hand, which gave gullible members of the public a cheap thrill. Yasha was a saviour to every television producer looking for a light entertainment programme tainted with a touch of the mysterious. From one studio, he was credited with stopping the watches and clocks of hundreds of people right across the country, simply by ....well, simply by doing very little apart from gazing vacantly out of the screen of a television set. Now a millionaire, he displayed his talents with careless abandon but there were those who wanted to expose him for what they thought he was... a fraud. Until this happened people, not only from Britain but also around the world, would go on building up his bank balance.

The task of serious minded scientists and journalists, I felt, was to produce evidence proving his powers were exaggerated and he was a clever magician at most. I considered Stephen's performances should be appraised in similar fashion as I was convinced he had orchestrated the domestic upheavals at his home and had supported these with a copycat public relations campaign drawn from Yasha Rashnin's armoury. It was about time the gloves came off.

4

The Swivelling Head

It didn't take much to raise Eric Driver's blood pressure to danger level and just a mention of Spicer's name could create enough hot air to put the newsroom into orbit. He blamed me for raising the temperature in the first place and had a novel method of protest; he would scribble the words 'attention ghost-hunting department' on any handout with weird origins and drop it into my in-tray. If it made him feel better, that was fair enough by me.

The fur threatened to fly again when during a fractious editorial conference I tried to convince Eric we should show an interest in a psychical research seminar taking place at the University during the down time. The advanced blurb spoke of serious study by an international team of experts into extra sensory perception, hypnosis and the latest suggestion that the human brain's left and right hemispheres had never been seriously studied. The new theory was that human beings had been wandering the earth for thousands of years not using part of their brain.

'We've got one or two here who would make good candidates for that experiment,' said Eric, a comment that might have been taken as a joke from other lips but not from Eric's. 'By the way, can we remember, this is the Trentbridge Evening News, not the New Science Journal,' he added sarcastically.

There was more than a hint of jealously in many of Eric's comments. Having decided to take a desk job to enhance his status and salary he truly missed the thrill of picking up the scent of a decent story. His sarcasm directed continuously at the Spicer investigation when it was at its peak told me he would really have liked to be out there joining in the chase.

Although working in a university town Eric had no time for

conferences and seminars. 'You can never understand what the silly buggers are talking about, if you do get it right they'll still claim they've been misquoted if it suits their purpose,' was a typical pre-conference judgment before he crossed the engagement off the diary. For good measure, he would invariably add: 'Very little seems to happen after these academic merry-go-rounds. When did they ever do anything other than talk?'

'Well, they talked enough about Newton's theories and spent hours chewing the cud over Darwin's assertions,' I reminded those at the daily editorial powwow, ' no one's going to suggest all that came to nothing, are they?'

These less than erudite observations silenced Eric for a minute or two and gave me the chance to advance the theory that serious consideration of the human brain and its complexities might put a spoke in the wheels of manipulative magicians claiming they were gifted with special connections to the spiritual world.

I knew Eric shared my distaste for sharp practice designed to exploit 'the ignorant masses' as he charmingly called them. So I set about winning him over by highlighting how we might take an active part in the summer seminar, providing stimulating copy during a period when local news dried up. One of the problems for experts in psychical research, I had discovered, was finding people who would make an honest and constructive contribution, resisting any inclination to cheat if things were not working out as they had hoped. Eagle-eyed observers were also in short supply.

The international conference of the Society of Psychical Research, scheduled to take place at the School of Divinity in the centre of town, had aroused my interest because it seemed like an occasion and a place where the participants would be adopting a serious approach to their task. Some 20 papers were to be presented covering almost every aspect of recent research including a report on 'house-shaking and poltergeists.' There was also to be a report on laboratory controlled testing of Yasha Rashnin's metal bending exploits.

Other areas of discussion, which looked promising in terms of providing copy, were going to be led by experts from London, Edinburgh, Cambridge, Nottingham and Freiburg, Germany, as well as from American universities. They intended to illuminate us on the results of experiments in psychokinesis, which I was told was the influence of mind directly on matter. If that wasn't enough to satisfy my curiosity then I could wait for the German expert, who would present a paper on political prophesy made in 1914 about European events between 1932 and 1945. To round things off there was to be an evening symposium on a much publicised poltergeist case in east London.

Bryan Pettifer, busy as he was organising the conference, suggested it would probably present him with good material for a research paper if he could set up a practical exercise with a touch of originality about it. The widespread publicity Stephen had attracted did not escape Bryan's notice and his proposition was we should spend time in the Spicer household using powers of observation of greater intensity than had so far been demonstrated.

'You may be considered acceptable but the Spicers won't let me near the place,' I pointed out, 'they know I suspect devious practices at the cottage and this tends to make me very unpopular with most members of the family.'

Bryan agreed this could be a problem but said he would make the first approach. He came back the next day with the surprising news that the Spicer family would tolerate my presence as it might serve to quell my scepticism. Bryan's plan was to spend an evening and part of the night in the house just quietly absorbing the atmosphere and keeping a close eye on the three younger members of the family.

'If this turns out to be anything like a similar experiment I carried out in Nottingham, we shall certainly need two pairs of eyes,' said Bryan. What I liked about this man was his refusal to be laboratory-bound. In his search for truth, he had already spent many hours following up alleged hauntings in various parts of the country. In most cases, he had produced negative reports but was always prepared to come clean if there was something he could not explain.

His special interest was in the possible survival of personality after bodily death. We had discussed this on several occasions but the outcome was always the same----Bryan keeping an open mind, me obstinately refusing to acknowledge even the possibility. 'Just imagine the uproar there would be if leaders like Gladstone or Disraeli made a come-back and started throwing their weight about,' I had mockingly observed. 'The Speaker in the House of Commons might want to rule them out-of-order but he would have his work cut out against angelic forces.'

It was frivolous remarks like this I had to be careful not to repeat at home. It may have been a joke as far as I was concerned but Penny was clearly disturbed by the constant references in our household to the supernatural. When it started to upset the sleep patterns of my wife and children, I knew it was time to distinguish clearly between what was happening at work and how I behaved in the domestic environment.

The night Penny woke up screaming was a memory not likely to go away in the hurry. She wasn't prone to nightmares as a general rule but on that occasion her fright was so intense I had to accept the possibility that events going on around her, the discussions, the letters, the phone calls, occasionally the arguments, could have infiltrated that part of the brain that provoked her to dream or, more seriously, to have nightmares.

'It was horrible,' she said as I attempted to pacify her, 'a face was looking at me through my dressing table mirror and it was…. swivelling.'

'Swivelling? Is that so strange? We all swivel from time to time, don't we?' I suggested, feebly trying to make light of an incident I later accepted had frightened Penny in a very serious way.

'You don't understand, it was going around the full 360 degrees and leering at me in a quite horrible way.'

Penny's nightmare did for a moment make me think that perhaps the investigations of the psychical research team might be more useful to the general populace if it examined the cause and effect of dreams. Why do we sometimes have nice dreams but more often than not, thoroughly nasty ones? It was, I decided, a subject to take up with Bryan at a more appropriate time.

I was to be given more cause to ponder over this when a few nights later I had an experience that certainly warranted some attention by those taking a closer look at the functions of the brain, especially at times when we think it is resting.

On the landing of our small house was a piano, which I liked to play without disturbing the children's homework or Penny when she wanted a quiet hour with a book or watching the television. The positioning of the piano, when we first took up residence, had created a Chaplinesque type scene. Too mean to call in the removal men, I co-opted three colleagues to help manoeuvre the dead-weight piano up a narrow staircase. It was a miracle no one finished up in the mortuary.

Farthest from my thoughts at the time was the possibility this instrument would feature in another night-time drama. In the early hours, probably three or four hours into a normal night's sleep, I awoke abruptly to hear the sound of piano hammers hitting strings, noisily but amateurishly, like a child coping with early exercises. 'Don't be ridiculous, I told myself, too much strong cheese at suppertime.' The tuneless notes continued unabated so lifting my legs over the side of the bed, I walked out of the bedroom door, with the intention of crossing the landing and visiting the bathroom. On the piano stool with his back to me was a man in full evening dress. He didn't turn but continued to fiddle with the keys. I was petrified and my hand froze on the handle of the bathroom door...then I woke up!

I lay in bed for a few tense seconds, then hearing no sound from the piano, got out of bed, walked across the landing and slammed down the lid over the keys as I passed. I realised the dream had been so powerful I was actually trying to reassure myself that the previous short walk to the bathroom really had been a dream. The next morning I had no problem in laughing off my own discomfort but had to admit the inquiries into poltergeists and the alleged return of Deepcote's long dead residents may have been the trigger for such a disturbing episode. I was only too pleased Penny had slept through my small, personal drama.

She did comment the next morning that I looked rather pale and drawn and it was about time I started to take it easier. Even my lively sons, having been told one time too many that their Dad was 'very tired', complained I was not so enthusiastic about joining them for a kick-about on the recreation ground.

Recollections of those domestically troubled times were going to stay with me for some time. What had started as a fascinating, but never vitally important local investigation, had turned into something bordering on obsession. More level-headed and less emotional members of our editorial team, who had stayed firmly on the sidelines, insisted repeatedly that Spicer was a seven-day wonder who would be dropped from media agendas once a more active autumnal news programme got into its stride. 'Just leave them all to get on with it' was the initial attitude of Eric and some of the sub-editors when we heard that two 'ghost hunters' had taken up residence in the Spicer home.

I was angry because the agreement with Patrick Spicer that Bryan and I could spend time at the cottage seemed to have been disregarded. Now the 'crime scene' was likely to be contaminated by two men Stephen's father described as 'experts' in the ways and habits of poltergeists. Our inquiries revealed that neither of these men had any academic experience in the scientific field they so confidently embraced. Any conclusions they came to were likely to be highly suspect but we decided to go ahead with our visit anyway, evaluating their procedures and then drawing our own conclusions.

****

Nigel Brackshaw, an author and Dennis Hart, who described himself as an inventor, wasted no time in telling us how they had recorded 50 unexplained happenings in the cottage over a period of a week but didn't seem to want to hang around to tell us more. They excused themselves by saying they had a train to catch but in case we were interested, we could look at their preliminary report left on the coffee table.

With the agreement of the Spicer parents we made ourselves at home in the cottage's comfortable, ground floor living-room but were already wondering how we could possibly keep an eye on Stephen and his two siblings as they went about their normal routines. We realised we had not considered how we would handle the night watch and this was a bad mistake. With all the co-operation in the world, it certainly wouldn't be possible to wander in and out of bedrooms where, according to all previous reports, most of the activity was likely to originate.

As we waited for Stephen to honour us with a visit from his room and for the twins to come home from school, it seemed a good moment while his mother was making tea in the kitchen, to examine the draft report of the two ghost hunters in whom the Spicers had put so much faith. They had written about crashing furniture, flying objects, mysterious noises and strange voices but we searched in vain for any substantial evidence of the events which led up to the incidents or who actually witnessed them.

'This is what we were discussing earlier,' Bryan reminded me while our hostess was still out of the room, 'So great is the desire of some self-styled researchers to believe, the possibility of serious scientific inquiry is completely obliterated.'

Turning over a few more pages of the report, I observed: 'They don't even say where each member of the family was situated when the disturbance started. The discovery of a piece of furniture some distance from its normal position in the cottage means nothing unless someone actually witnessed it moving from A to B.'

'And whether anyone might have been carrying it,' added Bryan, with a little more cynicism than he usually allowed himself.

I was beginning to realise how important it was to have someone of Bryan's experience at my side in these circumstances. He had warned right from the outset that Brackshaw and Hunt were the sort of men who would probably be quite happy to accept the explanation of any one member of the household without bothering to check it out.

'They want to believe, so they believe,' explained Bryan, 'but that doesn't necessarily rule out the chance that there is some sort of psychic phenomena going on in this building. If I didn't keep an open mind on these occasions, then I would be wasting my time trying to sustain a university research project which I want people to take seriously.'

I turned to another part of the report which dealt with strange voices heard by all members of the family usually late in the evening or in the early part of the night. Dennis Hart told how he had been invited into the bedroom of the girls and listened to adult sounding voices coming from the direction of the curtains. It was a guttural male voice and in Hart's opinion, could not have been manufactured by one of the girls.

Bryan thought this the most interesting part of the report because a number of recordings and a video tape had been compiled and the two men planned to give these a premiere at the forthcoming conference.

'Should provide an entertaining evening session, if nothing else' Bryan predicted, 'they'll face an audience of internationally recognised researchers and won't get an easy ride; some of the scientists who are coming would have made good barristers if they hadn't chosen science.'

A door banged somewhere in the house and a moment later a confident, cocky Stephen, stepped into the lounge with the flourish of an actor enjoying his first entrance. 'Gather you two guys want to write me off as a hoaxer, you'll have your work cut out, you know'. He threw himself into an armchair, gave both of us a look bordering on contempt and asked what we knew that others didn't.

'If we had made up our minds that you were a hoaxer we wouldn't be here,' said Bryan, 'If we come across anything that can't immediately be explained we shall be the first to admit it. Then we'll look for answers.'

'That may be the case with you but what about the scribbler you brought along with you; will he keep an open mind?'

Ignoring the fact that he was deliberately talking as though I wasn't in the room, I admitted I had been scathing in weeks gone by but with Bryan's help I was prepared to take a fresh look, first hand. 'If you're serious, Stephen, then this exercise might be of help to you. Surely you want explanations whether they turn out to be negative or positive?'

Bryan underlined his credentials by explaining why he had given up other projects to head a research team at Trentbridge University. 'I'm hoping you, Stephen, can make a valuable contribution. Something you should know, though, I've visited scores of allegedly haunted places and only a couple produced a scrap of evidence making me want to dig deeper. All the others were the product of lively imaginations or just fabrication.'

'You won't be thinking in terms of imagination after a while here, I can assure you,' replied a confident Stephen. 'I can guarantee you an experience or two which will have you scratching your heads.'

'Guarantee?' I chipped in, 'if what you have been experiencing in this house has any authenticity then surely that's just what you can't do. Poltergeists, if they exist, surely don't work to order.'

Turning on me angrily, Stephen wondered why his father had agreed to my presence in the cottage. 'You've already demonstrated your bias. Can't you understand that the phenomena we are talking about can simply evaporate before people with closed minds? And what I've read of your articles so far, your mind is more closed than most.'

'That's another cop out,' I retorted, in spite of my promise to behave, 'a ready excuse if nothing happens. All down to my unresponsive attitude, I suppose. I just don't wear it.'

'That's up to you,' said Stephen closing his eyes, 'but why not try to convince me you're different, a journalist who actually bothers to examine the evidence, rather than creating his own fiction using people like me as a fall guy.'

The three of us fell into a period of reflection. It gave me an opportunity to study our subject at close quarters, something I had not been able to do until now. Plenty of passport type photographs had appeared in various publications but none of them gave too much away about Stephen's personality. Now on the verge of his 20th birthday, he was probably considered good-looking by girls of his own age group but shoulder length hair, a weedy moustache and sparse facial growth didn't show him off at his best. Then it was probably all part of the guise self-styled psychics adopt.

My moment of contemplation was disturbed by the arrival of the twin sisters, who by this time were so blasé about curious visitors hanging about the place, they stalked into the kitchen without even bothering to say hello. They headed for the cold-water tap and as they poured a drink, a glass dislodged itself from somewhere and hit the floor with a splintering crash.

The cheeky face of Caroline popped around the door and with a wide grin, she told us not to get excited. 'That wasn't the poltergeist, just my clumsy sister dropping her drink by accident.' Bryan thanked her for being so frank but said it hadn't even crossed his mind that the noise had any mysterious origins.

This incident heralded what was to turn out to be a very frustrating session. Neither of us had worked out just how we should operate in someone else's home even though the parents seemed perfectly willing to let us wander. We had a light supper with the family comprising sandwiches, cakes and biscuits and for most of the time Mr Spicer, senior, talked about how the family had come to terms with what was happening to them. At first, they were scared but now realised 'the spiritual visitors meant us no harm so we've learned to live with them.'

Bryan and I exchanged glances, unseen by the rest of them, but we were already beginning to feel we were being led by the nose. This feeling was heightened when we realised one of the twins had left the room. No one commented on the fact until there was a scream followed by the sound of something falling step over step down the stairs. Dutifully, we all rushed out to witness a bedroom chair, two legs missing, in the middle of the downstairs hall.

We expected to see Veronica appear at the top of the stairs, confirming our suspicion that she was responsible for the crashing chair. Instead, she came out of the ground floor kitchen innocently asking: 'What's happened, is our little visitor playing tricks again?' Not the sort of remark one would expect from a frightened young girl.

This was not, we felt, the time to start an argument or express doubts. Now we were in the house we wanted to make as much good use of our time as we could. Later, when we compared notes, Bryan and I agreed there was opportunity for Veronica to transfer herself from upstairs to down; none of us had left the room for a number of seconds after the crash.

'Or perhaps she had one of those plastic, fire escape ladders rolled down from her bedroom window,' I speculated.

'Or maybe she levitated into position,' added Bryan, not too seriously.

For the rest of the evening I sat in the lounge and Bryan made himself comfortable sitting at a table in the hall. The girls disappeared several times over the next few hours but always came back in a manner, which made me think they were checking on us rather than the other way about. They made feeble attempts to distract us and certainly didn't like the way our gaze followed them around. A kitchen mop took flight on one occasion but when Caroline saw me standing at the door of the kitchen watching her she didn't even bother to claim it was anything abnormal.

Strangely, the young man we both wanted to see at close quarters kept himself well out of our way. His parents said he spent most evenings incarcerated in his room but we were welcome to tap on his door if we wanted an audience. We decided against this and for several hours fought to stay awake, with the intention of going into action if there were any unusual occurrences. There weren't any, we thought, but had to admit we dozed off in the early hours. That didn't do much for our reputations as researchers but we were sure any major disturbance would have jolted us into consciousness.

Morning came without anything to get excited about and the anti-climax was so great I didn't have much stomach for the buttered croissants and cold meats offered for breakfast. The girls, who had had very little to say to us since we entered their home, drifted off to school, father went to work and Stephen said he had an appointment in town and wanted to visit the library. We were left for a while with Stephen's mother who said we were quite welcome to look around before we left. I thought this a strange invitation; not many women would want visitors, one of whom she had met only the previous evening rummaging around her home before even the most elementary domestic chores had been completed.

It was, however, too good an invitation to overlook and while I kept Maureen Spicer engaged in conversation, Bryan went quietly upstairs and pushed open the door into Stephen's study-cum-bedroom.

Our friendly chat downstairs came to an end when Bryan, sounding quite startled, called out: 'You'd better both come and see this.'

I shot out of the room and up the stairs but the lady of the house—and this didn't occur to me until later---was in no hurry. It's likely that she finished her cup of coffee before she joined us in Stephen's room. When she did appear, she certainly didn't share our astonishment at what confronted us.

One of the walls, originally painted off-white, was now host to a painting that both Bryan and I felt we had seen in a magazine or perhaps on our travels, in an exhibition.

'I've got it,' said Bryan,' I'm no expert but that looks very much like an impressionist painting I saw at an exhibition in Paris. I seem to remember it was a Monet exhibition and this looks something like his water lily pond.'

48

'You're quite right,' said a female voice behind us, 'I'm impressed with your instant identification. It's Monet's "Waterlily pond and Japanese bridge" which is usually on show at the Museum d'Orsay.' Maureen Spicer had quietly followed us upstairs and now seemed keen to demonstrate her own knowledge of the art world.

This was the appearance of what would be the first of many automatic paintings but Mrs Spicer expressed no surprise or anger that one of the walls of her house had been used as a painter's canvas. Her calmness was unnatural, offering the information that she had studied art at college and was familiar with Claude Monet's work.

'Aren't you shocked,' I asked her, 'people don't get their bedrooms redecorated like this every day of the week.'

'No, not really, not after all that's happened here over the last few months. He's not plastered a wall before but Stephen's been telling us for some time about a force moving his hand. Until now it's been messages, not illustrations and paintings…this is new.'

'Did Stephen demonstrate any artistic ability at school?' Bryan wanted to know.

'I thought that would be the next question' said Mrs Spicer, 'you think it's a fake don't you?'

'No, I'm not saying that but any researcher worth his salt examines all possibilities before coming to a conclusion.'

'Well, rest assured, my son could not have produced this unaided. Art was his weakest subject at school; he could hardly draw a straight line, even with the aid of a ruler.'

Neither of us thought it was the time to pursue this revelation, there would be opportunities later. For the moment, we were content to examine this latest manifestation and look for any clues indicating its origin and the identity of its perpetrator. We found nothing.

In the months that followed our visit to the Spicer household, during which time many more automatic drawings appeared, a veritable queue of hack reporters, specialist writers and television reporters would beat a path to this part of the world, to be told by Stephen the artwork was aided by an unseen force over which he had no control. So many people were now visiting Deepcote, villagers jokingly threatened to set up a customs post and charge cross border dues.

5

Divinity School Chaos

Leaving the press pack to make what it could of Stephen's prolific collection of manifested artistry, Bryan and I set about lining up a panel of local academics who knew a thing or two about artists and their works. Both of us, appreciative of art in its many forms but lacking the knowledge to compile a serious critique, could not be anything but impressed by the skilful execution of the drawings, paintings and signatures spattered across walls of the small Trentbridgeshire cottage.

But was it craftsmanship of a high quality we were talking about? If not then there was nowhere else to go but back into the arms of believers in the psychic abilities of people like Stephen. It was a line of thought I dismissed out of hand but it was one that my keen university partner quite rightly would not rule out until he had fulfilled what he had undertaken to do...carry out thorough research.

'Don't be in too much of a hurry,' Bryan advised, 'try to forget you're a journalist for a while and sift the evidence like a pro. Listen to those who have been examining works of art for most of their lives.' Bryan had a low opinion of most of the material he came across in the national press and urged me to step back from the crowd and go about my inquiries in my own way.

'Don't give the psychic circus a chance to write you off along with all the other media bods they've fallen out with,' he urged.

Our next port of call was to the world-famous MacMillan Museum in the centre of Trentbridge. I had always intended to spend more time among its exhibits but invariably got busy and put it off. Now was the time to explore the potential of at least one of its departments. There was little doubt that we had on our doorstep people who could give samples of Stephen's work the sort of rigorous inspection needed in any serious attempt to clarify its origins.

Just as we were about to get started we received a hurried message from the Spicers that another rash of messages and signatures had appeared at the cottage. Had we tracked down experts who could give them answers? We had, but for a while we wanted to keep the promised participation of the MacMillan art experts to ourselves. Perhaps we were being unfair, but we felt that if Stephen didn't get glowing affirmation, the Spicers wouldn't waste any time in trying to rubbish it, no matter where it came from.

Dr Anthony Laing, Keeper of Paintings and Drawings, was our first point of contact. With a title like that, I was expecting to meet a stuffed-shirt individual with beady eyes and a monocle. So I was surprised to be confronted by a casually dressed man with a shock of untidy, ginger hair and a jolly expression which told us he thought life was to be enjoyed. He may not have been a typical specimen of Trentbridge academic life but his breadth of knowledge was monumental and his approach to the challenges we brought him was a great tonic for two struggling art sleuths.

'They're good, in fact excellent copies,' pronounced Dr Laing, 'but there are many people who have perfected the art of faking. What is this lad of yours claiming to have happened?'

I explained that Stephen had been telling the world he believed a number of artists, including Durer, Picasso, Matisse and Beardsley, had been moving his hand. He fancies his whole body is taken over by them and he has no control over what emerges. 'Well, he certainly demonstrates considerable draughtsmanship and ability,' said Laing, 'but I find it difficult to believe this young man completed these in the time span you have outlined. Didn't you say a lot more of his work appeared on the walls of his home?'

I confirmed that was so and the samples now before him were the few he had committed to paper. Dr Laing said he would have liked to visit the cottage but could not spare the time. Other members of the museum staff joined the informal panel gathering around Stephen's work and the general verdict was that his efforts were 'fascinating but not very convincing.' Almost to a man they declared that no recognised art expert would take them seriously.

'What makes you all so sure?' Bryan asked. Dr Laing urged him to take a closer look at the alleged Picasso. 'The lines lack the sureness and energy which was Picasso's outstanding characteristic. The Beardsley drawing of Salome,' he went on, 'is quite well known and was originally published under the title "The Dancer's Reward". It would be readily accessible to anyone wishing to study or copy it.'

Considerable interest was shown in a small Beatrix Potter style painting. One member of the group pointed to the signature in the bottom right hand corner of the canvas. This was unusual, he said, because Potter seldom used her name but preferred to mark her authorship with just three initials.

We then focused our attention on copies of the messages and signatures which were of special interest because some were supposedly produced through the power of Stephen's receptive arm, while many others, it was claimed, had appeared on a wall at a time when the room was empty and sometimes locked.

The offerings of Charles Chatsworth, the villager who lived in the house in the 17th century, had attracted the most attention because so much of his history could be verified. When Stephen came to publish his first book on his experiences ('The Hidden Force' sold in thousands in all parts of the world) he used his encounters with Chatsworth to convince sceptics there was no faking. By anyone's calculation, the speed with which the wall artistry appeared was breathtaking, no matter how it was delivered.

Stephen reported that within 24 hours of the first scrawl being discovered, another 30 materialised on the magnolia paintwork. They were making such a mess of the bedroom that Mr Spicer, probably not with a great deal of seriousness, insisted that his son contact Chatsworth to ask him 'if he would pay for the necessary redecoration.' Serious or not, the reply Stephen claimed to have received was blunt and negative. 'It's my house; I'll do what I like.'

According to his book, Stephen was also told by his persistent visitor from the past to check local records. 'You will find that all these names are of people who lived in the village and frequently visited me.' We don't know whether Stephen carried out this instruction or not but we followed the trail and true enough parish records did mention many of the names on the wall.

'Well isn't that the point?' said Anthony Laing, 'if this boy wanted to build a fantasy world he had only to pop along to the library and study the history of the village. No one would have thought it unusual for a young, studious man to be sitting at a desk making notes and if they had it is unlikely they would recall any of the detail.' He was right. Despite time spent talking to people who used the library regularly as well as the staff, no evidence could be found of Stephen either openly or surreptitiously raiding the local history section.

Putting together a strong case to prove Stephen's perfidy was turning out to be far more difficult than we had anticipated. We had to accept that our expectations of a quick and clean execution were now on hold.

To complicate the issue even further, a well-known psychologist arrived in town to maintain that perhaps Stephen was a catalyst—this wasn't the first case of its kind, we should remember. 'People should keep open minds,' he advised.

Riled by some of the bad publicity he was getting, Stephen also hit back with a letter that some publications felt they ought to use in the interests of balanced reporting. 'Journalists are supposed to be observant,' he wrote, 'hadn't any of them noticed many of the messages and signatures on my ceiling were upside down. Did they think I had the agility to suspend myself like a bat and still write legibly?'

It was a slick reply, typical of Stephen's ability to respond to any type of criticism. He certainly had the makings of a wily politician. But he did make mistakes and describing the wall illustrations as 'spirit graffiti' may have been one of them.

We turned to another of Bryan's friends, archivist, Robert Smythe, who had been studying parish records for years. He was welcomed at the cottage to inspect a collection of writings on the walls and in notebooks. His conclusions did nothing to appease the Spicers. He considered the samples put before him had the stamp of a modern writer who had looked at old signatures but had failed to grasp one or two salient points.

'In many of these cases the spelling of Christian names in the signatures is correct by modern standards,' said Robert, 'in practice that did not occur. Writing in the 17th and 18th centuries was not definitive. People spelled Christian names virtually the way they chose. A common practice was to use an abbreviated form. I didn't find one single abbreviation.'

To emphasise his point Mr Smythe pointed to one of the women's names and noted that the Christian name was represented as Kathleen. 'Kathleen is a modern name which arrived in England with the Irish in the 19th and early 20th centuries. Prior to this, the name 'Katharine' or 'Catharine' was popular. It would be highly unlikely that a Kathleen would have lived in Deepcote or anywhere else in the country in 1692--- the date which appeared below that signature.'

With all this additional ammunition in our armoury, Bryan and I began to feel a little more confident that progress was being made. We debated how Stephen would react if confronted with the sort of views these experts had been voicing. We agreed we should bide our time.

'If they're right then this boy is going to a hell of a lot of trouble to make a name for himself,' Bryan observed. 'The fabric he's created is truly amazing. He acts the part and looks totally devastated if anyone hints he might be cheating. To do all this and then publish a book about it….well, you've got to be determined and quite a good actor to boot.'

After the fun and games at Deepcote and the valuable discussions with the experts, we turned our attention to the international conference at the Divinity School. Bryan had a substantial organisational job on his hands but I was looking forward to getting further insight into the fascinating, sometimes crazy world of the psychical researcher. A few blatant publicity seekers would be there but substantially it was to be a gathering of people who wanted their subject taken seriously.

I was particularly looking forward to the presentation of the two spook chasers, Nigel Brackshaw and Dennis Hart. Although at our previous meeting, they seemed anxious to put distance between them and us they had promised we would see stunning videotape evidence at one of the conference sessions. Even if they dismissed me as a nonentity there would be plenty of people in the room who would know just how to prick the bubble, if indeed there was a bubble to be pricked.

The question I wanted answered was, 'are psychical researchers bound by the same strict rules as other scientists?' My impression so far was of a group of young men and women, fresh into their new research projects, ready to take large chunks of reported paranormal phenomena on face value and peddle it around the world. Bryan and his team promised to be the exception.

The conference started on a serious enough note---a string of technical and often obscure papers seeking to explore the secrets of the brain. However, I was not the only one who was looking forward to the promised display of evidence to be put forward by Messrs Brackshaw and Hart. Over coffee, delegates talked about little else.

They must have known they would face intense questioning by many of those gathered but the two men adopted an approach more suited to the stage than to a conference hall. The Deepcote case, as they had dubbed it, was the most exciting demonstration to date of poltergeist activity. Hart could hardly contain himself. He rattled off stories of crashing furniture, flying objects, mysterious noises and strange voices.

One video tape after another was flashed across a screen. They may have impressed Hart and his colleague but for those watching from the hall very little could be seen with enough clarity to identify what was going on. The exception was a tape featuring one of the Spicer sisters. Laughter broke out as the action on the tape appeared to uncover the efforts of a young girl to prove the voice emerging from her body was not under her control. What most of us saw was an attempt by a young girl to disguise the fact she was practising, or endeavouring to practice, a form of ventriloquism--- the struggle to keep her lips closed and speak at the same time did not go too well.

One of the European researchers was quickly on his feet: 'Could anyone seriously believe the grunts coming from that girl's body was anything other than part of an elaborate game?' he asked. 'Could this really be accepted as serious scientific evidence by men and women who devote much time and energy researching the paranormal?'

It was the first of several challenges; another came from a Belgium delegate who described the performance he was watching as more like a circus clown routine than a serious presentation by reputable researchers. Asked if there had been occasions when they thought they were being deceived, Hart said they didn't want to waste time considering the possibilities of fraud or cheating. 'Shouldn't that have been your first priority?' queried another of the delegates.

Blackshaw retorted: 'I have spent many hours in that house and I have seen these things happen....what you call fraud, I don't call fraud. Of the 50 incidents we witnessed I would say that 49 of them were genuine.' Hart leapt to his feet to support his colleague: 'If you have already made up your minds that poltergeists don't exist then why be members of this society?' he shouted.

These remarks further incensed many of those gathered and there were murmurs of agreement at one suggestion that recognised parameters for investigating a poltergeist case had been missed by a mile.

It was a relief when Bryan stepped onto the platform to present his paper and insisted the society wanted to see claims of paranormal phenomena subjected to the same rigorous standards of proof required for any other scientific discovery. 'If we do turn up sound evidence, of course we'll get excited about it. Until then the society plans to pursue paranormal claims mercilessly. Leaving them unchallenged erodes the spirit of scepticism that is healthy for both science and society,' he added with a considerable degree of passion.

During the coffee break, I heard two delegates discussing the activities of Yasha Rashnin, someone who I regarded as an entertainer more at home on the end of a seaside pier than in a science laboratory. But his popularity with the public was growing apace following television appearances, featuring not only his 'amazing' spoon bending capabilities but also his ability to bamboozle the nation into thinking he was stopping their clocks and watches and causing windows to crack.

One of the cuttings, found sandwiched between others in my Spicer collection, was an investigation into the capabilities of Yasha Rashin. He had reigned supreme for a number of years helped by television celebrities such as Harry Brightwell, who allowed him all the freedom he needed to present stunts of a very dubious nature. Interviewers usually sat open-mouthed as Yasha performed tricks that might have gone down well at a children's party but would probably have provoked cheeky comments like, 'I know how you did that.' The interviewers probably thought the same but they had their audience figures to consider.

Rashnin had a good run for his money before his performances were rubbished by a disillusioned manager who confessed he was part of a conspiracy to cheat. Angry about a pay dispute the man, who had initially hailed Rashnin as a miracle worker, decided to spill the beans. He told one of the country's respected science magazines: 'I acted as a confederate by sitting in the audience and signalling to the stage. One of the ploys was for me to move my cigarette in various directions to tell Yasha what he was supposed to be determining by extra sensory perception.

'I also helped him to take note of licence plate numbers of the audience's parked cars so that later in his performance he could baffle the owners by revealing, not only the registration numbers but also other details of the owner's vehicles. He then claimed it could all be put down to the wonders of extra sensory perception.'

These details and many more were contained in a magazine article, filed by me because all the pointers were suggesting Stephen Spicer was planning to move into the territory previously jealously guarded by the disgraced manipulator. His ambitions received a boost when it was reported that an appearance by Yasha in Coventry had been curtailed. He had been alerted to the fact that the front row of the meeting hall had been packed with members of the Magic Circle and he had refused to go on stage. Reporters and audience were told that there had been a bomb scare. The manager later learned he had been blamed for the cancellation of the show. Rashnin claimed he wanted to perform but his manager wouldn't allow him.

All these details had come vividly to mind as I waited for the conference to re-convene. My suspicion that Stephen might be seeking celebrity status by filling the television slots temporarily abandoned by Rashnin was later to be tested. For the time being, I was trying to keep my feet firmly on the ground so that I could assess the sincerity of those who had travelled large distances to attend the conference. They were a mixed bunch and very hard to fathom.

During the early debates, I noticed that Stephen had slipped in at the back of the hall. He got up and left when the challenges came thick and fast, not from journalists on this occasion, but from people who had spent years of their life looking at psychokinesis and related subjects. I was surprised when Stephen decided not to stay around to support the story of the two men who had spent so much time in his home.

The conference was just warming up with countless allegations that Rashnin had cheated his way into the gullible hearts of the British public when the school's fire alarm shattered the uneasy calm of the conference theatre. No flames, no smoke so every one stayed put until a worried caretaker burst through the swing doors shouting that it was not a false alarm and all the delegates had to bale out.

In true 'the show must go on' mode, the delegates gathered on the spacious quadrangle outside the school and continued their debate in informal groups. That was until a computer keyboard came hurtling down from an upstairs window and crashed at the feet of a startled Eastern European delegate.

'Not the sort of thing you expect to happen at a Divinity School' he observed, moving to a spot he considered might be safer if other missiles were to follow the first one. 'Perhaps the Lord is showing his displeasure at the nature of our discussions,' said one of his serious-faced university colleagues, 'after all we have been told enough times not to meddle with the occult.'

Conversations came to an abrupt halt and all eyes turned to the upstairs windows of the school, most faces showing curiosity rather than fear. Bryan was the first to make a move. He scurried into the building expecting to be met by the caretaker who had given the alarm.

No one appeared. I was close behind Bryan and followed him up the stairs two at a time.

The sight, which greeted us in the conference room, was truly alarming. We had only left it a few minutes earlier but in the short time it had been empty, it had been substantially trashed. A second computer, projection screens, files and carefully ordered rows of books had been thrown about; chairs and desks were on their side and those still upright seemed to be smeared with a grey, gluey substance. No one would be sitting on those for a while.

As a few of the fitter delegates started to return to the conference room one, from West Germany, suggested they might have been witnesses of a life-changing poltergeist activity. 'You've changed your mind,' remarked a fellow compatriot sardonically, 'Didn't you come here to tell us they don't exist?'

Above the excited chatter of the delegates, another sound attracted the attention of the more alert. Muffled shouts were coming from a cupboard in the corner of the room. Everyone stood like statues as Bryan marched across the floor and wrenched the door open. Looking rather sheepish, the caretaker who had raised the alarm, shuffled out. He was not bound in any way but said someone had thrown a sack over his head and frog-marched him into the cupboard before he had a chance to resist. It wasn't the sort of thing that happened to him every day, he insisted. 'No' he didn't get a chance to look at his assailant.

Around the leg of a table from which the first of the videos had been shown was a tangle of tape, twisted in such a way that it could never be shown again. Just to make sure the assailant had drenched it with copious amounts of glue. 'Someone didn't want the world to see any more evidence of what happened at the Spicer cottage,' I suggested, at the same time wondering why anyone would have gone to so much trouble to violate material of such dubious quality.

'How did they do it in that short space of time?' asked another of the delegates as he walked around the room prodding the fallen items with the end of his walking stick.

'This must be the work of more than one person.'

'But where did they come from?' asked Bryan 'We saw no suspicious characters around the school when we arrived and before the first session, front and back entrance doors were locked to stop people wandering in.

The caretaker agreed. No other doors were open and his instructions that morning were to admit only those with passes. 'One person could not have caused all this damage in the short time we were out of the conference hall,' suggested one elderly scientist, seriously out-of-breath after labouring up the steep staircase. He thought the perpetrators probably secreted themselves in the building overnight and released themselves during one of the more heated sessions.

'Perhaps they're still here,' I suggested. 'If they are they'll have me to cope with' said the caretaker, moving towards the door but then pausing to ask: 'Anyone willing to come with me?'

The incident created an atmosphere of tension and bewilderment. These were men and women who had presented themselves as serious scientists, most of whom would insist that nothing except cast iron proof would ever lead them to think they had had a visitor of uncertain origin. Yet, any observer picking up snippets of conversation would have been in no doubt that there were delegates present who were seriously thinking the scene of destruction in front of them had been caused by unnatural forces.

My thoughts went back to the moment when I had noticed Stephen, at first occupying a discreet position at the back of the hall, but then quietly slipping away. Had anyone else noticed his presence? Or were the delegates so preoccupied with what was going on at the front of the hall any activity elsewhere would have escaped their attention?

There was no time, I thought, for Stephen to return to the hall to create the amount of damage we were now witnessing. I was also puzzled by the lack of commotion during the time the hall was ransacked. Until the computer had landed at the delegate's feet, I could recollect hearing none of the bangs and crashes one would have expected if the deed was being carried out in a hurry.

The thought that we were dealing with something out of the ordinary was a passing one and I quickly reverted to the comforting analysis that always came to my rescue.....nothing ever happens in this world without an explanation. Told by my other half that there is a burglar in the kitchen, I pop downstairs and put the cat out. Confronted with so-called evidence of poltergeist activity, I look for bored youngsters (probably girls in their early teens) and come to my own conclusion.

The conference had to end at this point. The caretaker called the police. Statements were taken from delegates who had little to tell them apart from the obvious. My police contacts are valuable to me so I did tell them about Stephen being in the hall for a short time. I was concerned about being the informant but the inspector in charge confirmed he had no need to reveal whom he had been talking to. Later I heard that Stephen had been able to provide an alibi for his movements after leaving the school and this had been accepted.

I wondered what Bryan had made of the incident, which had destroyed his carefully prepared conference. In our discussion as we left the hall we found we had both come to similar conclusions---one group of delegates, albeit a minority group wanted to believe. They wanted to believe that this was an abnormal happening with paranormal connotations. Back in their own countries, they could look forward to many free lunches and maybe a dinner or two on the strength of their experiences in an English university town.

When I asked the police inspector, a month or so later if any of the delegates had been in touch to ask about possible developments such as an arrest, he said he had heard from no one. Not so surprising, I thought. Such hard evidence would not have been welcome while the wine was flowing and the free lunches were still being enjoyed.

I reminded Bryan of his promise that if he did experience any incident he couldn't explain, he would be the first to admit it. What had he made of the mess in the Divinity School, a mess that had taken five of us more than an hour to clear up?

Bryan didn't answer immediately. His hesitation seemed to indicate that for the first time he was genuinely puzzled.

'My inclination is to put it all down to a well-planned hoax by a bunch of students,' he suggested, 'they have been known to do clever and dangerous things. Remember when they suspended a small car from the towers of their college chapel? Getting in and out of the school would not have been a problem for the fit and agile.'

I thought he could be right but with no evidence to show that something like this had happened, I felt it judicious to keep our minds open until someone had inspected the premises to see where entrance was gained. As far as I could determine no one ever did

It was also my turn to admit I didn't have all the answers. What was it I had so arrogantly proclaimed on so many occasions---'there is an explanation for everything that happens in this world.' Well, there's always a first time......to be wrong that is.

6

Just a Trick

'Go on, it was a trick,' said the blushing waitress in a central London steak house, as she self consciously dropped a twisted, battered spoon into her apron pocket before disappearing into the restaurant kitchen.

'There you are,' said Herbert Corelli, a magician of formidable talent who had travelled from America to continue his crusade against pseudo-scientific phenomena, 'not everyone is taken in so easily.' This was one part of the Spicer investigation that didn't upset Penny or the boys. Dad's meeting with an internationally famous magician, who had once managed to release himself from one of America's top security prisons, fascinated them.

Corelli's journey to London had been brought about by endless claims from Rashnin that he could bend metal by electromagnetic radiation; Spicer's mushrooming notoriety had also attracted his attention. The claim that dead artists were using his physical body to remind the world how great they were opened up a new line of inquiry for this intrepid investigator.

Corelli had nothing against Rashnin or Spicer. 'I would just like them to admit they are good magicians, not paranormal miracle workers. They may have something that is a step beyond clever sleight of hand and mental manipulation. But if they won't offer themselves up for reliable laboratory testing we may never know.'

Staff of the Master Brewers in West London will never forget the visit they received from Corelli. They were convinced he was gradually demolishing the restaurant's stock of decent cutlery and one waitress hurriedly went in search of the manager. Another said her watch had gone haywire.

The spontaneous show was not a gimmick. Corelli wanted to

61

demonstrate to me and others who happened to be around that spoon bending and watch meddling were established magicians' tricks. I had also given him all the background to Spicer's automatic writing and he was not impressed. Nevertheless, he would reserve judgment until he had taken a closer look.

We discussed the many confident assertions made by people who claimed to monitor the activities of psychic prodigies. 'Young career-climbing scientists are often a pain in the neck,' was Corelli's frank opinion. 'They're so keen to make their mark they overlook the possibility that their subjects in an experiment are quite capable of cheating.'

Corelli believed it was a waste of time setting up complicated laboratory work unless you co-opted people with razor-sharp eyesight and an ability to concentrate for long periods. 'The key to a successful experiment is to make sure independent observers understand the subtle arts of deception and distraction. The magician uses them all the time to put his victims on the wrong foot but what you don't want is observers who allow themselves to fall under the spell,' added Corelli.

I witnessed the important part distraction plays in a magician's repertoire three or four times that day. The instruction to me was to stay alert and follow the movements of both magician and victim, concentrating on one, then the other, not both at the same time. If I lost my focus, I would be the one who would get distracted. I was able to see how the waitress fell instantly into Corelli's distraction trap and busied herself with all manner of little duties while he, with a twinkling eye, bent half a dozen spoons produced from his waistcoat, not from the restaurant's cutlery drawer.

A junior manager who came to see what was going on looked at the damage and angrily declared, 'You will have to pay for those, you know.' Poor man was quite taken back when we all laughed.

Later Corelli went with me to meet Stephen Spicer's publisher, Melanie, and more hilarious episodes gave me plenty of fodder for the article I was planning. Melanie, poor girl, was rather like the eager volunteer who goes on stage and feebly falls under the spell of a hypnotist. Hypnotism was not part of our investigation but that, too, would surely come under scrutiny in Bryan Pettifer's laboratories at some time in the future. Hypnotism was already a tool much used by entertainers, who were always very particular in their choice of victim. An unwilling or obstinate volunteer was very unlikely to fall under the spell, Corelli told me.

For the second time I was instructed by the magician to watch him carefully. There was hardly any need. His ploy this time was to get Melanie agitated by making a few mildly derogatory remarks about one of her publications and then persuade her to search her desk for evidence, which might support her contrary view. While she grovelled in a bottom drawer, protesting all the time that 'it is here somewhere,' Corelli moved at will away from and around her desk, unnoticed by her but watched with amusement by me.

'I've found it,' she announced triumphantly as she emerged from an uncomfortable squatting position. Straightening her back, she noticed that the spoon in the saucer of her tea cup was twisted into little knots, a piece of automatic writing had appeared on one of her visiting cards and items of office equipment had disappeared, to be found later in another room.

'But you didn't move,' said an incredulous Melanie, turning to me, seeking some support.

'He did,' I told her, 'but you were rather busy examining the contents of that bottom drawer.'

'Don't be too embarrassed,' said Corelli, trying to be conciliatory, 'most people are taken in...until they know what to look for. Damon had the advantage of a good briefing.'

Maybe I had, and I know I had kept items on Melanie's desk under my watchful eye, yet on two occasions a spoon had changed its shape (or rather, Corelli had re-patterned it) without me noticing. If it's easy to distract someone who has been alerted to the tricks of the trade, it doesn't take a lot of mental effort to see how much easier it is to trick those who have had their powers of concentration seriously disrupted. Corelli was good at doing that.

This was probably the moment when Melanie started to wonder whether material she had been responsible for publishing was all it was made out to be. But she wasn't going to muddy the waters at this stage. Too much was at stake. A lot of her own money had gone into the Spicer enterprise.

Corelli reminded us that similar techniques were adopted by Rashnin but there was an interesting variation, which he had put to the test in a practical way. Taking a leaf out of Rashnin's book, he participated in a radio programme and told thousands of listeners that because of his presence in the studio, people would find various pieces of their furniture would have suffered minor damage. Windowpanes would also crack while he was on air.

He asked everyone to check their windows and report on damage to furniture. Scores of people rushed to their telephones to report previously unnoticed scrapes and scratches on their dining room furniture and many said they had found a crack in a window. Later a check was carried out on people who had volunteered their home address. 'The window cracks were there right enough' explained Corelli, 'but often contained a dust deposit indicating the damage was not new but had been there for some time. Superficial damage to furniture was also in evidence but the blemishes had probably been there for weeks or longer. Some people just wanted to believe all this was down to me.'

That night when I gave an account of Corelli's little stunts, my family, particularly my sons, were in raptures. 'If you meet Mr Corelli again can we come?' they pleaded.

'How did he get away with it,' queried Marcus. Demonstrating a small boy's confidence, he said he was sure that he would have spotted Corelli's deception. I thought he probably might have done. He's a cunning little so-and-so.

I explained that magicians rarely revealed their secrets but Corelli wanted people to know that Spicer and Rashnin could be cheating when they claimed special psychic powers.

Penny was amazed by my account of what had happened at the publisher's office. 'Surely, Melanie should have been aware of what was going on around her. You don't have to be looking at someone directly to know they're shuffling about.' I thought she would probably have to see Corelli at work before she was fully convinced. In the meantime, she would have to take my word.

I wanted them to understand that Corelli was something more than a magician. He was a man with a mission. If I could convince my wife of this then she might be less inclined to think of my activities as merely an elaborate newspaper stunt. Corelli, I was able to explain, was a member of a committee set up to investigate the claims of paranormal activity and was elected onto the committee because of his insight into the idiosyncrasies of human behaviour. He was also responsible for a quite special publication about which one reviewer expressed undiluted admiration. Producing yet another tattered clipping, I quoted 'This book marks a turning point in a tidal wave of alleged psychic phenomena which has been threatening to engulf logical thinking. It almost qualifies as an introductory text to basic psychology.'

'What's psychology?' asked Ian, a good question from an eight-year-old but not one to be tackled after a mind-bending day at the office. I won myself a reprieve with a promise to talk about it on the way to Saturday's football match.

'All very well,' said Penny, 'but if people like watching this stuff they're not going to listen to two blokes they regard as a couple of old stick-in-the-muds. In their view you're just spoiling their fun.'

It was time to let the family into the secret of how Corelli was planning to throw down the gauntlet. 'What annoys him is how these people walk away from any attempt to examine the 'gifts' they so proudly claim to have. So Corelli is dangling a bait of 10,000 dollars, his own money, as a reward for any person who can demonstrate genuine paranormal activity. He's confident enough to think the money will never leave his bank account.'

'Can we come and watch?' asked Marcus and Ian enthusiastically and both were downcast when I explained that experiments carried out in 'lab' conditions could be hampered by an audience no matter how small or well-behaved.

'If anyone takes up the challenge, and we hope Stephen Spicer will, they'll have to face a panel of observers, including Corelli himself. If what I think will happen, happens that will be the moment my typewriter goes into overdrive,' I said optimistically.

I realised that once the account of my collaboration with Corelli was published, Stephen Spicer was likely to be a very angry young man and would probably refuse to meet me again. Drawing comparisons between him and his rival, which I intended to do, would be like red rag to a bull. Before publication, I was anxious to discuss with Stephen some of the more discreditable stories appearing on an almost twice-weekly basis. Did he intend to continue encouraging these outpouring from a sensation-seeking press or did he really want to start unravelling the mysteries of the paranormal? If he were serious, he would not back away from offers to test his 'gifts' under controlled conditions.

No request for an interview this time. I just turned up at the family cottage hoping to benefit from an element of surprise. I was the one who got the surprise. A young people's party was in progress and the drink was flowing freely. There was no sign of parents or sisters and Stephen was obviously making hay. Little chance of asking any serious questions on this occassion.

'Look who's here' said a tipsy Stephen, 'our very own correspondent from the local rag. Now you will all be able to see what I have to suffer.'

In a young people's gathering such as that was, I didn't expect to see anyone I knew. One face, however, was familiar, that of Stephen's publisher, Melanie Cooper. She gave me an embarrassed smile and then moved to a group on the other side of the room.

There was one other face well known to most people in Trentbridge. It was that of a minor television celebrity, Roger Hanks, who had started to make a name for himself with claims he could heal the sick. The minister of a local church had annoyed his flock by allowing this man to conduct occasional healing services. There had been letters to the editor in plenty, I recalled, from people who were angry that Roger Hanks had been allowed to go unchallenged after a number of preposterous claims.

Hanks, three parts to the wind like most people in the room, seemed oblivious to all that was going on around him; but perhaps his healing technique did require wrapping himself around two of the more glamorous girls in the room! He quickly disentangled when Stephen mischievously suggested if he wasn't careful, he could finish up on the front page of Trentbridge's own News of the World.

Turning off the music, Stephen announced that he wanted to tell his 'fans' about the latest extraordinary development in his extraordinary life. As I was still there I might as well listen, he said. 'I'm sure our star Trentbridge reporter will put his own slant on anything I say but you, my friends, can be judge and jury on the accuracy or otherwise of his reporting. He'll undoubtedly get it all wrong.'

Everyone in the room turned towards Stephen. The attention he commanded from his followers was mind-boggling. The chatter stopped and all eyes were focused on his face with an intensity that was disturbing.

'I had two visitors last week and none of you could possibly guess from whence they came,' said Stephen, pausing to give dramatic effect to the next part of his statement, 'they were emissaries from the Vatican who had read about me in some obscure publication. As a result, they wanted to find out whether I might be able to use my gifts to solve a particular problem.

'They probably won't admit it if you phone the Vatican, but it happened,' maintained Stephen. 'What they wanted me to do was throw some light on the state of the elderly Pope's health. They had heard from various sources that I could diagnose unsuspected ailments.'

'Oh, come off it,' said one of the less gullible party goers who had obviously had enough ale to ease his inhibitions, 'you're not telling us the Vatican sent two members of staff all the way from Rome to the village of Deepcote to utilise the skills of a 'spirit' doctor, you presumably?'

Since I had not been thrown out yet, I decided to join in the fun. 'You may like to know I checked this one out and was told by a Vatican spokesman that the visit of the emissaries to this country was purely social.

'That's ridiculous, don't listen to him,' said Stephen, beginning to return to his normal irascible self. 'Can you possibly imagine the Vatican going to all this trouble, just to make a social call… on me? What they were hoping for was that I could diagnose the Pope's ailment by the same method I demonstrated on television, using birth-dates, a few other personal details and a technique I don't intend to make public.'

The expressions on the faces of most people in the room told me they were well and truly under Stephen's spell. Most of them had watched the television show and had been impressed by Stephen's apparent ability to be quite personal about the state of health of people in the audience. None of them, it seemed, had considered the possibility that Stephen might have had a stooge in the audience, someone who could have talked with and closely observed the demeanour of people as they entered the auditorium. That, one supposes, would have been considered heresy in these circles.

'But what is the significance of the dates,' asked one young woman, who from her cross-legged position on the floor was having difficulty in getting her drink to stay in its glass, 'how can knowing birth dates lead you to sorting out someone's health problems?'

Stephen admitted this was something he wasn't sure about. 'Focusing on a particular date in the past and then feeding in details of the person I have been asked to investigate triggers off a process which has no real explanation. Then, as you all know, plenty happens in my life which I can't fully explain.'

Stephen was now getting into his stride, as usual enjoying the chance to speak to a captive audience. 'There are times when I sit down to write and find the handwriting totally different from my own. Often the words are those I would never use in the normal course of events.

'Our journalist friend here will snigger, I'm sure, but recently the name Thomas Parsons appeared at the end of a diagnosis spelt out in detail on my bedroom wall. I was completely baffled until receiving a cryptic message inviting me to search the records of the Royal Society of Medicine for the last quarter of the 19th century. I was told I would find something of interest. What came to light was a post mortem report in exactly the same handwriting as appeared in the message from Thomas Parsons.'

That was all we were going to learn about Dr Parsons that night. Stephen's little speech was suddenly interrupted by heavy banging on the front door and male voices shouting 'to open up.' Faces fixed on Stephen a few moments before, suddenly showed concern and the suspect content of the rooms ashtrays quickly vanished into the flames of the roaring lounge fire. Momentarily, the air carried the intoxicating smell of many discarded cannabis joints.

All invited guests were present so the likely explanation for the disturbance, if not caused by the police, was the unwelcome arrival of a crowd of unruly gatecrashers. Stephen's face clouded over and others in the room looked at each other anxiously. Like me, they had all read stories about the details of private parties being revealed either accidentally or with malicious intent.

'Don't open the door,' shouted Stephen to those who were propping up a wall in the hallway. It was too late. The back door had been left unlocked and before preventative action could be taken a bunch of seemingly inebriated males burst into the kitchen.

What struck me almost immediately was that although the men were waving cans of beer around and putting on a show of bad behaviour, it looked contrived and didn't fit the popular image of binge-drinking young adults, intent on spoiling someone else's private party. What was strange about their behaviour was having gained entrance and demonstrated their physical superiority they made an odd proposition. They wanted to talk to Stephen privately and they wouldn't break the place up if he came outside for a chat.

With what seemed like fatal naivety, Stephen agreed to the demand probably to avoid the fearful damage that could be inflicted on his parents' home if he didn't comply. He ignored my shouted plea to stay put.

Everyone sat in shocked silence for a few moments until someone decided dialling 999 was the most sensible thing to do. As the call was being made, I twitched the curtain just in time to see two cars disappearing around a bend in the road. The assumption was that Stephen was in one of them but bearing in mind his party was still in full swing his departure, it seemed, could hardly have been voluntary.

This was to be the first of two mysterious disappearances by Stephen.

The Saturday night incident converted into a reasonable story for the Monday editions but at the official level, there was very little concern about Stephen vanishing into the night.

The lack of interest had its roots in the fact that twice the police had been called to Deepcote to deal with over enthusiastic press activity and they were no longer amused by Stephen's antics. 'He'll reincarnate himself sometime, somewhere' was the cynical attitude of local CID officers who quickly made up their minds the disappearance was in some way planned, another stunt possibly. They felt their scepticism was justified a few days later when an anonymous caller reported Stephen was free, unharmed and had been seen many miles away in the West Country.

The stunt theory was generally accepted; even his mother's tearful appeal for information lacked sincerity and the story went off the boil. I was glad of the break, allowing me the opportunity to get back to what my colleagues deemed to be real work. Eric showed his spite by sending me off to Crown Court to cover the most boring fraud case in judicial history.

The Spicer story reactivated itself six or seven weeks later when a pile of clothes was found on one of Cornwall's most beautiful and popular beaches. Stephen's name was, by now, on the missing persons' list along with a description of what he had been wearing at the time of his disappearance. A cautious statement by the Cornish police suggested the clothes could have belonged to Stephen but they were far from sure. His parents were being contacted in the hope of a more positive identification.

If Eric had been at his news desk, I'm sure he would have vetoed a visit to Cornwall but he was away on a course for a few days so I despatched myself on a mission to find the missing psychic. To this day I'm not sure why, but I was certain he would turn up. Even before I set out on my journey this confidence took a bit of a knock when Stephen's parents, having travelled to Cornwall told the police the clothes did belong to their son.

The minute this news was released Stephen again became front-page material. Had he gone for a swim and got into difficulties or was it a classic suicide, removing his clothes and walking into the sea? All the theories, which were raked over, were in my view poppycock. Stephen was not the type to take an early morning bathe in a cold sea nor had he any reason to take his own life. With his rival out of the picture, he was having the time of his life and was certainly demonstrating that when I last saw him partying in his parents' cottage.

There were, however, plenty of unanswered questions. The so-called raid by middle-aged gatecrashers was so farcical, the more I thought about it the more unreal it became. Stephen left his assembled guests so meekly and apparently put up no sort of resistance before he was driven away. Certainly, I had heard no shouts of protest and there was no evidence of a struggle.

I was probably the only one thinking along these lines but I could not get it out of my mind that Stephen had been a willing victim. This lad, I felt, was too arrogant to think about destroying himself. What would the world possibly do without him?

I was going to have a lot to answer for, leaving the office without the guiding hands of senior newsroom staff on the tiller. But I sensed new developments likely to yield another slant on the Spicer saga. Anyway, there was nothing much happening in Trentbridge. Even the parrot had decided to behave itself.

The train journey allowed me to catch up on some reading, especially material dealing with a series of pseudo-scientific claims from various parts of the country. Nicholas Barnard, a professor of philosophy at Bridgnorth University, had only that month set up a committee to examine what he called the 'new nonsense' of spoon-bending, astrology, flying saucers, Lock Ness monsters and plants with the ability to think.

In a frank statement, Prof Barnard said their fears were not so much around the possibility of scientific misinformation, as about the social and political consequences of people believing cock-and-bull stories.

'There is always the danger that once irrationality grows, it will spread into other areas,' explained the professor. 'There is no guarantee that a society so infected by unreason will be able to resist even the most virulent programmes of dangerous ideological sects.'

This was music to my ears having spent several months fighting off criticism that I was wasting my time chasing a freak. I countered by maintaining that one of the worthwhile jobs of a local newspaper was to put a stop to the activities of those seeking to make their name by exploiting vulnerable people.

'Gullible people, you mean,' Eric had commented on many occasions. He had a point but there was satisfaction in hindering the activities of 'con-men' who usually targeted the weak, the poor and the elderly. I had no cast-iron proof that Stephen fell into this category but the evidence was building up.

I noted with some displeasure that Yasha Rashnin, had joined the Bridgnorth university committee and 'would challenge ruthlessly' all scientific claims he considered pseudo. He would be using his sharp eye to recognise sleight of hand and anybody found to be a fake would be exposed. Given more time, I might well have challenged the choice of Rashnin to do this work but I was on my way to the West Country and had enough on my plate establishing that Stephen Spicer was still alive if, in fact, that was the case.

Another encouraging development was that serious investigation into the paranormal seemed to be taking place on both sides of the Atlantic simultaneously. An American committee had been roused to fury by a television documentary titled 'Exploring the Unknown', which reported an outbreak of psychic phenomena as if it was backed up by firm facts.

The committee complained to the National Broadcasting Corporation that the show presented a totally biased point of view in a sensationalist manner and its members were backed on this occasion by many members of the public. Telephone lines to the Corporation had been blocked with protests. Carefully filing away this report, I treated myself to the thought that perhaps my pursuit of Stephen was not as frivolous as some of my work colleagues seemed to think it was.

I left the train at Bodmin and hired a car to take me to a part of the Cornish coastline, which was very familiar to me. Polzeath, Rock and Padstow had been favourite holiday spots during the early years of my marriage and many pleasant hours had been spent with my two sons on the wonderful expanse of sand at Polzeath.

The police at nearby Padstow were anxious to help but could tell me little I didn't already know. They were satisfied with the positive identification of Stephen's gear by his parents but in the absence of a body had to keep an open mind about the possibility of him still being alive.

'We've combed the beach daily,' a helpful station sergeant, Bill Howson, told me. 'The lifeboat crews have done their stuff, too, including thorough inspections of the many coves and caves down here. But so far nothing.'

'I'm sure he's still around somewhere,' I told Sgt Howson and asked whether a photograph had been circulated in the area.

'No, but one has appeared in the local paper and that produced no response at all,' added the sergeant, 'with his long straggly hair and distinctive features, plus the publicity he seems to be getting all over the country, I'm really surprised we've heard nothing.'

Having clarified that the bodies of people who drown on the Cornish coastline are usually washed up within three or four days, I thanked Sgt Howson for his help and stepped out into the Cornish sunshine, still convinced this was not the end of the Spicer story.

And it wasn't! I'd hardly moved 20 yards down the road before I noticed a very ancient Daimler parked with its two nearside wheels partly blocking the narrow pavement. I would have walked straight past it without another glance if the passenger door had not been pushed open in my path almost knocking me flat. For a moment, I thought I was going to be hustled into the back seat, gangster style but the guy who stepped out, although well built with bruised and battered features was dressed in a smart grey suit and spoke with almost gushing politeness.

'Gather we've similar interests,' he said, 'both wanting to find Stephen Spicer.'

'Well, I certainly would like to know his whereabouts if his body is not, as the police think, floating in the sea. But what's your interest? How did you know I was looking for him?'

'We have our spies, need to in my business.'

'And what is your business? How come you're looking for a man who lives several hundred miles from here? I probably don't need to tell you he disappeared mysteriously after a party in Trentbridge. Am I right in thinking that you may know something about that?'

'Maybe, but come back to my office and we'll talk about it.'

'I'm not going anywhere until you tell me what your business is and if you have knowledge of where he might be at the moment.'

My surprisingly gentle assailant, quite likely a retired boxer from a different age, rubbed his flattened nose pensively and swung on his car door for a few moments. 'I'm a bookie, properly registered, I tell you, under the name Billy Biggins and Partner. We're firmly on the straight and narrow. No funny business, if you see what I mean. They say bookies don't lose but me and me partner, Jim, were going through a rough patch. Then we saw in one of the papers something about a guy called Spicer. He reckoned he could look into the future and forecast all sorts of things.'

'So you went to Trentbridge and kidnapped him. Right?'

'No mate, wouldn't have risked that. Had too much to lose. We'd been talking to him for weeks and right from the start he seemed keen to see if he could forecast a few handy winners. Got the impression he liked the idea of floating around the country mixing with the racing crowd.'

'If you had it all buttoned up what was the gate-crashing drama for?' I asked in some bewilderment.

'Well, he seemed to be losing interest and we were losing money so we went along to his cottage intending to put the pressure on a bit. Pity about the party, knew nothing about that until we got there. When he came outside we didn't rough him up or anything like that, just reminded him we had a stake in his future. He didn't need a lot of persuasion to get into the car.'

'But you did use some force,' I suggested, 'he would never have walked out on his friends otherwise.'

I got no direct answer to that one, instead a detailed account of how Stephen had decided to join the partnership for a week or two to test his fortune-telling abilities. A couple of early successes got all three of them excited but Stephen was anxious that those back at home should not be aware of what he was doing. He slept on a mattress in the office and only went out when the partners travelled to a racecourse in their Daimler.

Billy told how it started to go wrong after a big telephone bet on a horse at Windsor went down the pan and Stephen claimed the other two had gone against his advice and picked a loser. 'Why have me around if you are not going to listen?' queried Stephen, but the partners swore they had put the cash on Stephen's chosen horse and he was trying to get off the hook for a bad forecast.

'The next day we came to open up and Stephen was gone, without a word,' said Billy, 'but he left a note saying he thought he could do very nicely on his own thank you very much. Ungrateful little bastard!'

I asked Billy whether he thought Stephen really did have something going for him. 'In the end I don't think he had any better chance of picking winners than you or me but he certainly got lucky for a while. He talked quite openly about the help he got "from the other side" but that help started to dry up, he said, because "the spirit" decided we were getting too greedy. I think the little swine decided to get it all wrong on purpose and then pushed off to make his own pile.'

'So you don't think he's dead either.'

'Good God, no. He just didn't want Jim and me around. I've read enough to know that leaving a pile of clothes on a beach is one way to tell the world you don't exist any more. It's usually done for insurance lolly but Stephen, I reckon, had other plans.'

'Where do you think he's gone then?'

'Your guess is as good as mine; if you find him tell him he owes us a couple of long-shot certainties to make up for all the trouble he's caused.'

I walked away wondering why Stephen should have got involved with a couple of hardened bookies, if he thought he had the insight to pick winners at the flick of a race card. He could have done it all on his own, unless he felt inside knowledge of the gambling world was still a necessity.

In other circumstances, this might have been another interesting way to test his abilities. Stephen facing a challenge to go through the card at Newmarket under research conditions. But that was cloud cuckoo land. He would say his gifts weren't given him to make other people rich and anyway he couldn't operate with a bunch of sceptical people watching his every move.

For the first time since getting involved in this madcap adventure, I was in danger of allowing myself to be caught up in flights of fancy. I knew perfectly well no one had ever succeeded in predicting future events. If there were psychic operators capable of doing so, what incredible chaos would be caused. Football pools operators would have to shut up shop and even the Stock Exchange might be ringing its bells in alarm. No, it was ridiculous. Stephen had found a recipe, clever enough to deceive those who wanted to think he had special powers and flexible enough to beat a hasty retreat if the going started to get tough. He also had to rely on some ample slices of good old-fashioned luck. That was my verdict and I would continue to stick to it in the absence of anything that proved the contrary.

By the time I got back to Trentbridge, my article on the Corelli demonstration had been published and the offer of 10,000 dollars to anyone who could convince a panel of experts of their unique psychic abilities was on the table. The hope was that Stephen would take up the challenge and if he refused everyone, we argued, even his most fervent supporters, would start to have their doubts. Or would they? Stephen was very adept at saying, when confronted with something he didn't want to do, that the circumstances weren't right. His friendly spirits couldn't operate if they felt antagonism from those around them. As far as he was concerned, it was the perfect escape route.

The next day I walked back into the office rather sheepishly, having to admit I had not solved the mystery of Stephen's disappearance.

'Wasn't he supposed to be kidnapped?' smirked Jeremy, a junior reporter who loved to cover up his own deficiencies by embarrassing his seniors.

'That was a presumption,' I foolishly tried to explain,' but it seems he managed to pull the wool over our eyes.'

'Your eyes you mean,' said Jeremy, presumably not caring that his punishment for insolence might be two days gathering dog show results.

This time I thought I would test this aggravating junior in another way. 'If you want to be a reporter you can ease yourself out of that desk and go and see Mr and Mrs Spicer. Find out if they have heard from their son. You had better not mention my name if you don't want the door slammed in your face.'

Jeremy returned within the hour having had the door slammed in his face. 'They'd seen your article about Corelli and weren't pleased. If I was from the same paper I could go to hell.'

'Did you check the neighbours? They might have seen him around. Suppose you didn't think of that?'

Jeremy brightened up. 'I did speak to one neighbour who spends a lot of time in his garden. He had seen a young man walking towards the cottage but was pretty sure it wasn't Stephen. He looked too respectable. The same day the parents went off carrying suitcases.'

For the first time, I felt I could reward Jeremy for his initiative and gave him another important task. 'Good work! While I spend a few hours putting this newsroom back together, you can speak to the CID. They must have become involved again since the discovery of Stephen's clothes.'

Jeremy was now demonstrating a few sparks of enthusiasm and came back to tell me a body had been found on a beach in the Polzeath region. I almost felt sorry for him when a call from the same department informed us it was definitely not the body of Stephen. All my efforts to bring the inquiry to a conclusion had failed so for the time being at least I had no excuse for not getting back to the daily grind.

Several years later, my untidy desk would offer up another little gem---a rejected expenses sheet along with a crumpled note signed by the editor explaining that the newspaper did not pay for unscheduled holidays to Cornwall. For the time being, Stephen and his activities would have to go on hold but not for long, of that I was quite sure.

7

Who Killed the President?

After a period of frantic activity trying to keep track of Stephen, then having to play my part in re-establishing office routines, the next two months seemed quite blissful. 'We still have a newspaper to get out,' Eric would remind me when he suspected I was sliding off to follow up another lead. Penny was happy to tell her friends she was now leading a less frantic family life, apart from the occasional late night telephone call. We both needed a time of relative calm as I had been on edge since returning from Cornwall with nothing to show for my trip except a lesson in how not to make a living on the racetrack.

While away, the feature inspired by Corelli's very public demonstration of the magician's arts had been published followed by angry rebuttals from Rashnin's agent as well as from some of Stephen's still loyal friends. His parents decided to keep themselves to themselves and I came to the conclusion they probably knew where he had gone but I would be the last person they would tell.

Proof of this came when from a secret location Stephen decided the Psychic News, a spiritualist paper claiming over 100,000 readers, would be a good vehicle to put sceptics like Corelli and me in our place. Fortunately, the newspaper carrying this report was sent to the office not my home and I was able to study it in work time without antagonising Penny or unsettling the children again. Some of the comments made about both of us, if they had been allowed to filter into the domestic domain, would almost certainly have disturbed the peace.

Stephen had obviously relished his interview with a kindly disposed member of the editorial team and had accused both of us of supporting a fanatical crusade rather than turning to the results of serious scientific investigation. He was incensed by Corelli's offer of $10,000 to anyone claiming they could provide verified evidence of genuine psychic activity. In Stephen's view, Corelli was the wrong man to mastermind a properly controlled experiment. 'No magician is able to reproduce results which a careful laboratory experiment, run by sympathetic scientists was capable of doing,' claimed Stephen. We thought him very foolish to refer to sympathetic scientists when what was wanted was quite the opposite.

Stephen was making it clear he was not going to take criticism lying down but I was anxious to avoid a slanging match at this stage. Family affairs could come first for a change. We had actually managed a day by the sea but never got the chance to dwell on the benefits of that brief excursion for very long. I walked into my office a couple of weeks later to find the switchboard operator frantically trying to link me up with a caller from the United States. Communication from country to country was still basic at that time, subject to long delays, poor reception and very expensive. Local newspapers didn't expect to get too many long distance calls.

Curiosity kept me at my desk instead of straying into another part of the building and when the phone rang the caller turned out to be Rod Bryson, a reporter working for the Chicago Herald. He was anxious to get background material on a psychic 'dickhead' named Stephen Spicer, who had made a brief but dramatic visit to the United States. Was I the right person to talk to?

I said he was probably on the right track because I had been pursuing Stephen for some months but had no idea he had left the country. Realising that co-operating with Bryson might yield good results for both of us, I gave him a brief summary of what had been happening in the UK, up to and including Spicer's flirtation with bookmakers in the depths of Cornwall. 'He told nobody over here about plans to visit the US, in fact, he's been behaving strangely for some considerable time even by Stephen's standards,' I told my American counterpart.

'Can probably help you there, buddy,' said Rod, who had been puzzling over the antics of a young Englishman, drawing attention to himself by claiming he knew who killed the American president.

'I thought we had all the head-cases this side of the Atlantic but he started telling all who'd listen, we'd messed up and hadn't put the finger on Kennedy's real killer. Our quirky press lapped it up and went along with his crazy claims. One nuthead reported he was getting his information from little green men up yonder.'

'He's not really saying that, is he?'

'Well, they didn't actually mention little green men but you know what I mean....poltergeists or sprites you call them over there, don't you?'

Rod said the more responsible among them knew he was using material from a document called *The Gemstone File*. He'd had a copy in his desk for many months. No author of the file had ever been named and there was general acceptance the author was a troublemaker with nothing in the way of evidence to back it up. 'Until now, no one has believed a word of it.'

'Until now? Has something happened to bring about a fresh appraisal?' I asked.

Rod explained that there was nothing concrete but his sources talked about uneasiness behind the scenes. Certain pieces of evidence were being turned over. Purely routine, he was told, but the boat was certainly being rocked.

'Where is Spicer now?' I inquired.

'Can't say for certain but seems he scurried out of the country, after some sort of threat. We've always thought the names in the file were put there just to cause trouble. But if someone is angry enough to put the frighteners on a zany, young Englishman, maybe we should think again.'

'Can you fax me a copy of the file, or will that cause problems?'

'No reason it should,' said Rod, 'but watch your back, perhaps your boy's gone in deeper than he intended. Doubt whether he understood the sort of material he was playing with.'

Rod also promised to send a couple of clippings from American newspapers, one from the New York Chronicle, another from the Washington Times. But even before this fascinating collection arrived, I got a call from one of Stephen's young supporters which, amazingly, demonstrated that Stephen was still hawking the 'real truth' about Kennedy's assassination to anyone he thought would listen. He probably mailed it before he was threatened and decided to return home.

As soon as I had my hands on Rod's fascinating faxes, I phoned Penny to say I would be late. Despite the incredulous claims made in the file, I thought it wise to mug up on the sort of information someone was endeavouring to throw into the ring. Better to go into battle well armed; if *The Gemstone File* was to be dismissed as rubbish then one had to be sure of the official version of events.

I remembered the Warren Commission had rejected claims of a possible Cuban connection and ruled that Oswald was Kennedy's sole assassin. But that didn't stop the conspiracy theories and the view of many that Oswald did not act alone. One item in Rod's package referred to the discovery of letters said to have been written to Oswald from Cuba, offering rewards for services rendered. Other conspirators were also mentioned with details of the rewards they would receive. Because the bureau had no agents in Cuba, there was no way to check the substance of the letters.

I had become so absorbed, I didn't notice Nigel Ferguson, rarely seen out of office hours, walk into the newsroom intending to return a pile of paperwork to editorial files. He had been to the Pentagon Club dinner and had been watching me for a while from a doorway at the back of the room. He wanted to know why I was still in the office at such a late hour. 'Don't usually see anyone here after 5.30.' His comment demonstrated just how little he knew about office routine or my personal habits.

I explained I had just received some potentially explosive information and I wanted a few moments peace and quiet to absorb it and decide on my next move.

'What sort of explosive information? Not anything to do with that Spicer fellow again by any chance? He's taken up a lot of your time this year, it's costing this company a packet.'

For a moment I thought he was about to suggest pulling the plug on the entire investigation and I was preparing for the worst when much to my surprise he said he thought we should keep the inquiry going until Spicer was found, dead or alive. 'Then I suggest we wrap it up before we get a rap over the knuckles from the Press Council for hounding the Spicers.'

I could have made out a case that far from hounding the Spicers they were the ones seeking publicity, pretending they didn't like it when it suited them, courting it when the outcome promised fame, glory....and money. But I didn't pursue that line of argument. It was late and I still had papers to read before I headed for home.

However, our brief conversation, although not bubbling with encouragement, had been important to me. It meant I could carry on with my inquiries, which now had the editor's endorsement, however grudging. It would be useful when Eric complained I was spending too much time chasing ghosts.

Glancing through *The Gemstone File* before setting out for home, I found myself wondering why such a discredited document was still a hot potato in the eyes of some individuals and organisations on the other side of the Atlantic. To Stephen, it was just another handy prop to convince supporters back in the UK he had received dramatic messages about the death of Kennedy from 'the other side.' It was understandable that its downgrading by those closer to the action would not have come to his notice. But if the file had been relegated so emphatically why would anyone have gone to the trouble of warning Stephen to shut up shop and make himself scarce?

On closer inspection, I came to the conclusion that an introduction to the file had been photocopied many times. In an amateur attempt to shield identity someone had gone to the trouble of cutting letters out of various publications and sticking them together to form the title: *A skeleton key to the Gemstone File---credit will go where credit is due after the mess has been cleaned up.*'

The file contained the sort of material I expected, multiple accusations of very shady practices by people and organisations who had no love for Kennedy and wanted to create their own power base. Greek shipping magnates, well-known Mafia gang members, big cheeses in the CIA, state senators, potential presidential candidates.... just about every ambitious political-climber, as well as others with dubious backgrounds, got a mention.

My main interest, though, was in the other part of the package from the States, three pieces of hand written A4, Stephen's attempt, I assumed from the signature, to tell the world that use of his special gifts could lead to knowledge of who was behind the death of Kennedy. It appeared to be the brief Stephen had used to impress people back in the UK and according to Rod had been found in the telephone booth of the hotel he had been staying at during his short visit to the States.

Who shot President John Kennedy! Was it really Lee Harvey Oswald? was the headline that could have come from any tabloid newspaper? What followed, if it had any substance at all, certainly would have disturbed certain notorious characters in the States especially if by accident or design, more likely the former, Stephen had stumbled across elements of the truth.

Stephen opened his revelations by telling his audience that the core of the matter was a power struggle, so far not alluded to by any commission or board of inquiry.

'Kennedy was assassinated chiefly because he had set up a group of 40 to fight Aquino Remigis, who had been shipping heroin and other drugs out of the Golden Triangle with the acquiescence of a known security agency. There were four shooters—Ubertino, Malachi, Berengar and Hemsley. Ubertino hit Kennedy twice with shots from a handgun. He was arrested but was released without being booked. Berengar hit Kennedy in the right side of the head, blowing out his brains with a rifle from behind a fence in the Knoll area. It was supposed to be a triangular ambush and Hubert Hemsley was the third man. He missed the president because Ubertino and Berengar had already hit him. Ten men were arrested after the shooting. None were booked and none are mentioned in the Warren report.'

Before signing the document and dating it 10/10/67, Stephen said he could reveal that Ubertino received $250,000 for his hit on Kennedy. Berengar's pay off included $109,000 from a San Francisco bank.

It was difficult to escape the feeling after studying this material that there just might be some elements of truth in parts of it. It was not my objective, however, to play around with that potential time bomb. The value of comparing the File with what Stephen had sent back to the UK was the proof it provided that Stephen had attempted a big cheat which had misfired. It didn't need a mastermind to see that Stephen had used the File in a rather school-boyish attempt to impress all his followers back at home. His mistake was not finding out that nearly every journalist in the Western World had received a copy of the File but had spiked it.

My eyes started to close. It was time I made my way home, so I filed the papers in a safe place---if one could designate a locked drawer in my old-fashioned desk a safe place--- and made for my car. I was still thinking about the content of Rod's package as I walked across the poorly lit car park at the side of the building and was about to put the key in the car lock when I noticed a Land Rover straddling the car park entrance. My first thought was that someone had parked awkwardly and would move away as soon as it was obvious I wanted to leave.

On a second glance I could see that there were two men in the vehicle and although the light was poor, one had long, untidy hair and the other, the driver, appeared to be a much older man. The reflection from a street lamp highlighted a distinguished head of grey hair. With the intention of asking the driver to move away from the entrance, I walked towards the car, but there was no time for conversation. The engine started up while I was yards away and the vehicle went off at speed. As it went through the gates, the passenger turned his head and looked straight at me. Without a shadow of a doubt, it was Stephen Spicer. I vaguely recognised the driver but could not be absolutely sure in poor light that it was Stephen's father.

What would have brought Stephen and his father to the gates of the newspaper so late in the evening? Could it have been to talk to my editor who had left the building 30 minutes or so before me? But that didn't make much sense because my boss and Patrick Spicer, both members of the Pentagon club, would surely have had plenty of time to talk at the dinner they had attended that evening. There was only one thing I could be certain of, the occupants of the car didn't want to talk to me. Living in times when the word conspiracy cropped up on a daily basis, I started to wonder whether I was becoming entangled in one.

My first task on arriving at the office the next day, was to send a dossier on Stephen, including the stories that had been written about him, to Rod, my new found contact in Chicago. Although Stephen had left the States, Rod wanted to look more carefully into the activities of those still showing nervousness whenever *The Gemstone File* made a reappearance.

I felt I should make some effort to discover more about the recent activities of Yasha Rashnin. He was obviously very angry about Stephen's interference with the comfortable little world he had created for himself. Perhaps their colliding interests held the key to some of the strange incidents of the past few weeks. The possibility of a personal war between them could not be ruled out.

A visit to the library and a painstaking search of a comprehensive index allowed me to turn up an article in the *Scientist* with the intriguing headline '**What price Rashnin now?**'

The content must have been a big blow to a man who thought he had the world at his feet. A well known scientist, Professor Peter Parkinson, who had been very impressed by Rashnin's 'gifts' in the early days had changed his mind dramatically about what he had previously called the 'Rashnin effect.' Five years previously Prof Parkinson had been completely taken in by Rashnin's performance, admitting that try as he did he could find no flaws in Yasha's claims. 'I felt as if the whole framework with which I viewed the world had suddenly been destroyed,' said the Professor. The U-turn came when after extensive laboratory tests on subjects with allegedly paranormal abilities, he dismissed the very existence of the phenomena.

The *Scientist,* in a leading article referred to Prof Parkinson's 'journey through the valley of irrationality.' It would be reassuring, the writer thought, if his conversion to rationality would have as great an impact as his gullible endorsement of Rashnin in the first place. But that, he added, seemed very unlikely.

Condemnation by someone respected in the scientific world must have had quite a devastating effect on Yasha Rashnin and the cancellation of some television appearances would have really hurt. If he thought Stephen was waiting in the wings to take his place on the international stage, then he might well think of ways in which he could destroy his rival's plausibility. In the States, Stephen had walked into some kind of trap and whether Yasha had set it up or not, he must have felt there was now an opportunity to cut the young 'psychic' down to size.

I had a number for Yasha's agent and decided the direct approach was probably the best one. I drew another blank. Yasha had gone away days before and the agent said he would not be available for at least a month. Before he left he talked about an important meeting in America, which would be vital to his future prospects and would return him to a position he believed was his natural right ....centre stage.

8

The Temptation to Cheat

With all trails having gone cold, all I could do was keep the newsroom ticking over and use the in-between times to catch up on some of the information arriving on my desk at regular intervals. It was becoming obvious that there was a clear division between people who dismissed paranormal activity as the product of a vivid imagination and those whose desire to connect with another world was so great they would happily suspend rational judgment.

Before going off to Cornwall I had responded to an article in *The Times* in which Andrew Pearce, known for his incisiveness and willingness to call a spade a spade, described a book on the natural and supernatural as an extraordinarily important and valuable work and added that the writers, including Spicer, had piled up a mountain of evidence, searchingly examined and scrupulously evaluated. It was a surprise to find a man of Pearce's intelligence and reputation being taken in so readily.

'I give you my word as one who has always, in these matters, trodden the tightrope of rigorous scepticism without ever swinging on the trapeze of dogmatic disbelief or being fired from the cannon of gullibility, that it is simply not possible, after reading this book for any fully sane person to deny that there have been a vast, and unaccountable number of supernatural happenings that cannot be rejected as the products of fake, hallucination, chance, misunderstanding or the effect of powers and senses already known to be possessed by human beings. '

It seemed like another attempt by Pearce to write the longest sentence in the history of journalism but it was not that which drove me to write to the editor suggesting that Pearce may have fallen from his tightrope of rigorous scepticism. He had suggested, amazingly, that scientists who tested the alleged abilities of Yasha Rashnin were afraid to release their conclusions in case their experiment proved his powers were genuine. I pointed out in my reply that there were scientists in Trentbridge, who were desperately keen to work with subjects who may have unexplained abilities but were invariably regarded as 'hostile' should they suggest a test which did not allow 'the psychic' an enormous amount of freedom. It was disappointing but I was not surprised that the newspaper did not consider my letter worthy of consideration. Perhaps I had been a little too dismissive of one of its star writers.

Another disappointment was my failure to convince Weekend Television that when Stephen appeared on the Grant Stephens programme they should have been more challenging. The producer exploded. 'If you can prove Spicer a fraud, then do so. This constant haranguing is an example of a time-honoured newspaper trick, trumping up a rumpus to fill space. Prove it or leave it alone.' We were in the process of proving it and we certainly were not going to leave it alone.

From the States came a letter enclosing a newspaper clipping with the headline: 'Could this man (Spicer by all accounts) really bug Chequers?' The origin of this one was uncertain. However, the writer was in no mood for compromise: He said the answer was almost certainly 'no' and complained about a society dominated by people with little science and little logic. 'I believe that an effort is required to stem this tide of pernicious fallacies in pseudo-religions and pseudo-sciences,' he added.

I started to wonder whether Stephen's disappearance might have had something to do with a growing awareness that his claims were being greeted with more widespread scepticism. The material landing in my tray gave reason to think this might be the case. Another example was a claim made by Stephen's supporters that he had managed to sabotage Timmy Clarkson's morning radio programme. The claim that Timmy had been taken off air for four minutes by paranormal influences didn't stand up to examination. Apparently, Spicer was in an unmanned studio in Trentbridge and had been given a key to let himself in. The theory was that he had decided to experiment with some of the switches in front of him and managed to break the connection between Trentbridge and London. Then, when back on air, he suggested that this was down to psychic vibrations.

Stephen's automatic drawings were also coming under the spotlight once again. One correspondent was fascinated by the presentation of a well-known Aubrey Beardsley work. If someone wanted to fake a well-known drawing, then Aubrey Beardsley would be the artist to engage with, he suggested. 'It is very possible to imitate Beardsley's mannered style with a little draughtsmanship,' he wrote, 'but for someone who claims he is unable to draw, they are extraordinary.'

Another controversy, which had been raging while I was away, was over a set of Clejuso handcuffs, said to be unbendable but apparently distorted by Spicer in one of his high profile demonstrations. In Spicer's first book, he wrote about high-ranking officers at Scotland Yard being 'quite flabbergasted' that someone had managed to bend the cuffs to such an extent he had been able to escape. The handcuffs were supposed to have been taken for examination at the police forensic laboratory at Brundel University. Problem was that there was no forensic laboratory at Brundel University. This, I felt, must have been the time when Stephen started to lie, thinking no one would bother to check his claims. He must have known he would come unstuck eventually, until then he would swan along on a cushion of self-confidence.

This appraisal of what the rest of the world was saying about the paranormal was interrupted by another call from Rod who was keeping a close eye on developments across the Atlantic. 'Guess you gotta hear about this,' said Rod in his usual drawl. 'Early on security guys just didn't want to know. Claimed they knew nothing about a UK citizen making wild statements about Kennedy's death. Now they've decided they want to talk to him.'

'Why ever would they want to do that?' I asked, 'They're not taking any of his 'intelligence from another world' stuff seriously, are they?'

'No they're not, it's not the paranormal they're interest in, they want to grab those responsible for giving your fella' *The Gemstone File.* Stephen Spicer, they say, was paid a bundle to use the file and contradict material in the Warren report. To begin with, security laughed it off. Then the word started to go around that the file might contain grains of truth. A few people in high places have got edgy. Any chance your guy will be coming back this way?'

'Very unlikely. He came home in a hurry because of threats; it'll take some persuading to get him to risk his neck again. Anyway, he's gone to ground and nobody knows where he's scuttled to. An extradition order wouldn't wash, either.'

'S'pose you're right, the guy's not done anything wrong. Not against the law, anyway.'

I promised Rod we hadn't dropped the story, just put it on ice until some new development revived it. When I put the phone down, I didn't imagine I would have to wait only 24 hours for another positive lead. It came gift-wrapped but wouldn't have interested the law enforcers in either country. The antics of a teenage psychic were a low priority in countries where serious crime figures were increasing in leaps and bounds.

Despite Bryan's sound advice not to rush my fences, I felt I was very close to the time when I would be able, with reasonable safety, to seal Stephen's fate. But I still needed a break, a piece of watertight information from a reliable source which would persuade the world it could do without the activities of people like Stephen Spicer. The break came in a most surprising way.

Whenever challenged about his automatic drawings Stephen always had an answer. He stressed in his first book and later to every journalist who sought to break down his defences that he possessed absolutely no artistic ability whatsoever. He could not draw neither could he paint.

In one of his books, he gave an emphatic assurance that he was no artist. 'I have no artistic ability in my conscious self,' he wrote, 'they made me go to art classes but I have never been able to paint or draw with the least competence. I have to state this to allay the suspicion that I am perpetrating a clever fraud. My parents, teachers and friends have all testified to the fact that I am hopelessly bad at drawing.'

A simple postcard, signed by a man who said he was an art teacher at Stephen's school and had had dealings with Stephen up to the age of eleven, arrived on my desk at a moment of personal despondency and gave me the sort of adrenalin rush one might have experienced from a tip that the town mayor had absconded with the university chancellor's wife.

The art teacher, Keith Donovan, had come across a couple of newspaper stories about Stephen's 'miracle activities' and was puzzled. He wrote, 'Stephen was a pupil at King Edward School. Two of us recall he had artistic ability and this prompted me to check the school magazine. One issue records that Stephen was joint winner of the Art Cup in July 1963.'

So that no one could claim he was being vindictive or making up stories to discredit Stephen he enclosed a copy of the magazine, which had the usual list of prize winners and an entry that recorded---*Art Cup: Spicer and Heppelswaite*. The cup was obviously shared but that did nothing to diminish the fact that Stephen was very much at home with a pencil, crayon or a paintbrush.

Reporters aren't supposed to get excited about anything but on this occasion I held the postcard aloft and shouted across the newsroom: 'Get a load of this lads. Yours truly has just hit the jackpot. Young Mr Spicer, with all his magic, won't be able to wriggle out of this one.'

The faces of five would-be journalists, raised momentarily from their much abused keyboards, all had that kind of expression which said: 'Here he goes again, mad as a hatter!' These were young men and women, some with university backgrounds, who thought with little or no effort they could change the world. Bristling with ambition in the early months, now they were happy if a phone call yielded a saucy quote from a visiting celebrity or a complaint about the town's rubbish collections. Where had the industry gone wrong?

Eric reacted in his usual deadpan manner. 'I'll take a punt,' he said, 'a letter from Spicer's grandmother saying he used to play with her tarot cards and regularly cruised up the garden on a broomstick?'

'Along those lines, Eric, but not as frivolous as that and a great deal more intriguing. Looks as if you may now have to give credit where credit is due. The time spent on chasing Spicer has not been wasted.'

'Let's have it, then. If it's that good perhaps I can get this crappy story about lack of parking spaces off the front page.'

I gave Eric a run down on the build up to this development, handed him the postcard bearing the damning evidence, and outlined how I thought Spicer had been relying on the creation of a fabric of lies and deception. 'Goodness knows how many people have been taken in and parted with well-earned cash thinking he could deliver them a small miracle. Apparently £150 was the going rate for whistling up an aunt or uncle, £200 for a wife and £300 for a long lost lover.'

'That much? Now pull the other one,' said Eric, still in need of some convincing.

Really encouraging was the fact that I had probably made a breakthrough with one of the juniors, young Jeremy, who unlike his colleagues was demonstrating some enthusiasm at last. 'Sounds good,' he said, 'sorry I joked about it.'

Eric was also warming to the situation and I thought this might be the moment to tell him about the two men, one of them probably Spicer, prowling around outside the office while I worked inside.

'Could be he intended, or his father intended, to start leaning on us,' suggested Eric, 'but what we don't know is whether they spoke to Ferguson and, if they did, whether they planned to apply some sort of pressure. Perhaps Spicer realised you were about to damage his lucrative career and thought he might persuade you to drop the story. He knew any sort of exposure could cost him hard cash and do nothing for his reputation.'

'But how did he know I was in the office that night?'

'Probably he didn't.... but hang on a minute. How long after everyone sloped off home did you eventually leave your desk and walk outside.'

'It was at least a couple of hours.'

'Well, then, someone in the office who doesn't love you would have had plenty of time to pass on a message that you were still at your desk and likely to be there for some time. Better keep an eye on Angela, our television wannabe, she got quite upset when you made fun of the Maharishi and his meditation classes. Thought you were demonstrating all your prejudices and went around the office telling everyone so.'

I didn't take Eric's warning too seriously until one morning I came in and found that someone had been rummaging through the drawer where I had kept a lot of sensitive material. Fortunately, most of it was history and had already been used in one way or another. I was relieved to find the school magazine announcing Stephen Spicer's art prize was still in my brief case, where it had been since I took it home to show Penny. I decided in future to be much more careful about what I left lying around. Caution would be even more important when I started to put together copy designed to shorten Stephen's colourful career. The world would be a better place, I told myself, without his activities or those of his rival, Yasha Rashnin.

It was encouraging to have Eric on my side rather than continually sniping from the sidelines. Now that things were hotting up, I was sure he would have liked to be more involved. But it was his decision to allow himself to be tied to a desk. Several of the younger reporters who had scoffed at the story in its early stages now decided they ought to be taking more of an interest, a good development from one point of view but I thought it best to keep them at arms length until we established whether we had a mole in our midst. For a while, I thought it wise to use the small interview room as my private study. No one objected. My status and reputation had certainly risen a bit.

It was time to see how the story might shape up and with so much material to work through I wished I had something more efficient than an old-fashioned Olivetti typewriter to work on. Smooth computerised newsrooms with super-fast keyboards were talked about endlessly but many more hurdles had to be surmounted before they became a reality.

Making sure I had a good supply of paper and carbon, I hit the keyboard with new enthusiasm:-

'*Before he set off on a tour of the United States earlier this year Stephen Spicer succumbed to a temptation which sooner or later faces most would-be psychic marvels… the temptation to cheat.*

'*Perhaps with a publicity stunt in mind, perhaps for financial reward, he decided to reveal through 'automatic writing' the contents of an alleged underground document known as 'The Gemstone File.'*

'*The file purports to answer the question "Who shot John Kennedy? Was it really Lee Harvey Oswald?" and links international figures, big business, gangsters and security forces in a plot which few had dared to hint at, let alone publish.*

'*Stephen did dare. Once in the United States he rattled off pages of the file and sent them back to the U.K. presumably hoping they would be accepted by the press and others as a sensational piece of automatic writing through the hands of the Western World's most gifted psychic.*

'*But Stephen failed to take two important considerations into account. One that respectable newspapers and magazines do not publish potentially libellous and scandalous material without making their own detailed inquiries; the other that the content of the File was fairly well-known to journalists on both sides of the Atlantic who were therefore able to make comparisons and draw their own conclusions.*

'*Oblivious to the notorious reputation of the file, Stephen started sending back extracts to the UK, thinking their impact would be such that his fame as a psychic with formidable powers would be considerably enhanced.*

'*His naïve publisher, Melanie Cooper was delighted and cheerfully went about her task of spreading the material as widely as she could. Then out of the blue, she received a panic telegram from Stephen. Marking it very urgent, he said he no longer wanted publicity on the*

Kennedy assassination revelations and ordered her to stop circulating the material already in her possession.

'But it was too late. Already more than one reporter had been comparing Stephen's version of events with the actual file. The image built up by this over ambitious and dishonest young man started to crumble with the speed of lightning. There was no doubt that had Stephen been playing it straight he could have presented his revelations as truly remarkable psychic phenomena and the financial rewards would have been beyond his wildest dreams. Instead, ridicule at all levels was going to be his fate.

'But that would come later. It was not the reason for his sudden decision to return home. One theory for his rush to leave the States was that he had trodden on some very sensitive toes, the toes of important law enforcers and maybe the toes of one or two unscrupulous law-breakers. America was waiting for the publication of 40,000 pages of material on the death of Kennedy, released under the Freedom of Information Act. Serious accusations would not be welcome as the administration made big efforts to put the past behind them and restore some normality back into the political scene.

'Two questions needed answering. Did someone with a keen desire to see some of the 'facts' of The Gemstone File published at a crucial time decide to use Stephen as a go-between? Did something happen in the States to frighten Stephen into an early departure? By leaving, he had abandoned a lucrative tour of at least a dozen universities.

'Intriguing questions but whatever the answers Stephen would appear to have been coaxed by someone into prostituting the 'psychic' gifts he had previously claimed to have. Or perhaps it was that at a very early age Stephen, having decided he had a special gift of sorts, started to work out how he could claim psychic abilities and take the world for a ride.

'If so, then Stephen's claim to be a genius might bear up to examination but not quite in the manner his books led us to believe. His genius could be said to lie in another direction, in his ability to mastermind a confidence trick of mind-boggling complexity.'

As I deliberated over the copy so far and sifted the monumental amount of material on file, the door opened and a junior reporter, grinning hugely, came in holding a mug of tea. 'Eric sent it, with the message that it's not the sort of service you can expect as a matter of course. Just once, he said, while genius burns.' I took this gesture as an acknowledgement that Eric rated the story and would have liked to be part of it rather than an observer.

I picked up one of Stephen's books, one that had sold thousands of copies around the world, intending to check out some of the claims he had made at that time and to put them to the test against what I already knew about his activities. Idly flicking over the pages, I came across probably the most hilarious claim made by Stephen early in his pursuit of fame. There were three photographs, which according to the caption featured a curious white cloud, circular in shape, above Stephen's head. The trouble was, there was no cloud. It was obviously one of Melanie's blunders, doing nothing for the cause of her young client. When clearing the book for publication she failed to notice that in all three photographs the white cloud had fallen victim to the guillotine. In cropping the picture this vital piece of evidence had been removed, almost certainly by accident.

Perhaps Stephen didn't notice either because at the end of his book he wrote about the white cloud in terms that suggested the omission had not been pointed out to him. In sweet innocence he wrote: 'It's possible to conclude that these are photographs of psychic energy emanating from me; and to recall that a white shape may have hovered above the heads of those other well-known psychics, I mean men of an entirely different and holy complexion, the saints.' The shape could have been the origin of the halo, Stephen had unashamedly added.

This sort of fantasy was probably encouraged by a Vatican diplomat serving in Western Europe who told a journalist that Stephen's extraordinary gifts were obviously the work of God. Although superb fodder for a publicity release this was one statement Stephen did not pass on to the rest of world. He often appeared to have a sudden attack of shyness when faced with incisive questioning on the source of his gifts.

He was not so bashful about claiming objects often materialised as a result of him making a wish---wood for a fire, gramophone records, even a bottle of beer and an apple pie when he felt hungry and thirsty on a train. This hint of a 'fishes and loaves' type miracle was one of Stephen's big mistakes. Many times when challenged he had to squirm free by saying it was not the sort of demonstration capable of being turned on and off like a tap.

Stephen made many more mistakes along the way but they were always overlooked by those who desperately wanted to believe in his gifts. Not for a long time did anyone bother to check the background of a self-styled expert graphologist who appeared on a Granada television programme. When they did, they found the woman described on the programme as the Official Examiner of Handwriting and Documents at the Central Criminal Court was not holding a title of that description at all. In fact, that title didn't exist.

When a Sotheby's expert was persuaded to examine an automatic drawing featured on television, his comment matched those made by our helpful museum experts. 'The drawing couldn't have fooled an expert but for someone who claims not to be able to draw, they are good.' He pointed out that some of the drawings were the wrong scale--more like copies of book illustrations.

As part of the substantial feature I was now preparing, I thought it right to deal with the question frequently asked in the newspaper's correspondence column and by some of my friends and colleagues also: 'Does Stephen Spicer cause anyone harm by making the claims he does? Couldn't his activities be written off as harmless fun?'

Even if my views were dismissed, I felt we should listen to responsible members of the university's Psychical Research Society. One of the society's teams was carrying out research in the fields of extra-sensory perception, telepathy and psychokinetic energy and its concern was that people like Spicer and Rashnin, in making a living out of presenting a popular and fabricated image of a serious subject, were harming research. On more than one occasion, possible ESP subjects had turned their backs on experiments for fear of being dubbed 'cranks.'

When I thought I had covered enough ground to fill an inside page as well as the front-page spread I expected to get, I dropped the story into the overnight tray, put another copy in a place of safety and made tracks for home, treating myself to a favourite pint of ale on the way. As that slid down a parched throat, I indulged in a little self-satisfied contemplation, looking forward to the impact my exposure was likely to have, not only in Trentbridge, but probably in London, other parts of the country and almost certainly in America.

9

Spiked!

Turning up at the office next day with high expectations, I was surprised to be met by Eric before I reached my desk. He had a dour expression on his face and suggested we found some privacy in the interview room. Nothing could have prepared me for what was coming next.

'You're not going to believe this. They've spiked your story.................'

'They've done what? Don't be so bloody ridiculous. You're winding me up.'

Eric pushed a scrappy piece of copy paper across the desk and I stared in disbelief at its content. It was from Ferguson's secretary, Sheila---a young woman who should have stayed at the supermarket check-out desk from whence she came----'The editor says your latest attack on Stephen Spicer is unfair on you, unfair on Spicer and his family and on us, so he's not using it.'

'Unfair! What's he getting at? A few days ago he was urging me on, even threatening to put someone else on the story if I didn't come up with something more concrete. Hell! it would be like leaving out the last chapter of a book...the man's gone mad...or he's been got at...he must have been got at....no self-respecting editor in the country would ditch a story like this at the last fence.'

My rage built to a level that was not healthy in a person recently diagnosed with high blood pressure.

I turned on Eric. 'What have you done about it? You're the news editor for God's sake, doesn't he listen to you any longer.'

'Simmer down, I'm right with you but letting your feelings get the better of you will do no good,' said Eric, sensing that I might be on the verge of doing or saying something I might later regret.

He explained that when asked for an explanation for this change of heart, Ferguson was very evasive. 'Just said he was the editor and there were occasions when he had to kill a story without having to explain his actions to the whole world let alone the newsroom.'

'He's crazy.' I jumped up from the desk announcing that I was going to see the old fool but Eric, now in the unfamiliar role of the wise old bird, urged me to stay put.

'You'll get nowhere by charging in there like a bull in a china shop, sit down a minute and let's try to fathom what we think has happened and what we can do about it.'

Despite our day-to-day warfare, I respected Eric's judgment on internal politics. He had fought a previous editor who tried to stop him publishing a story about a corrupt estate agent and he had won hands down.

'Who do you know in the Pentagon Club?' queried Eric. 'Their monthly meeting is due this week and they have a speaker from the council talking about pollution control. Not normally your line of country, I know, but it might be a good idea if you went along. We know Spicer's father is a member, so is the editor and they were all together at the last meeting. Thought it was my imagination at the time but when you produced a Spicer story that week he started to nit-pick over some of the detail which gave the impression he wasn't so keen on keeping up the campaign.'

'Hang on a minute, Eric, we may have a poor opinion of him but do we really think he's capable of allowing himself to be got at during a piddling little event like a luncheon for local businessmen?'

'Piddling it may be but you know as well as I do that that's where it all happens. It may start with a casual chat but a lot of back-scratching goes on around those nicely laid tables.'

Eric reminded me of the multiplying number of town planning scandals. 'Bet half of them take root over a couple of glasses of wine at a business lunch,' he said knowingly. Eric had a good memory and could tell you in some detail about most of the notorious local government corruption cases during the past 20 years. It was his speciality.

'So, the editor finds himself chatting to Spicer's dad and Spicer senior says he doesn't like all the bad publicity his son is receiving from the local rag. He must have been in that situation dozens of times. It's one of the perils of an editor's job. I just can't believe he would have allowed himself to be sucked into that sort of situation. There must be something else behind it,' I argued.

'There probably is,' said Eric, 'but if you want your story to see light of day you've got to find out who put the spanner in the works. Go to the next meeting and poke your nose in all the corners. Meanwhile, I'll make a few inquiries of my own.'

Eric went off to get on with the job of bringing out that day's paper; I sat stunned for a while trying to fathom what could have precipitated this extraordinary U-turn. It threatened to destroy a piece of work over which I had sweated blood. In no way should it finish up on the spike and I was determined it wouldn't. I could always sell it to any number of publications but that would probably leave me without a job and a mortgage still around my neck. Couldn't the silly fool see he was throwing away material that could do wonders for his paper's reputation? Something must have happened to make him side step the editorial principles he had grown up with. I wanted to charge into his office with all guns blazing but decided an outburst of temper would get me nowhere. I needed solid evidence if allegations of corruption were going to be thrown around.

It was a long time since I had attended a lunch for local executives, especially one noted for its stomach churning old pals' acts. If they bothered to invite a local reporter, it was usually to show off their ability to capture a celebrity speaker, albeit a local one. It did nothing for my temper when one of the members sneeringly queried whether my shorthand was up to scratch.

I was expecting to see Ferguson but he was conspicuous by his absence. I wondered if he had looked at the newsroom diary, noticed I was down to cover the event and decided to keep his distance. It could hardly have escaped his notice that I was breathing fire and probably capable of making a scene.

First things first. I had to listen to a talk on pollution, a boring recital containing absolutely nothing that I hadn't heard or read about many times before. It was not difficult to look interested and pretend I was taking copious notes while at the same time noting the names of as many people present as possible.

One of the local government officials present leaned across the table during coffee time and asked, 'where is your editor today? Unlike him not to put in an appearance.' He said there was something he wanted to discuss.

I gave him a vague answer but then remembered this official worked in the same department as Stephen's father. I quickly backtracked before he could turn away and engage others in conversation.

'There's another absentee isn't there? ....Patrick Spicer who works with you is a fairly regular attendee, I'm told. What's keeping him away, I wonder?'

I got the brush off, amounting to 'mind your own business' if not actually expressed in so many words. Looking around I started to count the number of local government officials and councillors present and came to the conclusions that they were a powerful cartel in this seemingly innoculous organisation. How convenient to be all together at regular luncheon meetings if unofficial, perhaps contentious matters, needed to be discussed. The events of the last few days had done nothing to dampen the cynical side of my nature.

There was good reason to have doubts about some of the local government officials present. It was not a story I had been personally involved in but I could hardly have been unaware of the huge planning row, which had been bubbling for months. The controversy was over the development of an important piece of land near the centre of the town.

I had enough on my plate without getting embroiled in a local planning matter and I would not have given this another thought had I not been accosted on my way back to the office. As I walked away from the luncheon venue, I heard someone running in my direction presumably keen to catch up with me. I turned and recognised my pursuer as one of the juniors in the planning department, Jeff Woods, a young man seemingly bent on making his name as a whistle-blower.

He had given me a sequence of tips in the past, some useful but others needing to be treated with care. I did warn him frequently that his future in local government was tenuous to say the least but he never took any notice.

'Got a good one for me this time have you Jeff? But don't you think running down the high street after me might attract attention?'

It was a waste of breath. Jeff, with an ambition to go into politics, felt he was serving the community. Face as red as a beetroot and his lungs working overtime, he gasped out the fact that he had been waiting for the luncheon meeting to end so that he could have a word with me well away from the council offices.

'What's so important, then, and how did you know I would be there today? I never cover that meeting as a rule.'

'I rang your news desk and asked who would be at the lunch as I had some information I wanted to pass on. When I heard it was you I decided to catch you as you left. You do move fast, though, I nearly lost you.'

Pushing me gently across the pavement into the doorway of a bookshop, Jeff took a few more deep breaths and said he had witnessed something in the planning office he thought I should know about.

'Are you sure you want to talk in a place as public as this? Anyone could walk by and start putting two and two together.'

'It's important enough to take a chance. Can't tell you a lot but I have been reading your pieces about Stephen Spicer, and have seen the mug-shot you've used on several occasions. So you can imagine how surprised I was to see him walk past my desk, heading for the office of the Chief Planning Officer.'

'Peter Barnwell, you mean, he wasn't at the luncheon today nor if I observed correctly was his deputy, Stephen Spicer's father.'

I liked Jeff very much but I sensed we were about to enter Alice in Wonderland territory. 'Are you about to suggest a link between these people? Planning has become a bit of a joke, I know, but not to the extent, surely, that a psychic could play any part in the planning procedure.'

Jeff said he was about to tell me before I interrupted that there were four people in Barnwell's office, the chief, his deputy, Stephen Spicer and one other who he didn't recognise at first but then remembered seeing in a photograph of Trentbridge News executives at some presentation or other.' I'm pretty damn sure it was your editor. I couldn't begin to understand why a local self-styled psychic was meeting planning chiefs in the presence of the local newspaper editor.'

Jeff turned his back to the pavement as a group of suited, businessmen chatting earnestly, walked by.

'Yes, they were at the luncheon, Jeff, I told you we ought to be careful but now we've come this far, finish the tale.'

'Well I've told you all I know apart from one peculiar incident towards the end of that meeting. Peter Barnwell, using the light coming through the glass panels of his office, held up a document which I knew to be a certificate from a Government Department issued when a council can prove a piece of land scheduled for development is free of pollution hazards. It's vital to get hold of this document, testifying the land has been raked clean and tested, before embarking on major development.'

'You couldn't have seen much through a panel of glass, how can you be certain it was the certificate you say it is?'

'I've handled scores of them in my time and they are quite distinctive. Clearly headed with the logo of a Government department, it has three signatures at the bottom and these are the signatures of men who have the power and the authority to clear the way for redevelopment. They have to be satisfied that nothing nasty remains on the site, which is going to make Mrs Brown's children ill or destroy Mr Brown's early potato crop.'

I began to see where Jeff's appraisal of the situation was heading. It still sounded pretty unlikely but I made a stab at what I thought he was about to tell me.

'You are about to suggest that Stephen, considered by some to be a master forger of signatures, could be used to make sure there was an authentic certificate available to prove this valuable piece of building land was free from pollution.'

'You must be psychic,' said Jeff with a broad grin. 'Stephen stepped forward and started to study the signatures from close quarters; I have a desk position which gives me a clear line of vision between where I sit and Barnwell's office. It's a legacy of the open plan designs so popular when the town hall was refurbished. A freak combination of shadow and light enables me to pick out lots of detail in anything held up against the glass at certain angles.'

'You can't possibly be one hundred per cent clear that you were looking at this particular document, surely? But assuming for the moment that you were what projects are in the pipeline which would need this sort of clearance?'

Jeff took another quick look around him and said he would have to go or he might be missed back at the office. As he went, he reminded me of a plan for 600 houses on a large site, once the location of an agricultural fertiliser factory. I had to search my memory to recall that there had been a mega controversy probably seven years before about the many thousands of pounds, which would have to be spent on making this site safe for housing development. After numerous inquiries and failure to satisfy a series of inspectors, the plan had been shelved.

Jeff's parting shot opened a potential can or worms. It was probably meant to. 'The plan's back on the drawing board,' he said, 'but nothing has happened on that site for the seven years it has been lying derelict. Pollution? It's still as polluted as it was on the day the factory was pulled down. But no new certificates have been applied for. I know that for a fact because it's usually my job to make the application and chase up the appropriate government department.'

One part of me wanted to dismiss the idea that the Spicer family could in some way be linked to underhand and illegal goings-on at the town hall. Yet I knew Jeff well enough to know he would not be making this up. Stephen with his distinctive hairstyle and obvious youthfulness would have looked very much out of place among the grey suited men of the planning department. And his identification of Ferguson, although not conclusive, was as positive as one could expect in the circumstances. The rather odd way Jeff had identified the pollution document created some doubt in my mind but on the other hand if handling this certificate was one of his main jobs, his observation had to be taken seriously.

Now that the seed of doubt had been sown, it was going to be difficult for me not to consider the possibility that Stephen's automatic writing skills could have been co-opted to produce two or three vitally important signatures. The planning executives would be taking an extraordinary risk but this sort of deception was not uncommon in many parts of the country. Huge sums of money often changed hands.

The possibility that Ferguson was involved in any way had left me stunned but now I would have to discover whether Spicer, senior, with his close connection to the Chief Planning Officer had been drawn into a lucrative little conspiracy. Little? With so much at stake and so many reputations on the line, the rewards would have to be considerable.

10

Exposure Looms

The possibility that I now had two big stories on my hands didn't escape me. But my dilemma would be how to give attention to one without impeding the progress of the other. I had come a long way with the Stephen Spicer saga and whatever else happened this had to be brought to a conclusion. However, corruption in local government planning circles was a hot potato and if the council was trying to by-pass regulations over the decontamination of a potential building site then priorities would have to be reassessed.

With these two important issues competing for my attention, for once I was not sure which path to follow. If I started making inquiries about the meeting in the town hall, a number of those involved might put up the shutters and fade into the background. Moreover, unless I had very good reason for wanting to know about an internal meeting, the chances were I would be told it was none of my business. Somehow or other I would have to get confirmation that Stephen was invited to that meeting and did accept the invitation. If this turned out to be so then the planning department would have a hard job explaining their interest in a young psychic celeb, far removed from the world of local planning.

Handling my editor's involvement in all this, if indeed there was involvement, was a tricky business to say the least. I didn't want to find myself suddenly without a job which I almost certainly would be if I didn't have a cast iron case against any of the culprits I might be planning to name. Usually I came across Ferguson at least once a week but our paths hadn't crossed for some considerable time and tentative inquiries revealed he had been out of his office for days on end. This was unusual in itself because he hated leaving editorial matters in the hands of his deputy for too long.

His absence meant he was not witness to an extraordinary chain of events but nobody, least of all Ferguson himself, could have guessed our young psychic genius was about to blow himself out of the water. Stephen had been out of the news for weeks and no one had been able to throw light on the circumstances, which caused him to leave the States in a panic.

He must have had more than a suspicion by now that exposure was in prospect. I had tried very hard to conceal the damning revelation of his art teacher but maybe not successfully. Sadly, there were people in my own office capable of going to considerable lengths to acquire and pass on a piece of information like that. Even this type of setback might not have worried Stephen to any great extent. He was so cocky about his ability to deal with all such situations, he was probably already furnishing himself with a well-rehearsed rebuttal. One thing you could say about Stephen, he was a fighter, a fighter who never contemplated throwing in the towel.

But everyone has his breaking point and Stephen's was about to come. Without any warning, a press statement was released nation-wide, bearing no address or contact number. It must have been written in the face of pressures that so far we had only been able to guess at.

It was a very short message:-

In no way do I wish to withdraw anything I have said or written about in the past but from now on I would like to be known as a mentalist and not as a psychic---a description I have always resented and never liked.

Certain events in America have made me reconsider my position and I feel that this is a better description of the work I am trying to do. I would like to be judged on what I am doing now, and will be doing in the future, not what I have been doing during the past four years.

I have no intention of explaining this any further so you will be wasting your time if you try to contact me.
Sincerely,
Stephen Spicer.

'What a hypocrite!' I screamed, but it was approaching lunchtime and no one was around to share my amazement, my disbelief and my joy. They had all de-camped to the office's favourite watering hole, the Crown and Thistle, just a few hundred yards away, so no one would want to talk business until the pints and pies had replenished impoverished stomachs.

In an almost involuntary movement, I reached out for Stephen's much-vaunted book that had been taking up space on my desk for longer than I could remember. Mentalist, whatever did that mean? He had never used that description in any previous references to himself. The battered university dictionary that also lived on my desk contained no mention of the word. Mental and mentally were there, of course, with a brief definition 'performed in the mind—intellectual' but mentalist was not an entry the publisher had considered. Later in the town library, I consulted a more academic publication but the best it could offer was *mentalism—process of mental action.*

I pondered over the reasons for this surprise statement and decided it must in some way be connected with his hasty retreat from the States? Having gone to ground since his abortive attempts to persuade the world he had received mind-boggling revelations on the identity of Kennedy's murderers no one, not even his closest friends, had been able to track him down.

After the shattering experience of seeing all my hard work committed to the spike, I now had in my possession a statement, which amounted to a confession making nonsense of 90 per cent of the content of Spicer's most popular book. It was unlikely he would be allowed to forget his repeated claims to be the Western World's most gifted psychic. One couldn't imagine how he would endure the ridicule.

Fortified by a couple of pints of the region's extra strong ale, Eric was almost as jubilant as I was. 'We've no need to show this one to the Editor. He's not around anyway. The Press Association will be putting this on the wire within the hour and we shall look bloody silly if we hold it back. Feel sorry for you, Damon, really I do. You had it all first and now it's being scattered far and wide.'

'Scattered maybe but not with all the background leading to the confession,' I observed, 'People won't have a clue why he threw in the towel if he sticks to his decision not to talk about it.' With Ferguson out of the way, we could now give our readers a chance to make up their own minds about Spicer's activities. Many eyebrows would be raised in Trentbridge at the revelation that as a kid Stephen had demonstrated some artistic talent.

Eric didn't waste any more time weighing up the pros and cons. 'Let's go for it! The lid is well and truly off and we have nothing to lose.'

'Much to gain, I hope. We're doing Ferguson a favour but I doubt whether he will see it that way,' I added.

Chief sub, Bill Anderson, was in broad agreement and decided he might as well be hung for a sheep as a lamb. 'If we are going to do this, let's do it in style,' he said.

When I saw the front page later in the day I could see he had been true to his word. It was an impressive display and although I had received a fair share of by-lines in my time, this was one that glowed brightly, like having your name up in lights in the West End..

It was time for a little reflection, time to match the extraordinary claims made by Stephen over a period of several years with his timid retreat from a position he had promoted so unscrupulously. I looked again in disbelief at what had been written on the sleeve of one of his best-selling books:-

"Twenty-one scientists, among them Britain's Nobel Prize winner in Physics, Dr Peter Burke, took part in extensive tests and experiments in Ontario and they were bowled over by the phenomena Stephen Spicer was able to demonstrate. They agreed that Stephen was the most gifted psychic they had ever come across. His abilities were described as 'absolutely unique' and the discovery of an entirely new brainwave pattern in Stephen has set a milestone in psychical research."

One reviewer of the book was determined to go one better---'*I can only describe Stephen as the most remarkable psychic phenomenon I have ever met. He really speaks the truth and nothing but the truth in this book!*'

I made a mental note to meet this man at some point in the future if he felt he could readily recognise the absolute truth. Not many before him, if any, had made that claim

I wondered what the reviewer would think when news of Stephen's confession reached him. Would he and others like him be able to accept that he was no wonder boy, rather a skilled operator in the art of deception? By telling the world he no longer wished to be regarded as a psychic, he totally invalidated all he had ever written in a variety of publications. His flowery descriptions of a disturbed life at home and school would create a sour taste in the mouths of even his most loyal supporters. As for our detractors, people who put their faith in Stephen Spicer and were convinced our criticism was unwarranted, it was unlikely we would hear from them again.

There were three people I wanted to talk to before putting the finishing touches to this story---Stephen's publisher, Melanie, who presumably had money riding on his next book as well as the problem of what to do with shelf-loads of previous publications, all heralding Stephen as a psychic; Corelli, the magician; and Stephen's great rival, Yasha Rashnin who would probably be laughing all the way to the bank (unless, of course, he was silly enough to allow himself to get tarred with the same brush).

It took no more than a three-minute conversation with Melanie to reduce her to tears, not that I had set out to do that. She was overwhelmed and shocked when she was presented with a copy of the press release. 'He didn't even bother to tell me what was happening,' she complained, 'but that didn't stop him blaming me for not handling *The Gemstone File* episode properly.'

Melanie's particular gripe was about the number of times she had denied, on his behalf, that any of his experiments were faked or any of the incidents described in his books were inventions. When he decided to take on the press himself his denials were vociferous, insisting everything he had done had been open and honest.

'The miserable little so-and-so, leaving me with all the mess to clear up and hundreds, possibly thousands, of pounds of debt,' she added bitterly. 'And to think not so long ago he promised I would be one of the beneficiaries of his fame and fortune. Sounds like a joke now.'

It was probably just as well that Ferguson had gone AWOL because he certainly would not have approved of my 30-minute call to Corelli in Arizona or my long conversation with Rod in Chicago. It was important to let them know what had been happening in the UK if I was to keep them on my side. All attempts to contact Yasha Rashnin failed. His staff said he was still out of the country and they had been unable to reach him. I was beginning to doubt whether they were telling the truth.

Corelli could hardly contain himself when I told him what had developed. But nothing had come to his notice about Stephen's curtailed stay in the States and if it had got into the press, he thought he would have been one of the first to hear about it.

'You know Damon; this guy of yours isn't very smart. I've repeated all the things he claims to do by the paranormal on one of our television channels over here. I wanted people to know that Rashnin, Spicer and many others may be competent magicians but should never be allowed to dupe people into thinking they are some sort of miracle workers. If only they were honest about it, we might be able to forgive them.'

I asked him what he thought about the new title Stephen had crowned himself with.'

'A mentalist? All that does is provide him with an escape route. It also allows him to change direction and maybe try a different variety of tomfoolery. Healing perhaps?'

I wanted to know if anyone had taken up his 10,000-dollar challenge to prove under strict conditions that some paranormal phenomena was genuine.

'A couple of not very bright customers came forward but they couldn't get over the first hurdle. I certainly am not lying awake at night worrying about finding a big hole in my bank account, I can assure you.'

Because of the high profile research he was doing Corelli found he was under fire from many in the opposite camp. Some were saying he was conducting a crusade against any phenomena, which couldn't be readily understood. This was an unfair criticism, which didn't bear up to examination. Corelli's campaign was to convince scientists that no serious research into parapsychology could be carried out successfully unless the possibility of cheating was ruled out.

It was real encouragement to me to know that someone of Corelli's stature---in another time and place he could have become a good journalist---was ready to back our findings. But we were still fearful that our missing editor would appear on the scene, wanting to quell attempts to revive the story he had vetoed. To our relief he stayed away from the office and his secretary said she had not heard from him for days. She had spoken to his wife, who was very evasive, and had told her not to worry; he had gone away for a short break.

So we went ahead. Bill Anderson knew how to write a good headline and didn't let me down on this occasion. When the people of Trentbridgeshire and far beyond retrieved their paper from the front door mat the next day the news confronting them was clear enough--'**I'm not a psychic, says Stephen Spicer…..please call me a mentalist.**'

To ram the point home we reprinted an extract from the best dictionary we could find stating that mentalism was a process of mental action, a definition that failed to impress the good people of Trentbridge. Its vagueness riled many and a record number of letters arrived that week, threatening to swamp the pages set aside for correspondence. Mental action? Many of them asked if that was all it amounted to then in a university town like Trentbridge there must be a few thousand people who might well qualify for a similar title.

A debate quickly hotted up on the question of whether Stephen had done harm by pretending to be something he wasn't. Some agreed it was all good clean fun but they were in a minority. One serious objection was that to claim to be guided by spirits would encourage the more sensitive and vulnerable in society to seek non-worldly guidance without considering the authenticity of the messenger or the source of the message.

Theologians, of which there were many in Trentbridge, pointed out that the Bible had much to say about the Holy Spirit (referred to, they emphasised, as the Holy Ghost in traditional editions) but warned against meddling in ways which would encourage evil spirits. One local vicar quoted figures that demonstrated how few people had any understanding of the part the Holy Spirit played in their lives. He hoped his pews would be filled the following Sunday when he would offer a full explanation of the Holy Trinity.

At this point in my life, I had little time for the ghostly or the godly but I had been sincere in wanting to learn more about the extraordinary brain patterns being examined in new research. I was enjoying my association with the university's department of parapsychology and in an odd sort of way, I could thank Stephen Spicer for that. But I had to remind myself from time to time that I was a journalist, with minimum scientific and theological knowledge, and that there was still serious work to be done in my own province.

Later I would come to realise that this was probably the time I started to look at the world in a somewhat different way, sparing time to think about such matters as the creation and its origins. Darwin was a star in Trentbridge circles and had every reason to be so. But couldn't the theory of evolution fit perfectly well into God's plan for his world? Not for many in Trentbridge it didn't. Those wedded to the Genesis story struggled when the geologists produced another rock sample that made a nonsense of previous calculations of the earth's origins. This debate, I decided, was for another day. I had enough earth-bound problems to cope with for the foreseeable future.

We all expected a very angry editor to come storming through the front office at any moment, but it didn't happen. Instead, we got a memo grudgingly accepting we had to go along with the crowd but stating he still felt it was a weak story we should have left alone. He added almost as an after thought that he had taken no leave recently and intended to be away for a couple of weeks.

Someone who had been busy in the meantime was my council

mole, Jeff. A call from him reminded me that the potentially explosive story on polluted land had been bubbling away and there had been a considerable amount of attention focused on the council's planning department. We arranged to meet this time in a far distant public house where neither of us was likely to be recognised.

'Why are you doing this?' I asked Jeff as soon as we had settled down with a pint and a packet of pork scratchings.

'Well, I hope you don't think it's a grudge or anything like that. In some ways I'm perfectly happy in my job and don't want to lose it. I just don't like to see people with responsible jobs and earning good money looking for ways to get even richer at the expense of people they are supposed to serve.'

'A noble sentiment to be sure. But you don't yet know if that is what they're doing,' I ventured, 'there could be a quite reasonable explanation. Have you been able to find out why Stephen Spicer visited the planning department?'

'No, but after waiting for a week I inquired about the pollution clearance certificate, which it was my usual job to handle but had not turned up in my in-tray. The answer I got was that the boss was dealing with this one, and it would come back to me for filing when all the other procedures had been carried out. That was suspicious in itself.

'Suspicion number two was the unannounced arrival of two men who were wearing civvies but who I recognised as being members of the Criminal Investigation Department. One minute they were in the front office, the next they had disappeared upstairs, not going to the office of the planning officer but to the Chief Executive. That meeting never went on record and when I made a jocular comment to the chief executive's secretary, she said sharply that I had better watch my p's and q's.'

Jeff had done his best but I couldn't expect him to take any more risks and told him to let matters rest for a while.

The plot thickened when one of my close friends, a teacher at a local school but at heart a frustrated journalist, said he had noticed a flurry of activity at the front door of Ferguson's home. They both lived in the same street and Keith, who spent a lot of time in his garden, didn't miss much. He wouldn't have taken much notice of two men who called while he was pulling weeds but as they walked up the path to Ferguson's house an alarm went off and one of the men rushed back to the vehicle to switch it off.

'I'm sure the car was an unmarked vehicle the police use when they don't want to advertise their presence,' said Keith, 'I'm certain about this because similar cars often called at my school when the police wanted to make discreet inquiries.'

This time I had more luck when seeking out a friendly contact in the CID. He confirmed that Ferguson had received a visit from two of his colleagues but because it was an on-going inquiry, there was no way he could tell me any more. Very much off the record, he hinted that Ferguson was just one of six local dignitaries who had been interviewed.

We didn't want to set alarm bells ringing unnecessarily so we decided to let matters take their course at least until we had something a little more solid to go on. Unsubstantiated allegations would get us nowhere and probably put our jobs in jeopardy.

We established that the Planning Chief was still at his desk but any questions were turned away with the time-honoured 'no comment', the response that always makes a journalist want to dig deeper. It was much the same story at the police station with little information coming from anyone, even from those officers who had been helpful in the past.

'Sorry, Damon' said one potential informant, usually free with his snippets from the inside. 'If there is anything going on, it is being kept very quiet.'

'What about the two detectives visiting county hall, surely their visit must have been recorded somewhere if it actually happened?' I suggested. Apparently, it wasn't and that just increased suspicion. All the pointers were towards a potentially sensitive inquiry, which was being kept under wraps. There was certainly a closing of ranks.

****

Disappearing acts were becoming a habit. As well as failing to trace Stephen Spicer or our wandering editor, we met the same dead ends when trying to contact Yasha Rashnin. If he had seen any of the bad publicity surrounding Stephen, it was reasonable to think he might regard himself as in the ascendancy once again. But no, he too had taken it into his head to cross the Atlantic and spend time with the ever-expanding psychic circus. The landscape in that part of the world was certainly considered more fertile than barren European pastures.

Before he went on his travels, he experienced a revival in his fortunes after a stunt in the Daily Gazette. The newspaper had produced an eye-catching front page giving Yasha the entire credit for 'getting the whole of Britain in a right old twist.' Totally oblivious to accusations of gross exaggeration, it reported that thousands of people had accepted the Gazette's invitation to join the world's most baffling man in a nationwide experiment. The newspaper's partner in this gimmick-ridden project was a down-market television company known for its 'anything goes' attitude to entertainment.

There was no mistaking its popularity. Hundreds of viewers jammed the station's telephone switchboard. The Gazette reported that broken clocks and watches started to work again. So did faulty electrical gadgets, old TV sets and broken toys; the list went on and on, suggesting that 'little miracles' had taken place as people concentrated on Rashnin's picture staring out at them from the television screen.

In a pre-recorded episode, Rashnin went to the top of the Blackpool Tower beaming out his special vibes in all directions; in a room below a housewife was seen pointing a torch with no batteries at a picture of Rashnin and those watching were convinced the torch burst into life. Other people in the room held distorted knives and forks in their hands and in every corner of the United Kingdom metal cutlery buckled and twisted into all sorts of shapes.

It was another cleverly engineered paranormal-type demonstration, which, as in the past, went completely unchallenged. Thousands rapturously endorsed his claims and this gave Rashnin the opportunity to re-establish himself in places where his star had fallen.

Rod, on the ball as always, advised me when Rashnin arrived in Chicago and sent a copy of a press statement, indicating he might have a hidden agenda with disturbing implications. Taking part in a series of experiments at well-known universities was the publicised purpose of his visit, but he seemed hell bent on making sure his rival Stephen Spicer would have a rough reception should he ever venture into the States again.

Demonstrating extraordinary self-confidence, he announced he would be co-operating with American scientists in an attempt to prove that psychic phenomenon was genuine and should be taken seriously. Then he set about queering Spicer's pitch with vivid accounts of how his rival had come unstuck in the UK.

'It may not have come to your notice yet but we have a cheat back home named Stephen Spicer who has contaminated serious scientific research,' said Rashnin trying to sound as if he was really angry, 'he played tricks with the public and when faced with exposure, declared he didn't want to be known as a psychic in future but as a "mentalist".'

Observers commented that the magician was perfecting another talent, amateur dramatics, such was the flowery way he set about denouncing his rival.

Rashnin maintained that the new description Spicer was attaching to his 'gift' was meaningless and simply poured more cold water on his claims to have something special to offer the world. Cockily he told the American media: 'I hope if he comes this way again you will give him the rough reception he deserves. Those of us who want to make progress in this important field could do without the hindrance of people like him.'

Then, incredibly, Rashnin seemed to walk blindly into a similar trap Stephen had stumbled into. Before a critical audience, he made rash promises about attempting to solve the mystery surrounding *The Gemstone File*. 'Stephen Spicer went about it entirely the wrong way,' he suggested, 'and squandered the chance to examine whether some of the detail in the File had any validity.'

The pressmen present were baffled. One was particularly indignant: 'you're not telling us you want to revive that discredited old story and quarrel with the Warren report just as Spicer tried to do?'

'I didn't come here with that intention but I cannot ignore the strong psychic vibes plaguing me since the day of my arrival.'

Some in the room thought this was Rashnin's idea of a joke but their smiles quickly disappeared when he added: 'There are people no longer with us who would like the truth to be known and I believe they see in me an unknown and untapped source of communication.'

He went on to say that he would like to put the messages he was receiving in front of men and women who were able to interpret such material and come to realistic conclusions. 'You have the people over here who, I gather, can do just that.'

According to Rod, about six members of the press corps walked out at this stage, one muttering that he would rather consult the fairies at the bottom of his garden. Rashnin just ignored their sudden exit and ploughed on regardless. Known for his thick skin, he always worked on the principle that while two or three newsmen were gathered together there was still a chance of some decent coverage the next day.

I hardly had time to digest these latest developments before Rod was back on the line. He thought I should know that Rashnin had been given a bad press initially but nearly all the media in the States wanted to follow up the promised experiments. 'Even the guys who walked out won't be able to ignore him. When the time comes, they'll hang on his every word. It sells print in the States.'

Rod promised to keep an eye on Rashnin's activities and I said I would let him know if Stephen turned up. I didn't expect this to happen any time soon because even his closest supporters, still reeling at an announcement which had shattered their dreams, were unaware of his movements.

And that was how the Spicer saga became deep-frozen until the early seventies. Stephen disappeared over the horizon on a cruise ship heading for the Greek Islands; our local CID curtailed their inquiries on the basis there wasn't enough evidence of corruption at the Town Hall (no forged certificate ever came to light); Rod lost some of his passionate interest in the story when he found Rashnin embedded in a California university, strangely reluctant to go ahead with his probe into *The Gemstone File*; and our editor's absence did have an explanation of sorts----he had been offered another job with a small weekly series of newspapers in the north of England. He did come back to Trentbridge for a short time but although I passed him in the car park and in the corridors of the office once in a while he never acknowledged me, a sign maybe that someone's conscience was giving him trouble?

For a while, I enjoyed the attention I got after receiving an award usually reserved for scribes with national reputations, but they say a reporter is only as good as his next story and my assignments became more insipid by the day. Management, worried about cash flows and falling advertising revenues, made it clear they wanted a quiet life. No pot stirring stories in other words, nothing that would give cause for an advertiser to withdraw his custom.

So life became very dull and regional newspapers continued their decline; only the free sheets delivered to every door prospered but it had become a struggle to trace any genuine editorial matter among the advertisements. Crushed by falling standards, Damon Jenkins' fighting spirit died, as did the motivation and desire of many of his colleagues. It would come to life again but not before many barren months had passed.

Part Two

11

(1970)

Adventurous Freelancing

Watching the Scottish coastline disappearing from 20,000ft and facing six tedious hours in a Boeing 747, I did start to wonder why I was leaving the security of a sound job and the comfort of a good home to embark on what could well turn out to be a very expensive wild goose chase.

Not much more than a month ago, I had been content to allow my journalistic career to slip quietly into semi-moribund mode, untroubled by controversy and content to bully young reporters between arguments with Eric. These were usually about the value of publishing dog show results or spending hours of a reporter's time listening to accounts of shattered relationships in divorce courts.

'People like to see their name in the paper so long as it's spelt correctly,' insisted Eric.

'Even when the world is being told they committed adultery,' I queried.

'More so these days, they're proud of it,' suggested Eric.

So that was another battle lost!

Until the unwelcomed intervention of his friend Christopher, Stephen Spicer had slipped into that corner of my memory labelled 'recent history'. Some interesting times were recorded there, some painful some stimulating, but one recognises early in the rush and tumble of newspaper life you cannot live on past glories.

The old enemy, Nigel Ferguson, had gone north and his place in the editorial chair had been taken by a laid-back character, Ian

Wainwright, whose sole aim was to appease management. He believed he could achieve this by censoring any editorial item likely to upset a potential advertiser. Estate agents were particularly well protected; they could break the few rules they had, upset countless buyers and sellers, confident that any complaint aimed in their direction would hit the buffers.

At one time, the Trentbridge News had a very popular consumer page, which fought battles on behalf of its readers, no matter how insignificant they may have seemed to the wider world. The column was axed so as not to upset local businessmen.

Town Hall officials were no longer troubled by inquisitive reporters. The planning chief, Peter Barnwell, on the brink of destruction at one time was still in situ, having long ago persuaded Jeff Woods his future lay elsewhere. It had been an upsetting few years, witnessing the cutting edge of local newspapers being systematically blunted. Publications prepared to take risks in the interests of their readers were gradually weakened or sacrificed for the greater profitability of the free sheet. Now a poorly written press release, eulogizing the wonders of a planning strategy, which would never leave the drawing board, stood more chance of an airing than exposure of anything smelling of corruption. In the 'frees' as they were called, a minimum amount of editorial content, more often of a frivolous nature, was permitted to create the illusion that newspapers still existed in the provinces.

No one bothered to spy on the Pentagon Club any longer, it wasn't worth it. Too many local establishment figures enjoyed a regular meeting with their chums and were astute at building a wall of silence if the occasion demanded it.

So what was I doing flying over the Atlantic? Following my bizarre encounter with Christopher Howell in the paper's front office, I had tried to convince the new editorial team it was worth spending a few pounds on reopening the Spicer story. If he had been kidnapped in the States, there could be newsworthy developments. 'Leave it to those who have the cash to splash about,' I was told, 'we have enough trouble meeting the weekly wage bill without sending reporters charging around the world on expenses.'

For a long while, I had been thinking about freelancing; only lethargy and a lack of confidence had stopped me taking the plunge. That, and the fact I still had a family to support and a wife who might not look kindly on her husband disappearing again to do his own thing. This time I was wrong. Instead of threatening divorce, something I probably deserved, Penny astounded me by suggesting a break from each other might be a good thing and perhaps at long last I could bring closure to the Spicer saga.

I had tried her patience to breaking point on more than one occasion and had been a particular pain when an allusive poltergeist and its young manipulator invaded our privacy.

Deep down, I greatly valued the devotion and tolerance she had displayed for a number of difficult years. But like so many scribes I was reasonably fluent on paper but short on words when it came to expressing gratitude and love verbally. So many marriages had broken down during the 60s and 70s and journalists usually came near the top of the list of unfaithful creatures, especially among those who spent weeks at a time abroad.

My own behaviour had not been exemplary. I had learned the hard way that casual flirting can lead to obsessional relationships, platonic maybe, but potentially extremely harmful if allowed to get out of hand. Our relationship had survived one grey period in our married lives and Penny had demonstrated, as always, that she was the steadying influence in the family. When she agreed to me hopping over to the States, I knew she would not have gone along with that proposition without weighing up all the pros and cons. Perhaps this was the time we both realised that in all relationships trust was the most important factor. And trust was something which had to be earned.

Leaving the security of my job at the Trentbridge News was a risk as I still had children who needed my financial input to see them through the rest of their education. But I would not be completely casting myself adrift; at least two major newspapers had said they would pay well if I could solve the mystery of Stephen's return to a country where his previous behaviour had had strange repercussions, There was also interest in the activities of Yasha Rashnin, who had caused a couple of psychic-style sensations in the States and then gone to ground.

The focus of his attention, as well as others with similar inclinations, was a rambling, deserted mansion buried in the heart of the Acadia National Park in Maine. Ghost stories usually stayed local but this one had reached the lairs of psychics in various parts of the world with the result that pilgrimages to Maine had become quite frequent. The magnet was repeated reports that a girl in a white wedding dress had been seen wandering the corridors of the mansion by a number of visitors, some endeavouring to sound convincing in describing their experiences but predictably others who wallowed in the drama with the deliberate aim of seeking publicity.

However, it was the worldwide reputation of the former residents of the mansion that ensured a never-ending fascination in all that went on deep down in the forest. The owner was Conrad McWhirter, a wealthy American motor industry tycoon, who relished the isolation of the mansion and would probably have become a recluse if it had not been for the deep affection he held for his daughter, Madeline.

His wife had been dead for many years but when his daughter announced that she had accepted a proposal of marriage, he decided on one last grand gesture before retiring and cutting himself off from the world. With no expense spared, he would make Madeline's wedding the social event of the year. It was never going to happen.

The tragedy which was about to overtake McWhirter, his daughter and the rest of the household, was one which plucked the heartstrings of people all over the world. Many tears would be shed internationally as the detail of Madeline's suicide forced other events, even wars and natural disasters, off the front pages.

Madeline, it was recounted, was waiting for her bridegroom to arrive from the United Kingdom aboard the ill-fated Titanic. When news of the devastating loss of life, particularly involving the male passengers, reached Madeline, she persuaded herself that her future husband would be among the survivors. Then the bodies started to be brought ashore further up the coastline at Halifax.

The anguished bride-to-be didn't even wait for confirmation of his death. Within 24 hours of hearing about the horrendous loss of life she was found hanging from the banisters of the mansion's ornate staircase, wearing the white dress she was due to be married in.

The sad story was one that local guides taking cruise visitors and others around the park capitalised on for many years and embellished lavishly if the weather closed in and the Cadillac Mountains disappeared in a swirling mist. I first heard it while on a short 'autumn colours' trip to New England and the surrounding area.

'Look down there,' the guide suggested, pointing towards a clump of trees near the water's edge. The top of an impressive mansion could just be seen through the dense vegetation. 'That was where Madeline McWhirter was waiting the arrival of her husband-to-be, British actor,

Albert Duncan, who was travelling across the Atlantic (the guide paused here for dramatic effect) on the ill-fated Titanic. All the wedding arrangements had been made and the planned ceremony and reception, for which no cost had been spared, was going to be the social event of the year. Some of the guests had already begun to gather in their mountain retreats.

'After the first shock news that the Titanic had struck an iceberg, Madeline clung to the hope that her fiancé might be saved until the bodies started to be brought ashore. She was distraught but no one, including her father, imagined she would end her life in such a gruesome manner.'

In a voice cracking with well-practised emotion, the guide in charge of our party ended his story with a flourish which would not have disgraced Laurence Olivier: 'After a traumatic evening trying to comfort Madeline, the McWhirters retired to their rooms and tried not to listen to the uncontrollable weeping coming from their daughter's bedroom. The next morning the whole household was awakened by the screams of a servant. She had found Madeline hanging from the banister wearing her wedding gown. All attempts to revive her failed.' The day before the wedding was due to take place guests were told of the tragedy and asked not to travel to the mansion

The story tended to send occupants of the coach into a moment or two of gloom, quickly dispelled as the Cadillac Mountain offered up the beautiful vistas it was internationally famous for.

I was carrying an account of the McWhirter family's virtual disintegration in a brief case full of background material brought with me for closer study. Hindered by the confines of aircraft cabin space, I hadn't noticed some of it had spilled into the lap of an elderly woman sharing my seat. One of the articles focusing on Madeline's death was particularly macabre and if I had been a little more attentive, I would have noticed her interest was rather more focused than one would have expected of a woman of her age.

I apologised for invading her space and started to gather up some of the other material now in danger of spreading itself far and wide. If what she had already seen was upsetting, she would certainly be seeking a new seat and fresh company if some of the other newspaper headlines in my assorted collection caught her eye.

I needn't have worried too much. 'I remember the story very well, only too well' she said introducing herself as Winifred Kelly, and giving me a surprise by revealing that a distant cousin had been due to attend the wedding but halted her plans on hearing of the tragedy.

I thought that perhaps I had stumbled across a good source of information but on comparing notes, it was obvious her connection with the McWhirter family was quite remote.

'What did you make of the media frenzy over the alleged appearance of Madeline's ghost?' I asked her.

'Nonsense, just nonsense, young man. Anywhere else in the world, the fuss wouldn't have lasted more than a few days. Americans have a weakness for stories about poltergeists and ghosts. They lap them up like a thirsty puppy.' She hastened to add that although she had been born in the States her American blood had been well watered down by long periods living in various parts of Europe.

We chatted for a while and found common ground on the gullibility of large sections of the human race. Removing another piece of newsprint containing details of *The Gemstone File* from her right knee, Winifred gave it the once over and then said brightly: 'You must lead a very interesting life. Have you been recruited to help the Americans find out who really killed their president?'

'Well, not exactly. My interest is more in people who think they can open up lines of communication between this world and the next.' Unable to face several more hours in my company, Winifred decided this was the moment to order a scotch and move to a vacant seat, which offered fewer distractions. She apologised and claimed she had nothing against me personally but she too had a number of magazines she wanted to read.

I returned to the task of getting myself fully updated on more recent developments, events that had finally convinced me to leave my regular job and take a chance on a spell of adventurous freelancing.

My American newspaper chum, Rod, had provided the trigger when he despatched material that demonstrated how the Americans were much more interested in the story than anyone in Britain. After a family from Texas had rented the McWhirter's mountain mansion and reported seeing a girl in a white dress walking the corridors, her face flooded with tears, a hungry press decided there was real meat here to feed the masses.

As other sightings were reported by subsequent visitors, the story travelled across country from Atlantic coast to the Pacific and the mansion started to become a place of pilgrimage for people with a variety of motives. Some took the reports of paranormal activity very seriously and installed all sorts of equipment to capture a glimpse of the girl in white; others were just curious tourists who had been fascinated by the stories told in travel guides or reported in American newspapers. After a while the McWhirters, who had taken up residence in another part of the island, decided enough was enough. They closed the mansion, put up a few inadequate security barriers to keep people out and instructed agents to find a buyer.

'The McWhirters were wasting their time,' Rod told me, during one of our frequent conversations before I left England, 'The spiritualists and the psychics wouldn't leave the place alone, neither would various sections of the media. But even you, Damon, may have difficulty in coming to terms with the latest development. In one of the bedrooms, the one that Madeline was said to have slept in, the selling agents came across another wall covered in 'automatic writings.'

'You're joking,' was my first reaction but I knew Rod wouldn't call me from the other side of the Atlantic just to pull my leg, 'no of course you're not, but you're not going to tell me the content of the writings are extracts from the *Gemstone File*, are you?'

'You've got it, chum. Its all back on the agenda, or back on the wall I should say, Kennedy, his assassins, the mafia, the CIA and the Warren inquiry. Somebody has been having a whale of a time and there was no one around to catch them, or it, at it!'

And that was the reason why I was now sitting on a Boeing 747 heading for Maine. The final spur was a short piece in the Bar Harbor local paper, also sent by Rod, which reported a flurry of activity as ghost hunters from various parts of North America and Europe headed for the mansion. This was an old cutting so an update on the current situation would be a priority.

If the interest was as described, then there was a good chance Messrs Spicer and Rashnin might have converged on the now notorious mountain residence in recent weeks. The bad feeling between them probably ruled out any likelihood they would have travelled there together but one of them, I figured, could well have been responsible for the automatic writing.

Yasha's extended visit to the States provided plenty of food for thought. Had he decided to pick up where Stephen left of? He was certainly made of tougher stuff and usually had a small posse of people around him capable of providing him with some protection. On the other hand, there was no evidence that Yasha was into automatic writing. Without artistic flair, he would have needed an accomplice to achieve artistic work on Stephen's level.

I spent the rest of the journey trying to compose some sort of strategy for my visit. I certainly didn't want to waste time, as from now on it was my money I would be spending. Rod had promised to set about discovering the whereabouts of Yasha Rashnin; I certainly wanted to get to the mansion as soon as possible so I could study the automatic drawings before someone decided to wipe the slate clean. With the help of Stephen's book illustrations and Bob Harding's photographs, I thought I would be in a good position to see whether the same hand was at work.

One of the 'writings' according to information supplied by Rod, was sent down the spiritual wire by none other than Kennedy's assassin, Lee Harvey Oswald, who himself died at the hands of small-time Mafia gangster, Jack Ruby. And there were other 'messages' which had probably been drawn from *The Gemstone File*. Whoever had decided to go down this route, obviously succumbed to a desire to spice it up.

Supplementing the *Gemstone* material was a number of messages purporting to have been 'sent' by someone who had perished aboard the *Titanic,* the 'unsinkable' liner. Rod thought there would be no shortage of people eager to manufacture a link between the suicide of the mansion's bride-to-be and the fiancé she lost on that tragic day. It wasn't the most pleasant of thoughts but I suspected the tourist guides would be rubbing their hands with glee. After the passing of so many years, the last thing they would have been expecting was a juicy update.

Both of these messages were going to be difficult to check out since it was unlikely I could get hold of any material written by Oswald to draw comparisons and there would be nothing of that sort from the Titanic archives. More likely, anything that might have been helpful was lying at the bottom of the Atlantic. Stephen had always been meticulous in researching his historic back-up material. Had the Cadillac Mountain bedroom wall defacer gone to the same amount of trouble? I wondered.

Now that I was on my way to examine the new scribblings and to assess the extent to which Stephen or Yasha might be responsible, I started to experience an unprofessional sort of emotion, which bordered on excitement. 'You'll get over it,' Eric would have said if he had been with me. But I knew he would dearly have loved to be my partner on this madcap excursion.

124

The on-board film coincidentally turned out to be one of the many about the Titanic. I felt my eyes starting to close but just as I was dozing off, I became aware of the film reaching that part of the story where a group of stoic musicians were said to have kept playing right up to the moment the Titanic went down.

The story of their bravery commanded my attention for the next few minutes but little did I realise I would soon be in strange surroundings looking at some chilling words attributed to one of these musicians. My reluctance to consider another dimension to our existence could have been about to face a serious challenge if I had not had in my luggage a fascinating book containing detailed stories told by Titanic survivors. Hopefully the book would help me counter any thoughts I might have had of giving credence to Stephen Spicer's more outrageous claims.

I had brought the book with me because Rod had alerted me to the content of some of the wall messages I was soon to examine. Looking away from the film, I turned to a page of *Titanic Survivor—memoirs of Violet Jessop who survived both the Titanic and Britannic Disasters.*' Violet's diary had been recently discovered and she was probably the only stewardess ever to have provided a detailed account of life aboard a cruise liner with predominantly male crews.

According to information Rod had provided, one message on the wall was signed by Wallace Hartley, violinist and orchestra leader on the Titanic, whose body was pulled from the sea with his music case still strapped across his chest. Many lines have been written about how the orchestra continued playing as the ship went down and some accounts have been coloured and exaggerated over the years. Wallace Hartley, in the bedroom wall scribble, apparently wanted to put his side of the story and had used, in the view of those eager to believe, the arm and hand of someone living to do the job for him.

The Jessop diaries would not have been so well known to folk in the States and an extract could easily have been adapted to suit the purposes of anyone intent on deception. That was why I had Violet's diaries with me. Rod, tongue in cheek, had hinted that there could be others in the watery Atlantic grave, who might be seeking contact with the real world. What about a bridegroom-to-be on his way to a glamorous wedding with the daughter of a wealthy American? This clearly was Rod living up to the image of the reporter prepared to lace the facts with a spoonful or two of fiction if it made for a better story.

As the credits of the film started to roll, I fell into a deep sleep and woke to find an attractive member of the cabin crew occupying the vacant seat beside me. Very gently she explained why she was there. I had caused some concern to passengers when I started shouting.

'Shouting?' I protested, 'It must have been someone else. I've been in a deep sleep.'

'Sleep, maybe,' she quietly informed me, 'but there was nothing deep about it. You made so much noise some of the passengers became very worried. They thought you might have some sort of mental problem.'

What was she talking about? Then it all came back. As I sipped the coffee brought to me by another bewildered but understanding stewardess, I had recall on the dream, much more a nightmare really, that had invaded my mind as the action on the screen drew to a close and I dropped off.

I was aboard the Titanic and as we waited for the inevitable, I was approached by a young man who asked me whether I believed in God. 'No I'm not sure that I do but just at this moment I'm wishing that I did,' was the reply I thought I had made in the dream.

'It's not too late, you know,' the young man had said, displaying incredible calmness in the face of the appalling catastrophe about to be visited upon us. He briefly explained---acknowledging that in the circumstances he didn't have too much time---that I had to seek God's forgiveness and say that in future I would put my faith in him.

This must have been the point when I started to share the terror of my nightmare with the other passengers.

'It was alarming to say the least,' said the stewardess. 'There was no panic or anything like that but I certainly had to calm the nerves of one or two passengers before I turned my attention to you.'

This was going to rate as one of life's most embarrassing moments. I half lifted myself out of my seat to look around and realised that everyone had stopped what they had been doing and all eyes seemed to be focused on me. Better, I thought, just to sit quietly and wait for the time when I could disappear into the obscurity of the airport lounge.

Try as I did to erase the dream, it wouldn't go away. The face of that young man, not recognisable as the image of a real-life friend or acquaintance, had been punched into my brain with extraordinary clarity. Strange he didn't wait for a response to his pertinent question but perhaps he perceived my heart was moving in the right direction.

Was it? Is it? Moving in the right direction? Did I have to come all this way on what might turn out to be a fool's errand to be reminded that God had always taken a back seat in my life and the day might come when I needed his help? And would I now take the hint and think about giving my life a fresh focus? The content of dreams do not usually last the day so I suspected I would have banished all these thoughts from my mind by nightfall. What a pity, if that was the case.

There was the usual rush to get off the 'plane at Bangor International Airport so I was able to sit back and let them all go. I was given a few strange looks as I collected baggage but was happy to think that I would never meet up with fellow passengers on this flight again.

Walking away from the airport's security zone, I was astonished to see among the cluster of hastily scribbled messages aimed at catching the eye of passengers in need of a lift, a piece of cardboard bearing the name of Stephen Spicer. That made no sense whatsoever. Stephen was already in the States and I could think of no reason why he would be needing a lift from Bangor airport unless he had planned to travel there on an internal flight arranged by one of his tour sponsors.

There was only one way to find out. I walked purposefully towards the young man holding the notice in the hope that he would be my passport to tracking down Stephen without days of endless inquiries.

'You're expecting to meet Stephen Spicer, I gather? He's a friend of mine. Do you know in which direction he might be heading?'

'You're not Stephen Spicer, then,' said the young man, stating the obvious. 'Can't help you.' With a look of panic on his face, he dropped his placard at my feet and sped away with the agility of a trained athlete. Something had scared him and in his rush to put distance between us, he allowed a brown envelope to slip from his jacket pocket. The fact that he made no attempt to recover it, I decided later, could have had something to do with the near presence of two 'heavies' who had been watching the incident from behind a newspaper stand. With little chance of matching the fleetness of foot of their quarry, they set off in pursuit but did not notice the brown envelope, which I was now able to recover from the airport floor.

Curious I certainly was, but it was important not to waste too much time arranging the next stage of my journey. I dropped the envelope into my brief case and headed for the ticket office.

There was a long line of people in front of me and I realised how silly I was not to examine the contents of the package. There might be something in it that would dictate my next steps, even change my agenda. Perched on the edge of my suitcase, I broke the seal and the first words I saw were *The Gemstone File, the truth about Kennedy's assassination.* Although the title was identical, it wasn't the same document I had seen previously and it appeared to have been produced by someone who wanted to blur its origins.

I may have travelled a couple of thousand miles from the scene of previous Spicer adventures, but it seemed that the content of the *File* was destined to follow in my wake. There would be time to compare the two versions later but for the moment, I felt it important to head for the mansion as speedily as possible to head off anyone who might have reason to mutilate or eradicate the wall messages. Without a visual inspection, which only I was in a position to make effectively, there would be no chance of attributing any of the graffiti to Stephen or Yasha, or perhaps ruling them both out altogether.

As I waited for the line of people in front of me to slim down, I took another look inside the envelope and noticed a crumpled piece of paper which I assumed was a message meant for Stephen. Smoothing it out, I read: '*Don't run away this time. We have important work for you to do. There is more in the file than meets the eye. You can help and make a name for yourself. Be ready for our next contact.*' The note was made up from letters cut from newspapers and magazines, a very unoriginal way of trying to conceal the identity of the sender.

Potentially disturbing in content, the note had been so carelessly handled and delivered, it was difficult to take it seriously. It was a reminder of the paper chase, which had taken place on the floor of my office following the visit of Stephen's worried friend. What was so amazing was that three years had passed since Stephen's first adventure in this part of the world. Now history was repeating itself and it was going to be important to find Stephen if he was still in the region and unaware of this second attempt to secure his services.

I spent almost an hour scanning the passengers teeming through Bangor airport just in case Stephen was still around. There was no one remotely resembling the long-haired psychic so I closed my brief case, collected my tickets and prepared to set out on the next stage of my journey.

12

Mistaken Identity

On my way to check the frequency of flights to the local Bar Harbor Airport, I passed a small office with tantalising posters inviting newly arrived visitors to take a ferry to Mount Desert Island and to the 47,000 acres of the Acadia National Park. Memories of this beautiful part of the world came flooding back and I had to curb a desire to travel slowly, crossing Frenchman Bay, enjoying at leisure the scenery which left such a lasting impression---the tall granite mountains, lush valleys and the charming cottages and chalets lining the banks of the bay.

My time was limited and if I was going to start making a living out of this plunge into the unknown then the last thing I could afford to do was get distracted from the job in hand. A freelance I may be, but if this mission was to yield dividends then I was not free to indulge myself, recapturing memories of a previous visit.

It was nearing the end of the season in this part of Maine but the seasonal shuttle across to the main part of the island was still operating. It took little more than an hour to complete my journey to Bar Harbor.

Although quite early in the day, I was able to pick up a hired car and decided to make the most of the seven or eight hours of daylight remaining. After reserving some modest accommodation near the town pier and acquiring useful local knowledge from Mary, the widowed owner of the house, I set out again but not before noticing that a few doors away I could enjoy a supper of fresh lobster. The advertising blurb was colourful and full of promise: *'Lobstermen are up with the sun each day to take in the daily catch and wooden sailboats still ply the deep waters of Frenchman Bay alongside more modern vessels.'*

The journalistic mind is a strange mechanism and tucks away all sorts of information, sometimes useful, often of no use whatsoever. Reading the dockside eulogies to the lobster, I remembered being told that in the 19th century this tasty crustacean was considered only good enough to use as fertilizer. Lobsters collected after a storm washed them ashore were usually fed to hired helps and domestic workers. There was another little titbit which my memory had preserved---although lobsters have 20,000 'eyes' they have terrible vision and communicate by smell and sensing movement with their antenna.

These quirky recalls probably resurfaced because even as I set out to fulfil the first part of my planned programme, I was thinking, prematurely perhaps, about the delights of a lobster supper, the first since my last visit to this part of the world.

I had to earn that supper, I told myself, by making strides to solve the mystery of why a deserted mansion in the Cadillac Mountain had proved such a magnet for people wanting to challenge the notion that once dead always dead. The mansion and its former occupants together must have seemed fertile territory to put their theories to the test.

My attempt to impose some self-discipline didn't make it any less painful to drive around the Park's Loop Road at a pace that made it difficult to absorb much of the beautiful scenery. Penny and I were still very much in the starry-eyed stage of our relationship when during a short visit we had wandered in the cool shade of the spruce-fir forest catching now and again the rat-a-tat of a woodpecker or a glimpse of a red squirrel darting along a tree trunk. I would also have liked to reach a spot where I could view the landmarks, which define Acadia's coast---Sandbeach, Thunder Hole and Otter Point. It would also have been pleasant to stop and investigate one of the park's groomed gravel carriage paths with their distinctive arch bridges constructed from pink granite. But perhaps I would have time later to explore and recapture happy memories.

After a while, it was necessary to leave the loop road and with the help of a local map handed to me on the ferry, seek a way down to the mansion, so placed that it would never be easy for the casual visitor to discover. The joy of being in the park and the feeling that perhaps I was on holiday after all was dampened when I noticed a Land Rover travelling not many feet from my back bumper. It must have been there for some time but in my relaxed state, I hadn't noticed it during the first part of the journey. Twice I stopped in lay-bys to see if it would pass but each time it, too, pulled up just out of hailing distance. It was not easy to see into the car, the fir trees cast shadows and the dark-tinted windows were an effective barrier.

According to the map, I was now within striking distance of the mansion and fancied I could see the tops of its very substantial gates. That, it turned out, was all I was going to be allowed to see for at that moment the peace and beauty of this idyllic corner of the world was shattered by a roar of engines and the appearance of cars and motorbikes from every direction. Men wearing balaclavas and carrying what looked like automatic weapons leapt from their vehicles and surrounded the Land Rover, which had been following me. As far as I could see, my four pursuers made no attempt to retaliate, not surprising in the view of the disparity in numbers and weaponry. This was not the way I had expected to start my investigations, one minute travelling through paradise, the next in close contact with a small army, heavily disguised and looking as though they meant business.

With a civil war breaking out around me, turning tranquillity into chaos, I realised that for the moment I was not the sole focus of attention. Peering into the gloom, it was just possible to see the four occupants of the Land Rover standing on the grass verge with hands above their heads. Those who had appeared so suddenly from the depths of the forest were surrounding them waving their weapons in menacing fashion.

In my rear view mirror, I could see they faced little resistance from the four big fellows I imagined were in some way connected with a local law enforcement agency but wore no uniform and carried no weapons as far as I could see. In fact, they allowed themselves to be led towards their own vehicle, now rolled into the bushes, and handcuffed to the door handles. Various items were thrown some distance into the forest, which I guessed might be keys to the vehicle or keys to the handcuffs. A walky-talky phone got the same treatment after being crushed under foot. I guessed that those in the car might be plain-clothes American cops but who were their attackers? They didn't seem to be particularly well organised, acting more like a tribe of Red Indian warriors surrounding a white man's wagon. The noise they were making reinforced this impression.

Suddenly attention turned back to me and it was now too late to speculate whether with greater presence of mind I could have jumped out of the car and disappeared into the forest. Still waving their weapons menacingly, three members of the victorious group approached my vehicle and helped themselves to seats, one sitting in the front, the other two in the back. Not a word was said but I had seen enough American movies to know these guys were not to be messed with. The atmosphere was such and their postures so threatening, I wasn't going to mount a challenge to their unruly behaviour.

My timid: 'Would you like to tell me what is happening?' was treated with what seemed to be contempt but could possibly have been put down to lack of understanding. 'Drive, follow black car' was the only response I got in an accent that gave me few clues as to its origin. Three more cars emerged from nowhere; hooded men abandoned their hiding places behind trees and bushes and piled into the vehicles. Off we went in a strange procession …but not for long. The man beside me must have come to the not too difficult conclusion that as the driver I would be able to memorise where we were going even if I was unfamiliar with the area. We changed seats and rough hands from the back of the car clumsily pulled a scarf over my eyes. I was not going to be allowed to see much more of the surrounding countryside, not on this journey anyway.

The car's interior filled with tobacco smoke of a pungent continental variety certainly not to be confused with the delicacy of a home-grown Craven A. I tried to make some sense of what was happening. My fellow passengers spoke in what I thought was Italian but with a regional twang that hindered my schoolboy understanding of the language. Through the bottom of my makeshift blindfold, I caught glimpses of the passing vegetation but nothing to indicate where we might be heading. We were climbing and in this corner of Acadia, there was really only one mountain to climb.

Remembering what had happened to Stephen Spicer on his first abortive attempt to tour American universities, there was real reason now to consider whether *The Gemstone File* might not be the harmless piece of garbage many had made it out to be. Could my dramatic detention under the noses of the island's law enforcement squad have something to do with the hidden mysteries of this much-maligned document? Perhaps I was the victim of mistaken identity. Maybe they thought I was Stephen Spicer or Yasha Rashnin but that didn't make sense since both men had been in the country long enough for positive identifications to be made. And I didn't look anything like either of them.

These thoughts prompted me to remember I was still carrying a copy of the file in the car and that wasn't going to help if I wanted to make out a case of mistaken identity. I could have left it back at my temporary lodgings but it was too late for thoughts of that kind now. I had memorised most of the content of the file so as the other passengers in the car didn't seem inclined to talk, I filled the time by mulling over some of the damaging accusations made in the document. Dismissed as preposterous by those who considered the Warren Commission had done its job, there were those who still found it troubling. Not knowing where I was going or who I was about to meet, I thought it sound policy to remind myself of any on-going conspiracy theories, whether justified or not. There were many but so far, not one had strayed beyond the columns of the less respectable newspapers.

The *Gemstone File* had never been given any credence by either the American or the English media, which demonstrated its corporate disdain by demoting it to the file reserved for dubious and subversive documents. My original verdict, now questionable in the light of recent developments, strongly supported the hoax theory. From my present position as a prisoner trapped in a carload of armed terrorists, I had reason to reassess this conclusion. My dream holiday island suddenly seemed to have an under-tow of unrest and intrigue quite out of character with its long-held idyllic image.

It was not unreasonable to start thinking how accusations in the File might now be getting under someone's skin but I had come to America to track down two self-opinionated magicians with a tendency to abuse whatever skills they had for financial gain. I was not in the business of doing battle with America's elite security forces or the criminal elements they habitually tangled with. That sort of exercise would have called for the combined efforts of a James Bond and a Watergate team, not a single, defenceless reporter from an English university town.

The file basically claimed that Lee Harvey Oswald had been set up as the 'patsy' or the fall guy who would be blamed and himself murdered in time to let three other members of the assassination gang off the hook. The detail it contained was mind-boggling and it didn't hold back from accusing a notorious Italian media giant, known for his Mafia links, of running a drugs operation out of the Golden Triangle. Kennedy had been put in the picture, according to the authors of the file, and had formed a team to break the operation.

Although the File had never gained any credibility, I started to wonder whether I had stumbled across an attempt to reopen the debate or, possibly, fallen foul of those who wanted to prevent the debate from being reopened. Making sense of the sequence of events since my arrival at Bar Harbor was impossible but one thought wouldn't go away---the possibility that that there was collaboration between known criminal forces and supposedly respectable local law enforcers. The forest skirmish could, on reflection, have been an elaborate piece of theatre.

A shiver went down my spine and it was not because the windows of the car had been left open. If Stephen, not the most robust sort of young man you are likely to meet but fairly determined in his quest to become famous, had three years ago felt it necessary to beat a hasty retreat from America after such a short visit, should I be doing the same, given the chance? History appeared to be repeating itself apart from the fact that I was now in an even more vulnerable situation than Stephen had been. My blindfold stopped me looking around the car but I began to sense this gang might include some of the characters Stephen had met on a previous occasion.

The time had come to take the initiative. 'Does anyone speak English in this car?' I asked. No response. 'Couldn't I be more helpful if you told me where we are going and what you want from me?' Silence again.

We travelled for what seemed like another 10 miles mainly uphill before a voice from the back seat gave me a hint of what was happening. In fractured English, he informed me: 'In some minutes we arrive there; then you talk to boss-man. He says if you come back.'

'Thanks, anyway, but where is "there" and what do you mean, "if I come back"?'

Now I really was nervous. Did he mean I wouldn't be coming back *this way* or was he telling me I could rule out any prospect of a return journey? All my life started to flash before me as they say it does when crisis hits. Suddenly it seemed a very long way from sedate, lovely old Trentbridge. What would Penny and the kids be doing now? No one at my old office would be concerned, they didn't even know where I was heading and editorial strategy would probably have moved on to arguments about whether rubbish should be recycled or incinerated.

I certainly hadn't bargained for what I was now walking into when I decided to go it alone and buy a ticket to Maine. The two main players in this complex drama, Stephen and Yasha his better known adversary, were now in the USA, possibly unaware of each other's presence and yet linked by events which could be a mystery to both of them. Both claimed they were capable of unfolding some of the secrets of the after life, while an eager investigative reporter queried the validity of their claims. Meanwhile all sorts of fringe players were deliberately putting spanners in the works to achieve their own purposes.

Where were the two lead players now? Stephen, who had decided to push his luck despite being frightened out of his wits on a previous occasion, was keeping his head well below the parapet; Yasha Rashnin was somewhere in the country, probably making hay while his rival stayed out of the limelight; I seemed to have attracted attention simply by poking my nose into places I was not wanted; the local police force appeared to be impotent and a bunch of hoodlums were causing mayhem for motives that were in no way clear.

I had to face the fact that I was no longer on my home patch pursuing lost parrots and trying to uncover the shady goings-on of council officials; somehow I had managed to get on the wrong side of people who could do me and others real harm, even to the point of murder. They don't carry guns for fun this side of the Atlantic, I reminded myself.

The car had stopped now and I was pulled unceremoniously out of the passenger seat and led none too gently across gravel and then grass before being pushed to my knees in what later turned out to be a garden shed at the end of a garden. I managed to loosen the rough and ready blindfold but before I could carry out an inspection of my surroundings, the door opened again and in walked a tall, swarthy guy with a John Wayne swagger. He was armed but not hooded which worried me somewhat since it raised the fear that if he was not worried about concealing his identity then I was not going anywhere in a hurry.

Despite his appearance, his accent was more that of an American academic than the rough and ready tones of a criminal gang leader. But there was something very unnatural about his use of language, much of it sounding as if it had been developed with the help of an easy-learning tape. If there had been a teapot on the table in the shed, I would not have been surprised if he had inquired whether I liked one or two lumps of sugar in my tea. But the meeting was never going to be conducted on that sort of sociable level.

'Well, Mr Spicer, we meet at last,' he said with more than a hint of menace in his voice, 'you have caused me much trouble…'

Completely taken back, my mouth must have opened wide and stayed that way for many seconds: 'did you call me Spicer?' I managed to say eventually, 'You're going to be a very angry man when I tell you I'm not Stephen Spicer. I'm a lowly, English newspaperman who foolishly, I'm beginning to believe, decided to come to this country, to try to find him.' I fumbled for my passport that fortunately was still in an inside pocket of my jacket and tossed it onto the floor in front of me.

I was right about him being upset. He demonstrated his discontent with the situation by exploding into incandescent rage. Throwing open the door of the shed, the sight of his henchmen sitting on a log casually smoking and joking among themselves really lit the fuse. 'Get inside here,' he screamed, but when they approached the door, he went to meet them with such force they all buckled and finished up in an unruly heap.

'Who in the hell do you think we've got in there?' he shouted, 'Did none of you meatheads think it might be a good idea to search him, you might have found his passport?' he said with the heaviest sarcasm he could muster. 'This is a wretched little English newspaper reporter, not the psychic wallah you were sent to collect.'

The air was blue for a full five minutes as they all argued about false information, mistaken identity and what could be done with me. That was a decision taken quickly.

'Put him back in the car, drive into the most dense part of the forest, drag him blindfolded down as many footpaths as you can find for at least half an hour and then dump him. Then keep away from me for as long as you think it will take me to calm down,' said their furious leader.

'And you can regard yourself lucky that I'm not in a bad mood today,' he said turning to me, 'a word of warning, though. If you say anything about this incident to the police or anyone else your chances of leaving this island in one piece are very slim.'

Despite this threat, I decided to push my luck. 'Why do you want to get your hands on Stephen Spicer so badly? He's my target as well but it would seem our motives for finding him are not quite the same.'

When I expressed surprise that none of them had seen photographs of Spicer, he flared again and putting his face uncomfortably close to mine spat out: 'We're in a forest, they don't deliver newspapers here.'

He told me to mind my own business about his motives and to remember that if I came across Spicer I had better not attempt to block their attempts to catch up with him. 'Leave the local police out of this. They're clumsy idiots. This may be a pretty island but don't fool yourself, nasty things happen here on a regular basis.'

The blindfold was replaced and within minutes we were driving

136

away from an area, I would have little chance of identifying. Ten minutes into the journey, I did hear the sound of sea crashing onto rocks but that wasn't much help because I remembered the island had many places where the Atlantic Ocean hit the land with tremendous power.

The scenic drive my blindfold kept me from enjoying did provide some more thinking time and I re-lived the last 15 minutes or so trying to remember anything that would identify my captors. The impeccable diction of the leader offered no clues and his appearance was neutral. He could have been English, American, Canadian but not Asian, Greek or Eastern. His henchmen were almost certainly Italian so the possibility of them being Mafia thugs could not be ruled out. One of the accusations in *The Gemstone File* revolved around shipping drugs out of the Golden Triangle. But it was difficult to connect that sort of operation with a gang of crooks holed up in a retreat on the Cadillac Mountain. There had to be some other explanation. And why this interest in Stephen Spicer? How could he possibly help them in whatever operation they were trying to pull off?

The inquiry into Kennedy's death may have been wrapped up officially but there could be all sorts of reasons why certain people would not want the pot stirred again, bringing unsavoury accusations back to the surface. My assumption, when I arrived on the island, was that it was the local police who were following me until they themselves were set upon. Now I wondered whether the Land Rover's passengers were from a different category of law enforcement, the CIA, FBI or one of the other organisations mentioned in the File. There was one fact I couldn't get away from and that was the intense desire of some individuals and organisations to get to grips with Stephen Spicer.

He no longer fitted the image of zany psychic, interested only in making 'contact' with those we quaintly describe as 'having passed away.' My priority was to try to unravel the tangled web enveloping the life of this young man. His first visit to the States and his sudden retreat, although now history might well have been brought about by genuine fear. That would explain why the moment he arrived back in his own country he scorned the title of psychic and disappeared. Initially, it was accepted that this second visit, some three years later, was to meet up with like-minded people and spend time at the notorious mansion investigating the reported appearances of the deceased bride-to-be. Why others with a different agenda had tried to intercept him was the mystery needing to be solved if Stephen was not going to come to harm.

My thoughts were disrupted by the sudden swerving of the car as the driver pulled up in an unnecessarily abrupt fashion. He had been stung by his boss's bad humour and was still demonstrating his annoyance. There were no goodbyes. I was bundled out and frog-marched away from the road for the prescribed half-an-hour route march. Whether it was to the north, south, east or west, I had no idea. No help came from my captors who literally tossed me into a bush and disappeared.

Not so many hours before I had been feeling sad at not having the time to re-acquaint myself with a part of the world I remembered so fondly. Now a trifle unexpectedly, I had an opportunity to explore the delights of the Cadillac Mountain, but one could hardly say the circumstances were ideal. To my relief I realised that the local map I had acquired on arrival was still in an inside pocket but it was going to be of little use unless I could find something or someone to give me my bearings.

Tired and not a little hungry by now, I sat under a fir tree and listened....listened for the sound of car engines, the shrill grinding of woodcutters' saws, moving water or anything that would provide a clue. But there was nothing, just a silence that on any other occasion would have been welcomed. Despite what had happened earlier I planned to head for the mansion and hoped my second attempt to visit it would not create the rumpus it did the first time. I would not be approaching by car this time, the vehicle having been left in the care of my captors. Somehow, I couldn't see them returning it to the hire car company. On the other hand, not to do so might well draw unwelcomed attention to themselves.

My best chance of picking up a sense of direction was to keep walking until I came across one of the carriage roads—described I remembered by my tour guide as a unique feature of the forest. There were over 40 miles of them. It seemed best to head downhill rather than up, so I got wearily to my feet and looked for a gap through the thick blanket of fir trees. Every now and again, I stopped if I thought I heard sounds of life but it usually turned out to be the movements of one or other of the Park's natural inhabitants.

It was getting darker and a storm seemed imminent so it was a relief to stumble across what appeared to be a flight of stone steps rearranged from the loose rock scree. Some distance away I could now hear the sound of the sea and as I headed in that direction I saw the top of a small wooden hut and from within came the noise of hammer on metal.

138

It was a tremendous relief to find someone native to the area but I knew I would have to be careful about what I said of strange happenings further up the mountain. A call by radiophone to the police station below might be intercepted, setting off all sorts of activity, dangerous to myself and others.

Saying I had got lost on a lone hike seemed to be the best explanation so I knocked, pushed open the door and found a ranger attempting to straighten a piece of iron which had served as a lock to the door. He looked a little surprised but grinned and said: 'Lost, I s'ppose, you gotta be the tenth hiker I've got out of a mess this season. Don't see too many visitors as winter comes on, mind you, the snow stacks up in these parts,' he informed me.

He assumed I had come from one of the camping grounds that open during the summer months and started to explain which path to take to get back there before it was dark. That wasn't what I had in mind but as my original plans were now in shreds it seemed a good idea to find the campsite and beg for a place to lay down my head for the night; there was sure to be some sort of spare accommodation at this end of the season.

It took another hour to reach the camp but my luck was in and I was able to get temporary use of a small-unoccupied trailer. It wasn't luxury but I felt a lot better after the site manager had taken pity on me and produced a hamburger and a can of cool beer.

'You, English?' he inquired as he pulled the top off his own can. 'I'm Hank. You're lucky to find me around. Season's good as over, and I'm already startin' to smell m' Ma's cooking. Not seen home for four months.' His expression indicated that, with some reason, he was more than a little suspicious about a guy, without a rucksack or any kind of walking gear, who had just appeared out of the trees.

'Not many from your parts come round this time of year. Strange, mind you, because two days past an old English gent, at least seventy I'd guess, upreet and perky, stopped off just like you have. You're not lookin' for McWhirter's mansion as well ar'yu?'

Before I could plead guilty, Hank explained that interest in the mansion had zoomed since some magazine resurrected an old story about it being haunted. 'Tourist guides been feedin' off that piece of nonsense for yers. Locals not too happy at first, but they kinda liked the dollars coming with it.'

'Sorry to be boring but the mansion is my destination, too. I'm trying to catch up with a young man who came this way and has landed himself in all sorts of trouble. He claims people talk to him from the grave and probably thinks he can make contact with members of the McWhirter family.'

'You're not up for that rubbish, are you?' said Hank, who despite our short acquaintanceship had decided we could be on first-name terms. 'The old boy, I was tellin' yu about, a rite posh gent, was off his head about the place; kept sayin' he was needin' to straighten things out with the lass he was hitchin' up to. Didn't happen it seems. We was sharin' a can like we're doin' now when tears started rollin' down his cheeks. Never seen a guy cry like that, tried to cheer him but no good, he just shunted off back to his van. I could hear him blubbin' for quite some time.'

'So what happened to him?'

'Next mornin', went to the van to offer him a waffle and coffee but he'd vanished. Didn't think much about it after that. Now you've turned up just like he did.'

'Well, I haven't cried yet but you are sure about this man's age? In his seventies, you said? You haven't seen a much younger man, an arty type with long hair. He would have been showing interest in the mansion as well.'

Hank, shaking his head in disbelief at the thought of a continuing invasion of mad Englishmen, said no arty types had come his way and probably hoping for a period of peace and quiet, said he would show me the quickest way down the mountain. 'Easy to get to the mansion but don't seem a good plan with cops all over the place,' he warned, 'don't ask me what they're doin'. Would guess more serious things needed 'tendin' to. But if you're takin' chances, I'll show you the way in the mornin'.'

Armed with accurate directions this time, it took me less than three quarters of an hour to get within sight of what clearly was the roof of a large property. This time I was on foot but still didn't know whether security patrols would be in the grounds. I doubted whether there would be as they obviously thought keeping an eye on roads near the mansion fulfilled their undertaking.

I carefully pushed my way through bushes, once quite beautifully manicured I suspect, but now badly overgrown and tangled. It didn't seem a good idea to go marching up to the front door, but all attempts at finding an easy passage to the rear of the premises met with no success so I returned to the front of the building and attacked the large iron knocker on the door with gusto. If any of the selling agents responded, I could pretend to be there as a prospective purchaser. To my surprise, the little amount of force needed to operate the knocker was enough to open the door without applying any more pressure. An invitation to enter? As there had been no response to my urgent hammering, helping myself to free admission seemed not entirely unreasonable. I pushed the door wider and walked in.

13

Writing on the Wall

It is not unusual to find that a neglected, deserted building deprived of any sort of human care and attention, exudes an atmosphere chilling to even the toughest of characters. If it has a history of past tragedies, even the most levelheaded will find it difficult to put dark thoughts entirely to the back of their mind. My own vulnerability exposed itself as I took the plunge and walked across a cavernous reception hall towards a staircase of impressive, almost majestic, proportions.

Some of the windows hadn't been tightly shut and the tattered remains of curtains billowed out as the wind caught each in turn. The faint but disturbing noises around me were probably made by birds, bats or vermin allowed to take up residence some months past and never discouraged. Standing in the hall, steeling myself to make the ascent into the upper rooms, I noticed a small white card lying on the floor, so prominently placed it was certain no one could walk past it without at least a glance. It was a business card but without a name, just an address, Mountberry Lane, Bar Harbor, and a logo which had been carelessly blacked out. It was my first and only clue to what might be happening in this sinister building and in the area around. I put it in my wallet thinking that if I had no other leads, Mountberry Lane would be my next port of call.

As I put a tentative foot on the first step of the stairway, I told myself boldness was the order of the day if, having travelled so many miles, I was to solve a multi-faceted mystery. It was Rod who had kept me informed but rather belatedly it occurred to me I had never asked him if he was eye-witness to recent events or was merely passing on the information second hand. That was a bad omission and another mistake was not to encourage him to leave the comfort of his office and join me in this god-forsaken place. The atmosphere was so oppressive any companionship would have gone a long way towards making this part of the expedition less nerve wracking.

At the top of the stairs I was faced by a long corridor, off which were probably seven or eight rooms. The corridor still had the remains of light fittings at intervals but everything else had been stripped. The paintwork, now a dirty fawn, had many patchwork squares, revealing that this passageway did at one time house a selection of paintings. Every step I took on the bare, wooden flooring echoed along the corridor, adding to my disquiet.

Without a more precise plan, my only course of action was to inspect each room in turn, in the hope of finding evidence of the wall artistry Rod had talked about. It had never crossed my mind that I would have anything like the hair-raising experiences other visitors to this building had talked about. However, now that I was here without any friendly company, not even my trusty photographer, Bob Harding, I started to feel an uneasiness that was completely foreign to my nature. Stop being so damned stupid, Damon, I kept telling myself. This is not the time to start getting the heebie-jeebies.

If I did come across the phenomena, known as automatic writing what would it prove? If Stephen had faked it in England then there was a good chance someone could have followed his example in this remote mansion where human activity had been at a minimum for a very long time. Gathering evidence of any kind should be a much easier task here than in a cottage which was still a home to five people or more.

I had to remind myself that the purpose of my mission was to find Stephen Spicer and learn more about the activities of his rival Yasha Rashnin. Ghost hunting was not on the agenda. Despite his international reputation and easy identification, Rashnin had evaded everyone's radar and had not been seen for many months. Rod said that the popular papers in the States had been full of his exploits for a time, then nothing. He seemed to have vanished again. At least two universities cancelled meetings with Rashnin as chief speaker because he could not be traced weeks before the event was due to take place.

After extensive publicity about the history of this deserted mansion, I was quite surprised to find myself on my own. Whatever forces patrolled the periphery roads must be doing a good job and perhaps it was only those arriving on foot that had a chance of penetrating their defences. Also surprising was the fact that no one had made any attempt to make the place look attractive to a prospective purchaser. It had very little going for it except, of course, its position in a delightful corner of the National Park.

Room after room served up nothing to attract my attention but half way down the corridor on the seaward side, a door resisted my attempts to push it open. It didn't seem to be locked by bolt or key, just jammed. A hefty shove with a shoulder made little difference so I risked causing damage by lunging at it with one foot raised. It gave under this pressure and I finished up in a heap on the floor inside.

As I looked up from my spread-eagled position, I noticed every inch of one wall was covered in messages and drawings. Eager as I was to inspect them in detail, I turned my attention first to a chair that was lying on the floor in several pieces. It had obviously been put under the handle of the door but could hardly have been a serious attempt to stop anyone entering. What did fascinate me, however, was how the person who put it there got out of the room. I looked out of the only window. It was a long way down and there was no drainpipe that I could see.

Cynic or not, I knew this was an occasion when I would have to work hard to keep my imagination in check. The surroundings, the atmosphere the vacuity of the place, all conspired to put a sensitive soul in a spin. But I was not a sensitive soul, was I?

I took out of my pocket a few crushed photographs of Stephen's handiwork back in England—goodness only knows why I hadn't kept them in a protective file but they would have been difficult to carry around. Then, as I thought back to the events of the past 24 hours, I realised I was lucky to have anything with me at all. Most of my background material brought from England was still in the back of the hired car. If discovered, as it would have been by now, my captors could well be sorry they let me out of their sight. The first thing they would have found would have been a copy of *The Gemstone File*.

As I eased myself into a sitting position on the floor, the nearest of the messages to catch my eye was without any doubt an excerpt from the File but it wasn't in the small, neat handwriting I remembered seeing on the wall of Stephen's cottage.

The piece before me seemed to start at the heart of the document and a glance to left and right confirmed this. The writer had obviously decided to 'publish' in serial form so the story started at the one end of the room and carried on until the writer ran out of space at the other. He had then written in cheeky fashion—'readers interested in the next episode will find a continuation in the blue room, please exit and turn left.'

In other circumstances, all of this could have been considered on the level of a student prank, the sort of thing to liven up a university rag day. But an element of light-heartedness was missing; to me at any rate this room and the building in general gave off vibes which disturbed the ordinary soul. Perhaps this was a common reaction for anyone plunging alone into a deserted building where tragedy and sorrow were endemic.

If Rod or Eric had been here, we would probably have been carrying out our investigation in much lighter vein, an attitude that Stephen would not have approved of. If we had later complained that there was nothing out-of-the-ordinary to report he would no doubt have explained that a frivolous approach to the job in hand would have instantly killed off any resident 'presence'. It would not have been appreciated if one of us had suggested that perhaps ghosts lacked a sense of humour.

There was certainly nothing light-hearted about any of the entries on the bedroom walls. The one immediately in front of me stated:

'*Strattiano shot from a second-story window in the Dal-Tex building across the street from the Texas School Book Depository, apparently using a hand gun. He is an excellent shot with a pistol. Strattiano hit Kennedy twice, in the back of the head. The Dallas Police Department is in the Dal-Tex building. Strattiano and his back-ups were "arrested", driven away from the Dal-Tex building in a police car. He was released without being booked.*'

I moved a few feet to the left of this disturbing message and realised that the accusations came thick and fast in *The Gemstone File* and there was no doubt that they conveyed a feeling of authenticity. But someone who wanted to cause trouble would work hard to get the tone of his document just right. My eyes opened a little wider at an earlier panel, still in the same handwriting:-

'*Lee Harvey Oswald with links to both the ultra-right and to the Communists was designated as the patsy. He was supposed to shoot at Governor Connally, and he did. Each of the four shooters---Oswald, Browning, Strattiano and Postelli---had a timer and a back-up man. Back-up men were supposed to pick up the shells and get rid of the guns. Timers would give the signal to shoot.*'

145

None of this made much sense to anyone who had found the findings of the Warren Commission satisfactory but the File contained material which people and organisations, desperate for closure of the controversy surrounding Kennedy's death, would rather not have seen in the public domain. Endless conspiracy theories repeated enough times inevitably draw the comment from some quarters that there is rarely smoke without fire.

Quite puzzling was the fact that three years after Stephen had been sent packing the first time around, there was still all sorts of activity on Mount Desert Island apparently involving criminal elements as well as those responsible for law enforcement. Could any of them have been really worried about the movements and activities of a couple of psychic oddballs?

Some obviously were. No matter how hard intelligence officers in the lower ranks may have tried to relegate the file to the 'no action required' tray those in high places, clearly concerned, would have taken great exception to the suggestion that:-

'...a South American drug-dealing multi millionaire was so confident of his control over police, media, FBI, CIA, Secret Police and the U. S. judicial system that he had JFK murdered before the eyes of the nation, then systematically bought off, killed off, or frightened off, all witnesses.'

One young man who had taken fright was Stephen Spicer who unbelievably had now returned to the States for a second time for a reason not yet made clear. I came to a quick conclusion that these wall messages had not been penned by Stephen, who used his artistic skills (or the other sort of skill which he claimed to have) to produce very neat, precise work usually bearing someone's signature. What I was looking at now seemed to have been composed in a hurry by someone who was not too worried about the visual impact. In Stephen's bedroom, I remember, the automatic writings were not lined up neatly but sometimes ranged over the ceiling or in other places that were not readily accessible. If Stephen had been here, then he would have probably walked away, I decided, disgusted at the amateurism of the perpetrator.

Taking out pencil and paper, I made rough notes of the contents of the messages on the wall and then stepped out into the corridor intending to check whether there had been similar 'happenings' in any of the other rooms. The next two were undisturbed but a third one appeared to have been secured not, I felt this time, by a chair forced under the inside handle but by a key. This was not a door I could penetrate without causing damage and I knew there was no chance of looking into it from the outside unless I came across a ladder in the grounds.

Standing in the corridor, wondering if there was any other evidence I could gather about recent visitors, I suddenly had a disturbing feeling that perhaps I was not alone, that I was not the only one stalking the corridors of this lonely mansion. At first, the noises were indistinct but then sounded as if someone, moving very carefully, was trying to walk on bare floorboards without making a noise. Then, as though giving up the attempt to remain unnoticed, the 'intruder' scurried the last few steps, threw open a back door and exited into the garden.

I reached a window just in time to see a figure cross the lawn and disappear into a backdrop of fir and pine trees. He was visible just long enough for me to realise he was no youngster, rather a man in his late sixties or even early seventies. For that age, he moved with surprising agility.

It was easy to decide who this person certainly wasn't, hardly a lone security man at that age, a real estate agent or a prospective buyer. There was something incongruous about a man of senior citizen status creeping around an empty mansion and then beating a hasty retreat on being discovered. My conversation with the campsite manager a few hours earlier came to mind; he had spoken of another Englishman, quite elderly, who had turned up at the camp but offered little information to explain his presence in the middle of a forest.

I wandered back into the room with the unconventional wall decorations in the hope that something might emerge, which would point to a recent visit by one of my intended quarries. There was nothing. It didn't seem like Stephen's work and why would Yasha Rashnin have made a journey here to ape the work of his rival? Surely, he would have thought of something original, something to catch the public eye and give him useful and dramatic publicity.

I slowly made my way along the corridor and down the stairs thinking that if my visit to the States wasn't to be wasted then I needed a breakthrough of some sort and soon. I considered a call to my American reporter chum to persuade him to join me in the hunt. But he would need something solid to convince his editorial chiefs that it was worth him making the long journey to Maine. Alternatively, a visit to Mountberry

Lane in Bar Harbour might give me the lead I needed so badly. For the time being, the birds and rats could have this unfriendly mansion to themselves.

14

Hell Sampled

Less uncomfortable now than when first setting foot in the mansion, I paused in the main hall and focused on the spot where the visiting card had been so prominently deposited. It was reasonable to assume the card with its minimum amount of information had been planted for someone's benefit, possibly mine. No one, however, knew when I would turn up at the mansion, certainly not after my original plans had been thrown into disarray. But if the information on the card was not meant for me, who was it meant for?

The mysterious man who had fled on realising he was not alone in the mansion still intrigued me for he could have been responsible for dropping the card in such an obvious position. But I had enough on my plate looking for my two elusive miscreants without mounting another search for a bewildered old gentleman. For the time being, anyway, I would have to accept I would not be adding to my knowledge of that particular character.

A desire to return to the fresh air of the forest outside was now very strong and with the light fading, I realised I faced another difficult hike back to Bar Harbor. It was, I thought, a short distance from the mansion but I was still not sure of the island's geography and without anything on wheels, the walk would take time.

I had a last unproductive look around the ground floor rooms and then headed for the front door. About to leave, I noticed for the first time that there was a door in the far corner of the reception hall leading into what appeared to be a cellar. It was ajar and a feeble light burned somewhere below, presumably forgotten by the last visitor to the mansion. A single bulb was sending out just about enough light to make a flight of stone steps less hazardous and I felt I would not be exhausting all possibilities of finding useful information if I didn't take a quick look below before going on my way.

Nearer the foot of the steps, the light seemed brighter, bright enough anyway to take a look around. An attempt appeared to have been made to turn the cellar into an area that could be lived in for a while, albeit with very basic facilities. A table and chair of simple origins took centre stage and a small, very uncomfortable looking camp bed along one of the walls was the only other piece of furniture. It had a mattress of sorts, a bright yellow cushion more suited to a drawing room divan and a rather grubby duvet.

A little shiver went down my spine as I noticed several items on the table that could have been someone's idea of a simple survival kit--- three cartons of long-life fruit juice, a sliced loaf of bread, two packets of digestive biscuits and a big blue book that looked as if its content could be on the heavy side. As my eyes became accustomed to the poor but just adequate lighting, I could see there was a collection of buckets and bowls tucked away in one corner. I tried the tap on a tiny, tin basin and water spurted out erratically. I concluded that any extended length of stay in these dingy confines would not be a pleasant experience and couldn't conceive why anyone would have equipped it in this way.

My imagination was in danger of running out of control and it seemed the right moment to take my leave and pursue my inquiries in more amenable surroundings. Why a small corner of a deserted mansion had been furnished in such unfriendly fashion was a question to be left on hold for the time being.

As I turned on my heel and put a foot on the first step, I was jolted by a sound that did nothing for my composure---the noise of metal scraping on flagstones. To my horror, the door at the top of the stairs was slowly closing. Never had I negotiated a set of stairs so quickly. I hit the last step with the agility of a long jumper and simultaneously lunged against the heavy iron door. It was too late, the door slotted into place with the solid crunch of a prison gate closing in the Tower of London.

Of course, there had to be a handle somewhere. No one who lived here in the past would have wanted to be parted from dinner party guests during a quest to recover a good bottle of wine from the cellar. I was wrong. There was no simple lever or handle that would allow me to leave easily.

Nothing I could write in the future about my life would ever adequately describe the panic I felt at that dreadful moment. Fruitlessly, I hammered on the door with my fists, forgetting I had just carried out an inspection of the entire building and found no signs of life apart from an old man who had scampered off into the forest. He wasn't likely to return.

All the less agreeable newspaper stories I had covered in the past came to mind and way out in front in terms of horror was the discovery of the body of a pensioner in his front room. The coroner decided he must have been dead for at least six weeks. Everyone in his street searched desperately for an excuse as to why they had not noticed his absence and the unfortunate milkman said he thought the occupant must have gone to stay with his daughter. That was until the stench of decay started to spread to surrounding properties.

Could that happen to me? Of course not, I told myself, even Eric Driver might start to wonder whether something dreadful had occurred if no news leaked back that I was creating some sort of upheaval in one of the united states. We had become more friendly following my departure from the newspaper and until I left English shores we talked on the phone at least once a month. Penny would certainly raise the alarm eventually and if this mansion were up for sale or in the rental market, some land agent representative would surely be checking the condition of the premises. Would my shouts be heard on the other side of this formidable door?

I tried not to think too hard about why the door had closed. It was a heavy, iron-reinforced door hardly likely to be moved by a draught. And the possibility of someone concealing themselves in the wide-open spaces of the ground floor was very remote. Normally in denial about anything supernatural (television's sci-fi material always left me cold), I gave no credence to any answer which remotely pointed in the direction of hidden and unexplained forces. But perhaps all my dealings with Stephen and his strange friends were beginning to have an effect. Not very convincingly, I told myself this was not the time or place to evoke thoughts of the paranormal. There was always an answer to all such incidents. The door had been badly hung, probably, or there had been some warping of the supports because the house had been left empty and without heat for so long.

All I could sensibly do was try to stay calm, use my ears especially during the day and be ready to create a rumpus if the smallest of sounds came from upstairs. Easily said, not so easy to do. Food supplies were so meagre, I would have to ration myself meticulously. The lighting was poor, the camp bed looked uncomfortable and the toilet facilities---

151

presumably the buckets I had noticed on first entering the cellar--- were not going to enhance the already sticky atmosphere of the cellar.

Calm? How could anyone stay calm in a situation like this? The thumping of my heart and a dull headache added to all the discomforts and without realising what I was doing, I ran up the stone staircase and started hitting the iron door frantically. On hands and knees I tried to look through the tiniest of gaps at the base, swallowed a mouthful of dust for my efforts but saw no sign of anything like human activity. I lay on the top step for a full five minutes and made a mammoth effort to pull myself together. From the steps I embarked on a second inspection of what my unknown gaolers had felt would be sufficient for my immediate needs. The table's content was too well ordered to have been left there randomly. The food was sparse, the liquid predictable but how kind of them to think I might become bored if I didn't have something to read. But one book! Not a selection, not even a choice between three or four paperbacks.

I walked slowly back down the stairs and picked up the one isolated piece of reading material which I hoped would contain something capable of taking my mind off my desperate situation.

Initially, I didn't know whether to laugh or cry. The embossed gold print told me my solitary piece of available literature was a Bible but not the sort to be found on a family bookshelf or even in a church pew. This one looked very formidable indeed, twice as thick as the Sunday school bibles I vaguely remembered. It was certainly not the sort of tome I would have turned to with relish if there had been a copy of a newspaper, any old newspaper, in the cellar.

Having taken a small amount of nourishment and worked out how best to handle the primitive toilet arrangements, I pulled the book towards me and inspected the wording on the inside cover. A bible it certainly was, but a bible with a difference. Not the sort I would have encountered in my youth when many hours on a Sunday were spent in the choir stalls of the local church playing noughts and crosses.

It was an enormous volume containing far more material than I remembered the old and new testaments having. Flicking over the pages I was able to establish it had all the well-known stuff written by Matthew, Mark Luke and John but it was a study bible, a new international version, it said, and would probably be used, I decided, by people who were thinking of going into the church and wanted something to study in greater depth than was normal.

As I turned pages at random, I remembered a stormy dinner party conversation I had had with a group of friends--- Jeremy Mackintosh, a devout Christian, Peter Hodgson, a confirmed atheist, and several others falling somewhere in between. It had started friendly enough but as the wine flowed, a dispute broke out over who would be going to heaven and who would be going to hell. Jeremy had put the cat among the pigeons by hinting he was probably the only one in the room who would be going to heaven.

'You arrogant sod,' was the far from polite reaction of Keith, one of the non-committed guests. 'What makes you think you're so privileged?'

Jeremy explained with the enthusiasm of a recent convert who had been waiting his chance to share the message that the Bible was God's word. Be it on our own heads if we didn't confess our sins, ask for forgiveness and commit our life to Jesus Christ. If we didn't the heavenly gates would slam in our faces. 'Frankly, what more should you expect if you spend a life demonstrating utter disdain for God and the world he created,' added Jeremy with a passion which had started to overflow.

The confidence fervent evangelicals have about their future and their determination to bring Jesus Christ into the conversation at every opportunity had in the past, always made me feel uncomfortable in the same way preachers, standing on street corners screaming about sin and the devil, got under my skin. Their efforts seemed futile but maybe they hoped even the most stony-faced passer-by might sub-consciously take note of at least one of their warnings.

I probably fell into the category of the majority of people living in the Western world who thought there might be a God somewhere in the way beyond but channelled any serious thoughts of a vengeful master handing out punishments by the bucket load or a loving God welcoming his chosen few, firmly onto the back-burner. It was something I could always come back to later in life when time was not the essence. Jeremy told me over and over again, that would be too late but like many pig-headed, over confident young men, I didn't listen. Nobody, not even God, was going to control my life. I didn't need that sort of interference.

Such arrogance and self-confidence does have a habit of evaporating when everything around you starts to collapse. So far in my varied and interesting life, I had been fortunate but would there be a time in the future when in pain or distress I would be crying out for the help that so far I had so carelessly rejected? Had that time just arrived?

Quite suddenly and with perfect timing, the dream I had experienced not so many days ago on the last leg of a transatlantic flight, came flooding back into my troubled mind. So much had happened since arriving in Mount Desert Island, there had been no time to reflect on the incident which had given a jolt to fellow passengers and the cabin crew.

Was there so much difference between that hellish moment people had faced on the Titanic and the situation I was facing now? Of course there was---my experience was wrapped up in a dream; Titanic passengers didn't wake up, they stared death in the face. Now it was my turn to face up to a real-life drama. But I still couldn't visualise the moment when on my knees I might seek God's help.

It was sinisterly quiet and chilly in the cellar and I could not expunge from my mind the thought that it had been deliberately equipped to allow an occupant to survive for a limited period. What sort of person had been here before me and for what purpose? There were no clues, no messages scribbled on the walls or initials scratched into the table in front of me. The mansion itself had a sad history but nothing to suggest that the cellar had been used as a temporary prison. Neither were there any wine racks, ruling out the possibility that good vintages had been stored here recently.

In a determined effort to look on the bright side, I told myself that back in the homeland, I had a very busy job and active family needing lots of attention and here for the first time I had been presented with something not readily available in the turmoil of everyday life---time for contemplation and evaluation without distractions. If I could control my emotions, particularly fear, this was a chance to take stock. But could I steady my nerves and concentrate under these conditions? Someone would come to the mansion eventually. I just had to be patient.

Every time the single light bulb flickered, I flinched expecting it to add to my discomfort by plunging me into darkness. My supply of cigarettes had run out long before I reached the mansion and the pangs of an addict were starting to grip. Couldn't the sick bastard who set up this hell-hole have at least left me a bottle of bourbon or a few cans of American beer?

I started to dwell on what it might be like to starve to death. Was there any way I could end things on my own terms? But how? By hitting myself over the head with a bucket? Perhaps not, bearing in mind what it would contain after a few days. These were dour, desperate thoughts but just as panic again threatened to swamp me, my eyes fixed on the one piece of reading material in the cellar. If death was on the agenda, my agenda, then it surely must contain some useful guidance.

But what did I believe in, if anything? Was I destined for a fiery hell? ---surely not, there was nothing I had done which deserved that sort of punishment. Perhaps if we ignored God during our earthly tenure, I reasoned, there would be no welcome in heaven and we would just cease to exist in any form----a state that several of my dinner party friends seemed to think was highly desirable. But if that was the case what was the point of the struggles we had been through; why did we build up relationships, some so strong that it seemed nothing could break them? How about the beauty of creation, the mystery of the cosmos the fascination of the seasons, all that couldn't have happened by accident, brought about by a big bang billions of years ago? Could it?

It was a funny time and place to think about crocus bulbs but the memory of finding a box of them hidden under rubbish in my garage during a particularly cold start to winter hadn't ever left me. They'd been there for several years so a decision to dispose of them on the compost heap didn't require a great deal of thought. Next spring purple and yellow crocuses pushed their way through the muck and I remember standing alongside the rotting vegetation, shivering with the cold but marvelling at what for the first time in my life looked like a small miracle. This was a moment when I should have paused and taken stock but the 'phone rang and life hurried on.

I pulled the big blue book towards me. The concordance, or index as most people would call it, was new territory as far as I was concerned but with time on my hands perhaps I could discipline myself sufficiently to consider some of the big questions so often relegated to that time in the future, that never comes.

Heaven and hell came to mind as a starting point. They were mentioned at school but never really explained. Jesus rarely got a look in, except at Christmas time when the crib was pulled out of a dusty cupboard and parents were asked to turn their children into shepherds, wise men, sheep, even a donkey. In many homes, it was the parents who asked the children why their teachers wanted them to grow wings.

Seeking assurance that hell was not my most likely destiny I flicked over the reference pages to check where it featured in the Bible. Would I really find threats of being thrown alive into a fiery furnace and left there for an endless number of years suffering excruciating pain? This dire prospect probably lodged in my mind as a result of watching a piece of depressing television drama. It certainly hadn't been as a result of serious reading of the Bible.

Hell, given 14 references in the index, was featured between *held (hold)* and *helmet*. No problem with helmet, even someone of my limited theological education vaguely remembered reference to the *helmet of salvation*. Of the apostles, Matthew had the most to say if I wanted positive guidance on the nature of hell and who went there. The crazy and inappropriate thought went through my mind that this could be useful material at the next gathering of my friends, if I ever got out of this place.

The index reference that worried me most was the single word 'judgment'. It appeared many times and confirmed that no one would escape it. Those who thought they would be extinguished like an exhausted candle at death and have nothing else to worry about were in for a shock.

I thumbed through many hundreds of other references, not having the nerve to turn to some of them. Away from the gung-ho atmosphere of the dinner party table, I was displaying shocking cowardice. I was afraid of what I would read and was still insisting to myself that I was in control.

I came to the conclusion that if I was to acquire fruitful understanding of this book I was holding, I would need some serious help when and if I returned to the world outside. For a start, I had never considered judgment apart from the sort handed out by judges in a British court. Devine judgment had never come into my calculations. Already, there was one positive from this unscheduled, personal examination of life's meaning. Tensions eased just ever so slightly as I stopped dwelling on my present predicament.

What might I turn to next? Adultery came to mind, something that was considered a serious misdemeanour in my parents' days but much less likely to rock the boat in the years approaching the millennium. It had become just one more of those aggravating little rules happily abandoned by a modern, selfish society. That attitude, I found, didn't match up too well with what had been written in the book of the apostle, Matthew:

'You have heard that it was said, "Do not commit adultery. But I tell you that anyone who looks at a woman lustfully has already committed adultery with her in his heart".'

Ouch! That hurts. Could anyone in the editorial department of the *News*, let alone those who regularly gather around my dining room table, ever claim not to have looked at a member of the opposite sex *lustfully*. There was worse to come:

'If your right eye causes you to sin, gouge it out and throw it away. It is better for you to lose one part of your body than for your whole body to go into hell.'

Now this was one of those parts of the Bible that enraged many people and if I had not been incarcerated, the covers of this book would have been slammed shut and I would have vigorously rejected any thoughts of punishing myself by attacking areas of my precious body.

Was Jesus, recognised as a great teacher even among faiths which followed a different path, suggesting we should disfigure ourselves or was there some way in which we could understand this to be, if not a piece of deliberate exaggeration, a method of underlining the seriousness of sin?

Sin---I had the feeling, as I turned the pages, that it wouldn't be long before this word crash-landed into my lap, instantly providing a reminder of another regular dinner table discussion about the nature of sin and particularly original sin. At least two of my female friends had problems with the concept of original sin. 'How can anyone say a tiny baby of a few weeks is saturated in sin?' was their question, echoed time and time again by other mothers who see only little angels gurgling happily in the comfort of their prams. Some mothers may change their minds a few years later but the general perception of the newborn babe is of a bundle of innocence and joy.

With every new biblical reference drawn from this unfamiliar index, the population of heaven started to look more and more threadbare. The conditions for getting there were so tough I couldn't think of anyone I knew who would have an automatic passport. As for my present accommodation, getting colder and more putrid by the hour, I was beginning to feel this might be my introduction to a living hell. Many times, I had heard people say with some conviction that we don't have to leave the earth to find hell. It is here, right on our doorstep.

One of the few stories I remembered from my Sunday school days was that of the rich man and Lazarus. This was a tale, which really shocked me, but instead of making me thirst for real understanding, it had the unfortunate effect of making me dive for cover. The time was right and the material was available to take another look at this frightening story----frightening that is for everyone like me who had a lukewarm attitude towards the power of God.

With the help of the concordance, I was quickly able to locate Jesus' cautionary story, leaving little doubt about the future of those who concentrate on lining their own pockets at the expense of the poor. The rich man gets no name in Luke's account. He is just described as being dressed in purple and fine linen and living a life of luxury. At his gate is Lazarus *'covered with sores and longing to eat what fell from the rich man's table. Even the dogs came and licked his sores.'*

Both men died at about the same time, the poor man going to meet the prophet, Abraham in heaven; the rich man condemned to a life of torment in hell. I may have been thinking that my cellar experience was dire but it was a picnic compared with the fate of the rich man. Escape was a possibility for me, he had no way out. But what made my blood really freeze, I remember, was hearing of the desperate attempts of the rich man to make up for lost ground and bow to God's will when it was too late.

The story goes on to recount how the rich man looked up from the blazing fires of his eternal home and pleaded with the prophet Abraham to *'have pity on me and send Lazarus to dip the tip of his finger in water and cool my tongue, because I am in agony in this fire.'*

Any one of us in that hopeless and helpless situation would probably make a similar request but how many of us in the prime of life ever think it necessary even to consider the possibility of our lives coming under judgment? Even if we did, we would probably seek to water it down by assuring ourselves that God would not be that harsh. As a young man, I might have had some sympathy with my atheist friend, who would have told me the Lazarus story was just another myth created by the founders of the Christian church to keep its flock in order.

I had started to believe that this period in such unpleasant and threatening surroundings was my Lazarus experience. Except for me there was still time to put matters right. There was now a compulsion to read on, not just to pass the time but in the very real hope that I could gain a better understanding of how I should lead my life in the future. If I had my forced occupation in a cellar to thank for this then all well and good. So far, my life had been devoted to the pursuit of becoming a 'rich' man---rich in the sense of putting career and its material rewards first. The moment for reappraisal was undoubtedly long overdue. So what had been Abraham's final indictment:

'Son remember that in your lifetime you received your good things, while Lazarus received bad things, but now he is comforted here and you are in agony. And besides all this, between us and you a great chasm has been fixed so that those who want to go from here to you cannot, nor can anyone cross over from there to us.'

Shocking as this story may have seemed, worse was to come. Even if I had fouled up in God's eyes, surely I would be allowed to warn my beloved family not to make the same mistakes. But no, said Abraham, I should have taken care of that when I had the chance as a father. The rich man's request was that Lazarus should be sent to his home to warn his five brothers of the torment they faced if they scoffed at the prospect of finishing up in hell and continued to live a selfish life. Abraham said it was too late, the rich man had had his chance.

Was that it then? A choice between living a life according to God's word or ignoring him and going your own way. The small light in the cellar flickered reminding me that if the bulb failed I really would be in a place of darkness. It recovered, enabling me to think very carefully about the implications of this fearful warning.

It was not sympathy that Abraham offered, rather an enforcement of the stark message he had been delivering, There was hope for the five brothers if they rejected their selfish existence and started to demonstrate their concern for the less fortunate people around them. In desperation the rich man, who probably never opened a Bible let alone encouraged his brothers to do so, registered one last plea. He was sure that if someone from the dead went to them they would repent.

Abraham's reply was emphatic and one not to be ignored by anyone thinking these decisions can be made casually and in their own time:

'If they do not listen to Moses and the Prophets, they will not be convinced even if someone rises from the dead.'

It was possible I had read this verse sometime in the past but in terms of understanding its deep significance, this was the first time. Study God's word and take it to heart, this was saying, because if you don't make the effort now then even if you are told God's son gave his own life and later was raised from the dead for your benefit, you will not be convinced.

So why did Christ have to suffer an excruciating death to save me? I would seek the answer to that question the next day, I told myself, putting aside the fact that it would have been much wiser to get on with the job there and then. Who could say what tomorrow would bring or even if it would arrive at all?

I turned out the light thinking that in some way energy might be saved and lay on my not very comfortable camp bed re-running the verses over in my mind until I fell asleep. A Damascus type conversion it was not likely to be. But something was stirring in a brain previously well sterilised against spiritual revelation by the pressures and bustle of the material world. I could hardly believe I had to be incarcerated in the cellar of a deserted mansion many miles from home before I started to make a serious assessment of whether I was in charge of my life or perhaps had a creator to answer to.

It seemed a strange moment to think of Stephen Spicer and the complicated life he had led. Or perhaps it wasn't. In deciding whether any of his activities were worth the time and effort of serious analysis, all sorts of new questions arose if heaven and hell were brought into the equation. For so many years, I had considered myself the sceptical, pragmatic journalist who didn't believe in anything unless proof was laid on the table before him. To any sane person, Stephen's 'spirit-controlled' drawings were the work of human hands; his encounter with poltergeists figments of the imagination, his wall messages orchestrated to feed an individual's desire to......to what? Probably to believe that there is something beyond the cares of a world torn by strife and conflict; that contact could be made with a much-loved relative or friend, someone they could look forward to meeting one day outside the recognised cosmos.

Now I had another problem. Having got this far studying a book I had not set eyes on for years I realised I wouldn't get much deeper into it before coming across the word spirit, not only the Holy Spirit but also references to evil spirits. A logical argument says that if God is somewhere 'up there' then so are some of the evil spirits who are helping the devil to fulfil his ambition to bring the world and its people to its knees.

Where does that leave me? In a word mystified. Now I am wondering whether Stephen Spicer might have gifts, a brain that operates in a different manner to the majority. Even if that were now a possibility, there would still be the question of whether he was abusing his gifts for his own gain. There would also be the question of whether the spirits he says he communicates with are good ones, bad ones or invented.

All these disturbing and totally mixed-up thoughts were interrupted by what I thought was a noise coming from directly above my head. Leaping off the camp bed, I switched on the light, ran up the stairs, shouted and banged as heavily as I could on the impenetrable iron door. I then kept quiet, pressing my ear against the cold metal to pick up any sound that could have been associated with human activity. Not a hint.

After a few more shouts, a couple more resolute thumps hard enough to jar my wrist, I dejectedly returned to my tiny prison and consoled myself with a few remaining biscuits and a small cup of orange juice. Thinking of all the stories I had read in my youth about people stranded on deserted islands or on large seas in small boats, I decided to treat my meagre supplies with respect. How long they would have to last me, I daren't think about. Unlike people trapped on dessert islands, there was nowhere for me to wander in search of coconuts and edible fruit, no chance to fish for my dinner.

It was hardly the most luxurious meal I had ever tasted but it refreshed me enough to think of taking another look at the book that had started to challenge my prejudices and make me consider the possibility that someone, somewhere was in charge of my life. However, that could only be the case if I acknowledged the existence of a force greater than anything we could muster up on this planet.

Instead of turning to the index, I opened the book at random and immediately stumbled across a passage that made a clear distinction between people who had been chosen by God and promised eternal life and the rest (the vast majority I calculated with a heavy heart) who were destined for hell.

This chilling message reminded me of a debate I once had with Penny about the fate of the large band of people who had no particular beliefs but led what most people would consider useful lives, often willing to put aside their own problems and help others they felt were in greater need. The exchange came after one of our rare visits to church when the sermon had broached the subject of eternity and the privileged few who would experience it.

Penny was so upset; she threatened not to bother with church again. 'I just cannot accept,' I remember her saying, 'that if there is a loving

161

God he will create such an unfair division between those who believe in him and those who don't.'

'Unfair?' I queried at the time, 'if God created us who are we to say how he should treat us.'

That was probably one of the few times I had gone to God's defence and Penny was far from impressed. She berated the preacher for insisting that the followers of Jesus Christ would go to heaven, the rest would be despatched to the raging fires of hell. 'What about all those good people who may not have found God but devote their lives to helping others?' she asked, still unable to contain her anger.

Penny claimed many of her friends fell into that category. If the preacher were right then billions of people from every part of the globe and from many generations would end up scorching in a lake of sulphur that could not be extinguished. 'Some of these people probably spent the last few years of their life taking meals to the elderly or sitting by the bed of a relative who was dangerously ill, I just can't believe....I can't believe,' Penny was getting more and more upset, 'that God would want to have that scene of horror constantly before him.'

It was some years ago but I remembered I sympathised with Penny's view on that occasion. In an attempt to counter her anger I told her I preferred to believe that those who never accepted God into their lives would just disappear on the day they died. No one could expect to be received into the membership of a realm they had never believed in. 'You wouldn't be welcomed as a full member of a golf club if you didn't like the game and never played it,' I had feebly argued.

What I was reading now, however, destroyed the notion of 'preferring to believe' in something or other. When life is busy and full it is easy enough to think one is in control of one's life, but not so straight forward when the storm clouds are gathering.

Sleep would not come easily on the following night so I opened the Bible once again, consulted the concordance, then turned to a part of one of Peter's letters headed *Making One's Calling and Election Sure*. It listed all those wonderful qualities like kindness and perseverance and coupled them with a promise that a rich welcome into the eternal kingdom was waiting for those who served Jesus Christ.

Thanks to the efforts of a Sunday school teacher long forgotten, I didn't have to seek out a concordance note on Jesus Christ but remembered with some sadness a poll carried out by one English newspaper, revealing that a very small number of children had a firm grasp of who he is or what he has done for them. As a boy, I would not have fared well in that poll. Time served in a church choir would hardly have warranted many bonus points. Important to me now was an assessment of how my recent experiences might affect my future, assuming that I still had one to look forward to. Was I on the brink of getting the message? A hint that I might be was that the feelings of panic and sheer, unadulterated fear originally felt when the cellar door closed, were now moderating little by little.

I was particularly heartened by another promise in this chapter that *'the Lord knows how to rescue godly men from trials.'* My challenge was to discover how I could be rated a godly man. Surely, it wouldn't be easy.

Two more days passed in reasonable comfort but as the food and drink supplies dwindled anxiety started to grow no matter how many verses of the Bible I consulted.

Sleeping was becoming a problem; the unending silence was unnerving. In my more composed moments, not too many of them at this stage, I thought how much I would have enjoyed a quiet hour or two when the boys were young and noisy. Now I was thinking about them and Penny in quite a different way. Hopefully, they would not be aware of my predicament until I was in a position to tell them about it. 'Please Lord, help me get out of this place' I found myself praying. Perhaps that was the moment I set out on my Christian journey proper. Time would tell.

I rolled off the camp bed, feeling stiff and rheumatic, put on the light and glanced casually towards the stairs. Mirages in the dessert are common but they don't usually happen in cellars. No, I was not mistaken. The door was open. With three bounds, I was up the stairs and threw my body at the iron door before anyone could shut it again. Anyone? What was I thinking about? A quick look into the hallway on the other side of the door revealed no evidence of human presence. That didn't really register until later. I was out and my relief was so great that all I could do was sit on the floor and cry.

15

Out of the Frying Pan.......

Weeping uncontrollably was not something I had given into for a very long time; the lack of witnesses was certainly a relief but there was no immediate unravelling of the mixture of emotions whirling around inside my head. Tears of relief they certainly were, but mingled, I fancy, with one or two of another kind...maybe a few tears of joy, too. Not wanting the dramatic turmoil of events in the cellar to evaporate too quickly, I wandered into the garden, found a seat and mulled them over.

A spectator might have thought I was praying earnestly but I was not ready for that yet. My prayer in the cellar was of the sort most people offer when they are in serious trouble. I now had a lot more thinking to do before I could make a rational appraisal of my week in isolation. Whatever the future had in store, it seemed a good idea to retain for more detailed consideration some of the more startling pieces of scripture I had been introduced to. In all I had read, however puzzling on the surface, there seemed to be continuity and purpose exhibited which for the moment I couldn't conclusively fathom. At least one of my regular dinner party friends would have said it was no accident. I vouched my neglected copy of the Bible would be dusted off and elevated to a more prominent place on my bookshelf. Penny would be surprised!

For the present, I had work to do if I was to survive as a freelance journalist. As yet, I hadn't come within spitting distance of covering the fare out to the States let alone the fare back home. Taking a quick look back at the mansion, a sorry pile of masonry in the gathering gloom, I set off through a gap in the woods and took to a path, which I felt sure, would lead to Bar Harbor. It was a long and tiring walk eventually connecting with the Loop Road before a welcome sign indicated that I was a short distance from the centre of the town.

'Thought you were lost for good,' said a welcoming Mary, showing me to the room I had booked earlier. 'We do lose the occasional Englishman who thinks he can dodge the waves at Thunder Hole, but guess you're too old and wise to mess about at that sort of caper.'

'Too cautious, rather than too wise,' I suggested, remembering how horribly cold the water was when foolishly trying to swim on my last visit. 'I must say I didn't relish your freezing sea. I withdrew quickly after the tentative dipping of a big toe.' Mary laughed and said I should have consulted the locals.

I decided not to say anything about my adventures in the forest or my unexpected imprisonment. Mary, understandably curious about my prolonged absence, might come to the conclusion I was not a safe person to have under her roof if I went into too much detail. After a quick wash and brush-up, I headed for the establishment promising the best lobster roll in Bar Harbor. A pint of English beer would have gone down well at this point but I settled for a root beer and blueberry soda (described on the menu as 'awesome'). The waiter said he would leave me to make up my own mind about the awesomeness of root beer mixed with blueberry.

It was a delight to sit there enjoying mouth-watering chunks of lobster and listening to the chatter of people who had done a normal day's work. I was beginning to put the more puzzling aspects of my adventure into some sort of perspective, when a swarthy character clumped his way to the counter and in an unmistakable accent, similar to that which I had encountered the previous day, ordered a lobster roll. By hiding behind the map I was studying, I was able to stay out of sight, but precautions were unnecessary as he quickly made his purchase and left in a hurry.

'Do you know who that was; there can't be too many accents like that on the island?' I said to the local who had served him.

'Not the case buddy, we've had quite a few of them around this year. They hang out up in the Cadillacs, say they like the fishing here and whale watching. They don't come down into town too often. Usually to pick up a lobster when they do.'

I decided not to linger in case another of my kidnappers turned up but I was also concerned about the unidentified group that followed me out of town from the airport. The little I had seen of them gave me no firm assurance that they had anything to do with the island's law enforcement network. The more I thought about it the more doubtful this possibility became. Whatever the answer, the safest policy for the moment seemed to be to keep my head down. I didn't want to do anything to draw attention to myself.

There were many questions I would have liked answered. I was puzzled by the apparent freedom granted to undesirables on this small and pleasant isle. If the clash I had witnessed was genuine then one might have expected to see a major operation in the mountain area to clear out aggressive and unwanted forces. I had seen nothing to suggest a manhunt might be in progress.

I slept well that night, enjoyed Mary's breakfast of homemade oatmeal bread and rhubarb jam and then followed her instructions to Mountberry Lane. She had expressed surprise that I wanted to go to that part of the town, which was run-down and 'had a bit of a reputation.' She didn't elaborate.

It was only as I was walking down the first part of the street that I realised there was no house number on the card, left so prominently for any visitor to the mansion to pick up. That seemed to be a major problem but having walked the lane a couple of times I noticed there was one house, which stood back from the rest and was partially obscured from the road by trees. It had an unoccupied look about it, rubbish in the garden and heavy curtains drawn at every window. I suppose I should have made some polite inquiries at the properties nearby but it was quite early and a short prowl around the empty house should not, I felt, cause any alarm. Nobody seemed to have started their day.

Walking to the back of the house, the questions started to buzz around in my head again. Why should someone have left a doctored business card in a position where it was obviously going to be noticed by the first person who walked across that hall? It was a message to someone, perhaps me but that was unlikely. No one on the island knew I was about to arrive on the scene? Few, if any, would have been witness to my wanderings around the forest. If I didn't know where I was going for most of the time, they certainly wouldn't. Then there was the mysterious elderly gent I had seen hurrying off into the forest; for the moment there was no way I could fit him into the picture. His behaviour gave the impression he didn't want to hang around to be seen by me or anyone else.

The life of a journalist is unconventional by any standards but I had never before found myself in a position where I had to break and enter two properties within the space of 48 hours. My actions were not entirely criminal as in both cases there was little breaking-in to do. This time a kitchen window had been left open. Or had it? Glass on the window seal and kitchen implements scattered on the floor pointed to the possibility that someone had already travelled this way recently.

If ever there was a moment for discretion this must have been it. But fools and reporters never learn and once again, I stepped into unknown territory without giving a thought as to what I might find or what the consequences might be. It was a terrible mistake. Negotiating the jagged pieces of glass still left in the window frame was difficult enough. Getting onto the kitchen floor without sustaining injury brought new hazards. Sliding from my perch on the edge of a kitchen top, my foot reached the floor but slid away as it struck a slimy patch. I put a hand down to lever myself back into an upright position and found I was sitting in the middle of, not the remains of someone's greasy breakfast, but a pool of blood.

My first thought was that whoever had broken in before me had cut his hand on the broken glass still lying around. That seemed very unlikely in view of my next grisly discovery; there were bloody footsteps leading across the kitchen floor and connecting with another set at the foot of a flight of stairs. Pausing for a moment or two, I started to think that my sanity might seriously be questioned. Within hours of undergoing one of the most alarming and puzzling experiences any human being could endure, here I was with one foot on the bottom of another staircase and a bloodstained one at that.

I should not have mounted those stairs; something was very wrong in this house and a call to the police was the obvious next step. I was in a strange country, I kept telling myself, not dealing with local coppers who knew me as well as their station colleagues....get out and sound the alarm, you idiot! Maybe the reason I didn't was the thought that I had blood on my shoes, blood on my hands and blood on my clothes. A touch incriminating, to put it mildly.

There had been times when my police contacts back in Trentbridge had let me onto a crime scene, probably out of some bizarre desire to test my nerve and sensibilities, but nothing I had witnessed before could have prepared me for the horror confronting me as I opened a first floor bedroom door on the landing of this empty house in quiet and respectable Bar Harbor.

A man's body, or what was left of it, was spread-eagled across a bed, hands outstretched, in what seemed like a last desperate plea to his killer. The room was saturated in blood, so much that one wondered if it could all have come from one body. Few murderers left their weapons at the scene of a crime but lying on the floor was an automatic pistol, plus silencer apparently carelessly discarded. It looked as if the entire contents of that weapon had been unloaded into the victim's body. The stench in the room was so overwhelming, it was clear the body had festered there for some considerable time.

I knew I had to get help and very quickly, but for what seemed like many minutes but was probably seconds, I stood at the bedroom door trying to fathom what sort of person would want to destroy another human being in this way.

With the product of my nausea threatening to add to the gore spattered around this room, all I wanted to do was to breathe fresh air, but having been lured to this place by a strategically placed business card, I needed to know whose body it was lying on the bed of another deserted house. Someone had steered me in the direction of Mountberry Lane and I needed to know why.

The room was quite dark but for a moment, the sun came from behind a cloud and sent a beam of feeble light across the bed. It was strong enough to give me the next great shock of the day. As well as bullet holes, the body was scorched, blackened as though someone had tried to burn it. But there was no sign of fire in the room, no sign that an attempt had been made to destroy the evidence, house and all. Apart from a few black streaks, the face had escaped the worst of the mutilation and just before the sun disappeared behind a cloud, I was able to make a positive identification. It was the body of a man who had appeared on British and American television many times. I was looking at the remains of Yasha Rashnin who had set off for the States many months previously and after one or two television appearances on this side of the Atlantic had vanished without trace. Now I had found him.

Panic overwhelmed me. Blood on my shoes, blood on my hands and in the same room as the remains of a man who had acquired celebrity status all over the world. I was totally traumatised. Any thoughts of leaving the scene in a hurry were quashed by the sound of sirens, many of them and seemingly coming from all directions. It sounded like a small army converging, alerted probably by a neighbour who had seen me climb through the kitchen window.

There was no point in running. There was nowhere to run to. Beginning to realise just how much I was in shock, I walked slowly down the stairs and opened the front door just as four burly cops were about to make a noisy and forceful entry. So accustomed were they to manhandling desperadoes, they were quite taken back when confronted by a not very tough looking guy, unarmed, covered in blood and with a terrified expression on his face.

But they woke up quickly and while two of them charged up the stairway shouting well-rehearsed warnings, the other two put me through the routine I had witnessed on television on so many occasions---head hitting the police car roof with enough force to dent the bodywork, hands and arms drawn painfully into positions making resistance impossible.

'Nasty sight up there,' said one of the law-men as he reappeared at the front door, calling for any forensic help the Bar Harbor's small force could muster. 'Take that guy's shoes now, there's bloody shoe prints all over the place, must be his. We can strip him back at headquarters.'

Forced into the back seat in that familiar 'you're going nowhere chum' kind of way I had only a few minutes to digest what had happened and try to form an explanation that would save me from agonising months or years in an American jail. 'My God,' I thought, 'they sometimes keep you on ice over here while they argue endlessly over what the charge will be.' As things stood at the moment, they weren't going to have too much trouble finding the right book to throw at me. My one hope was that the origin of the business card which led me to Mountberry Lane might provide them with another line of inquiry.

'I know it looks bad,' I said feebly as I was pushed very aggressively into an interview room.

'You can say that again chum,' a gruff but authoritative voice said as I was piloted brusquely towards a table and a couple of chairs in the centre of the room. The way was cleared for a big man, unshaven and from the way he was rubbing his eyes, not long out of bed, who said he was Police Chief Barkway, undoubtedly a man who didn't like to be disturbed before mid-day. Dealing with a dishevelled Englishman covered in blood was not his idea of a pre-lunch activity. The general conversation around me seemed to indicate his junior officers were secretly congratulating themselves on an open and shut case and merely wanted a simple confession recorded on tape. Then, one got the impression, they could go back to activities of a more mundane but less stressful nature.

'What the hell you doing in Bar Harbor, anyway? Did you come all this way to take revenge on this guy? What did he do to upset you that much?'

The highest-ranking cop on this island, maybe, but he was certainly not the brightest. It suddenly occurred to him that he had no idea who the victim was. They had found no passport or any other identification and apparently there was no record of any foreigners (apart from tourists) coming to the town during recent months.

The shock of the last few hours was still affecting my ability to think clearly but I had to start defending myself quickly and decisively if I was not going to spend many uncomfortable nights in a cell.

A clear explanation of my reasons for being in Bar Harbor and a detailed account of what had happened to me during the last few days seemed to be the sensible way forward. But I was still trying to work out whether the police chief and his team now grilling me were the same group who followed me from the airport to the mansion. I didn't recognise any of them but the speed with which my pursuers were overwhelmed in the forest gave me no opportunity to register faces.

It was a relief that they seemed prepared to listen to me, for a while anyway. 'I realise I have some explaining to do but this guy did not upset me and I was not here looking for revenge on him or anyone else. But I can tell you who he is. His face is well known in most parts of the world and quite familiar here in the States. But I guess you guys don't spend much time examining the exploits of jerks who claim to be psychic miracle workers.'

'No, we don't and no way we're starting now,' warned Chief Barkway, 'speed it up, we're listening but it's not going to make any difference. Unless you come up with something real good you're (what do you say in the UK) in for the high jump. We don't like people being shot up in this town; it's bad for the tourist trade. This isn't Chicago, yu know.'

Hoping my interrogators would show a little more patience, I started from the beginning and first explained that the corpse on their hands appeared to be Yasha Rashnin, who described himself as a psychic but whom many believed was just a talented magician. I explained some of the tricks he got up to on the world's television screens and how he had come across the Atlantic some time ago because he thought there were more lucrative pastures in the United States.

'You should be able to find out quite easily what he did during his early months over here, but according to my contacts he disappeared about six months ago. Nothing else was heard of him until a rumour spread that he was heading for Mount Desert Island to join other crackpots, hoping to make contact with the lady in the white dress, haunting your infamous mansion down the road.'

'OK, but if that's true, where do you come into all this? Why did you start headin' in the same direction?' asked Chief Barkway.

'If you want the whole story then please give me a bit more time. It's very complicated.'

In some detail, I explained my background and said I had given up my job on a local English newspaper to discover what had happened, not to Yasha Rashnin in particular, but to another popular entertainer-cum-psychic, Stephen Spicer, who had also returned to the US without telling anyone the reason for his trip. I pointed out that he was my target because he had been involved in some dubious activities in the UK and no one could understand why he was heading for the States a second time.

'Hold it, this guy Spicer returned to the US…for a second time? What was he doing here the first time?'

I thought carefully before answering this question because my immediate future might depend on it. Bearing in mind what had happened to me on my arrival at Bangor airport, it seemed likely that the interest was not in the arrival of a small-time regional journalist, rather in the possibility of meeting up with Stephen Spicer. The common denominator could be *The Gemstone File.* A lot of mud had been thrown around after the Kennedy assassination and maybe *The File* was still causing some of that mud to stick. Crazy as it seemed to me at the time, there were people in the States who believed Stephen's antics could still cause concern in establishment circles. There were also people named in *The File* who might be angry about accusations tossed around with careless abandon.

What I had not yet fathomed because so far I had had so little time to fathom anything, was whether the four passengers in the vehicle that followed me from the airport to the mansion came from this station, the one in which I was now being held or whether other forces were at work. Even more intriguing was the identity of the gang that appeared suddenly from the inner depths of the forest. Who were they and why was it they seemed to have a free run of the island and cause all sorts of problems seemingly without attracting the attention of the law? But I was getting ahead of myself. First, I had to find a way of persuading my captors that they had got hold of the wrong man.

Before I could carry on with my story, Chief Barkway, chipped in.

'So it seems we have two English schmucks over here both chasing the ghost of a girl who topped herself a long time ago and a mad English newshound who thinks their activities are worth travelling hundreds of miles to uncover. You're going to have to do better than that, chum.'

'OK let me answer your question about Spicer's first visit to the States,' I said trying to keep the dialogue going for as long a possible. The trouble I was experiencing was that in these surroundings, it all sounded rather ridiculous and the disbelieving looks on my inquisitors' faces didn't help much.

It was going to be even more difficult explaining the part *The Gemstone File* played in all this but I suspected they were probably aware of its contents. My assumption proved correct because they showed no surprise and asked no questions when I mentioned the File.

I continued in as convincing a manner as I could muster under the circumstances. 'Stephen Spicer thought he had been dealt a winning hand when the file came into his possession and as he was coming to the States on a lecture tour he planned to use it as a way to convince his supporters back home he had very special powers indeed.'

Still no questions from my inquisitors so I carried on. 'I know all that stuff in *The Gemstone File,* throwing around accusations like confetti, may sound pretty stupid to you but the point was that once having pretended over the air and in newspapers that he was receiving this information from "the other side", someone was upset enough to put the frighteners on him, with enough persuasion to send him scuttling back home.'

'Hold it for a moment, let's try to get back to what's happened here. Got a stiff on our hands, remember?' said Chief Barkway, who by now was less brittle and showing some genuine interest, 'you say it's not Stephen Spicer, but another tricky customer, Yasha Rashnin. What's the tie-up between these two? Why were they over here together? Were they buddies?'

'Anything but' I said forgetting that the mind of a police officer might well interpret this response in such a way as to give him another suspect. This is exactly what it did.

'So we have rivals, gettin' in each other's way,' said the Chief, 'if you didn't do this, and I'm still not persuaded you didn't, then Mr Spicer might be the one with a big enough chip on his shoulder to kill.'

Rather feebly, I tried to explain that I didn't think Stephen was the sort who'd kill anyone but I could see little attention was being paid to my opinion. If they were going to let me off the hook, they would really want someone else in their sights.

So much was happening in such a short space of time, I realised I had said nothing about my experience at the airport or my time in the forest hide-away. I was about to raise these issues when I noticed that documents I thought had been left on the back seat of the hired car---*The Gemstone File* and the threatening note among them--- were on Barkway's desk. What were they doing there? Had they been handed in by the car hirers after their vehicle had been returned or was there some link between the gang in the forest and the local police force?

As we talked, Barkway kept shuffling the papers he had somehow acquired and I detected some uneasiness as he turned up the File and the threatening note. He made no comment, just pushed them to one side. I thought I would push my luck, as the tide seemed to be turning slightly in my favour.

'Was it you guys who followed me from the airport and then had a bit of a dust up with a small army near the mansion…' I wasn't allowed to finish my question.

'We're doing the quizzing here,' said the Chief, 'just remember you're not out of trouble yet. You'll be our guest for a while; we'll check out your story in the mornin'. After that, we'll decide what to do with you. One piece of good news… passport control says you've got a clean sheet. Sleep well!' Police Chief Barkway then left me to the discomforts of his cellblock.

It was my first night in police custody although there must have been occasions in my careers when I came close. A lesson to be learned was to be extra careful about what you do in countries where you are not known. After another lobster sandwich for supper—I suppose you could get fed up with them---I ran over in my mind the dreadful events of the day, trying to make sure I would make no mistakes when the inevitable interrogation resumed.

So many things didn't add up. There was a strange atmosphere on the island and a feeling that various groups, maybe official as well as unofficial, were being given a great deal of freedom to do their own thing. How come that a quite serious confrontation could take place near the McWhirter mansion and the local police either knew nothing about it or did not want to admit any involvement. Who were the group of thugs who came out of the forest like Robin Hood's merry men and were allowed to go about their business with little hindrance?

Also mystifying was the fact that they seemed to have an established headquarters. I wasn't there for long but long enough to get the feeling they felt secure and confident enough to come and go at will.

Perfectly clear was that this gang wanted to get its hands on Stephen Spicer and thought they had him when they picked me up by mistake. But why did they want him if his only reason for visiting the Cadillac Mountain mansion was to test his sensory perceptions in surroundings with a tragic history? There had to be more to it than that. Some agencies or individuals must have thought he could be useful to them in one way or another. But in some other quarters he might well have been seen as a threat.

And what was Rashnin doing on the island and how long had he been here? That seemed at this stage to be the key question. If he had met up with American psychics and scientists, it was most unlikely they would have wished him any ill will. He may have been responsible for the scribbles on the mansion's bedroom walls but they were so crude few would have been impressed. He might even have put them there as a joke or an attempt to make Stephen Spicer look silly. By this time, he could have discovered his 'rival' was in the country and was still determined to spike his guns in some way.

Another more sinister possibility came to mind. One of Stephen's seemingly tall stories had been along the lines that the British Secret Service had for a time wondered whether they might channel his unusual sensory capabilities towards interfering with defence and power mechanisms. Their interest had been sparked at the time by an experiment resulting, allegedly, in radio and computer links being disturbed.

Yasha, who considered interfering with communication links was his province, was said to have been jealous about the publicity Stephen had received and had set off for America telling his friends his powers, frequently demonstrated by bending metal, meddling with television services and even tampering with electrical supplies, might be more valued by the intelligence agencies of the world's most powerful country. One reasonably respectable publication had reported: 'At one extreme Yasha Rashnin could simply be exposed as a fraud; at the other, missiles could be knocked out of the sky by mind power alone.' Yasha told his friends that he would prove once and for all that he was no fraud.

Rod had reported to me that Rashnin had attended two or three meetings at well-know universities, presumably to prove his credentials, and then disappeared. There was a gap of six months or so between his last known public appearance and the time of his death so there would be many, including the police, who would want to know what he had been doing during the intervening period.

I must have been exhausted as in the middle of this analysis and despite my surroundings I fell into a deep sleep.

16

Off the Hook

Thankfully, I was not visited by demons of any denomination during the night and I woke feeling remarkably refreshed. On the surface, there was no cause for optimism about the day ahead but as I tried to come to terms with the sparse facilities of my police cell, I did have the comforting thought that their task of casting me as a vicious killer might be more difficult than they first thought. They would look for a motive in vain. Reporters might not be popular with the general public or the police but statistically, at any rate, they were not known for their violent behaviour.

Since leaving the mansion, serious contemplation on my experience in the cellar had to be put on hold because of the pace of events springing from the discovery of Yasha Rashnin's body. Of all the crime scenes I had visited over the years, none presented a scene of carnage as vile as that in Mountberry Lane. It would take me many years to rid myself of those images, if in fact they could ever be completely dispelled.

With time to ponder, I might find links between the two experiences, one of those being a sharp reminder that I do not have control of my life or the events that feature in it; another underlining the devastating effects evil can have on the lives of those who succumb to its undisputed power. Any previous certainties I may have thought I possessed were totally quashed.

More than adequate compensation, however, was the thought that when I next opened the Book I had neglected for so long--- hopefully in the comfort of my own home--- I would start to discover a peace of mind previously denied me by a life-style of my own devising.

Even so, it was not the time to jump to conclusions and I was still some way from embracing the possibility of divine intervention. Or I thought I was until the next sequence of events stirred in me a deep-down feeling that they could not have taken place without a helping hand from somewhere.

The sound of Police Chief Barkway's raised voice some way down the corridor was not reassuring. Being compelled to come on duty at an early hour could only mean trouble for me. But I was mistaken. The cell door was thrown open by one of his office-bound juniors and instead of the angry demeanour so pronounced the night before, I detected the hint of a smile on the big man's face as he marched in.

'You'll be pleased to know you couldn't have killed Rashnin,' announced Chief Barkway, 'as much as we would like to wrap up this affair by lunchtime, it seems we have more work to do.'

Completely taken back, and trying not to look too jubilant, I inquired: 'When during the night did you get a visit from my guardian angel, then?'

'It was simpler than that,' said the chief still managing to maintain signs of his better humour. 'I only have one reliable forensic man on the island but he's rarely wrong. Rashnin didn't die at Mountberry Lane; he was taken there and dumped. The burns on his body were most likely caused by contact with high powered electrical apparatus. He'd been dead for some time.'

'So what about the bullet wounds?'

'These were pumped into him later. The killer wanted us to think it was a shooting.'

'I thought bodies didn't bleed much after they were dead, how come the vast amounts of blood I managed to submerge myself in?'

'The blood you paddled in didn't belong to the body; it was an animal's blood possibly from the local abattoir. The killers had to be pretty stupid to guess they could get away with that.'

'Where does Mountberry Lane come into the picture,' I wanted to know, 'and why the card left in the mansion, pointing the finder in the direction of that building?'

Chief Barkway explained that the small gang of criminals, still causing him a headache, used the Mountberry Lane house as their headquarters until they thought their presence was raising suspicion. Then they pulled out, retreated into the forest and managed to conceal themselves for some considerable time

'I don't think that card was meant for you,' said Barkway, 'the same headcase who spattered the blood probably dropped the card in the mansion deliberately, thinking it would fall into the hands of one of your ghost hunters, hopefully Stephen Spicer who they wanted to get their hands on. If he went to Mountberry Lane they would be waiting for him.'

'Nobody was there when I went in,' I observed, 'unless they were hiding in one of the other rooms.'

'They weren't far away, be sure of that. They beat it when the neighbour saw you breaking in and called us.'

Barkway said the card I picked up belonged to a small café owner who once had a business at the end of the lane. I wanted to know what they were doing about the gang in the forest but it was made clear I had had all the information I was going to get from this source.

'So I can go?' I said hopefully.

'You can but you have a job to do for us. You owe us something for the nice way we've treated you,' said the police chief with a sickly grin. He hadn't demonstrated the carefree side of his character in the early stages of our acquaintanceship. However, it wasn't the moment to argue.

'We suspect, Stephen Spicer, will try to link up with you. He's the one we want to question now.'

'He's not your man' I started to say, but I was wasting my breath.

'That's not for you to decide. In our book he's got to be involved in some way or other and until he comes up with some good reasons why he's on Mount Desert Island and explains his movements, he's top of our list.'

My mind was now going round in circles. The idea that Stephen might be involved in killing Yasha Rashnin was preposterous. He might not have been his greatest admirer but an act like that was out of the question. Though, even as I dismissed the possibility as rubbish, a disturbing thought came to mind. Both these men had been credited, rightly or wrongly, with having unusual brain patterns that could interfere with all sorts of modern communications paraphernalia.

It had all started harmlessly enough with Yasha bending spoons and messing up peoples' television sets and radios, mainly as entertainment stunts. But Stephen took it a stage further, claiming metal bending and ESP demonstrations were kid's stuff. He would provide proof that he had a hot line to the spirit world. Contacting important 'dead' people, who wanted to correct the history books, made good material for his publications but when he started to 'resurrect' more modern figures who disputed the findings of official inquiries and commissions, trouble beckoned. The possibility was that he became a nuisance in the eyes of some law enforcement agencies and a likely accomplice, albeit an unwilling one, as far as some criminal elements were concerned. Unknown at this stage was which of Stephen's two claims to fame, communication disruption or digging up the past, might have attracted the attention of undesirable elements. Perhaps both were on someone's agenda.

Chief Barkway broke into my thoughts by not asking me but telling me what he was going to do next. He was going to let me go but only if I agreed to co-operate in the search for Stephen Spicer.

'You're going to be the bait,' said the uncompromising lawman, 'It might not be how you do things back in Blighty but you seem to be the most likely guy to lead us to our main suspect.'

I pointed out that Stephen may be their number one suspect but had they considered the possibility that the crowd of ruffians roaming free in the forest, having squandered the unusual skills of Rashnin, might now want Stephen as a replacement?' Again Chief Barkway demonstrated his ability not to answer a straight question. He left the cell without saying another word. There was something about this man's vagueness and casual attitude that made me feel uneasy.

He had treated me well enough in the end but I couldn't put the thought out of my mind that he might be dancing to someone else's tune. He returned a short while later to say I was to be handed over to intelligence agents, who had already made inquiries in the UK. They would have questions to ask and would then decide my fate.

I had no idea who they had been talking to but wondered whether Eric now had a story to enliven the front page of my old newspaper. Yasha's death, details of which I was told had been released, would have top billing to be sure but many of my former colleagues would be amusing themselves with the revelation that I had been suspected of a gruesome murder and locked up for a term. Dark humour was one of the less endearing characteristics of many journalists.

My shoes and trousers were returned, superficially cleaned but still unpleasant enough to make me want to go in search of a complete change. A request to return to my lodging was turned down and wearing the bottom half of an old police uniform, I found myself being driven back into the Cadillac Mountain with little idea of what was ahead of me.

My guess was that I would be dropped off somewhere in the region of the McWhirter mansion but we had not been travelling for more than a few minutes before I realised we were going in a different direction, along parts of the Loop Road I didn't recognise. Then I recalled why I didn't remember them; on the last occasion, I had been blindfolded.

We pulled up at a gate I did remember; it was at the end of the drive to the property briefly visited by me involuntarily a short while ago. I was marched up to the front door, which opened immediately, but not by any of the characters, I had met there before. Working industriously in rooms on the ground floor were men in scenes-of-crime boiler suits. The bunch of toughs that had dragged me here on a previous occasion were no longer in evidence. In the short time I had been away dramatic developments must have taken place but no one seemed in a hurry to offer an explanation.

An extensive search was taking place on the ground floor and through a small gap, I could just see into one room, which was still strewn with electrical equipment, including what looked like a portable generator. A strange piece of equipment to have in the lounge of a picturesque forest residence!

While I was trying to manoeuvre myself into a position to see even more, a grey-suited American, his potentially smart appearance spoiled by the bulging weaponry in his inside pocket, walked out of the room and introduced himself as Special Agent, Jasper Clarke.

'Intriguing, isn't it, more like a laboratory than the front room of a country house,' suggested Agent Clarke.

'Fascinating, yes, but can you tell me what the hell is going on?' I've been chased, kidnapped and arrested; threatened with a murder charge, not without some reason I admit, and then dumped in this remote part of the Cadillac Mountains for a second time.'

'A second time?' queried the agent.

'Yes, there's been a change of occupancy since I last visited,' I said sarcastically, 'what have you done with the previous residents?' Spotting damage to the walls that could have been caused by a small explosion, I observed: 'Looks as though you've been fighting a small war up here, not something you would expect in one of America's most popular and "quiet" tourist areas.'

'You can have an explanation but first we need to have a promise that you're prepared to cooperate.' Clarke said he was sorry about my encounter with hoodlums, who they had been watching closely but obviously not closely enough. The gang had been using the forest residence since vacating their Mountberry Lane hide-away. What was now visible was the aftermath of a range of experiments with electrical equipment. Hence the generator.

'Can you put me out of my misery about the drama which greeted me on my arrival in Bar Harbor? I didn't expect to be followed by strong-armed policemen and then surrounded by a gang of terrorists who appeared to have the freedom of the forest.'

The agent, who obviously prided himself in the efficient running of his team, was embarrassed by having to explain that this was one occasion when things didn't go according to plan The four guys in the Land Rover were not local police but part of his team, which had been given the task of following a British journalist to see what had brought him to Mount Desert Island.

'We had been told you were on your way, like many others, to chase a ghost in our notorious mansion. But we didn't buy that. We thought you may have special reasons for meeting up with Stephen Spicer and if we stayed on your tail, you would lead us to him. This young man has been giving us quite a headache and we wanted to find out just what he was up to. My men were under orders to play it cool and were not heavily armed. That's why they didn't put up a fight when suddenly submerged by men with an impressive armoury. If they had drawn their light weapons there would probably have been considerable bloodshed.'

Jasper Clarke said they had their reasons for not pouncing on the gang immediately and for keeping the local police in the dark about the discovery of their new HQ. It backfired when a walker passed close to the building and heard a cacophony of peculiar noises coming from what appeared to be a private house.

'He reported this to the police in Bar Harbor and instead of coming to us first, they over-reacted. Unfortunately, one of their panic messages was picked up by the gang and they started to evacuate very quickly. They just had time to grab some of their equipment enabling them, they hoped, to carry on their experiments elsewhere and disappeared into the forest. Or rather over the forest, we know they use a helicopter. They won't get away for long, this is not a huge island and is quite difficult to leave unnoticed.'

'But what were they doing and why up here?' I asked. Clarke beckoned me to follow him into the room I had seen briefly when I arrived. Apart from the generator, there were all sorts of electrical gadgets that meant little to a failed O-level physics student. Despite my unfamiliarity with this kind of equipment, Clarke obviously thought I might be of use, maybe as some sort of decoy. Stupidly not thinking of the possible consequences, I agreed to co-operate, if for no other reason than it might be a passport to a saleable story at the end of the day. I'm sure my peers back in England would have queried my sanity. They would have been right, of course. I hadn't even asked about the possible dangers.

As soon as I had put my signature to the bottom of a very long form--- the American equivalent of Britain's official secrets act--- Clarke went into a fuller explanation: 'The crowd in this house, as you will see just by looking around, were obviously working on an extraordinary project, one they probably thought could pay handsome dividends in the future. Their problem, apparently, was they couldn't find the right person to do the magic for them.'

'Come again! To do what for them?'

'Well, you'll know something about this because you've had dealings with two men who seem to have persuaded the scientific world, or at least a small part of it, that they can interfere with communications systems or tamper with energy supplies simply by using the power of the brain. This may turn out to be absolute rubbish but when people in top positions get worried about it, it becomes our job to sort it out.'

Not quite believing that a major world power would get sucked in so easily, I explained that magic was the last word I would have used. Research in the UK had not been very thorough and there was little to back up some of the claims being made. 'It now seems,' I said displaying some bewilderment, 'I am being asked to reconsider the theory that some people have brains which emit waves powerful enough to cripple important installations.'

'That's how it is,' said Clarke demonstrating his casual acceptance of the situation. I was surprised Clarke had been willing to take me into his confidence in such magnanimous fashion but I guessed he already knew I was the one most likely to lead him to Stephen Spicer. I was beginning to feel sorry for the poor lad; he could never have realised what he was walking into.

More surprises were still to come. 'We've done a bit of homework on your background,' Clarke revealed, 'we know you're a nosey but effective journalist and unlike many of the charlatans around here can use your brain to get to the bottom of things. Perhaps you've been wasting your life, you might have made a better cop,' he suggested in an undisguised attempt to flatter me.

'But what neither of you realised was that you were stepping into treacherous territory, omitting to take into account the variety of sinister forces at work in many parts of the world. That was why your English friend didn't hang around last time. Almost certainly, he was threatened. What induced him to walk back into a similar situation again we can only speculate about at this stage.'

'One rather important matter you haven't mentioned is the death of Yasha Rashnin. Where does he fit into the picture?

'He probably had no idea initially he was being targeted. But once he started to demonstrate his skills at a variety of universities, there were people on both sides of the law who began thinking his energies could be put to other uses. Even some of our top scientists refused to accept that they were probably being duped by a clever magician. They preferred to believe he might have the power to transmit powerful brain vibrations in such a way as to mess up an enemy's security systems.'

I reminded Clarke that this theory had been examined in the UK without any satisfactory conclusions being reached. For obvious reasons few details had ever been released but unofficial reports suggested that there was little or no substance in the claims which had been made.

Clarke said there had been similar scepticism in the States until electromagnetic radiation was brought into the equation. This, it was thought, opened up new trains of thought.

'It also opened another can of worms. I gather even your cautious MI5 crowd got worried about it at one stage,' suggested Clarke, 'We're concerned because we've already had one demonstration of what can happen, or rather what can go wrong, if people play around with something they don't really understand.

'A week or so ago there was a major electricity blow-out here on the island and there was no obvious reason for it. Then they closely examined the grid and found one pylon deep in the forest had been tampered with. They also found the remnants of a shirt, so burned that it was barely recognisable as a piece of clothing. That was when they decided to call us in.'

'Us being who?' I inquired.

'All you need to know is that we are a branch of the CIA. We wouldn't be involved if information had not come our way that more than one country was showing abnormal interest in a couple of English self-styled psychics, initially regarded as freaks. The incident in the forest involving the island's electricity supply had us all running around in circles. People wanted answers including top officials in the White House. '

'Well, one of the freaks you mentioned is no more; he had an unwelcomed encounter with an electricity pylon, I gather.'

'That would appear to be what happened. Initially,we left the matter with the local police to carry out normal inquiries. That was a mistake. Nothing happened until Barkway reported this week that they had found a body with gunshot wounds and severe burns. Sorry you had to walk into that,' added the CIA man, 'but you did us a favour. The body might have stayed in that empty house for a long time yet.'

'So, am I allowed to ask if you think Yasha Rashnin was part of an experiment in the forest and got his fingers......sorry, I didn't mean to say that. It just slipped out.'

Clarke couldn't avoid a weak smile but wasted little time in getting on with what was becoming more like a briefing. 'Almost certainly Rashnin's services were obtained in some way or other by the crowd who had taken over this house. What they obviously had in mind was a series of experiments. All this stuff you see around you points to that. When they decided to put their experiments to a practical test, that was when they ran into trouble.'

Details of what actually happened out in the forest were still sketchy, said Clarke, but preliminary investigations pointed to the possibility that when they attempted to use Rashnin's alleged powers, something went horribly wrong. Clarke thought the experiment itself might have killed Rashnin. The blood and the bullet injuries were a clumsy attempt to put investigators off the scent.

'Where does Stephen Spicer fit into the picture? I asked, 'Come to think of it where do I now fit into it? I'm grateful for the clear picture of events you have given me but I'm not used to the law taking me into its confidence quite like this. There must be a catch in it somewhere.'

'Well, we do have a reason. We think you may be able to help us with another, even more serious aspect of this inquiry but you must be aware all of this is classified. No sensational stories wired back to the UK under any circumstances.'

'OK, but you are going to let me tell this story at some stage, I hope? I need to make a living, you know.'

'You'll have your story eventually. Just be patient and wait until one or two very dangerous people are under lock and key. It's going to be in your interests as well because if you fall into their hands a second time the outcome may be nasty. Are you prepared to go along with us? We'll be right behind you but won't be able to eliminate the dangers completely.'

I gave Clarke the assurances he wanted. Deeply entrenched as I was in this adventure, the depth of which I could not possibly have imagined a few weeks before, there was no going back. The promise of a story told with the backing of America's top security organisation, was also appealing to a freelance still looking for his first break and his first hard-earned fee.

Although now more or less in the picture about recent activities in and around Mount Desert Island, my surprisingly friendly agent still had another part of the story he wanted me to be aware of in case it impacted on recent developments.

'Tell me, did the story about the Russian super-trawler sinking off the coast of Nova Scotia taking with it a pile of Russian surveillance equipment, reach your ears in the UK?' Clarke wanted to know.

I said I did dimly recall such an incident but the story only lasted a day or two and then disappeared off the front pages. 'Weren't there accusations from the Russians that it had been sunk by an American warship?' I queried

'Quite so, and there was also a ridiculous theory traded by the Russians that the sinking was a revenge attack for the suspected sabotage of an American cruiser which went down off the North Cape with 140 men on board. Helped by grieving relatives, rumours multiplied and relatives in Russia and here demanded answers.

'Both sides pleaded innocence but both sides went to extraordinary lengths to try to locate their vessels. Most attention fell on the Russian efforts because they displayed a degree of desperation, which indicated the gear that sank with the ship was pretty important to them. The efforts of both countries failed to yield results and the incidents might have passed into history if two celebrity psychics, Rashnin and Spicer hadn't started rival bids to use their powers to help in the search.'

The details of this incident started to come to mind although I had no recollection of Stephen Spicer's involvement. I recalled it all happened at a time when scepticism had started to grow apace in the UK, even in the tabloids. The silly season had long passed and there were political scandals galore to keep editors happy.

In America, Clarke now told me, there had been a very different reaction. Relatives of the lost American crew, hotly in pursuit of an official inquiry, saw the possible revelations of psychics in a far more positive light. If nothing else, it might put the authorities under pressure to open a full-scale investigation. Quite surprisingly, the Russians, usually so practical and down to earth, had also been convinced that psychic phenomena might be brought into play to reach their valuable property lying on the bed of the Atlantic. All routes seem to lead to Mount Desert Island, probably because of its convenient location near the spot where the Russian ship sank. Its dense forest areas and the fact it was known as a quiet tourist spot with, at that time, little in the way of stifling internal security also proved attractive to official as well as unofficial investigators.

'We didn't know what had hit us at the time,' said Clarke, 'suddenly the island was alive with immigrants of the illegal, as well as legal variety. The job of the local police wasn't helped either by all the attention which had built up again around the 'haunted' mansion, bringing men and women claiming legitimate scientific interest. And then into all this walked two, not one, English psychics stating their only interest was in the mansion but seemingly having other agendas of a far more serious nature, probably forced upon them by opposing factions.

'It didn't stop there, even. Just to complicate matters we then discovered there was a male septuagenarian hobbling around the island showing a particular interest in the mansion. We couldn't bring ourselves to believe this old chap was a Russian spy but we have been keeping an eye on him. For a while, we even toyed with the idea he might have something to do with the death of Yasha Rashnin. On top of all that, you arrive bringing another copy of that bloody stupid *Gemstone File* with you.

'Is it bloody stupid?' I asked, 'I'm beginning to think there are people this side of the Atlantic who are still disturbed by some of its content.'

'Of course it's stupid,' said Clarke irritably. 'It's become the 20th century way of stirring up trouble. Throw around a few accusations and hope some of them stick. Your man Spicer walked right into it on his first visit over here. He should have worked it out a lot earlier that someone was using him.'

'He did in the end,' I suggested, 'because he arrived back home in a hurry and told the world he didn't want to be known as a psychic any longer. What totally took me by surprise was the appearance of one of his friends on my doorstep three years later telling me Spicer had gone back to America again. Why do you think he came back?'

Clarke pointed out that it was all very different the second time. Both men started shouting their mouths off about how they could interfere with all sorts of installations and security officials started to think they ought to check it out, if for no other reason than to eliminate outlandish claims by people who said they had these special powers.

'The sunken cruiser stories just added to all the confusion. Great, no doubt, for you reporters but a nightmare for us. There are people in the Pentagon who still think we have Russian spies on the island and they insist we keep looking.'

Getting back to present day affairs, I asked whether there was any doubt about how Rashnin died.

'It looks as though the same gang, who grabbed you in error, persuaded Rashnin to help them with the experiment I have been describing. Wrecking a country's electricity grid or even part of it might well appeal to terrorist organisations anywhere in the world. Meddling with radar installations might be even more attractive to some undesirable elements. The little bunch we have on the island (certainly not Russian spies whatever the Pentagon says) go about their work in a pretty amateurish sort of way but they've still managed to create too many problems for my liking. We'll mop them up over the next week or so, as soon as we have gathered what information we can from this place.'

'If they thought they had their hands on Stephen Spicer when they grabbed me, what's the theory? ---a straight-forward replacement for the departed Yasha Rashnin? They took a risk coming out of hiding didn't they?'

Clarke thought there was more to it than that. 'By the time you were on your way, they had worked out that Spicer, who was already on the island, should have been their prize in the first place. In their own dealings with Rashnin they had realised he was something of a fraud, his powers were nothing like they had been built up to be.'

'Do you think they killed him, then?'

'Maybe, but probably not intentionally, the burns on his body point more to an experiment that went wrong.'

Feeling it was time I reciprocated, I endeavoured to give Clarke a broad picture of what Rashnin had been famous for in the UK. He had been identified by one of America's best-known magicians as a man with deft skill but one who couldn't resist dressing up his performances as something far more significant than a collection of tricks. He was arrogant and boastful and probably thought he was quite capable of corrupting a vital part of an electricity grid without hurting himself.

Spicer, on the other hand, had been very brash in the early days, even writing books, so badly researched that a five-year-old could have spotted the inconsistencies. I thought his success could partly be attributed to a British press desperately eager to endorse whatever he did just to acquire sensational copy. His refusal to offer himself up for supervised experiments compounded the theory that he, too, was taking his audiences for a ride.

Clarke listened intently but stuck stubbornly to his theory that Spicer could have been tempted to throw in his lot with the same gang who brought about Rashnin's demise. 'I suspect he might be with them now,' said Clarke, 'when they went looking for him at the airport they mixed him up with you but the game has changed since then.'

Not expecting an answer, I asked Clarke whether it was his men who had watched me approach the young man with a placard at Bangor airport.

His frankness had not dried up: 'That was one of our successes. Despite his speedy get-away we did catch up with him. He was one of the youngest members of the gang and gave us some invaluable information about the people he was working with. He was terrified and is going to need our protection for a while.'

Clarke thought the boy had been told to go to the Bar Harbor airport but went to Bangor by mistake.

I was sure they were wrong about Stephen Spicer's possible involvement but having so far failed to meet up with him, I had no positive evidence that would get him off the hook. It was one of those times when it seemed better to keep one's theories to oneself.

'So how do you want to use me? Flattered as I am to be seconded by the US security services, I am anxious to complete my own little mission, make a penny or two out of the international press and get back to my family.'

'We won't keep you around longer than necessary but just remember you could still be languishing in that cell down the road. Our priority is to get our hands on Spicer. You may think he's not our man but we believe he has a lot to answer for.'

'OK, so how do I go about this? I'm not sure unless he is very frightened, that Stephen will want to see me. We're not exactly good friends.'

Clarke said the plan was to drop me within a reasonable distance of the mansion, far enough away to make it look as if I had arrived there on foot. They'd make it known locally that an English journalist had travelled to the island to talk to scientists equipped with special gear capable of recording the midnight walks of the lady in the white wedding dress.

I didn't think much of the plan because if Stephen was up to no good he wouldn't come within miles of the mansion. Clarke thought differently so after allowing me a night's sleep he would send transport to my lodgings the next day to put me down near the mansion.

'Make sure, then, I don't get kidnapped a second time,' I urged him, 'I don't fancy telling my story from a hospital bed or, on the really black side, being washed ashore at Thunder Hole.'

'We'll take care of you, we won't be far away,' Clarke promised. 'By the way if you bump into the elderly wanderer just let him continue wandering. We had a suspicion he and Spicer might meet, so thought it worthwhile to leave him on the loose to see what transpired.'

I still wasn't convinced. My assessment was that some aspects of law enforcement and security on this island would make the Keystone Cops look efficient. But I was too far down the road now to start changing horses. I had to go along with their plans or head back to the UK frustrated and penniless.

17

Shades of the Titanic

Back in my lodgings, I realised that although several days had passed since my arrival at Bar Harbor there had been no time to take in my surroundings or to review the progress of what was turning out to be the zaniest journalistic mission of my career. With a few hours to myself, I had a chance to mull over the fast-moving events of the last few days. How, I asked myself, had my original mission to discover the whereabouts of Stephen Spicer moved furiously forward to a point where I was now agreeing to become a decoy for a branch of an American security agency? Sandwiched between all this was a session in a dank, dark cellar where many of my preconceived notions about life and death had been challenged. Thank goodness, I didn't have to account for my actions to an editor or to my wife. Both would have had serious doubts about my state of mind.

By now, I had hoped I would be sending copy back to the UK giving colourful accounts of the activities of Stephen Spicer, as well as news on the movements and activities of the elusive Yasha Rashnin. But Jasper Clarke had firmly tied my hands. I either had to go along with him or throw caution to the winds and risk a heavy penalty, probably more detention or even prosecution. There was no doubt that the murder of Rashnin would now be dominating the front pages in England and I was probably losing my chance to sell my personal story. But I had been in the newspaper game long enough to know a promise not to interfere with police inquiries was a promise not to be broken. Being offered first bite of the cherry after inquiries had been completed was incentive enough to remain discreet at this stage.

From my window, I had a good view of the bay and spent a while watching the fishermen moving between their colourful buoys setting their lobster traps. People were heading out for an evening walk along the historic Shore Path, from which they hoped to get a better view of the *Cunard Venturer*, one of the many cruise liners that made Frenchman Bay an important port of call. I wondered why quite so many were gathering at the town pier but then surmised that this was probably the *Venturer's* first visit to Bar Harbor. There was always a good turnout to see the latest cruise liner and I was tempted to down tools and join them.

The light was fading, so putting this thought aside, I extracted the copy of Violet Jessop's Titanic diaries from my suitcase, and started to enjoy some of her simple, captivating recollections of life as a stewardess. Although a humble woman, with little education, she wrote very vividly and movingly about the conditions on the Titanic, before and after people had been ordered to the lifeboats. Until now, I had no reason to suspect the story of the distraught bride-to-be and her reaction to the loss of her would-be husband was flawed in any way. Madeline McWhirter's suicide, as far as I could gather, was an historic fact but the fate of the British actor crossing the Atlantic for his wedding ceremony not so clear. Most bodies dragged from the sea were identified but Albert Duncan was never found.

Tiredness was beginning to take its toll and the diaries slipped through my fingers as my eyes started to close. The thud of the book hitting the floor jolted me back into consciousness and for the first time since listening to the tourist guide's version of the tragedy all those years ago, telling his party about the death of the girl in the white dress, I wondered why there had not been more speculation about the fate of the man she was about to marry. Somebody must have asked the question: 'Why was his the only body not recovered?'

I would not be striding the corridors of the mansion tomorrow with expectations of finding an answer to that question, nor of encountering an apparition of a woman in white moving from room to room without the need to open doors. Nevertheless, my senses had been stirred enough on my previous visit not to be quite so cynical about paranormal claims. I had to remind myself that back in my own university town and in many parts of America serious research was being carried out into the vagaries of the human brain and the many different ways human beings reacted to certain situations.

Even allowing for the recent jolt to my thinking about the ultimate fate of the human soul, I still found it impossible to take on board the possibility that Stephen Spicer and his like could have any sort of link with 'the other side' as they liked to call it. And yet demons and a devil were mentioned enough times in the Bible to make serious study of their characteristics and behaviour an exercise not to be scorned at.

In danger of nodding off again, I leant forward to pick up the diaries. The pages had opened at a point where the author had given a dramatic account of how hundreds of Titanic passengers had faced the possibility of a watery death, many of them calmly and stoically. It was the moment when women and children were instructed to take to the boats and there must have been many, especially the ill-fated men left on board, who found themselves praying for the first time. It is an accepted fact that everyone, even atheists, pray at desperate times in their life.

My attention was caught by Violet Jessop's description of the behaviour of male passengers, the majority caring only for the safety of their womenfolk and children. There was, however, one exception. As I read through this passage, the possibility of any link between the human drama at the McWhirter mansion and what had happened aboard the Titanic couldn't have been further from my mind, until a final paragraph described the panic of one particular male passenger. Violet wrote:-

'A few women near me started to cry loudly when they realised a parting had to take place, their husbands standing silently by. They were Poles and could not understand a word of English. Surely a terrible plight to be among a crowd in such a situation and not be able to understand anything that is being said.

Boats were now being lowered more rapidly and a crowd of foreigners was brought forward by a steward from the third class. They dashed eagerly, as one man, over to a boat, almost more than the officer could control. But he regained order and managed to get the boat away. It descended slowly, uncertainly at first, now one end up and then the other. Some men nearby were throwing things over the side---deck chairs, rafts or any wooden thing lying nearby.

Suddenly, the crowd of people beside me parted. A man dashed to the ship's side, and before anyone could stop him, hurled himself into the descending boat. There was a murmur of amazement and disapproval.'

If Stephen or any of his psychic friends had been around, they would probably have told me that the page with this account didn't open by accident but was pre-determined. I was not in a frame of mind to draw any such conclusion.

I was, however, profoundly affected by one coincidence. I had travelled to a part of the world where there were still strong reminders of the Titanic's tragic demise---certainly not on my mind when I set out--- and in my luggage was a book by a woman who recorded her experiences in great detail. As well as her memories of those terrible moments when the ship had to be abandoned, Violet Jessop described the scenes of grief, as people waited for Titanic's survivors to be brought ashore. Not far away from Bar Harbor, at Halifax, was a cemetery where many passengers, mostly male, were buried and not so very far to the east the Titanic still lay on the seabed. Some would have seen these facts as interesting clues to the origin of the stories that had built up around the McWhirter mansion. Such thoughts had not entered my mind. They would soon.

I put the book down, treated myself to a shower, asked my understanding landlady to send up a modest breakfast before Clarke's man arrived, and went to bed. I did have an unpleasant dream reminiscent of the one experienced on my journey out. Thankfully, it didn't last long and I enjoyed a measure of good quality sleep before the dawn started to break.

I was dropped off as arranged within a mile of the mansion and decided to approach and enter the building in much the same way as I had before. This time I was relying on Clarke and his squad to make sure no one impeded my progress. The gang responsible for my kidnapping would surely not dare to show themselves now they had become the hunted rather than the hunter.

The deadly hush that hung over the garden and building on my last visit to the mansion had not changed; bird song seemed absent and inside there was the same damp coldness common to buildings left empty for long periods but particularly chilling in any place with an unhappy history. The extent to which the imagination plays a part in creating these feelings probably boils down to individual temperaments. On the ground floor, at least, all seemed to be as it was a few days ago. It did surprise me, however, that those given charge of the building never seemed to lock it up.

Taking the very briefest glance at the cellar door, now closed, I headed for the room with the automatic writing and here I was in for yet another surprise. All around was evidence of another visitor, and one that didn't bother to cover his tracks. Crayons of various colours lay on the floor, some trodden on, making a mess on the wooden floorboards.

But it was the walls, which had been given a thorough working over. Many of *The Gemstone File* entries were barely readable. Some, those in coloured crayon had been partially rubbed out; others had been subject to destructive scribbling of the sort one might associate with the actions of an ill-disciplined child. The distortions did not worry me greatly because I had already come to the conclusion the writings in this room were not of the same artistic merit as those decorating the walls back in Stephen's cottage. But who would want to travel many miles to a remote mansion to vent their feelings in this manner?

As I wandered to the far end of the room, I became aware that one wall, unmarked on my previous visit as far as I could remember, now had a message totally unrelated to anything in *The Gemstone File*. It was signed Wallace Hartley and I was immediately struck by the thought that this was a name I had come across since leaving English shores. It didn't take me too long to recall that this was another name mentioned by Violet Jessop in her diaries. Hartley was the orchestra leader and musical director on the Titanic and had died with hundreds of other male passengers.

Although some of the material could well have been lifted from the diaries, details were included which Violet couldn't have recorded because she was in a lifeboat when the Titanic finally disappeared under the waves. Something else didn't ring true. The message was purportedly signed by Hartley but written as though he was an eyewitness, not the man at the heart of the drama:

'*Hartley was instructed to move the players forward into the boat deck lobby atop the main staircase. The seven could continue playing as before because an upright piano was located permanently there. After having completed several selections, Hartley moved his men once more. Temporarily dismissed, they all trooped below, all the way down to E Deck, to don overcoats and lifejackets before reassembling at their third venue of the night...*'

The writing broke off at this point and I wondered why, if this was intended to be accepted as a genuine 'other side' message, it was not written in the first person. Instead, it read just like an excerpt from

194

the diaries. Perhaps the scribbler, recognising his stupidity, suddenly curtailed his foolish attempt to deceive.

The diaries of Violet Jessop recorded in vivid detail the musicians' activities and musical programme on the night of the sinking but written accounts vary on the type of music they were playing at the crucial hour. Just why this mattered so much to historians is anyone's guess but arguments continue to this day as to whether it was hymn tunes they were playing or popular ragtime to keep up the spirits of the passengers.

It was the message on the opposite wall that caught my eye on this second visit. Again, it was signed by Wallace Hartley but the signature looked nothing like the other one in the same room. The content was also different and actually contested the other version:

'*I have read the rubbish opposite and want you to know that this was put there by a human hand. I watched him at work, trying to copy something from a piece of paper and then attempting to rub it out with a handkerchief. To scare him I knocked over an ornament because I felt he was attempting to discredit us unfortunate beings who cannot escape the world despite the demise of our physical bodies. For the record, I can tell you that six of us played the final lament on the Titanic. One musician had to drop out because no piano was available on deck. We did play hymns including Nearer My God to Thee, heard by many in the lifeboats, but we also played familiar tunes which passengers had danced to or listened to ever since Southampton'*--- Wallace Hartley.*

Sitting cross-legged in the middle of the floor, I tried to put all the bits and pieces together and come to some conclusion about this collection of bizarre messages, which filled the walls of the room. The possibilities were endless. Was the first message written by a prankster who fled when an ornament crashed to the floor? Did Rashnin find his way to the mansion and decide to make Stephen look stupid? Did Stephen pay a visit and obliterate some of the material because he felt it to be a poor imitation of his own work? Or should we start embracing the thought that at least one of the messages was written by Wallace Hartley's departed spirit?

While all these possibilities and several more were buzzing around in my brain, I spotted more scrawls partly obscured by an old wardrobe at the far end of the room. Wondering how much more of this spooky nonsense I could take, I approached with caution and was just able to read:

'*I came back, darling, just once because I thought you would be here somewhere...I didn't find you...where are you?...tell me, please tell me, if you can.*' Faint, so faint that it was hardly discernible, was the name *Maddie.*

Assuming this was not a genuine message from the departed bride-to-be, Madeline---and I had still not approached a point in my thinking that would suggest it might be---then who would have had the desire to keep persuading others he had the gift of communicating with long-departed loved ones? The 'Maddie' message was neat, unlike the other 'automatic' writings in the room, and suddenly I felt certain Stephen had been here. This was his sort of work but just whom was he trying to impress? The message seemed to indicate that Maddie was looking for her long lost lover. But why would Maddie's spirit, even with all the benefits of perception granted to those in the spiritual world, think she would find the man she might have married in the almost derelict remains of her former home?

My experience in the cellar had obviously had greater impact than I first imagined because I found myself wondering whether research would eventually prove there is a dynamic force in some people allowing them to use their brain in a way most of us would find incomprehensible. I could still recall one of the papers presented at the Divinity School in Trentbridge, which dismissed the mesmeric trance state (hypnosis) as occultism. Some delegates protested that the materialist arguments could no longer be sustained and appealed to scientists to demonstrate some humility when considering the possibility of paranormal phenomena.

I set off along the corridor towards the stairs wondering how Stephen could have broken through the police cordon to reach the mansion if, in fact, I was right and he had paid a recent visit. I was surprised that so little attention appeared to have been paid to the building by either the police or the selling agents. My problem now was how to get to Stephen and talk to him before he was taken into custody, which seemed inevitable. That could be a tall order.

I walked towards the back of the mansion intending to take the back staircase; then remembered the locked room I had ignored on my previous visit. I casually tried the door handle as I passed and to my surprise, it yielded to the slightest pressure. Coming from within was a faint almost indescribable sound, something between a moan and a chant which did nothing for my already jangled nerves.

Gently, I pushed the door far enough to see into the room and there seated on a rickety chair with his back to me was an elderly man with long, white hair. If this had been night-time not early morning, I might well have thought I was getting my first introduction to a real ghost! In front of him was an improvised, portable altar, not bearing a cross but decorated with flowers arranged around a portrait in a silver frame.

The moaning came from the mouth of the old man, who I felt sure was the same person I had seen disappearing into the forest on my last visit. He was holding a miniature recorder, which was emitting sombre background music, probably a monastery chant. He did not hear me at first and I was afraid of what his reaction would be if he suddenly became aware of my presence. This time I didn't want him to disappear, I wanted to encourage him to stay around and talk.

Not to cause him to panic, I went back into the corridor, walked a few yards in the other direction and then approached noisily, knocking on doors and allowing my feet the freedom to hit the wooden floorboards as they would normally. I don't know who was the most scared, him or me. Despite his age, he sprang from the chair energetically enough to send it skidding in my direction.

'Don't be frightened,' I tried to assure him, 'I'm not going to harm you but I would like to know why on a previous visit you scurried off when you heard me in the corridor. I don't think either of us have a right to be here, so from that point of view we're on equal terms.'

The old man walked away towards one of the windows facing out onto the rear gardens and seemed to be taking time to recover from the shock of being discovered going through his private ritual. When he turned to face me I could see he had been crying and even before either of us could utter a word, tears started to roll down his face again. I would claim that I am not easily lost for words but I was struggling on this occasion.

'Can I help you in any way?' I asked feebly, 'would it be better if we went into the garden and talked? I'm a good listener.'

'It wouldn't do any good' the old man croaked as he picked up a small suitcase and started packing away his portable shrine, 'comfort of any sort is in short supply in the world I have created for myself. Coming to Bar Harbor was my last chance to find peace of mind, or that is what I thought when I booked a passage on the liner you see in the bay.'

'The *Venturer* you mean? Excuse me for saying so but at your time of life wasn't that a slow way of coming to a place you hoped would dispel bad memories or whatever it is that is causing you so much distress.'

'None of your business,' the old man snapped, pulling out a large white handkerchief and wiping away a few remaining tears.

'Sorry, I just thought that speaking to a stranger about your problems is sometimes a better remedy than bottling them up.'

'You couldn't possibly understand. How do you off-load a secret part of your life to people who only want to condemn you? I've tried a few times over the years but I'm usually told to go away and stew in my own juice, I've only myself to blame.'

As he pushed by me, menacingly swinging his suitcase and heading for the staircase on which we had nearly met the first time, I tried once more to engage him in conversation: 'I won't tell you to stew in your own juice,' I promised, 'I just think we might be able to help each other. I've got myself into a bit of a mess these last few days and you may be able to throw some light on one or two of my problems.'

I watched him descend the stairs, his gait indicating that he was probably even older than I thought he was. He went out into the garden and was about to make a similar exit into the forest when he turned, walked towards me and then headed for the only seat left in the garden, a very rotten, wooden affair that looked barely capable of holding one body let alone two. I decided this was a half-hearted invitation to join him, an invitation I certainly didn't want to turn down.

18

A Coward's Confession

The old man, weariness beginning to overtake him, flopped onto one end of the garden seat and risking the possibility of it disintegrating, I took up occupation of what space was left at the other end. We sat for a while in complete silence. He was the first to speak. 'It won't mean anything to you or anyone else after all this time but in the early part of my life I was an actor with a reputation for being a bit of a ladies' man. That, as you can see, was a very long time ago. He paused again as if trying to pluck up courage to continue his story. 'I suppose you want to know what I was doing in that room up there. I thought I would never have to explain my actions to anyone because I found it easy to tuck myself out of sight. That was until you managed to creep up on me.

'I suppose you know who this mansion once belonged to? Henry McWhirter, one of America's top motor industry bosses, lived here with his family in the early part of the century. He had two daughters, Madeline and Beatrice, but Maddie was the apple of his eye. I had met them all when they were on a trip to Europe. They came to Stratford where I was a middle-of-the road member of the Shakespeare Company. I say middle of the road because although I had been quite well-known in repertory theatre, I never made it into the star billing category.'

So many questions were building up in my mind but the old man, already struggling to control his emotions, looked as if he might vanish into the wood again unless I curbed my impatience. I had started to ask a question but stopped when he admonished me. 'Please, now that I've started, let me finish. I guess you must be a reporter of some sort but I don't think I care about that any longer.'

He took another long pause, got up, walked around the seat, sat down again and then continued. 'The McWhirters came to see me playing *Malvolio* in *Twelfth Night*. Mr McWhirter was looked upon as a possible sponsor and the whole family came to a lavish public relations events. To cut a long story short Madeline and I fell in love, our romance blossomed but because of my busy career, I was able to make only one visit to this mansion. I was here long enough to propose and to my surprise, her father approved of the match. It was arranged that we would marry in the spring of 1912.'

It was a date that would have meant little to me if I had not been reading Violet's diaries. But now imprinted on my mind was the date the Titanic had gone to its watery grave---April 15, 1912.

'You're not going to tell me you were sailing on the Titanic, are you? Hardly any men survived and those that did were mainly crew members who knew how to launch and handle a lifeboat,' I said feeding off the knowledge I had acquired from Violet's diary.

The mere mention of the cruiser's name threatened to open the floodgates again but he pulled himself together and to my amazement, I found myself listening to a variation of the story a tourist guide had recounted on my previous short visit to Maine. Only this time it had a personal touch, the story was coming from the mouth of a very old man who was able to spell out amazing detail that only someone very closely connected to the family would have had access to. It was the story of the young daughter of a prosperous family who had killed herself following the apparent loss of her bridegroom-to-be aboard the Titanic.

In this previously beautiful but now over-grown and weed infested garden, I looked searchingly into the face of a man who looked totally bewildered and a long way from home. No, I told myself, what I was thinking was ridiculous. This guy may be ancient but the imagination would have to be stretched to breaking point to believe there was a link between him and a young bride-to-be, so desperate at her loss that she ended her life in the home of her own family.

He, in turn, was concentrating on my quizzical expression, guessing that probably I was adding two and two and beginning to make four. Maybe he was also thinking it was time to get things off his chest, to a stranger rather than a friend or colleague with a tendency to be judgmental. It was beginning to dawn on him, maybe, that if long-standing wounds were to be healed, he had to take this stranger into his confidence and explain the cause and nature of those wounds. That, I could now see, was the dilemma he was trying to come to terms with.

Could he open up a part of his life, the consequences of which he had bottled up for so long?

I was expecting a dramatic story but not one quite as heart-rending as the one slowly unfolding before me. 'Yes, I was aboard the Titanic,' he started to explain, 'yes I was on my way to join my bride-to-be. But long before we set sail I had started to wonder whether I was doing the right thing. Madeline and I were still very young and had seen so little of each other; we had never had time to cement our relationship. It was still based on a few romantic nights at Stratford and walks through the Cadillac Mountain during my one visit to the island.'

In faltering voice, Albert spoke of the variety of distractions that were common to all luxury liners but multiplied ten-fold on the glorious Titanic. One of the distractions was a very good-looking girl, travelling with her mother, both probably packed off by a rich Daddy while he enjoyed himself at home. 'The daughter made a b-line for me and for the first few days, we met on the dance floor where the music and the atmosphere took its toll. Our dancing became more and more intimate and it wasn't long before we were seeking the delights of an intimate stroll away from a crowded ballroom. Hand in hand on a deck, swaying enough to throw us closer together was still, in my book, pretty harmless stuff but I suppose I realised even then that it wasn't going to stop there.'

Albert said the inevitable seduction followed the usual pattern except that he never quite made up his mind whether he was seducing her or she was seducing him. Her behaviour since the start of the trip had suggested the latter. 'I was putty in her hands and when she returned from a trip to the bathroom, wearing, or almost wearing, the sort of diaphanous nightdress you only see in top-flight fashion magazines, I was done for. The nightcap on top of the wine already consumed broke down any remaining barriers and we had sex in a desperate sort of way.'

Albert admitted there was no meaningful relationship, no love, just high-octane sex that seemed great at the time but gave him a terrible hangover caused, not by alcohol, but by deep-seated guilt. Within minutes of untwining himself from her embrace, he started some serious self-recrimination: 'What have you done?' I asked myself, for God's sake you were on your way to get married.'

To this point, I had listened intently but there was one question I was bursting to ask: 'What were you doing on the *Titanic* anyway? It was a strange, slow and expensive way of travelling to be at the side of your bride-to-be. Didn't she raise any objections? Naïve as she might have been, she must have been aware of the pitfalls?'

Albert, looking more and more bereft as he unwound the details of his sad history, explained that he had joined the *Titanic* as part of a group of actors who were to provide the passengers, mainly wealthy, with one act plays or sketches as part of the entertainment programme. 'I thought it would be a great experience and although the money was not an issue, I would be earning a few pounds rather than paying for my passage.'

During the pauses in his story, I had already started to wonder how it came about that 50 years or more after the most dramatic of all sea disasters, I was sitting in a garden many hundreds of miles from the UK talking to an old man, who by all accounts should have been dead. Most of the male passengers had gone down with the liner when it struck an iceberg in 1912. How did this man, sitting beside me manage to escape? Tears began to gather again but I could see he was doing his utmost to control his emotions.

'So how did you survive? Were you one of the lucky male passengers asked to help crew a lifeboat or were you pulled from the freezing sea in the nick of time. I was under the impression that no one who fell or jumped into the ice cold water managed to live for more than a few minutes, is that so?'

Even as I posed this question, the description in Violet's diaries of the panic-stricken male passenger came vividly back to mind--- '*Suddenly the crowd of people beside me parted. A man dashed to the ship's side and before anyone could stop him, hurled himself into the descending boat. There was a murmur of amazement and disapproval.*'

Without really realising it, I had voiced those last few words, loud enough for Albert to hear---'there was a murmur of amazement and disapproval.' It wasn't meant as an accusation, just an acknowledgement of what I thought Albert might be trying to tell me.

It was a terrible mistake on my part to let these words slip out at that particular moment. Albert's whole body tensed and he demanded to know what I was saying. 'You weren't there. You don't know what happened. You just want to turn this into another story, don't you? Making things up as you go along. That's what your profession does all the time, isn't it?'

There was only one way out now and that was to tell Albert I had come across an account of how passengers acted during the final minutes of the liner's existence. One crew member had described how a male passenger had elbowed his way through the crowd on the ship's rail and hurled himself into one of the lifeboats. 'In no way was I implying I thought you were that person,' I said in an effort to placate this hypersensitive old man.

'Well, you're well on your way to that exclusive I'm sure you're looking for,' said Albert, now looking totally devastated and pathetically frail. 'Yes, I was the foul person who pushed everyone aside and leapt into the already over-loaded lifeboat.............'

Albert couldn't continue. His uncontrollable tears fell onto the grass in mini-waterfall volumes. Probably for the first time in his career, this cynical journalist found himself putting an arm around the shoulders of the person he was interviewing. Pity photographer, Bob Harding, wasn't around. It would have been the picture of a lifetime, one that might have lifted journalists out of the top spot in the league of most despised professions. It was confirmation of something that maybe only our closest friends really know that most of us have a soft spot. It just stays buried most of the time.

Two or three minutes must have passed before I felt Albert was in any sort of condition to continue and wind up his story. For his sake, it was something he was going to have to do.

'So I presume the boat you jumped into brought you to safety? What made you decide not to continue your journey and head for Mount Cadillac?' Even as I asked this question, I realised it could rate as just about the most unfeeling and idiotic question I had ever asked or was likely to ask.

Albert realised that, too, but decided it was probably best to finish his tale, in the hope that the telling of it could lead to a calmer state of mind than he had experienced for many a long year.

'When the *Carpathia*—that was the ship that eventually picked us all up---arrived back in New York, there was absolute chaos as sympathisers and media teams battled to get close to those who had survived. I had already decided any future I might have had with Maddie was no more. My infidelity was bad enough but my cowardly action in leaping into a boat as other men said final goodbyes to their wives and loved ones would soon be uncovered if I stayed around. Fortunately, the people I had shared a lifeboat with did not recognise me and I judged that if I disappeared quickly enough it would be assumed I had drowned with the other 1500 victims.'

'So where did you go? And why this trip to the Cadillac Mountain half a century later?'

'Eventually, after living rough in the States for several months I returned to England and changed my name. I was able to join a relatively unknown repertory company and travel around England anonymously. I didn't read many newspapers, certainly not any from America, and so I didn't get to know the story of Maddie's suicide for several years. Eventually, I came across her father's obituary in which there was a brief reference to Maddie's short and tragic life and the reason for her suicide. I learned later that the press had dug out a few details about me from their files, accepted that I had not survived the *Titanic* tragedy and told the world that Madeline McWhirter had died from a broken heart.'

'......and they were still telling that story when I first came to Maine and was touring the Cadillac Mountain. You haven't answered the other part of my question, why come back now?'

'You know how it happens, one of your lot in search of an angle, decides the story will excite less scrupulous sections of the media, and produces a new colourful version whenever there is a bit of space to fill.'

Many years after his return to his home country, he had read in one publication that the McWhirter mansion was becoming a centre of attention in the psychic community. 'A couple of house agents, by this time despairing of ever finding a conventional buyer, fanned the flames by saying Madeline had been seen walking the corridors of the mansion in a white dress. In desperation, they were trying to appeal to a small minority of house-hunters who get a thrill out of living in a "haunted" house. More than one potential buyer said the building had a forbidding atmosphere and a couple of Hollywood minor "celebs", seeking publicity no doubt, claimed they had an encounter with a young woman who just evaporated when they attempted to speak to her.'

Albert said the shock of reading these reports, whether inventions or not, brought memories flooding back and after one terrifying nightmare came to the conclusion some sort of exorcism was needed. 'I planned to pose as an interested buyer, cross the Atlantic and make a return visit to the mansion. I'm beginning to realise what a fool I was, but at that time I started to believe the only way of ridding myself of guilt was to make some sort of contact with Maddie. I even spent a half day in the local library reading spiritualist magazines and convincing myself there was "another place" and my intended might be there. This feeling was heightened on my second visit to the mansion when, given the freedom of the place by the selling agent, I walked into one of the rooms and found alongside many bizarre wall scribblings, a brief message that appeared to have been written by someone's departed spirit. In my emotional state, I convinced myself this was genuine.'

Albert then described how he returned to the mansion with a few objects he thought might enable a contact to be made. This was what the book in his local library said one had to do. The package he put together included a tape of music he thought could sooth his mind and make him more receptive. Nothing happened. Then on a third visit, he heard someone faintly whistling and walked into a room where to his amazement a young man with a crayon in his hand was adding to the mass of material already covering large sections of the wall.

'I asked him what he was doing there and he claimed to be a serious researcher looking into reports that the mansion was haunted. He astounded me when he said he could reach people who had departed and when I eagerly told him about Maddie he said there was a possible chance he could contact her. It was something he had done for other people in the past,' he assured me.

'A young man, can you describe him to me?' I asked. Albert did this without difficulty and it was obvious he had had a meeting with Stephen Spicer. 'What did he suggest you do? Was the shrine his idea?'

'No, but he said I was moving along the right lines. How wrong he was. When you burst into the room no doubt you could see it wasn't working very well. I was beginning to believe this was my punishment; never to be allowed to free my conscience from the torment it had been in all these years.'

As we drifted into a period of silence, with me trying desperately to think how I could help this sad man, I remembered a small piece of paper that had fallen out of the cellar Bible. It had been used as a marker. I had no time to study it in detail but recalled it was a tract on forgiveness that I had stuffed into my pocket as I scurried frantically up the cellar staircase. To my surprise, it was still there.

Albert was lost in his thoughts and in no hurry to continue our conversation so I was able to take a closer look at the words on this scrap of paper and realised it might contain just the sort of message Albert needed.

'Albert, it may sound crazy but I think I may have found something which could give you comfort. You have buried secrets in your heart for years and have come all this way because you think you might meet up with Madeline in some way and ask her to forgive you. What maybe you have to understand is that Madeline can't forgive you whatever spiritualists or psychics try to tell you. Forgiveness has to come from a very different source, a fact I started to come to terms with very recently.' Attempting to put the tract into Albert's hand, I suggested the words expressed there might help him find the peace he was seeking.

Albert's expression told me he thought he was about to get another sermon. 'You're talking in riddles. Don't try to humour me,' he said angrily. 'How can that bit of paper help me? More pious words, I imagine.'

'I don't know whether you're going to find them pious or not, but they could help you in a way they have started to help me.'

I explained to Albert how I had been accidentally shut away for a week with only a Bible to keep me company and how it had moved me to review the sort of life I have been leading and dwell upon a few home truths.

'I think I know where you're going,' said Albert, 'but don't bother; I had all that stuff about Jesus as a boy and I started to believe. But when I most needed him, he let me down. Where was he when all those people died on the *Titanic* and where was he when I was trying to put my life back together after the disaster?'

Now I'm in trouble, I thought, how can someone who a week or two ago would have made more or less the same point begin to say something useful to a man who had been suffering mental torture for half a century? If the experience in the cellar meant anything, I was about to get the first real test of my understanding and my sincerity.

'I don't want to preach Albert, I have neither the wisdom nor the ability to do so but perhaps we were both meant to come together to share our problems at this point in our lives.'

Albert looked as though he was about to walk away in disgust again but then changed his mind and said: 'OK, then, let's have it. What little pearl of wisdom did you dig out of your cellar?'

'It is by an *author unknown,* and its about forgiveness,' I said as I tried to smooth the creased paper in order to get better sight of the words. 'It says it takes only a few seconds to open up profound wounds in those we love but it can take many years to heal them.'

'You don't have to tell me that,' mumbled Albert, 'I've lived my life trying to cope with a gaping wound.'

'Yes, I know,' I said, trying not to sound irritated, 'but your wound was caused by yourself. You were in control, or thought you were, you decided to take a leisurely trip on the Titanic, you allowed a relationship to develop on board, it was you who lost your courage and decided to jump into the lifeboat.'

'Shut up! How dare you judge me? You have no idea of the terror we were all experiencing on that terrible day. In my shoes you might have done exactly the same thing.'

'I may well have done,' I volunteered, 'but I'm only trying to point out that there might be a solution to our problems even if they have festered for years. And I don't think trying to reach someone you have harmed and is no longer in this world is the answer. What my recent experience taught me is I have to look beyond the trivial matters filling my life and think a little bit more about others who are less fortunate.'

'Like me? Don't think that is going to get you anywhere. I'm just a hopeless case. Bet the next thing you are going to say is that I should pray. I've tried that but God is never around when I want him. After all I've done, he is never going to forgive me anyway.'

There was so much I wanted to say in reply but I felt totally inadequate and realised I would have to put my own house in order before I could help someone so bruised by life as Albert was. I would need to seek forgiveness myself before having the conviction to help people like Albert, who felt his dreadful behaviour gave him no chance. Would I be able to convince first myself and then someone like him that the door was always open? It sounded simple enough in theory. But in practice?

Albert handed me back the tract on forgiveness and as he did so I noticed the message had an important footnote. It stressed the importance of forgiving one another but that was not all. We had to go one stage further: '*We must also learn to forgive ourselves,*' it said.

'Perhaps even at your late stage in life, this is something you must make a priority,' I suggested. For the first time, there was a hint of relief on Albert's craggy face. 'At least that's worth thinking about,' he said.

That was about as far as we were going to get, bearing in mind it was very much a case of the blind leading the blind. However, there was one piece of information I wanted from Albert before we parted. 'What about the scribblings on the wall supposedly from Maddie and people aboard the Titanic. Who was responsible for these?'

'Most of it was done by that psychic fellow. He sent me out of the room and when I came back, it was all there, apart from the one message I had added, hoping Madeline would respond. I think I now know what a futile gesture that was. I still wonder, though, where he got all his information about the last hours of the Titanic.'

'I think I can answer that query for you,' I said taking a copy of Violet's diaries from my pocket.

19

The Witch of Endor

Without another word, Albert got up from his seat and walked towards the trees as he had done on a previous occasion. But this time he turned at the edge of the forest and called out: 'Thanks for listening, I'll think about what you've been telling me but it won't make any difference, I'm quite sure of that.'

'Give it a chance,' I shouted,' before it's too late.' He waved and disappeared. I sat for a while trying to convince myself that perhaps I had been of some help. Maybe I was on my way to becoming a Christian of the genuine sort but it was probably a little premature to be trying my hand at evangelism. I had done my best.

There were still matters I wanted to clear up in the mansion without the added complication of someone like Albert on site. Making a short detour to satisfy myself my movements were not being observed, I passed through the mansion's front door, still wondering why no attempt had been made to make the building secure. I had very mixed feelings about carrying out another sortie because the panic of being locked away in the cellar was too recent a memory just to cast aside. My prejudices, my contorted values, my preconceptions were still suffering from the battering they had taken. Not before time, some might have said, but still painful. One conviction remained unshaken. Communication with the dead was not an option for anyone. And nothing could persuade me I would be meeting Maddie's ghost on this second visit to the mansion.

I walked into the same eerie silence I had found so disturbing during the previous exploration but one of the reasons for this second visit was to focus on the automatic writings to see if there were any clues, missed the first time, about their creator. I also had to remember I was there as bait to trap Stephen---an enforced role I didn't relish or intend to take seriously.

The mansion was a big place to search but having briskly walked both corridors and opened all doors, believing by now that the only likely visitor would have been Stephen Spicer, I found no one.

Descending the staircase once again, I had to pass the cellar door before releasing myself back into the fresh air. Taking a quick look at the entrance to my recent prison, I was surprised to see that the door was firmly shut because I was convinced I had left it open after making my escape. It was another indication that someone had been in the building since my first visit.

Just the sight of the door gave me a queasy feeling. I certainly had no intention of putting one foot on those steps again, even though I was curious to know whether the set-up down below might have changed in any way.

There was no business card prominently placed on this occasion but I could hardly miss a small slip of paper sticking out an inch or two below the door's bottom edge. Glancing around in furtive manner, I bent and retrieved the paper, which had been squeezed through the tiniest of gaps. Written on it in a shaky hand were the words: *I'm trapped. Please get me out!*

Remembering what the discovery of a card had led to not many days previously, my first instinct was to turn on my heel and head for the forest. How could I be sure, I thought irrationally, if I opened that door whether by one means or another I would finish up inside enduring another period of enforced solitude. But journalists aren't meant to be reluctant adventurers, timid to the point of not following up a possible lead. A lead? What was I thinking about? This wasn't nice friendly Trentbridge; it was a very strange residence in the heart of a beautiful but disconcerting forest area. The Cadillac Mountain, once idealised by me, had already offered up enough nasty surprises to last a lifetime but so far little material or evidence I could mould into a story.

Looking about me to make sure no one was lurking in the shadows, I grabbed the same large chair, which I had thought would protect my point of exit on a previous occasion, opened the door purposefully and once again jammed the chair against it. Still determined not to walk down the stone steps, I stood at the top and shouted: 'Anyone down there?'

There was movement as someone or something crossed the tiny beam of light which had been my salvation a week or so back. As my eyes became accustomed to the dimness of the cellar, I realised that sitting at the table was a man who immediately looked familiar because of his long, straggly hair and generally dishevelled appearance. My search covering many hundreds of miles had come to an end. In the most extraordinary circumstances I could now meet and talk with Stephen Spicer once more. The man who had managed to keep out of my way despite chasing him through towns and villages of two countries was looking up at me in so casual a manner, one might have thought we regularly met in distant cellars.

It was an odd coming together. Stephen didn't leap up the stairs as I had done when freedom beckoned. 'Oh, its you' he said almost in a whisper and then returned his gaze to the one item still lying on the table….the big blue book which had been my only companion. It was open at a place even I knew must be the pages of Revelations, that disturbing final section of the Bible which frightens so many because of the seemingly brutal way it sorts out the wheat from the chaff.

Making absolutely sure that the chair was firmly embedded in the bottom of the cellar door, I advanced a few steps downwards and asked Stephen if he was all right. Had he been in the cellar long? A more vital question than it first seemed because if his imprisonment could be measured in days rather than hours, it left me in some doubt about who had mutilated the first floor wall writings.

I should have been used to the unexpected by now; not however for the remarkable confrontation which took place during my second visit to the McWhirters' cellar. The first experience had been alarming enough; the second would have tested the resilience of a Bishop. Instead of attempting to explain what had been happening to him or indicating curiosity about my presence in America Stephen, seemingly in no way desperate to regain his freedom, chose to tell me about his own detailed inspection of parts of the Bible. I tried to say something similar had happened to me but he did not appear to be listening, it was as though his mind had passed into another world, hopefully not the one he had claimed experience of in the past.

It seemed pointless to stand talking to him from the middle of the stone staircase, so taking yet another worried glance at the position of the iron door, I walked down the last few steps and perched myself on the end of the table. Stephen looked up at me and this time there was a stronger hint of recognition on his face.

Still avoiding any explanation of what had happened to him or showing any interest in my sudden appearance, he said quietly: 'I've had rather an interesting experience but I don't expect you'll understand,' he paused, laying his hand on the book before him, and adding: 'I doubt whether the Bible was essential reading at the journalists' training college'.

It did not seem to be the time or place to discuss the inadequate training of would-be journalists or their atheist tendencies and I couldn't wait to hear Stephen's account of his incarceration in my cellar. My cellar? Well, its influence and what happened there did seem likely to stay with me for the rest of my life.

With a serenity that hardly seemed real, Stephen continued his account: 'I was petrified at first, realising I had accidently locked myself in this hideous hell-hole with no apparent means of escape. Bits of food and drink were left lying around so I helped myself and then prowled around attempting to find ways of getting out. There was really nothing I could do except wait and listen for anyone who might come to the mansion...perhaps the security guys, who I knew were hanging around, or a prospective buyer.'

'Then I noticed this hefty volume lying in front of me. It seemed odd that the only reading material in this inhospitable place was a Bible. Couldn't they have left a couple of Readers' Digests, a Time magazine or something a bit more interesting? I hadn't looked at a Bible since my Sunday school days and that was a version specially written for kids.'

I was tempted to chip in with my own experiences sitting on the same chair at the same table. But I felt restrained from doing so and thought it probably better to allow Stephen to get his story off his chest before delving into all the other circumstances which had brought us together in this most unlikely of places.

'Tell me, then. What did you do? Decide that perhaps there was something to be gained from taking a close look at what your local vicar would have told you was the word of God?'

'Yes, I suppose some sort of thought like that went through my mind but I was distracted by words on a scrap of paper which had been used as a marker.' Stephen said the scrap seemed to have been torn from some sort of commentary and maintained the Bible was the world's best selling book. Not only had it survived, it had thrived despite being banned, burned, and ridiculed.

'My first reaction,' said Stephen, 'was that this was a piece of gross exaggeration, many secular books must have sold more, but why make a claim like that unless there were some facts to back it up. There was writing on the note, too, an instruction from someone or other to pick up the Bible and turn to the first book of Samuel, to a particular chapter and to particular verses. Who was meant to follow this advice?' he had wondered.

I continued to resist the temptation to interrupt and share my own experiences because I felt I was learning so much by listening to a man, who not so long ago was impressing his clients by 'making contact with spirits in another world.' I was also fascinated by the improvised bookmarker that had fallen into Stephen's hands. I was sure this hadn't been between the pages of the Bible I had studied. The thought occurred to me that someone could have visited the cellar and rearranged its contents. But surely not?

As I made a serious attempt to control my own meandering thoughts, I had to acknowledge that Stephen by one means or another had been directed towards words, which by no stretch of the imagination could have been considered his normal reading material.

'Did you follow the instruction to go to the book of Samuel? Or did you feel you had had enough of God by this time?' I asked.

'Oh yes, I turned to Samuel all right, not expecting to be confronted by a passage containing serious warnings which seemed aimed at me personally. The last few years of my life have been spent dabbling with intrusive spirits and here in the Bible was a chapter devoted to spiritists, mediums and, to my absolute surprise, a witch. Saul and the Witch of Endor was the heading to the chapter.'

The expression on my face would certainly have been one of amazement but Stephen didn't seem to notice. He had been pointed (dare we ask, by whom?) in a very different direction to the one I had taken just a week or so before. He had found himself rummaging around in a part of the Old Testament I must admit I had never come across. Nor had he.

'So what did you make of it?' I asked, trying not to sound too impatient and over inquisitive. 'I've never believed in ghosts or their younger poltergeist relatives but these apparitions were your bread and butter not so long ago. Did the Bible's slant worry you in any way? Did you think it ridiculous or were you challenged?'

Stephen explained how, having turned to Samuel, he found a hand-written note in the margin recommending the finder of these instructions to look at a section of Leviticus.

'I was staggered and not a little frightened, to find a passage headed *Detestable Practices*. I know some say the Old Testament was a device to frighten people into rejecting the devil. Maybe I would have said something similar at one time. But I would think twice before expressing that opinion after reading this warning:-

Let no one be found among you who sacrifices his son or daughter in the fire (Stephen couldn't resist interrupting himself at this point: Did they really do that, he asked me? But he didn't wait for an answer) *let no-one be found among you who practises divination or sorcery, interprets omens, engages in witchcraft or casts spells or is a medium or spiritist or who consults the dead. Anyone who does these things is detestable to the Lord).'*

Stephen was getting more and more wound up by the second: 'If that wasn't enough, just to press home the point Leviticus, whoever he was, said: *"Do not turn to mediums or seek out spiritists for you will be defiled by them"* and a little later *"I will set my face against the person who turns to mediums and spiritists to prostitute himself by following them, and I will cut them off from his people".'*

This was serious stuff. Stephen had found his way to a series of quite obscure passages in the Bible, obscure to most people but very relevant to a man who had made claims (and a large amount of money in the process) by reaching out to 'the other side'.

Overwhelmed by a mixture of apprehension and excitement, Stephen started telling me how Samuel had died and King Saul, no longer able to turn to the prophet, expelled mediums and spiritists from the land.

'Hang on,' I pleaded, 'aren't you going off at a bit of a tangent. Shall we try to bring things forward by at least 2000 years?'

No hope, Stephen was on a roll and was certainly not going to give up. He agreed the story started to get quite complicated and wondered whether it might be a little too involved for the likes of me. I ignored his barbed personal observation.

For a beginner Stephen was doing quite well but in his newfound enthusiasm, he was obviously getting out of his depth. And yes, I was in danger of drowning, too.

But he was certainly demonstrating perseverance. 'From then on the story gets even more difficult to understand,' said Stephen, correctly assessing that I was not going to be of much help. His clipped summary was that Saul, now scared to death by the Philistine army, changes his mind and in his desperation tells his attendants to go out and find a medium. One is found at Endor and Saul starts to act in the craziest manner. He disguises himself and sets out to meet the witch of Endor. Having found her, he asks her to consult a spirit of his choice and tells her to 'bring up Samuel.'

Was this really in the Bible or was a slightly deranged Stephen Spicer making it up? My ignorance was being exposed. With better background knowledge, I might have been able to contribute something useful at this stage. That wasn't going to happen but it was becoming clear to me now why this Old Testament story had struck a chord with Stephen.

It was also making me think about the extraordinary circumstances under which this young man had been brought to this particular passage in the Bible.

For the first time he was being made to think about what he had been doing during the latter half of his teens. Perhaps one or two incidents in his life were now being shown up in quite a different light. They could open up a door of understanding or, God forbid, unhinge him even further. I hoped the latter wouldn't be the case.

Seeing that I had become a little distracted, Stephen asked me almost angrily, 'Do you want me to go on or not?' I assured him that I did and again drew back from any attempt to start a discussion.

'Saul then asked the Witch of Endor what she was seeing. She replied: "I see a spirit coming up out of the ground." Saul immediately asked her to explain what he looked like. "An old man wearing a robe is coming up," she said. Saul knew it was Samuel and he prostrated himself with his face to the ground.'

It might seem shameful now but at the time, I had to exercise considerable self-control not to burst out laughing. Stephen, however, was not seeing anything amusing about an old man in a robe rising out of the ground. Looking quite gaunt, he stumbled on with the rest of the story, summarising how Samuel insisted that Saul should tell him why he had disturbed him 'by bringing him up.' Perhaps it was

Samuel's final rebuke which jolted Stephen into reflecting on the claims he had made to 'clients' about bringing messages from long departed relatives.

'Why do you consult me?' asked Samuel, 'now that the Lord has turned away from you and become your enemy. The Lord has torn the kingdom out of your hands and given it to one of your neighbours---to David.'

By any reckoning the worlds of Stephen and Saul were light years apart but Stephen obviously thought he detected some sort of warning. 'Doesn't give me much hope if what I have been doing has displeased him up there,' said Stephen lifting his eyes skyward.

'Think of it another way,' I said in an attempt to encourage, 'if this really has affected you so deeply, this could be the beginning of a new stage in your life.' I didn't say that the same applied to me because at that point I hadn't had a chance to tell him my story. I wondered whether he would believe it.

For the next few minutes, it seemed like hours, we sat in silence each weighing his thoughts. The atmosphere in the cellar was getting oppressive and I decided it was time to persuade Stephen to free himself from his prison and go with me out into the fresh air. He did come, tucking the big blue book under his arm as he moved towards the staircase. At the top, I gave the improvised doorstop a friendly tap but Stephen walked on apparently not wanting to acknowledge, let alone celebrate, his timely escape.

In an endeavour to jolt him back into the real world, I turned and looked down the stone staircase and said in as casual a voice as I could muster: 'What you don't know yet is that I shared a similar experience; I spent a week or more down there doing much what you've been doing. That book under your arm was my only companion, too.'

'You're not serious, why did you wait 'til now to tell me?' said Stephen expressing genuine astonishment.

'You were so carried away, you didn't give me a chance,' I reminded him, 'First, let's get away from this place and find somewhere more congenial to talk but before we go can I ask you a question? Have you asked yourself who shut the door?'

'Who shut the door? Not until this moment, I haven't. You're not telling me you couldn't find a way out either?'

'That's just what I am telling you. It might have happened once by accident but what are the odds against it happening a second time?

Maybe that's something we both have to consider very carefully,' I said as we walked out into the freshness of an autumnal evening. Certainly, neither of us felt inclined to go back to test the door's mechanism and to my surprise Stephen refrained from mentioning the possibility of any paranormal intervention.

20

Two Green Bottles

Relieved to be out of the cellar, we wandered back into that part of the garden where I had spent time with Albert. I gave Stephen a summary of what the old man had told me about their meeting, including the promise to create a spiritual link with his beloved Maddie. 'Did you? Did you really raise this poor man's hopes by pretending---even as I used this word I realised it would probably anger Stephen---by pretending you were reaching out to his long lost fiancé. Wasn't that an extremely cruel thing to do?'

'Pretending? Was I pretending? You say I was but are you really in a position to judge?' asked Stephen, 'Maybe I do possess some kind of energy source which others don't have. What I feel I must do now is decide if I have been using it responsibly. The answer to that is almost certainly 'no'. You will tell me, I'm sure, that I've seriously abused it. Or maybe you are still convinced it can all be put down to an over active imagination?'

It had taken some time but Stephen suddenly realised he hadn't asked me anything about my incarceration in the cellar. 'You found yourself with only the Bible to read, you say. Which bits did you study? Don't imagine an invisible hand pointed out which way you should go.'

'Maybe you won't believe this but I, too, felt I was being gently pushed or pulled in a certain direction. I probably wasn't as calm as you and it took me some time to detect a pattern to my unplanned biblical lesson.'

Stephen listened intently as I described how I used the comprehensive index to check out points made at some of my regular dinner parties.

'Did you really invite people who wanted to talk about sin and the devil? I thought journalists would only be interested in discussing their latest conquests, like wrecking the lives of people like me.'

'Well, you're wrong. Privately, we can be quite serious. One of the most heated arguments we had over the cheese and port was about who qualified for heaven and who didn't. The fur really flew on that occasion.'

Stephen thought this might be a good moment to put my life under his spotlight. 'Have you considered your refusal to believe in anything supernatural could be your sticking point? If your flirtation with the Bible was as meaningful as mine, perhaps you also have some reassessing to do. A good starting point might be to decide if you think there is evidence that spirits do exist, good ones as well as bad.'

I was starting to see Stephen in a refreshing new light. Perhaps the time had come for both of us to re-examine our unyielding view of the world and compare our experiences in the mansion's cellar to see if we had learned anything. However, it was not the moment for this type of detailed appraisal. We were tired, still a little frightened and as confused as one another.

'What do we do now?' asked Stephen, as we set off for yet another walk through the forest back to Bar Harbor, 'the few bits and pieces of grub left in the cellar were hardly sufficient for a growing lad. I could eat a horse just now. Pie and chips would go down well, unless you suggest something better on that huge expense account you brought with you.' Little did he know.

So much had happened so quickly I realised I had told Stephen nothing about finding the body of his rival, Yasha Rashnin. It came as a shock to him as I unravelled all the gory details and an even greater shock when I told him he had been number one suspect. That danger might have passed but he was still suspected of joining forces with a group of saboteurs.

'How ridiculous!' said Stephen angrily, 'I've not been anywhere near people like that. After my past experiences, I was doing my best to steer clear of trouble. My only contact with Rashnin was about a year ago when we both turned up on the same platform at a university in Colorado. The minute I saw a crowd of reporters and a television camera, I knew they would try to fabricate an argument to heighten the entertainment value of whatever coverage they were planning.'

Stephen felt the media 'mob' had become restless when they realised they couldn't put the two of them at each others throats. Instead, they were being asked to recognise that in some areas of research there were elements of agreement 'We both believed we had some sort of energy the majority of the population didn't have,' we told them, 'but they didn't want to accept we were seeking to use that force in ways that would benefit, not disrupt the world.'

'Surely,' I suggested to Stephen, 'you're not surprised some people were sceptical. Until now you've both courted criticism by making wild claims. Neither our sadly deceased friend or you were prepared to put those powers to a serious test, at least not one likely to be endorsed by reputable scientists.'

I warned Stephen that if he didn't move quickly he might have that test forced upon him. The CIA still wanted to know what happened on his previous visit to the States and why he came back three years later. 'They're not buying the story that you came over here in search of a ghost.'

'Then what do they think I've been up to?' asked Stephen.

'They have a notion that your real motive for returning to the States was to join a group carrying out experiments on ways of interfering with power supplies and vital national security systems

'Twaddle! I went through all this in the UK and no firm conclusions were ever reached,' Stephen reminded me. 'The scientists involved finished up arguing among themselves and decided to put the issue on ice. In Britain that probably means shelving it for good.'

I told Stephen I didn't think the Americans would be in any way impressed by conclusions reached in the UK and they would want to carry out their own tests. 'When you were suspected of killing Rashnin they thought they could detain you for as long as they liked. Unable to do that any longer they're looking for another excuse to make you stay around.'

I thought Stephen had to decide whether he was prepared to put himself in their hands or attempt to leave the country. It might be better for his health if he made himself scarce but that would not be easy from an island where border controls, in and out, would have probably been considerably strengthened.

We walked in silence for a while each mulling over the developments that had engulfed both of us during the past week. It seemed a good moment to clear up one mystery (a mystery for me and several others besides) of why Stephen had left the States in a hurry three years ago and immediately said he no longer wanted to be referred to as a psychic.

Stephen did not clam up as I thought he might but took his time in deciding what he would say to me. This was not a period in his life in which he could now take any pride, he said apologetically. He had been an utter idiot to think he could use the information in *The Gemstone File* as a method of building up his reputation as a psychic. Nevertheless, that was a verdict on himself which had taken a long time in coming.

'It was probably just as well that the File was a fake. If it hadn't been scattered among you journalists and dismissed as dangerous nonsense, I might have made an even bigger fool of myself. As soon as I arrived in the States, I guessed I was being used as a fall guy by people who didn't care whether any of its contents was true or not. They just wanted to cause trouble and were prepared to use any means at their disposal. I fell right into the trap.'

'So you decided to head for home and dramatically denounce yourself, without even a pause for thought. Why?'

Stephen, looking very repentant, said he realised he had been carried away by all the attention he had been receiving and started to cheat in order to make his television appearances more exciting.

'I was by no means the first to do this but it started to dawn on me that by doing so I had thrown away the chance of becoming a serious subject for paranormal research. And this was what I wanted to be. I knew there was something different, something possibly quite remarkable lurking within me and as a result of my stupid capers there was never going to be an opportunity to put that theory to the test. Disappearing for a while seemed the right thing to do but I always thought the time might come when I could get serious again. An invitation from an American university surprised me in view of my previous history but seemed to be opening new doors. The invite and the accompanying paperwork looked genuine enough but as soon as I set foot in this country for the second time, I realised the promised lecture tour might be a cover to get me involved in far more sinister activities. A suggestion that I should visit this mansion in Maine surprised me but that was something I wanted to do anyway so I went along with it.

'You were certainly right about the sinister activities but I doubt whether a reputable university would have become involved. I suspect your itinerary was published somewhere, allowing undesirables to get in on the act.'

I was about to explain that not too far away a gang of hoodlums were planning more of those sinister activities he had been telling me about, when my voice was drowned by the whirling blades of a helicopter hovering overhead. I hardly gave it a second glance; it was probably Clarke's men looking after our welfare. They wanted to get their hands on Stephen for sure but there was little I could do to prevent that.

We walked another mile or so into a clearing and as we did so were suddenly surrounded by a crowd of ruffians similar to those who had formed a welcoming committee when I arrived on the island. They didn't give the impression they had come to protect us. Neither did they want to hang about and ushered us towards their transport. I just had time to see that guns were in evidence before blindfolds were thrown over our heads and hands tied behind our backs. Our shouts of protest were ignored and we were frog-marched off with no one attempting to offer any sort of explanation. I was furious but my annoyance was more directed at Clarke who had promised to stay local and alert in readiness for my possible meeting with Stephen.

As we were pushed unceremoniously into the helicopter, I wondered why Clarke had allowed this to happen. It was his plan to get me back into the area around the mansion and his men were supposed to be in position to stop anything like this taking place. Or was I a sucker and again being used as bait? I imagined Clarke would be of the opinion reporters were expendable but what about Stephen? They wanted to get their hands on him badly enough.

Our demands to know where we were being taken and suggestions that the CIA were not far behind broke no ice. The blindfolds were pulled a little tighter each time we asked a question. I did detect we went over sea for a while and were heading east. Racking my brains to remember where the nearest land would be, having left the mainland, I guessed we might be heading in the direction of Nova Scotia. This turned out to be correct.

As the helicopter came into land, I could hear the sound of the sea lashing against rocks but the journey had not ended yet. Crushed into the back seat of a car, we travelled for another half hour or so, at no time losing the sound of the sea. At our journey's end, we were allowed to see nothing until the blindfolds were ripped off in what appeared to be the basement of a run-down country house. 'Oh, no, not another cellar, please,' I said aloud but no one was listening.

The first thing I saw was an array of electrical equipment similar to that uncovered by Clarke and his team in the Cadillac Mountain forest retreat. If Stephen and I were now in the hands of the same group who managed to operate undetected in the Cadillac Mountain for so long, then it was highly unlikely their plans had anything to do with drug smuggling out of the Golden Triangle or discovering President Kennedy's real killer. Something equally as sinister was occupying their time and if they had a hand in the death of Yasha Rashnin, then Stephen and I were in very dangerous waters. This was a bunch who obviously believed human life was very cheap.

Even as that thought went through my mind, the man who had confronted me on my previous encounter with his gang in the forest, walked into the cellar, swaggering towards us with an expression indicating he was enjoying a moment of triumph.

'So we meet again, Mr Reporter and this time I can thank you for leading us, at last, to the man we really wanted to get our hands on.'

'You talking about me?' Stephen asked with amazing calmness bearing in mind that he, not I, was the target. 'I can't imagine what possible help I could be to you. I'm just a magician.' With danger beckoning, this was a sensible retort but I couldn't resist a sideways look of surprise, almost amusement, at the man who had tried so hard for so long to prove his abilities were many grades above the status of magician.

'A magician, you may consider yourself to be when its convenient,' our captor observed, 'but we know there are people in high places on both sides of the Atlantic who are convinced you have something else to offer. We did our homework as well, Mr Spicer, and found your involvement with the British Security Service most interesting. We tried to meet up with you three years ago but for some reason you took fright and rushed home.'

They were surprised, he said, when Stephen decided to return but his timing had been impeccable. 'Your arrival coincided with news that more conventional experiments in jamming electrical and radar installations from considerable distances had failed. How good it was of you to return just in time for us to take advantage of your unique gifts. We hear you are probably a man capable of doing quite a lot of damage in the right circumstances.'

He admitted they had made a mistake in thinking Rashnin had similar abilities. 'We couldn't put our hands on you at the time so we gave him the job, a job he wasn't allowed to turn down.'

'And he died in the process,' I chipped in, 'don't you think you've done enough damage. The CIA know all about you and there's no way they're going to leave you on the loose for very much longer.'

'Really? said the gang's eloquent leader, 'then you're in for another shock. We made sure their air transport was put out of action. They tried to follow us but had an argument with the top of a tree. We'll be well out of the way before they can mount any sort of rescue attempt.'

Stephen glanced across at me, his expression giving away the fact he considered this a frightening piece of news. I was in no position to disagree. Our only chance seemed to be if Stephen could convince them his powers were not of the sort that would help them with their dangerous experiments. But that was not likely to work. If they didn't care about the safety of Yasha Rashnin, they certainly weren't going to worry about Stephen's future. And if he refused, they might well dump both of us, probably into the sea.

'You have absolutely no choice,' said our captor 'help us or take the consequences. I don't think I have to spell out what those consequences will be. Good night gentlemen, we'll start work tomorrow.' With that, he announced he was posting two guards at the door and walked out.

'What do you think he actually means when he says we'll start work tomorrow?' asked Stephen, as I tried to take in our surroundings and decide what sort of prison we were now in. It seemed ironic that after putting in so much effort to find Stephen, we had now been banged up together by a group of crazed men prone to taking action first and asking questions afterwards.

'If they treat you in the same way as they did Rashnin, they'll take you out to some remote installation---in Yasha's case it was an electricity pylon---and get you to demonstrate your 'bending' powers. Except that in this case it won't be a spoon they will want you to bend but a piece of metal or wire that is vital to the functioning of whatever it is they want to interfere with.'

'Who are they? Did you ever have a chance to find out?'

'Not really. My suspicion is they're a gang of criminals, not very bright ones, who have convinced themselves they can sell their ability to disrupt communications to any nation or criminal organisation in the business of sabotage.'

I had to admit some surprise when Stephen burst out laughing; a sort of nervous laughter, which I thought, was his attempt to break the tension. 'I couldn't do that even if they brought in red hot irons... it's a trick, it's a magician's trick perfected by Yasha Rashnin, copied by me and probably by quite a few others as well.'

Remembering Corelli's demonstration in a London restaurant, it was my turn to decide whether to laugh or cry. 'Do you mean I've come all the way to America, been chased around the countryside by a bunch of maniacs and now face being chucked over a cliff just to get you to admit what I already knew, that you are a fake.'

'Steady on, it's not quite like that. Some people like Rashnin and I do, or did in his case, have brain patterns that seem to be able to pick up and transmit disruptive waves. And they're not always disruptive; most of us accept that extra sensory perception and hypnotism are real enough to warrant serious study. But the spoon bending, malfunctioning of clocks and the apparent prediction of major tragedies has always been part of a magician's armoury.'

Stephen said that in his case it probably started when he became aware of vibes in the family cottage that triggered off strange thoughts and happenings he could not understand. 'This was not imagination, I can assure you. I was really frightened at first but my parents decided it was schoolboy nightmares. I shared some of my fears with my sisters but I now realise they decided to make fun of me and were probably responsible for some of the more bizarre happenings.'

Stephen said he knew he was different from other children but admitted he was in too much of a hurry and too greedy to allow proper research to throw up answers. 'Carried away on a wave of publicity, I decided to speed things up a bit. I started to cheat which is what many who call themselves spiritists and psychics eventually finish up doing.'

'So can we write off poltergeist incidents as poppycock?' I asked, feeling that I had to bring this semi-confession to a conclusion before our captors gave us a chance to experience the spirit world at first hand.

'Not always,' said Stephen a trifle defensively, 'there were strange happenings in the cottage and at my boarding school but once you succumb to a tendency to exaggerate there are plenty of characters in the media (present company excepted, of course) who will fan the flames. Then it's not long before things get out of hand.'

I could barely believe what I was hearing and for a moment wondered what the research team back at Trentbridge University would make of this conversation. Their chances of receiving further generous grants might well be put in jeopardy. For the moment, however, we had a more serious dilemma to cope with. If we didn't manage to escape, nobody would be around to tell the tale. On this occasion, I didn't imagine the door would mysteriously open and we would walk free. But even as I dismissed that possibility, I felt a twinge of guilt. What happened to those early signs of a developing faith? Were they evaporating already?

Perhaps I did say a discreet prayer but decided that any help from above would have to be accompanied by some practical effort down below. I stalked the room we were in and noticed that unlike the basement cellar in the mansion, this room contained a few objects that could be put to some practical purpose. My attention was drawn to a couple of heavy green bottles, the sort that probably once contained a substantial quantity of beer or cider.

'Stephen, we can either sit here and wait for doomsday or we can do something about our situation. I don't know about you but I'm in favour of a bit of decisive action; maybe we can imitate one of those dramatic scenes we see on British television most evenings of the week.'

A car had driven away earlier and there seemed to be a good chance that most of the gang were holing up somewhere else, leaving just two of their number to look after us.

'Armed to the teeth, no doubt,' said Stephen drily.

'That's almost certain but they're probably not particularly bright either, so let's take the sort of action Dick Barton, a favourite old radio character of mine would have taken, and get the hell out of this place.'

'What do you suggest then?' asked Stephen, 'something stupid like creating a scene, arming ourselves with the two bottles you are holding and then thumping them over the head when they come to investigate.'

'Yes, something like that. Take courage, Dick Barton used to do it three times a week and once on Sundays.'

Stephen observed that Dick Barton, whoever he might be, was not around to offer a helping hand and even if he had been the chances of my plan working were slim indeed. Almost as stupid, he thought, but probably with a better chance of success, would be to try to take the hinges off the door.

'Hand-to-hand combat is not one of my strong points. I didn't do National Service, like you probably did.'

'I did but I never came within a thousand miles of the enemy. I am probably no more adept at this sort of thing than you but I don't fancy hanging around 'til the morning waiting to see what they intend to do to us.'

Stephen still tried to talk me out of it. He certainly was not the violent type but he, too, realised that if we waited for the daylight our prospects were grim. Eventually he said, 'OK, let's go for it,' trying to sound brave.

If our crazy plan did work and the chances were slim, we would laugh about it in years to come. But nothing seemed remotely amusing at this point. I said I would play the sick man, lying on the floor groaning in agony and with the bottle hopefully out of sight, but handy. While I was dealing with number one terrorist, Stephen would stand behind the door and bring the bottle down on the head of the second man with as much force as he could muster. Simple the plan may have been but we could both see that our number would be up if we got it wrong.

As though we were setting a scene in a stage drama, we marked out our positions and for a moment stood looking at each other trying not to display signs of fear. For two men who had never hit anyone over the head in anger at any time in their lives it was a terrifying moment.

'Let's have a prayer,' I suggested

'You're not serious, are you?' said Stephen

'Yes, I am. This could be our last minutes on this earth and I can't think of a better moment to say to God, we're sorry we messed up but if we live we'll try to do better.'

'Sounds a bit OTT, but ok it can't do any harm.'

'And if we're sincere it may do a lot of good,' I added.

I hadn't done a lot of praying in my life but a simple plea for help should not, I felt, give me too much trouble. I did recognise, however, that I was again joining the multitudes who give God short shrift for most of their lives but are quick to turn to him in times of trouble.

As planned, I started to groan as loudly and as realistically as possible, an effort that would have reduced a drama teacher to tears. No response at first so I stepped up the volume and the door burst open. Only one of the men came in waving his gun menacingly, walked towards me and prodded me with his foot. I hadn't taken into account that he probably didn't speak a word of English and I wouldn't be able to describe the extent of my suffering.

He hadn't spotted Stephen, yet, but where was the other guy? I couldn't attack this one before his mate made an appearance. We seemed to stay statuesque for a very long time but it could only have been seconds. Out of the corner of my eye I saw a second figure appearing through the door but hardly far enough to put him in Stephen's firing line.

It was now or never. I raised the bottle and hit my assailant with enough force to bring him down like the giant falling off Jack's beanstalk. His gun went shooting across the floor but I then realised Stephen was having difficulty carrying out his piece of calculated aggression. The second gangster, having seen what I had done to his mate, approached me obviously intending to shoot at close range. As he lifted his gun, Stephen shouted and charged in our direction. This was enough to make the second gunman hesitate and turn but Stephen's delivery with the bottle was slightly off target and glanced off his shoulder rather than putting a dent in his head. It was however, enough force to make him loosen his grip on the gun and the sequence that followed would have done justice to a Buster Keaton black and white movie. We both went for him with our respective bottles and so very nearly struck each other. Fortunately, the gunman was so confused by this time he obligingly allowed us to have a second try and this time neither of us missed.

I knew little about guns but I thought it no bad idea to recover one of them in case of future trouble. At least I could look dangerous. A large key had fallen on the floor during our battle so we grabbed that, made a sharp exit, securely locked the door before walking cautiously out into the night air. It was only then we realised we didn't have the flimsiest idea of where we were or what direction to take in search of safety.

21

Celebrity Status

A hazardous walk was ahead of us. We could hear waves crashing onto the shore and in the darkness realised we needed to find some sort of path heading in an easterly direction. Walking straight over the edge of a cliff was the greatest danger, especially as we had not been able to equip ourselves with a torch and were not wearing suitable footwear.

'Do you think they'll come after us?' Stephen asked. The tremor in his voice told me he had not recovered from the shock of our farcical but dramatic escape. I tried to reassure him we had not killed anyone but I don't think he was convinced.

It was their possession of a helicopter that worried me. They could scan a lot of ground in a short space of time and knew we couldn't travel very far or very fast. Keeping Stephen's spirits up was a priority. 'Hopefully, they won't be able to guess the direction we're heading,' I conjectured, in an attempt to put Stephen's mind at rest, 'if we can reach some sort of civilisation by morning, they'll have difficulty in spotting us from the air.'

So we walked and walked, sheer tiredness being the enemy now. Later, when we were able to look at a map we decided our temporary prison had been somewhere near Peggy's Cove. If that was so then we must have been dodging the pitfalls of the cliff edge for many miles. There was a path set back from the sea but we never found it. With dawn breaking, we saw lights in the distance, enough to suggest we were approaching quite a large centre of population. It turned out to be Halifax, a feature of which, I remembered, was a citadel symbolizing British domination in the New World. The battlements around the citadel were a welcome sight and now that we were in a more populated area, we felt safer from discovery by any overhead helicopter search.

Our immediate problem was to find someone in authority to listen to our story and not write us off as illegal immigrants. A few people were making their way to work so getting directions to the police headquarters was no problem. Once there our task was to get someone in authority to listen to an account of our strange adventures and take them seriously. We had been stripped of most of our belongings along the way but our captors had missed one important item, my driving licence that at least confirmed who I was and where I had come from.

The desk officer took a while concluding we were not insane before packing us off to a security department in the same building. A man who said he was Jim Fiske, another 'special' agent, took us into a small interview room and listened attentively to our story, not interrupting with any kind of comment until we had both finished.

'Quite a story,' he said, 'but you realise you're lucky to still be alive. One or two others haven't been so fortunate recently.'

'So you go along with our story? We were worried you would write us off as a couple of illegals.'

'Might well have done so on another day, but most of what you have said ties in with what we already know about these hoodlums. We could have pounced on them at any time but we wanted to know more about them and who were their paymasters. So we have been patient.'

We told him what the leader of the gang had said about the CIA team helicopter coming to grief. 'Don't worry about that,' he assured us. 'No one was hurt and our own helicopter parked here in Nova Scotia was quickly pressed into service.'

'Will you catch up with them soon or will they have done another disappearing trick?'

'That's already in hand. As soon as you reported in, we had an armed team on the way. I suspect your captors didn't come after you, as you feared. They almost certainly headed for another hiding place. They're inclined not to hang around where they're not wanted.'

'But what about all the equipment they burden themselves with. What do they do with that?'

'It's not so much as you think. It fits comfortably into the back of their helicopter. We've got a fix on them now, thanks to you. In fact, you have done us a favour. They'll be under lock and key, or dead, before the week's out.'

The agent offered to get us taken back to Maine, something we had to do even if it was only to pick up a few personal belongings. He promised an escort but didn't think we would be troubled again by any member of the gang.

'We were told that last time. Think we'll take up your offer of an escort, if it's all the same to you. We've had enough excitement to last us for a while,' I added.

I was still curious about the role police chief Barkway had been playing in the drama. In the hope of some sort of explanation, I suggested the local force had not been particularly active. In fact, the group holed up in the forest seemed to have a free run of the island.

'That was part of the strategy,' Jim Fiske willingly revealed. 'Once we knew they were using Bar Harbor as their headquarters, we gave them their heads for a while. It was all going well until you two guys put a spanner in the works. And no one anticipated the death of Yasha Rashnin. That was a tragedy which came out of the blue and really complicated matters. We're real sorry about that but Rashnin's presence on the Island was not picked up initially.'

Neither of us were quite sure why, but before we left Halifax we asked for a couple of hours grace to visit the Fairview Lawn Cemetery, where 129 Titanic passengers were buried. There was a time when I would not have gone for a stroll through a cemetery accompanied by someone with Stephen's background. It would have been difficult not to imagine he was trying to make 'connections' with a few departed souls. After the events of the past weeks, however, I felt Stephen had changed and was beginning to look at the world in a more mature way. There was hard evidence that he was facing up to a few of the realities of life rather than flirting with the fantasies.

Time would tell and as we walked around the graves inspecting names and messages, I felt his motives for being there could have been similar to mine, curiosity, yes, but also a deep-down realisation that perhaps cemetery occupation was not quite as permanent as we had always believed. There was something else to look forward to, maybe.

The plethora of gravestones around me brought to mind a story in the Old Testament I had glanced at in the cellar but promised myself a more detailed inspection before the memory faded. It had described bones left on the floor of a valley and the question had been asked: '*Can these bones live?*' In no way would this have been Sunday school material. God had said quite specifically that he would breathe into the bones and make the flesh come to life. If my memory served me correctly, the passage had concluded with the words: *'Then you will know I am the Lord.'*

Stephen was looking at me curiously and I realised I had been murmuring these lines under my breath. 'I think we shall both need a psychologist as well as a Bible teacher to sort us out when we get home,' he predicted, 'few are going to recognise us as the people they knew before we left.'

We had one last surprise before leaving Nova Scotia. Back at the police headquarters, we were greeted by a small squad of media people who had picked up flimsy details of our unconventional arrival on their patch. Police contacts had let slip, on purpose I suspect, that the actions of two weird Englishmen had enabled them to swoop on a gang of terrorists before they could do serious damage to the infrastructure of Northern America and possibly Canada as well.

It started to look as if celebrity status was around the corner as questions came thick and fast from American journalists and English stringers. I hoped we had said enough, but not too much, to keep the story alive. Then as we were winding up, I noticed that one Yankee scribbler was not joining in. As the others started to run out of questions and a few of them stood up to leave, my English politeness prompted me to ask the silent reporter if there was any way I could help him.

'This time I think I may be able to help you buddy,' he said and as he spoke, I recognised the voice. It was the same heavy drawl I had heard many times in transatlantic calls from Rod, my Chicago chum who had kept me up-to-date with developments on the American side in the early stages of the Spicer saga.

'Rod, you old son of a bitch you've left it a bit late to join the party haven't you?'

'Sorry buddy, they wouldn't let me leave the city until I could convince them some good copy was in prospect.'

'I'm glad, then, we were able to spice it up a bit but how far and wide has the story gone? Are there still some pickings left for me to help pay for this crazy escapade?'

'Good deal more than a few pickings,' said Rod and he named four major English nationals who were after exclusive rights. 'They've all had the guts of the story slipped out by US intelligence sources but now they want it from the horse's mouth. You're the horse! They're bending over backwards for more on the murder of Yasha Rashnin; the cops here are staying pretty tight lipped.'

It was great to meet Rod at last and to get such good news but now I had to weigh up whether my payback would be better with an exclusive or from a general release. It would depend on the offers.

The Halifax police still in a spirit of co-operation gave me the use of one of their small interview rooms and a call to the Sunday Herald brought me an offer of more than I could earn in six months slog on the Trentbridge News. They would up their fee if I were prepared to lace the piece with material unlikely to come from official sources. I would have to think about that once free from the CIA's apron strings.

The outcome of a call to Jasper Clarke turned out to be more straightforward than I expected. I found him surprisingly relaxed about the detail I wanted to use, almost to the point of being frivolous about the activities of the Cadillac hoodlums, as he liked to call them. 'Bunch of amateurs,' was his comment but he did add that they would get the book thrown at them for the death of Yasha Rashnin.

Feeling freer to let my hair down, I started scribbling and a couple of hours later made a very long call to the Sunday Herald. It was great to think they were paying. I felt good.

This was my launching as a freelance. When I set out to cross the 'pond', I had no expectation of my first story being fought over by London editors. Now I had a name, a reputation and a by-line that would serve me well in the future. But there would be no room for complacency. My next story would probably be a hard sell unless I put my head on the block again. Next time, if there was a next time, I might be less eager to throw caution to the winds.

The journey back to Bar Harbor was uneventful. Stephen only had the clothes he stood up in but I wanted to return to my lodgings to gather up odds and ends as well as some paperwork. Stephen was invited to stay and we thought it better to have a good night's sleep before deciding how we were going to get home.

In the bay, the cruise liner *Cunard Venturer* was still anchored and we were told it had been held up because of emergency repairs in the engine room. This turned out to be good news for us because passengers in a hurry had sought other means of getting back to the UK. A number of cabins were now available at much reduced cost and having remembered my family would still be away in our holiday caravan for another couple of weeks, I decided to take the slower trip home.

After all, I argued, I was now a freelance and about to pocket my first fee of a size I could hardly have imagined a few weeks ago. I would also have time to mull over all that had happened in the cellar. That experience in itself might yield another feature with even greater possibilities than the exploits of Stephen Spicer. Whether anyone would believe it was another matter. Eric would probably dissolve into hysterics if I told him I had become a Christian.

There was much to consider, however, before trusting my thoughts to paper. Not least, the mystery of how twice within a few days an iron door had slammed on unwilling occupants of the mansion's unfriendly cavern. And who would believe that two men with such different outlooks on life would have, not only shared similar experiences, but as a result found themselves on a similar road of discovery.

There would be advantages in having Stephen travelling on the same liner but I was not ready to share a cabin, even if a few pounds could have been saved. What I needed and I suspected Stephen needed as well, was some thinking time. Would the events of the past few weeks have a permanent effect or quickly dim as the more demanding, as well as the more attractive, elements of modern life tightened their grip again?

It had not occurred to the island's security officials that we might depart by sea and we embarked without hindrance. My one regret was that I was leaving a beautiful part of the world without taking time out to enjoy it properly. But the cheap cabin offer was too good to miss.

We went our own ways for the first day, enjoying much needed relaxation after our recent experiences. The sea trip would last six days so there would be a chance to lock swords again---this time without drawing blood hopefully---after both of us had had time to recalibrate our brains. When Stephen did come knocking at my cabin door it was to tell me he had found a Gideon Bible in the bedside cabinet. It had been one of the first things I had noticed as well, an unlikely observation by either of us if we had been travelling to America on the same liner a week or two back.

Stephen wanted to tell me he had found the Old Testament piece I had been muttering about in the cemetery. It came from Ezekiel and the passage had the curious title *The Valley of Dry Bones*.

'My schoolboy understanding is that the soul goes to heaven if you're lucky and our bodies become a small pile of dust,' observed Stephen, 'this passage seems to indicate some bodies are put together again. Can you believe that?'

'No, I don't think I can at the moment. If we want to pursue the answer to that sort of question I reckon we'll need some help with the basics.'

'Where do you think that help will come from?' asked Stephen. 'It certainly was in short supply at my school. I don't remember The Old Testament getting much of a mention. We might have had a lecture on the seven deadlies but that was about it.'

Squatting on the edge of the beds in the tiny cabin, we both started dredging our memories and came to the conclusion that scripture didn't rate very highly in either of our schools. I recalled a religious education teacher in my secondary school who was nicknamed 'Pop' by the boys and constantly the victim of practical jokes.

There was nothing to be proud of during my days as a choirboy either, time often spent playing silly games in the choir stalls or flirting with the girls who occasionally came to church with their flamboyantly, irreverent parents. Every service was the same and I recall with shame the day I upset the vicar by suggesting he could make a recording of the service and replay it each week. Then he wouldn't have to plough through the same old psalms time and time again.

He told us to listen more carefully to the regular readings. It was God's word, he said, and would help us to lead better lives. But we all agreed the language was funny and difficult to follow. No one bothered to explain it to us. The vicar urged us to listen to the sermons but we often didn't understand them either.

The highlight for me was the choir, especially when I was asked to sing a solo. My mother and father came on those days but rarely put in an appearance during the rest of year, apart from weddings and funerals. They ran a business on a shoestring and with very little help; leisure time was at a premium and for them going to church was rated a casual and occasional activity.

'What are you saying, then, that we're not going to get much benefit from going to church, surely not?' said Stephen, but at the same time admitting he wasn't much of a judge because the Spicers rarely went to church as a family.

All these were negative thoughts and I pondered for a moment on how we could take home something more positive from our recent experiences. The time we had spent on our first serious inspection of the Bible had made us think, but I felt something very important was missing.

'What do you think that is?' asked Stephen

'My feeling is we still have to understand the need to make a sincere and lasting commitment. Without a genuine faith, all the knowledge in the world will not get us anywhere.'

We lapsed into a period of silence again before Stephen admitted he had probably always realised there was a spiritual dimension to life but had gone the wrong way about putting a handle on it. His 'mystical' experiences in his early teens went to his head, he thought, and blurred his focus.

I had to admit to similar deficiencies, in my case being too busy, too preoccupied, and too self-centred to think about life's big issues.

'I wonder how many people on the Titanic left it too late,' I reflected, as I remembered we must have been sailing through the piece of ocean where the mighty liner lay on the seabed. The captain had said over the ship's loud speaker system that he usually followed a course further south but the tail-end of a hurricane forced him to keep to the north. His concern was to make life more comfortable for all passengers but especially those with seasickness tendencies.

The description of the liner's last moments in Violet Jessop's diaries was still on my mind, one of the reasons being that although our encounter with gangsters now seemed like a scene from a Gilbert and Sullivan opera we had had moments, two in fact, when we thought our end was near.

'Wish you hadn't mentioned the Titanic,' said Stephen, 'the bridge also reported we would be heading into a force eight gale tomorrow.'

'Well, at least there's no ice around at this time of the year,' I said confidently, 'a force eight is nothing to worry about in a ship like this.'

Sensing that Stephen might be getting the jitters, I changed the subject and our mood by discussing life aboard ship, the food, the entertainment and the good-natured attitudes of the crew. But there was one passenger we had both seen at different times during the day, and for Stephen, in particular, this had been an alarming encounter.

We were both sure we had glimpsed Albert, the sad bridegroom-to-be, who we had talked with in the mansion. I knew he had arrived by ship so it was logical that he would be going home in the same way as he had come. I just hoped the captain's decision to put us on a course that took us virtually over the wreck of the Titanic had not reached his ears.

'I feel terrible about it now but when I saw him heading down the deck towards me, head down, I dropped into a deckchair and covered my face,' confided Stephen. 'What was I to say to him? During our first meeting, I was trying to convince him I could get in touch with Maddie but that message on the wall had no substance to it at all. I was just showing off. Now I'm ashamed. Perhaps there was a time when I imagined I could display some special powers but certainly not on this occasion.'

'So what are you going to do?' I asked him, 'keep out of his way or try to explain?'

'Try to explain, how could I do that? Can't see him being generous with his forgiveness and there's no reason why he should be.'

I tried to reassure Stephen because I felt I had made a small break through with Albert before he walked off into the forest the second time. There seemed to be a real chance he had started to pull himself together.

That verdict was to be severely tested later when Stephen and I were wandering the deck as darkness closed in. We were walking towards the back of the ship joking that neither of us could remember all the correct merchant navy terms for back, front, left side and right side, when we saw the figure of a man sitting on the boat rail looking down into the Atlantic.

'That's a bit dangerous isn't it?' remarked Stephen very quietly, 'didn't they tell us not to sit on a rail?'

'They did,' I said peering through the fading light and getting a clearer view of the man as we approached. 'You know, I think he's about to jump or is certainly thinking about it.'

'Oh Lor'! What shall we do? If we frighten him he might just go,' said Stephen, freezing to the spot. 'That is Albert, you know, what were you saying earlier about sailing over the spot where the Titanic lies on the sea-bed?' he whispered

'Well, there's certainly no time to analyse the situation, we've got to get him off that rail. If he goes in, there's no way a boat like this can turn round or stop in a hurry. In the darkness he would disappear within minutes'

I suggested we carried on walking very slowly as though we had not noticed him, saying nothing until we were quite close. We advanced a dozen steps or so and then stopped within feet of him.

'You OK, Albert?' I asked when almost in touching distance, 'it looks a bit precarious sitting up there like that'. Getting no response, I leaned on the rail tried to give the impression I was just enjoying the light of the moon dancing on the waves and said as casually as I could, 'you do remember me don't you? We met at the mansion. Talked about the reasons why we were both there.'

The next few moments were going to be crucial. There was no question of making a grab for him because if he were seriously thinking of jumping, he would be gone before we could get a firm hold.

Albert turned his head at a slight angle towards me and I could see he had been crying. 'I should be down there with those men who stayed aboard and waited for the end. It's difficult to live with, being a coward and betraying the girl you loved. I should have paid the price years ago' he smiled grimly and added: 'Better late than never.'

I thought that was it but after shifting forward a couple more inches he paused just long enough for me to put an arm around him. My hope was that it would be seen more as a gesture of comfort rather than a rescue attempt. Stephen had quietly moved to the other side of him and we were able to ease him back onto the deck. He burst into tears again: 'Still a coward, you see. Why didn't you push, not pull? I could have joined them, men with the guts to go down with the ship.'

'Because that would prove nothing,' I ventured, desperately searching for words that would sooth not worsen the situation. Nothing you do will bring Maddie back. You can't say sorry to her or the other Titanic passengers from the bottom of the sea. However, there may be a chance to say sorry in a different sort of way. You're getting on a bit but still have time to put matters right.'

'With God you mean.' Albert grabbed hold of me and in quavering voice asked whether I still believed what I had told him in the mansion garden.

'Of course I do. You may see me as a rotten reporter but I promise you, I wouldn't start playing with your emotions just to get a story out of you.'

'In that case will you pray with me?' Albert asked.

Stephen and I looked at each other in a slight state of panic. Neither of us had done much praying in our lives and the little bit of knowledge both of us had gained in the cellar had not gone deep enough to produce a spontaneous response. Or that was what we thought. When we discussed it later, we both felt that at that moment we had been given a little help, definitely from a good spirit on this occasion.

I asked God to forgive Albert and strengthen him to face the world in the months ahead; Stephen completely blew me away and made Albert burst into tears again when he prayed that Maddie was in heaven and

Albert would be able to ask her to forgive him when they met again.

'I don't know which affected me most,' I told Stephen later, 'Albert's sudden request for prayer or the words you found on the spur of the moment to give the poor old chap hope. You reduced both of us to tears.'

'Perhaps we should go to confirmation classes when we get home,' said Stephen with a broad smile. 'That would give them all something to talk about. I can see the headline now: **Psychic and his persecutor seek God's forgiveness.**'

Simultaneously, we both burst out laughing despite attempts to stifle our mirth. I wondered whether this was something we should be laughing about. Stephen had no problem: 'Maybe God will see the funny side of the situation---two guys, seriously at each others throats for long periods suddenly dropping on their knees and seeking forgiveness. He'll probably wish it happened more often.'

When we went to Albert's cabin to check he had fully recovered we made him promise not to do anything silly during the rest of the trip. He seemed calmer and said he would think over all we had said and all that happened.

'I'm sorry about the mess I made of the wall writings. After our conversation in the garden I went back into the mansion, checked that you had returned to the ground floor and then vented my feelings on the wall with a damp rag left lying around by another determined desecrator. I thought I was getting my own back on the fellow who promised to put me in touch with Maddie.'

Tears and the poor lighting on deck had prevented Albert from recognising Stephen. Now in the brightness of his cabin, the former actor realised he was face to face with the man who had claimed he could reach out and put him in touch with his long departed fiancé.

'Do you still think you could reach her?' asked Albert but then answered his own question: 'Of course, you couldn't. Do you still intend to play that hurtful little game when you get back to the UK?'

Stephen was contrite. 'No more, I can assure you. I did think at one stage I could help people like you but not any longer, I was stretching out way beyond myself.'

With that confession the world's 'most gifted psychic' was making it quite clear he intended to take serious decisions on how he wanted to lead the rest of his life. 'If I do discover new gifts and am tempted to abuse them, Albert, I shall think of you and remember it's not a good thing to risk pushing people over the edge.'

Stephen hadn't realised he had served up a dreadful pun quite unintentionally. But Albert noticed. His face relaxed, he smiled and said one of the things he needed to get back was his sense of humour. We were surprised when he asked if we could meet again before docking at Southampton but agreed to talk at any time, now or in the future.

The rest of the voyage was uneventful, something of a relief after all the excitement of the past couple of weeks. Cruising, a new experience for both of us, did give us a chance to meditate seriously, not only on what had happened in the cellar but also on fragments of the Bible, which we hoped would give us a different slant on life. We still argued about sin but that was a promising sign. Neither of us considered ourselves good but then we didn't consider ourselves bad either. Well not too bad!

Stephen recalled one passage in the Bible—he couldn't remember exactly where it was---which said however hard we tried, we couldn't bridge the gap between God and us by our own good deeds or even by religious activities. 'If that's so what do we do?' asked Stephen, 'I find that very confusing.'

I picked up the Gideon bible from the bedside table, flicked idly through it for a moment or two but then turned to John's gospel because I remembered my dinner party friend advising me that if I ever wanted to know more about Christianity this was the gospel I should read.

Perhaps it was the chapter many people turned to eventually but there was no doubt chapter 14 packed a punch. 'Listen to this Stephen. It's the verse we probably all skip over at first reading because we find it a bit scary:-

'*Jesus said: "I am the way and the truth and the life. No one comes to the Father except through me. If you really knew me, you would know my Father as well".*'

'Does this bring us to the heart of the matter, do you think? That we should be concentrating more on Jesus and the sacrifice he made for us on the Cross and stop thinking God is happy to hang around and wait until we decide to give him our attention.'

Stephen went very quiet for the next minute or two, then admitted he had received some instruction on the Trinity in the past but all he had now was a hazy recollection of the details. 'The phrase three-in-one comes to mind but I never could understand how God, Jesus and the Holy Spirit came in one package.'

I had to admit I had given little attention to the spiritual side of my life at any stage. 'For me Jesus only ever came into the reckoning at Christmas time when the school trotted out the stable, the toy donkey and sheep and we all dressed up as angels, shepherds and wise men. Beyond that Jesus was rarely mentioned at school.'

It was probably an unfair conclusion to come to but the gaps left in our understanding by those who were responsible for teaching and inspiring us, meant too many of us went through life thinking either we were not good enough to go to heaven or needed to pass some sort of test of our good deeds to be even considered.

It was getting late and we both decided that the questions we were raising were getting more challenging by the minute. We were not going to get all the answers at the drop of a hat but we promised ourselves we would not let worldly pursuits take over and dominate our lives in the same way as they had done in the past. Neither of us claimed anything like a Damascus Road-type conversion but we agreed something was happening which was already generating a feeling of expectation.

Before going back to his cabin Stephen, looking very sheepish said there was one more thing he wanted to get off his chest. 'I was behind all that chaos at the Divinity School,' he admitted. 'The police accepted my alibi but I don't think they wanted to get involved. In their view it was a university matter and it wasn't the job of the police to sort out student japes unless life was endangered.'

'Was it a stunt?' I asked him, 'Why would you want to wreck a conference designed to come up with some of the answers you were seeking?'

Stephen said at the time he had had enough of so-called paranormal researchers and the two 'madmen, Hart and Brackshaw were the last straw. 'It takes a thief to catch a thief and I knew they were staging the whole episode for their own benefit. They didn't know I was watching them as closely as they were supposed to be watching me. I must say they would have made quite a good living as furniture removers!'

Stephen said it suited his purpose to go along with them for a while but he thought they deserved to be taught a lesson. He had also come to the conclusion that several delegates invited to the conference were phoney.

I resisted the temptation to say that he was a good one to talk and instead asked Stephen to satisfy my curiosity about how they managed to invade the School.

'Students are clever at this sort of thing as I expect you have noticed.

It was along the lines suggested. We found an attic window and climbed into a roof space during the night with a fair amount of equipment.'

'How did you manage to do it so quietly and so quickly?'

'We were well rehearsed, it was like a military operation.'

'Do you now regret what you did?' I asked.

'Not really. It kept the paranormal pot boiling and just think of the fun all those researchers had telling the story to their friends when they returned to their own countries.'

I suppose I should have reprimanded him but then I had no more reason to do so than the local cops who turned a blind eye. I went to sleep that night starting to look forward intensely to seeing my wife and family again. Would they see any difference in me? I wondered. I guessed Stephen's Mum and Dad were in for a bit of a surprise.

As we travelled slowly down the Solent we started to relish the thought of home comforts and planned a quick get-away soon after docking. But there was one surprise still to come, a reception party which neither of us had anticipated. News of our exploits had travelled and the media had already weighed up the possibilities of a dockside bust-up between the psychic and his pursuer. They certainly demonstrated their flexibility when it was apparent that a kind of peace had been declared.

Without any understanding of what had happened, they were happy to turn the story on its head and make something out of the rapprochement. I was also happy to play it cool. I had a living to make and I was hoping my story still had legs. Rather than relegating it to yesterday's news, the Sunday Herald piece seemed to have generated more interest.

We were about to break away from the dockside scrum when a smartly dressed guy who turned out to be a top civil servant in one of the security branches approached Stephen and took him to one side. They talked for about ten minutes and I stayed diplomatically in the background. When the pinstriped suit had disappeared, Stephen couldn't wait to tell me what he had been saying.

'I don't think you're going to approve of this but I've just been asked to take part in a series of experiments to help a team of Government scientists. I told him I no longer made any claims to special psychic phenomena but they're still convinced I may have brain patterns different to most other people…and they want to investigate.'

'You said "no thanks" of course.' But one look at Stephen's face told me his interest had already been ignited.' Whatever you do leave me out of this one,' I pleaded, 'If this ship was returning to America, I'd be tempted to hop back on board. There's only so much a man can take.'

At that moment, a voice coming over the top of the crowd sounded familiar. 'Glad that you're back safe and sound,' shouted Christopher Howell, coming forward to meet his old friend. Catching sight of me he looked positively embarrassed when I inquired in a loud voice whether he was still in a position to tell me who killed President Kennedy.

'Well, it grabbed your attention and the end result is good. Stephen is back home with us safe and sound,' he said, making no attempt to hide his delight. Then to my surprise, he handed me a small package, which he said, would amuse me and be a souvenir of sorts.

Giving his friend a hug, he described how worried they had all been following some of the alarming reports coming back from the States They did, however, enjoy the most recent story about how we had outwitted a gang of criminals.

Christopher demonstrated that he was still looking after his friend's interest. 'Sounds as if you are going to be as busy as ever, they want to see if you have a sixth sense that might help the Government solve a few problems,' he divulged

'Did you hear that?' Stephen shouted to me as I was about to walk away,

'Yes, but I feel I've had quite enough trouble with your other five senses, thanks all the same. You're on your own if you want to play games with the sixth one.'

I turned to Stephen one more time and shouted: 'Don't forget our date with the Bishop. You may have an even greater need for a bit of celestial help. The Government is nowhere near as forgiving as Him upstairs, remember that.'

We'd meet again I was sure, but for the moment my thoughts were with Penny and the boys. I just hoped Penny would not be angry about the way I had indiscriminately plunged myself into trouble in the interests of a good story. The views she had expressed after that rare sermon we had listened to were not going to rest easily with my new outlook. Perhaps I would have to shut her in the kitchen with a Bible.

I called a taxi and headed for the station, remembering there was still plenty of work to be done. There was no office to go to on Monday morning but that was actually a relief. My old Olivetti typewriter would be red hot by the end of the month.

In the train, I remembered the present from Christopher. Removing the brown paper, I opened a small box and found two rubber stamps still bearing signs of the red ink previously applied. As I collapsed in laughter, others in the carriage dropped their newspapers in surprise. 'It's nothing really,' I explained, 'just a couple of souvenir ornaments to put on my mantelpiece.' And with almost school-boyish delight, I stamped the carriage window with words that would keep the guards and cleaners guessing for weeks---*Secret and Confidential* on one window *Top Secret* on another.

Lightning Source UK Ltd.
Milton Keynes UK
30 April 2010
153557UK00001B/89/P